A WICKED KIND OF HUSBAND

MIA VINCY

Inner Ballad Press

A Wicked Kind of Husband

Copyright © 2018 by Inner Ballad Press

Ebook ISBN: 978-1-925882-00-1

Print ISBN: 978-1-925882-01-8

CONTENT WARNING: EARLY PREGNANCY LOSS

Cover design: Studio Bukovero

Editing: Inner Ballad Press

For author information, visit www.miavincy.com.

A WICKED KIND OF HUSBAND

CHAPTER 1

The trouble began with brandy.

Or perhaps it was fairer to say—fairer to the brandy, at least, which ought not be blamed for all human failings—that the trouble was already there, and the brandy simply brought it to light.

Cassandra was not personally familiar with the effects of brandy, but as she stood in the doorway to the ballroom at midnight, watching Lucy sing and dance alone in the pool of light cast by a candelabra, it was clear to her that drink was involved.

First clue: Lucy did not dance with her usual grace. Rather, her waltz—if it could be called a waltz—was punctuated by hiccup-like hops and skips. It did not help that she wore one of their mother's ornate gowns from the previous century. The gown's skirts, blue with gold brocade, were three times as wide as Lucy and trailed on the floor, threatening to trip her up. Lacy sleeves flared out over her forearms and one of Mama's old wigs wobbled on her head.

Second clue: Lucy was singing a bawdy song about a lass

losing her virginity. That was not surprising in itself, but she sang it off-key, and only one thing made Lucy sing off-key.

Which brought Cassandra to the third and most obvious clue: The brandy bottle that Lucy clutched like a dance partner.

Cassandra sighed, causing the flame of her candle to flicker. If she were less tired, after having passed yet another evening staring futilely into the fire in Papa's study, she might have found the sight comical, but there had been too many scenes like this one in the past year. Not that Lucy needed brandy to make a scene. But clearly, it helped.

"Cassandra!" Lucy cried, spotting her. "Am I not splendid?"

She whirled to a stop and flung out her arms. The remaining cognac sloshed in its bottle, and her wig toppled onto the floor, landing dangerously close to the candelabra.

Then, arms still extended, she began to spin.

Brandy, plus spinning, plus long skirts, plus naked flame. This was not going to end well.

"Splendid is one word that comes to mind," Cassandra said, moving toward her. "I can think of a few others too."

"I'm going to London!" Lucy announced, still spinning. "I'll go to court and become the king's mistress!"

"They say he's mad, so you may well appeal to him." Cassandra held out her free hand. "Why don't you give me that bottle now?"

Lucy stopped spinning, stumbled, and took a defiant swig. "What do you think it's like, being a mistress?"

"I hope neither of us ever finds out."

"Ha! You don't even know what it's like to be a wife, Mrs. DeWitt, and you've been married two years!"

After another swig, Lucy lurched into a reel and bellowed out a new song, something about avoiding the pain of wedded life because "a Wench is better than a Wife."

Oh dear.

Most of the time, Cassandra felt that she was managing.

She took care not to brood over the past or worry about the future. She remembered to be grateful for what she had, and buried her yearning for what she could never have. She kept the estate running profitably and the household running smoothly and faced every situation with a smile. She even kept her mother's wretched goat out of the rosebushes. Most of the time.

Yes, most of the time, she managed.

This was not one of those times.

"Give me the brandy, Lucy."

With a shriek, Lucy leaped away and the inevitable happened: Her skirts caught under her feet, the bottle flew out of her hand and smashed against the wall, and she crashed onto the hard floor. Brandy fumes filled the air and the flames quivered with anticipation.

Cassandra darted forward, hoping her sister wasn't hurt, but Lucy's shoulders were shaking with laughter. And at least the brandy was no longer a problem. Really, Cassandra was making excellent progress.

"Shall we go up to bed, now, oh splendid one?" she said.

Lucy looked up, her dark hair tumbling about her shoulders, her beautiful face slack from drink. "I want more branny! It was Papa's branny, you know."

"Yes, I know. But the brandy is upstairs," Cassandra lied. "So let's go up."

Somehow, Cassandra managed to coax Lucy up the stairs without either of them breaking their neck or setting anything on fire. As they neared the top step, Cassandra cast a longing look down the dark hallway, to the haven of Lucy's bedroom. Almost there.

"The branny is French. I wanna be French," Lucy said. "The French have more fun!"

"No doubt."

"England is boring. Sunne Park is boring. Cassandra is booooooring."

"And Lucy is bosky."

"Bosky!" Lucy crowed, as she stumbled up the last step. "Bosky! Bosky! Bosky!"

"Hush. You'll wake Emily and Mr. Newell and Mama."

"Nothing will wake Mama. She's been asleep for years."

In vino veritas.

Cassandra said nothing and concentrated on maneuvering Lucy around the landing. Fortunately, Lucy had forgotten about the next round of brandy. She had also forgotten how to walk. She tripped and slid, Cassandra barely catching her before they both went tumbling down the stairs.

"Come on, Miss Bosky." She hauled Lucy to the safety of the hallway. "Let's put you to bed before you get yourself killed."

"Was Charlie bosky when he got himself killed? Was Papa bosky when he got himself killed?"

Abruptly, Cassandra let go of her sister, but Lucy stayed on her feet, swaying. The light from the candle showed Lucy's face was hard, the way she got sometimes these days: hard and bright like crystal. For too long they stared at each other, the flame flickering between them. It was Lucy who looked away first and burst into a shriek of loud laughter.

A door opened: Emily's bedroom. Cassandra could just make out the pale oval of Emily's face through the crack. Mama's door stayed shut. Mr. Newell would be awake, no doubt, in his room around the corner, but he would have enough sense not to emerge.

Lucy picked up her skirts and danced down the hall to her own door.

"I'm going to run away to Ireland!" she yelled.

Cassandra followed after her. "Haven't the Irish suffered enough?"

"Maybe a pirate will kidnap me. If I'm lucky."

"If we're all lucky."

Finally, Lucy stumbled into her room. The momentum carried her to the bed, and she clung to a bedpost, swaying. Cassandra put down the candlestick with meticulous care.

"Let's get you out of that gown." How jaunty she sounded. Perhaps she would laugh too, if she raided Papa's brandy stash.

"Poor Mother Cassandra! Whatever will you do with me? With naughty, bosky, tipsy Lucy."

"There is only one thing I can do," Cassandra said, still with her forced cheerfulness. "I shall sell you at the market."

"Sell me?" Lucy spun around, eyes wide. "How much do you think I could fetch?"

"You're so pretty in that gown, I wouldn't accept a penny under twenty pounds."

"Twenty pounds." Lucy repeated it dreamily, but then her demeanor changed again. She leaned toward Cassandra, her teeth bared like a wild animal. "Ha! I wish you *would* sell me. At least then I could get away. You want to keep me here to grow old and ugly and boring like you, you with your husband who's so ashamed of you he never even visits. Just because your life is already over, you want us to be miserable too. I hate you!"

Lucy's spite was so vicious that Cassandra lost her breath in a hiss, which meant she had no breath to yell too, to scream that she was trying, didn't Lucy see that she was trying, that their family had been unraveling like bad sewing for years, and she was trying to keep it from unraveling further, but she didn't know how, she had no idea, she didn't ask for this, but this was what they had. And how dare Lucy mock her marriage to Mr. DeWitt! So what if her husband was a stranger? Papa had chosen him, Papa said he was a good man, and Papa said she had to be married to inherit Sunne Park, so they weren't cast out if Papa died. She'd done it for all of them, and she wouldn't regret it, none of it, and if she never saw her husband and couldn't remember his face, it was best this way, it was best it was best it was best.

But as always, her lips stayed locked. Screaming and theatrics were Lucy's forte. Cassandra was the calm and sensible one.

Besides, this was her problem, not Lucy's, and there was already something so terribly broken in Lucy. Something that Cassandra didn't understand and didn't know how to fix.

The silence crackled around them, until Lucy released another wild laugh, whirled away, and tripped. Mercifully, she fell facedown on the bed. Even more mercifully, she stayed there.

"Is Lucy all right?" came a soft voice from the doorway. Cassandra briefly squeezed her eyes shut before turning to smile at Emily, who was using both hands to torment the end of her long red plait. Dear, sweet Emily. Fourteen going on ten. "Is she drunk?"

"She'll have a bit of a headache tomorrow," Cassandra said. Oh, so jaunty, so cheerful. Yes, she could be cheerful. Most of the time.

"Better an aching head than an aching heart," Emily said.

"What?!"

"That's what Lucy says."

"Heavens."

"I've never been drunk," Emily volunteered.

"I should hope not."

"Have you?"

"No. It's not a nice thing for a lady to do."

She reached out to pull Emily into a hug, but her little sister backed away.

"She just wants to enjoy herself!" Emily cried. "Why can't you let her? Why are you so mean?"

Emily ran back to her room and slammed the door behind her. Cassandra breathed deeply and let her go. One sister at a time.

Her smile was real, though, when she spied the fresh violets on Lucy's bedside table and inhaled their sweet scent. Cassandra had found the violets only that morning, bursting up under the hedgerows along the laneway. The sun had broken out several times during the day, and what with the larks singing and the magpies building their nests, she had been intoxicated by the delicious excitement that came with the early spring. She had gathered scores of the violets and put them in everyone's rooms, so they could all feel the new season.

Lucy probably hadn't noticed.

A dark mark on Lucy's foot caught her attention: a small smear of blood. Lucy must have caught a shard of glass after all. She'd not mentioned the pain. Perhaps she never felt it. Perhaps there was something to say for getting drunk.

"Oh, I remember that gown. I wore it the night of the Beaumont ball," she heard her mother say from the doorway. Mama had awoken after all. Cassandra turned and studied her. It was hard to tell in the dim light, but Mama seemed lucid. "The night I met your father, when we laughed and danced and fell in love." Mama pressed her hands together and sighed happily. "That's all Lucy wants, you know. You should let her enjoy her youth."

"*Et tu*, Mama?"

"I beg your pardon, dear?"

"Nothing."

Her mother gazed into the distance and when she looked back

at Cassandra, she wore that radiant smile that neither age nor grief could dim. "You will look so beautiful when you make your debut, Miranda, and you will find such a wonderful husband. Nothing less than a duke for you!"

Cassandra smiled and smiled, because what else could she do? Four daughters *was* a lot to keep straight. It was only to be expected that Mama would get them confused. "I'm Cassandra, Mama. And Miranda and I already have husbands."

Neither of whom was wonderful, or a duke, but still.

"Ye-es," her mother said uncertainly.

Then she smiled again, started warbling a song, and wandered back to her room. Cassandra would check on her later too.

First, Lucy. She tugged the heavy dress off Lucy's floppy limbs and wrestled her into a bed jacket over her chemise for warmth. She rolled off her stockings, gently washed away the blood, and checked for shards, finding none. She would check again in the morning.

When Lucy was snoring delicately under the covers, Cassandra placed the dirty cloth and blood-stained stocking next to the basin on the dressing table, went out, and shut the door. She hesitated. Already she regretted leaving the cloth and stocking like that—a petty, passive reproach that was beneath her—but she did not want to go back into that room. Not after what Lucy had said.

No. It was not the words. It was the look in her eyes. That look of utter hatred.

Gripping her candlestick, Cassandra headed back along the hallway, cold, dark, and lined with closed doors. At the empty master bedroom, she paused. She imagined the door opening, imagined Papa standing there, beaming as he always did, with his cheeks pink and his thinning red hair in a mess. "Well, Cassandra, my dear, what's our Princess Lucy done this time?" he would say fondly. "Let's go steal some cake and you can tell me all about it."

"Oh Papa," Cassandra whispered to the door. "I am trying to look after them for you, but they don't make it easy. Why did you have to..."

She sighed and looked back down the deserted hallway. Sunne Park had stood for three hundred years, but she wouldn't be surprised if it all came tumbling down, brick by red brick, right now, as she stood here. Their family had always seemed so solid, laughing, loving, beautiful, popular, with Mama and Papa at their center, and then Miranda and Charlie and Cassandra and Lucy and Emily. Yet one by one, everyone was disappearing, claimed by death or marriage or melancholy. She had been trying to hold the rest of them together, but they did not want to be held.

It was time for Lucy to go. Last Season, they were still in mourning for Papa, and Cassandra had been foolish, cowardly, and yes, selfish, to think she could delay yet again. First Lucy and then Emily: Sooner or later, they would both go and leave her here with Mama, and the sooner they went, the better for them. She and Mama would be fine here alone. She loved Sunne Park, and she loved her mother, and that was enough.

Most of the time.

CASSANDRA PULLED HERSELF TOGETHER, walked around the corner to Mr. Newell's room, and tapped on the door.

"Mr. Newell?" she called softly. "I know you're awake. You cannot have slept through that."

Faint rustlings and rumblings issued from within, and then the door opened to reveal her secretary, candle in hand, somber dressing gown fastened primly over his round middle. His kind face was creased with sleep and his nightcap was askew on his adorable bald head. He glanced nervously over her shoulder down the hallway. Not one of the world's fearless soldiers, was Mr. Newell.

"Mrs. DeWitt? How can I be of assistance? Miss Lucy, is she..."

"We must make plans, you and I, to go to London."

"London?" He straightened his nightcap, only to tilt it again when he pulled his hand away. "But Mr. DeWitt prefers you to remain here."

"I believe his actual words were that he couldn't have his wife running around the country and I ought to stay where I was put." At least, those were the words in the letter that Mr. Newell brought after she last expressed a desire to go to London. According to Mr. Newell, Cassandra's husband dictated all his letters to a legion of secretaries, who thoughtfully edited out the curses. "Unfortunately for Mr. DeWitt, the situation calls for me to be..." She paused dramatically. "A *nuisance*."

"A nuisance. Yes. Ha ha," Mr. Newell said, looking dismayed.

"*Altogether too much of a nuisance:*" That was the phrase Mr. DeWitt had used to describe Cassandra and her family in Mr. Newell's letter of introduction, nearly two years ago now. Cassandra had not meant to be a nuisance to her husband. It was simply that her father's unexpected death, less than a month after their equally unexpected marriage, meant that she—and therefore he—owned Sunne Park and she had naively assumed he might want to, well, if not actively manage the estate, perhaps, ah, visit it? Maybe, at least, say, once?

"*I have four factories, three estates, one thousand employees, and a growing fleet,*" had come her husband's reply. "*I do not have time to attend to one measly cottage in the depths of Warwickshire. Surely Mrs. DeWitt can figure out how to prune the rosebushes and feed the pigs all by herself.*"

Never mind that Sunne Park was a fine Tudor mansion on one

thousand acres of rich farmland, whose pigs were the most sought-after breeding stock in the middle of England.

Never mind that Mr. DeWitt was based in Birmingham, which was less than a day's travel away.

"*We agreed to a marriage in name only,*" he had added. "*Mrs. DeWitt has my name; I cannot see what else she can want from me.*"

Nevertheless, he had sent Mr. Newell, newly hired as Secretary In Charge Of Matrimonial Affairs, along with a bright-eyed gray kitten, the latter included "*so,*" Mr. DeWitt wrote, "*the wife doesn't get lonely and do something foolish.*"

Charming man, her husband-in-name-only.

Really, Cassandra was perfectly content to have nothing to do with him, as his letters indicated that he was ill-mannered, and the scandal sheets indicated that he was ill-behaved. She knew little more about him now than she had on their wedding day— the only time she had ever seen him. Joshua DeWitt was a wealthy widower and the illegitimate son of an earl, Papa had told her, when he sat her down in his study and asked her to marry Mr. DeWitt, a week after they learned that Cassandra's betrothed, the cheerful and charming Viscount Bolderwood, had eloped with someone else.

"Joshua is a good man, for all his ways," Papa had said. "I wouldn't marry you off to someone I didn't trust. With your brother Charlie gone, the lawyers insist the only way for a daughter to inherit this estate is if she is married, and I know Joshua will take care of you all when I'm dead."

Cassandra had laughed at him. "Heavens, Papa! Why do you talk of dying? You are in excellent health."

But Papa had pleaded, so she married Mr. DeWitt, and a month later, Papa was dead. Though if Mr. DeWitt was a good man, she had seen little evidence of it.

Yet she was grateful for Mr. Newell, whose avuncular manner

and infinite patience made him a favorite with Emily and Lucy. As for Mr. Twit...

A soft head butted her knee and a pair of cat's eyes gleamed at her in the dim light. Mr. Twit, purring vigorously, rubbed against her calves, telling her to go to bed.

"The fact is, Mr. Newell, it is past time to launch Lucy into London society. In the circumstances, I think it best that I seek my grandmother's assistance. And as the duchess will be in London for the Season, there must I go too."

Mr. Newell shifted uncomfortably. "You must understand that Mr. DeWitt—he does not mince words. Once he decides something, he expects it to happen. He was very firm in saying no to you before."

Given how much control a husband could legally wield over his wife, Cassandra counted herself fortunate that Mr. DeWitt ignored her so thoroughly, and that his only requirements were that she ignore him back and stay where she was put.

Which she was willing to do. Most of the time.

"Unfortunately for Mr. DeWitt, Lucy's need to be in society is greater than his need to pretend I do not exist."

"Perhaps a letter to your grandmother would suffice."

"I had considered that but..." Four times a year, Cassandra dutifully wrote to the duchess, and her grandmother dutifully wrote back. The sole purpose of the letters was to acknowledge each other's continuing existence. "Our relations are strained, so it is best I see her in person. You will not be blamed for my actions," she added. "You need not fear Mr. DeWitt."

"I don't fear him," Mr. Newell hastened to say. "He is not unkind. He is merely...not restful. He will send you straight home."

"Not if he does not know I am there." Mr. Twit flopped onto her feet and she stooped to scratch the cat's neck. "You say he travels frequently and you are always advised of his schedule, are you not? We simply have to find a time this Season when he is not in London."

"Hm. I did receive word he is planning a trip to Liverpool. How long do you propose to stay?"

"I need only to convince my grandmother to take Lucy," she said. "If we plan it properly, we'll never see Mr. DeWitt at all."

CHAPTER 2

"Mr. DeWitt is everything that a husband ought to be," Cassandra said to her friend Arabella as they strolled through London's Hyde Park on a fine afternoon three weeks later. "He is conveniently rich, extremely generous, and always somewhere else."

Cassandra ignored Arabella's amused if skeptical glance, and concentrated on the marvels around her. On one side of them lay Rotten Row, with its cacophony of horses and carriages; on the other lay the waters of the Serpentine; and pressing all around them were the thousands of people in London who possessed both colorful finery and the leisure time in which to display it.

"Stroll," however, was an optimistic description of their progress. Navigating the crowd required something more like a slow, improvised quadrille: a *chassé* to the right, a *glissade* to the left, and then perhaps a small *sissone*.

Unless, of course, one was Arabella, Lady Hardbury, in front of whom space magically opened up.

"Absence is a quality that many women appreciate in their

husbands," Arabella said. "I have not been married to Hardbury long enough to appreciate it in him, but I daresay the time will come when we divide up the country and ensure we are always at opposite ends of it."

"I cannot imagine that, besotted as you two are."

"There is that. Besides, what on earth would I do for entertainment if my husband were not nearby to provoke?"

A pair of pastel-clad young ladies approached, hugging each other's arms as they opened their mouths to address Arabella. Cassandra readied her smile—finally, a conversation!—but Arabella merely lifted her chin and looked them over disdainfully. The ladies discovered an urgent need to be on the other side of the park and hurried away. Arabella smiled with satisfaction and strolled on.

"Why can we not talk to them?" Cassandra asked.

"They are not interesting enough."

"Arabella, you promised me conversation." Cassandra stopped in rebellion and narrowly avoided colliding with a trio of elegant gentlemen, who almost fell over in their haste to bow to Arabella and escape. "How am I supposed to forge connections if you do not allow me to talk to anyone?"

"Not any conversation will do." Arabella scanned the crowd, her uncommon height giving her an enviable view. "Most importantly, so long as you are with me, you will be seen."

Indeed, everyone wanted a glimpse of Arabella, who, since her marriage to the Marquess of Hardbury, had scaled the slopes of London society and planted her flag firmly at the peak. Those around them watched her while pretending not to, their expressions a mix of longing and fear, and they turned to each other to whisper words that bobbed through the air amid the colorful feathers and parasols, words like "Lady Hardbury" and "Cassandra Lightwell" and "DeWitt" and "Bolderwood."

"By 'seen', of course, you mean 'gossiped about'," Cassandra said. "I suppose it cannot be avoided."

"It *must* not be avoided. If one is not gossiped about, then one does not exist. What with this promenade and your appearance in my box at the theater tonight, every morning call in every drawing room tomorrow will feature your name."

"Gosh. What proportion of each call might I merit? A whole minute?"

"Don't flatter yourself, Cassandra. You are not *that* interesting." Arabella slid her an amused sideways look. "Although with your family history...perhaps half a minute? Multiply that by, say, three thousand conversations, at a very modest estimate—that's fifteen hundred minutes. Most people would kiss a monkey if it would garner them half that much attention."

"Why, that's...Twenty-five hours of gossip, on me alone." Cassandra twirled her parasol and smiled at the world. "How marvelous I am, to make such a generous contribution to society."

Society! Oh, how exciting to be in a crowd again! The last time she walked in Hyde Park, she had been Miss Cassandra Lightwell, engaged to Harry, Lord Bolderwood, and Charlie and Papa were still alive. And then—Well, that was then, and this was now. And now, she had nearly three weeks before Mr. DeWitt was due to return from his trip to Liverpool, and she meant to put every minute of it to good use.

Which was what she thought was the purpose of this walk: to smooth her way back into society, for Lucy to follow. Yet she felt less like a participant than a visitor at a menagerie, with Arabella as her guide.

"That fellow over there"—Arabella indicated a fashionable gentleman whose cravat was tied with such complexity it must have required a good three hours—"was last week found guilty of criminal conversation with Lord Oliver's wife. The jury set the damages at nearly twenty thousand pounds, which of course he cannot afford. The red-haired woman there is Lady Yardley"—a plump, vivacious lady in her thirties with a circle of admirers—"who almost outdid me at the Ladies' Debating Society the other day. And that handsome gentleman riding the fine bay mare would suit you nicely as a lover."

Cassandra stumbled and turned the misstep into a *jeté* to avoid tumbling over. "I beg your pardon?"

"So you are paying attention." Arabella laughed softly. Which was lovely. Arabella had rarely laughed before her marriage. "Anyway, 'tis not as though your marriage vows mean anything, since you married only to secure your inheritance, and he—Why did he marry you again?"

"Because Papa asked him to. But I would not take a lover simply because I can, or because Mr. DeWitt is rumored to do so. Why on earth would a woman go to bed with a man if it were not required?"

"Because it's...Oh, never mind. I have seen your Mr. DeWitt," she went on, "although he has not yet been introduced to me. No one knows what to make of him. They recoil because he is an industrialist, but receive him because his investments make them rich. They say he is no gentleman, but cannot forget that his father is an earl and that he would have been earl one day too, had his father's bigamy not rendered him illegitimate. Meanwhile, he goes where he pleases, says what he pleases, and no one dares get in his way. And," Arabella added, slyness creeping into her tone, "he is very good-looking."

Was he? At their only meeting, on their wedding day two years ago, Cassandra had hardly looked at him. She had still been heartbroken after Harry jilted her and grieving for the future she had lost.

"I remember him only as being dark and abrupt," she said. "I assumed he was as uncomfortable as I at marrying a stranger."

It was the waiting that Cassandra remembered, mostly. First, in the drawing room of Mr. DeWitt's Birmingham townhouse, waiting for the groom to show up to his own wedding. Papa chatted with the vicar, all the while flapping the special license that he had cajoled from the archbishop. The drawing room had the stale air of disuse, and an out-of-time clock persistently ticked away the last minutes of her spinsterhood. Finally, her groom blew in like a gale, and Papa had barely performed the introductions when Mr. DeWitt turned to the vicar, clapped his hands once, and said, "Let's get on with it, then. I don't have all day."

And later, oh good heavens, later. She had waited then too, huddled under blankets in the dark, for him to do what had to be done to complete the marriage. "Let's make this as quick and painless as possible," he said when he came to her bedroom—not exactly what a virgin wanted to hear from her groom on their wedding night. She squeezed her eyes tight shut throughout. His hands were gentle and warm and not unpleasant, and several times he told her to relax and she almost did, but then the act itself...

It wasn't painless, but it was mercifully quick, and she breathed through it while he stilled and cursed. When he got out of bed, she lay motionless and didn't look at him, not even when he spoke: "I doubt you enjoyed that very much," he said. "If it's any consolation, I didn't enjoy it either. It's best this way." She didn't ask what he meant; she wanted him only to leave, which he did, and he had already gone out when she rose the next morning, and she and Papa went straight back to Sunne Park and she never saw him again.

THEY HAD NOT GONE MUCH FURTHER when Arabella clutched Cassandra's elbow and steered them in another direction, saying, "Let us veer away now."

"Who are we running from?" Cassandra asked.

"*I* am running from nobody. *You* are choosing to avoid an encounter with Lady Bolderwood. No, don't look now."

Somehow, Cassandra kept moving, on limbs so light they might have floated away.

"I am right in assuming you don't wish to meet Lady Bolderwood?" Arabella asked.

"I suppose I cannot avoid it, but thank you, I should rather not do so today."

Nevertheless, Cassandra could not resist glancing at the Viscountess Bolderwood, the woman who had stolen her life. She saw a pale lady in an elaborate yellow outfit that showed off her small, well-shaped figure to great advantage.

"She is pretty," she ventured.

"She has the kind of face that seems pretty, until you look closely and realize she is nothing of the sort."

"And very fashionable."

"Lord and Lady Bolderwood do run with the fashionable crowd," Arabella said. "Whether they can afford to is another matter. I hear they are living off the gaming tables now and their debts mount daily."

Malicious glee danced through her. She tried to quell it but, well, the woman *had* eloped with Cassandra's betrothed while Cassandra was still in mourning for her brother.

"I shall not gossip about her," she said resolutely.

Arabella was unchastened. "We must be allowed to discuss other people's failings. How else are we to reconcile ourselves to our own? And come now, Cassandra, we both know you are not nearly as good as you pretend. Are you not a little glad that the woman who made off with your former betrothed is suffering some hardship?"

"Even better that Harry is suffering. Lord Bolderwood, I mean," Cassandra confessed. "I blame him for being stolen more than I blame her for stealing him."

"When you do end up meeting them, be sure to mention your husband's great wealth."

"How vulgar!"

"But how entertaining." Arabella threw her a wicked look and then smiled at someone over her shoulder. "Oh look, there is the Duke of Dammerton, with the lovely Miss Seaton. I hear he is courting her, and her family is reluctant because of his divorce. There, my dear, is precisely the conversation you need."

IT WAS a good ten years since Cassandra had last seen Leopold Halton, now the sixth Duke of Dammerton, who used to be a regular visitor to her neighbors, the Bells. In those years, he had inherited a dukedom, grown bigger, and chalked up a scandalous marriage and divorce, but he still wore the same air of distraction covering a sharp mind.

"How do you do, Lady Hardbury," His Grace said to Arabella, with a gracious nod that she deigned to return. "And Miss Cassandra—I mean, Mrs. DeWitt." He offered a sleepy half-smile. "Delighted to see you again. DeWitt never mentioned you were coming to London."

How confounding to hear her husband spoken of thus; it was as if he were a real person after all.

"Mr. DeWitt is a very busy man," she said. "I'm sure he has much more interesting things to talk about."

"I cannot imagine any topic of conversation more interesting than our womenfolk. Heaven knows Hardbury never shuts up about his wife." He indicated his companion with a gallant sweep of his arm. "Are you acquainted with Miss Seaton?"

Introductions were made and agreeable small talk began. They had not long exchanged pleasantries when Cassandra became aware of a disturbance nearby, an extra buzzing above the hubbub of the crowd. She turned to see a tall, dark-haired gentleman charging through the throng toward them, brandishing a roll of papers in one hand.

"Damn you, Dammerton!" the man said when he was still several yards away, apparently not one whit bothered that he interrupted, that he addressed a duke so rudely, that he used such language in the presence of ladies. "Why can you not stay in one blasted place so I don't have to waste my time looking for you?"

"Perhaps you should get a little bell," the duke suggested, unfazed. "You could ring it and summon me back from wherever I have drifted off to."

"Excellent idea!" The man pivoted and barked a syllable at the dapper, dark-skinned gentleman who sauntered after him with an expression of wry amusement. "Make a note. Bells to summon people from a distance."

It was rude to stare, but Cassandra could not look away. Even after the man came to a stop, the air around him continued to move like a whirlwind, and the thrill of all that energy slid under her skin. His clothes were of excellent quality, from his boots, to his fitted buckskins, to the dark coat tailored perfectly for his uncommonly broad shoulders. Yet those boots were dusty, and his cravat was knotted too simply to be fashionable, and—most shocking—the lower part of his chiseled face was covered with dark stubble, as one might expect of a workman or someone so dissolute that he was better acquainted with the bottle than with his razor. A fine beaver hat covered his dark hair, and a gold hoop glittered in his left earlobe, and she did not know what to make of him at all.

"Listen, Dammerton. I heard the most thrilling news in Bristol," the man went on. "My man in Somerset, working with new science out of Denmark—electrical power, I tell you! They are getting closer all the time."

The duke cleared his throat pointedly and gestured at the ladies. "Perhaps, given the company...?"

"The company?" The man frowned and looked around vaguely, as if seeking evidence of this mysterious company, until his gaze followed the length of Dammerton's arm and landed on the three ladies.

"And?" He sounded genuinely confused, but then he said "Sod the company!", which shocking language caused Miss Seaton to gasp.

Arabella nudged Cassandra with her elbow, but Cassandra didn't dare look at her friend; watching other people behave badly was one of Arabella's favorite sports. Cassandra could only stare at this oddly magnetic man, whose astonishing rudeness made him as repellent as his energy made him attractive.

"There is not a minute to waste! Steam is great, gas is grand, but to harness electricity? It will alter civilization for all time!"

The man's dark eyes were bright with excitement, and he waved his hands so emphatically he almost hit Miss Seaton with his roll of paper.

Again, Arabella nudged Cassandra, more sharply this time. Again, she ignored her.

"I don't doubt it," Dammerton said. "But the company...You might want to..."

"What? What?"

"Be more polite," Cassandra said, without thinking. Oh dear:

She was so used to managing her sisters that she had become impolite too.

But the stranger merely gave his head a little shake and started up again, as if Cassandra had not spoken.

"Devil take you, Dammerton. The most exciting period in history and you want me to chatter with ladies for the sake of being *polite*? Time is short enough as it is without wasting more on nonsense like that."

Well, this was too much!

"If you spent less time complaining about how little time you have, sir, perhaps you would have more time to be polite," Cassandra said, in the amiable, cajoling tone she used on Lucy.

His frown deepened and he whipped his head around to look at her, his eyes roaming wildly over her face. She endured the insolent examination stubbornly, dimly astonished that she was embarking on a public squabble with an ill-mannered, disheveled stranger.

"Did you *scold* me?" he said.

"I wish only to point out that being polite takes less time than complaining about being polite."

Arabella now gripped her arm, in a most unlikely fashion, but Cassandra could not turn away from that intense, dark gaze.

His Grace chuckled. "She's got you there," he said.

"It is a matter of efficiency," the man said. "Already you have wasted more of my time."

"Had you greeted us politely, *neither* of us would be wasting this time."

"Had I greeted you politely, you would have taken that as an invitation to blather on about balls and bonnets and I don't know what. And what are you laughing at now, Dammerton?"

He swung back around and glared at the duke, who grinned

amiably. A horrid suspicion began to dawn, what with the duke's sly amusement, and Arabella's sharp-fingered grip, and Miss Seaton's wide eyes, and that strange fizzing sensation under Cassandra's skin.

No, it was not possible.

"You two make an adorable couple," the duke said.

The man snorted. "Spare me your matchmaking. I'm already married."

"As am I," Cassandra said automatically, her head beginning to float away, her eyes fixed on His Grace's cravat pin so she wouldn't have to look at the man. The dark, abrupt, ill-mannered man.

No. No. No.

"I realize you are both married." The duke looked from one to the other. "But do you realize you are married to each other?"

No.

Cassandra closed her eyes. The clamor of the crowd withdrew to a great distance. Somewhere, someone played a French horn. It was too hot in here. Her gown was too small. But she was not inside, and she could not shut out the world, or the sunlight on her eyelids, or the man vibrating beside her.

Her husband.

She took a deep breath and opened her eyes, and found him studying her with a frown.

So. This was her husband. Mr. Joshua DeWitt. Of course it was. In hindsight, it was obvious, although she never imagined he would be in London, and he had been clean-shaven at their wedding, and hatless, and if he had worn that dreadful earring then, she had not looked at him long enough to notice. But even if she had forgotten his strong, bold features, she ought not have forgotten his manner, as dynamic as if lightning bounced around inside him.

Both having conducted their inspections, their eyes met briefly with a jolt of that lightning, and then he looked heavenward with a heavy sigh.

Cassandra became aware again of their audience, which had swelled markedly: Passersby were clearly fascinated by a group that included a scandalous duke, an intimidating marchioness, and a married couple who had never been seen together—and who had not even recognized each other.

Her quota of gossip may have doubled—but not in a way that she wanted.

She summoned up an amiable smile. "Of course we realize it, Your Grace," she said. "One cannot be married for two years without being aware of it." She flicked a pointed glance somewhere near her husband's profile and leaned in confidentially. "Especially to a man such as this. One does tend to notice him."

The duke looked back and forth between them. "You did not even acknowledge each other," he pointed out.

Cassandra slipped her fingers into the crook of her husband's elbow. He jerked, as if bitten, but she held on and he settled. She risked a glance at him: He was frowning at her hand on his sleeve as though it were some odd creature. She ignored him. Ignored the feel of his body beside hers. All that lightning. Oh dear, this man had bedded her. Briefly and uncomfortably, but his body and hers had...Oh dear. How did couples face each other over the breakfast table?

"We have already seen each other today," Cassandra explained, lying with shocking ease. "We do not need to greet each other afresh every time. That, Your Grace, would be inefficient and we're all aware of Mr. DeWitt's love of efficiency."

She gave his arm a little pat, smiled hard, and waited, breath held, for him to cooperate.

Then, to her relief, he patted her hand in turn.

"Well said, Mrs. DeWitt." He punctuated his words with jabs of the roll of papers in his free hand. "I know who she is, she knows who I am, and we hardly need to remind each other of that at every point during the day."

"You see, we are completely in tune with each other," Cassandra lied. "The less time we waste on redundant greetings, the more time we have to argue about manners. My husband's lack of them, particularly."

"I wish you luck, Mrs. DeWitt," the duke said wryly.

Cassandra glanced at Arabella, whose face was alive with repressed laughter. Arabella made a little moue with her mouth —"I did try to warn you," she might have been saying.

"This is all very charming," Mr. DeWitt said briskly. "But my, ah, *wife*, ha ha, and I need a private chat. Say your farewells, my *dear*. She will return to Warwickshire tomorrow."

But before she could say those farewells—or anything more at all—he was moving away, sweeping her along with him in a current that she could not resist.

CHAPTER 3

J oshua tried to reconcile this bright, amiable-looking woman with Lord Charles Lightwell's daughter, the plain, subdued girl he had married two years earlier. He could see something of her father in her, not necessarily in her features but in her air of open warmth, the sense that she welcomed everyone. That made her appealing, beyond her looks, which were pleasant if not beautiful.

Her hair was brown and her eyes were green, unless they were brown too; he couldn't tell and didn't much care either way. She had a stupid parasol and a stupider bonnet, but her green outfit at least was clever: Its bodice was cut in a way that showed she had a superb bosom, but not in such a way that anyone could accuse her of drawing attention to said bosom.

Brown hair—Amiable smile—Absurd emphasis on manners —Wife—Not where she was meant to be: That was all he knew about her, and all he needed to know.

To her credit, she came along with him easily enough, her

hand tucked into his elbow as though they were fully civilized people. Good: The sooner they got home, the sooner he could send her back to Warwickshire where she belonged.

"Das!" Joshua twisted to find the secretary sauntering a few yards behind them. At least *someone* was where he was meant to be. "Get a hackney."

"Will do."

His wife turned too. "Is he—"

"Don't ask. I'm tired of people asking." Joshua kept them moving toward Hyde Park Corner. "He's Bengali. He knew Bram somehow and wanted to come over here for some reason."

"I was going to ask…Oh, never mind. Mr. Das." She released Joshua's arm and, to be particularly annoying, walked back to the secretary. Das stopped too, still afflicted by those excellent manners that Joshua had failed to cure him of. "In the absence of a proper introduction, may I say that I'm pleased to meet you," she said.

Das bowed. "The pleasure is all mine, Mrs. DeWitt."

"I assume you are the Mr. Das about whom Mr. Newell has spoken so highly?"

"Mr. Newell is too generous."

"What are you my husband's secretary for?"

"Oh for crying out loud! Enough chitchat." Joshua strode back to them. "He's Secretary For Doing Whatever The Blazes I Tell Him. And I told you to get me a hackney. Now. Go. Go!"

He waved in the direction of the gate and went to grip his wife's upper arm. But she simply maneuvered her fingers back into the crook of his elbow and, when he tried to pull away, kept her feet planted firmly under the devious cover of her skirts. He couldn't march off now without yanking her along behind him. Huh. Clever, that.

"That cannot be the official job title," she said to Das, as calmly as if they weren't playing tug-of-war with Joshua's elbow.

"No, madam," Das said with great dignity. "I believe the official title is 'Secretary For Managing Whims and Getting Yelled At A Lot'."

She laughed and Joshua muttered "Very funny," and tried not to notice how warming his wife's laugh was. Reminiscent of Lord Charles but more...feminine.

"You must need a sense of humor in your position, Mr. Das."

"I think we have that in common, Mrs. DeWitt."

"Enough," Joshua said. "You are not Secretary For Making Stupid Jokes and you are not Secretary For Flirting With My Wife. If you must flirt with her, do it later, on your own time. Now. Get that carriage."

Das complied, but Mrs. DeWitt would not be hurried. Joshua forced himself to slow down, gritting his teeth and slicing the air with his precious papers, while she looked about in apparent delight, her fingers tucked into the crook of his elbow, her shoulder bumping against his arm, her skirts brushing his legs.

He glanced at her profile: that faint rose coloring her cheeks, that hint of a welcoming smile. To make matters worse, she was deploying that feminine floral fragrance that certain women used to create havoc.

"You're meant to be in Warwickshire," he said.

"You're meant to be in Liverpool."

"I did not give you permission to come to London."

"I did not ask your permission."

He stopped so abruptly that it took her a few steps to stop too, and her hand slipped from his arm. She looked back at him questioningly.

"You should," he said. In a single stride, he drew level with her again. Once more, she took his elbow and they moved on, although he was no longer sure who was leading whom. "Let me explain, Mrs. DeWitt, how marriage works."

"Oh, please do, Mr. DeWitt, I'm all agog."

"I am the husband, so I make the rules to suit me."

"And I am the wife, so I change the rules to suit me."

She must not say things like that. Bad enough that she had shown up here at all, as a real person. Even worse that she was attractive. If she proved likable also, that would be disastrous.

No, not disastrous. He was not a man who tolerated disaster. He was a man who punched disaster on the nose, then checked its pockets for coins and bonbons. But disruptive. Yes. Disruptive. A wife did not fit into his life, and the fact that he had a wife was nothing more than a minor inconvenience. Never mind: She might be likable, but he was not, and as soon as she discovered that, she would leave of her own accord and everything could go back to normal.

"You seem puzzled," said his disruptive wife, as they reached the gate. "Have I said something to puzzle you?"

"Most of what you say puzzles me. It's almost as though you have a mind of your own."

"Please don't vex yourself. I'll try not to use it too often."

He ignored her look as he searched for Das and the hackney amid the furious tangle of London traffic. In front of them, a pair of enterprising lads inserted a dog into the traffic to worsen the snarl, and then charged a coin or two to relieve it.

"Who is Bram?" she asked.

"What?"

"You mentioned that Mr. Das knew someone called Bram."

"One of my brothers. He lives in India."

"You have brothers," she said. "And now we are getting to know each other. Isn't that lovely?"

"No. Here's Das now." He pointed with his papers. "Stop dawdling, woman."

In the carriage, Joshua threw himself into the seat opposite his wife and glared at her. She had to sit forward a bit because of her stupid bonnet, and she used the parasol, closed now in a froth of ruffles, to steady herself as the hackney lurched into motion.

"I had forgotten how exciting London is," she said.

"Enjoy it while you can. You're going home tomorrow." He drummed his fingers on the roll of paper on his lap. "Now what are you smiling at?"

"Mr. Newell warned me that you are not restful."

"Restful?" He snorted. "I have no need of rest. I never get tired."

"You are fortunate. Sometimes I get very tired indeed."

She spoke so quietly he almost didn't hear the words. A question rose to his lips but he bit it back. Go around asking people why they were sad and the next thing you knew, your life would be all tangled up in theirs, and that never went well for anyone.

"Then go home to your cottage and get some rest, and leave me in peace."

"Oh, Mr. DeWitt, if only it were that simple."

She returned her attention to the window.

Joshua stared at her profile, his thoughts leaping and bouncing. That was nothing unusual. He always had thoughts bouncing around in his head, but usually they were like two dozen couples in a country dance, moving together, taking turns to hop or leap or clap or turn. Now they were stumbling, getting out of time, falling over each other. He would not ask what made her sad and weary.

He would *not*.

He leaned back, closed his eyes, and pulled his wayward thoughts into order. Electrical power—Patents—Investors—Potential—Excitement—Lust—Wife—

Damn.

Ah but—Lady Yardley had signaled her interest—Lord Yardley had signaled his lack of interest—He could find Lady Yardley and—Wife.

His eyes flew open and he sat upright.

No. Not now. He couldn't start an affair with another woman when his wife was nearby. And he definitely couldn't bed his wife. Ah well, never mind. He didn't have time for an affair anyway. Celibacy had not killed him yet.

"You're prettier than I remember," he said.

She turned her bright eyes back to him, looking amused and amiable. In truth, he hardly remembered much about her at all. She'd kept her head bowed throughout their short wedding ceremony, and he'd avoided looking at her anyway. And the other part had taken place in the shadows, both of them with eyes shut and thinking of something else.

"How charming of you to say so," she said. "I recall you expressed some disappointment on our wedding day, that you had heard the Lightwell sisters were beauties when I am not."

"I can't see anyone going to war over you, but you're not completely embarrassing. How old are you anyway? Nineteen? Twenty?"

"Twenty-two."

"That old."

He tried to remember twenty-two. It was only six years ago but it felt like a lifetime. Samuel had been two then, and Rachel brought him into the offices, saying it was never too soon for him to learn. That was the year they risked everything by purchasing and outfitting new factories, and ended up tripling their fortune. That was the year they watched Samuel discovering the world, and they vowed never to employ children in a way that might snuff out that spark. And Rachel must have been twenty-two when he first came to work in her father's office. But she had been the boss's daughter, and he was only fourteen then and too scared and angry to notice her, let alone imagine that, five years after he arrived, she'd marry him, and another five years after that, she'd be dead.

"Mr. DeWitt?" His wife wore a concerned expression. "Are you all right? I hope I did not upset you."

"Of course you upset me. You've upset everything. Go home."

"I'm afraid that I can't do that. You see, I have…"

"What? What?"

"Sisters."

"Sisters."

Ah. Yes. Lord Charles had mentioned daughters. Joshua couldn't remember how many, only that it was a lot, and that they all risked being destitute if Joshua didn't marry one of them, since Charlie was dead and daughters had to be married to inherit, and the one that was already married was a stepdaughter, and the one that was nearly married had been jilted, and all the others were too young.

Even now, his house might be overrun by giggling creatures in white gowns and colorful ribbons. He shuddered.

"Tell me there aren't more of you," he said. "Does my house have an infestation of sisters?"

"Only me, for now."

"For now!"

"I mean to strengthen relations with my grandmother and—"

"Not the duchess!"

"You see, my sister—"

"No."

"Because my mother—"

"No."

"My other sister—"

"No."

"Then my *father*."

She lifted her chin, with a hard look, proving that amiable did not mean soft.

"I had a debt to your father," he said after a moment. "I discharged that debt by marrying you, ensuring your inheritance, and providing for your family's material needs."

"And we are all very grateful. But—"

"The agreement was that I *get* married to you. It was not to *be* married to you."

"Unfortunately, one does tend to follow the other."

"We can be married at a distance," he said. "Our marriage has been highly satisfactory so far."

"Mr. DeWitt. That will not do." Now she was all stern and matronly. "My sister must make her debut, and I must persuade my grandmother to accommodate her. You need not be involved. I am more than happy that we lead separate lives. I only ask that you do not obstruct me or engage in behavior that will adversely affect her social position. Once this is done, I shall return to Sunne Park and you can go back to doing what you do best. Which, as I understand it, involves making money, offending people, and cuckolding lords."

JOSHUA'S MIND did a rare thing: It went blank. Only for the blink of an eye, but nevertheless. Then the thoughts came rushing back in.

Honesty: What a surprise. Politeness and honesty tended to be mutually exclusive, and Cassandra appeared to be the epitome of politeness. He loathed politeness, the way people went around ignoring the truth when it made them uncomfortable. Pretending that if they couched something unpleasant in delicate language, then it was no longer unpleasant.

Yet here she was, mentioning things that the polite did not mention.

It almost made her interesting.

He leaned back and stretched out his legs so that his boots flirted with her skirts. The blush on her cheeks had deepened but she met his eyes with calm defiance.

"Are you saying I have your permission, Mrs. DeWitt?" he said. "To conduct affairs, that is."

"What you have, sir, is my complete indifference. I ask only that you be discreet, as your behavior reflects on my sisters and me. We have sufficient disadvantages, in the circumstances."

"Circumstances?"

"A series of minor scandals in my family. And your...birth."

"Nothing wrong with my birth," he snapped. "I have it on good authority that I came out in the usual way, with lots of blood and screaming." He leaned forward and took a childish delight when she straightened her already straight shoulders. "I think what you meant to say is that I'm the bastard son of a bigamist earl and that kind of thing tends to upset people." He threw himself back against the squabs. "The 'bastard son' part of it, I mean. They're all fine with the 'bigamist earl' part."

Her lips tightened, which was a shame, because they were rather lovely full lips, on a rather lovely wide mouth.

"If you'd like to put it like that," she said.

But why discuss his father? This affairs business was much more intriguing.

"So you truly don't mind if I take a lover?"

"It is not a wife's position to mind. Ours is not the model of a faithful, loving marriage that my parents demonstrated, but—"

"Faithful! Your parents. Ha!"

A slew of emotions chased each other across her face: Shock? Disbelief? Sorrow? Fear? Then her features settled into cool dignity, her demeanor a reminder that she was the granddaughter of a duke, thank you very much.

"You will not pollute my memory of my parents' marriage with your own sordid views," she said. "Fidelity was a cornerstone of their relationship and of our family."

The truth writhed inside him but he held it in. The naive darling truly believed her father had been faithful to her mother. Ah, well. No need to rob her of her illusions. It hardly mattered anymore.

"As for your own behavior, Mr. DeWitt: I do not believe you have been celibate since our wedding day and either way, it is of no concern to me. I'm sure your self-regard will not be diminished if I point out that you are no more to me than a stranger who pays the bills. For which, I say again, we are all grateful. Besides, I'd much rather you bother other men's wives, if it means you leave me alone."

Excellent: She didn't want him; he didn't want her. Finally they agreed on something. Their wedding night had been nothing short of awful, however necessary. His first wedding night, now: *That* had been marvelous. He had been nineteen, then, and touching a woman for the first time and he was very, *very* enthusiastic. And Rachel had some experience and was not shy in telling him what she liked and what to do, and they were already friends. But with this wife, Cassandra...

No. What was done was done, and it was best that way.

"That was not my best performance," he said, sounding gruff and stilted to his own ears.

"I hadn't realized one scored points."

"We had a duty. I discharged my duty like a gentleman and you bore yours like a lady."

"England must be very proud."

Perhaps he should have been more tender with her. Talked to her or something. But he had been as gentle as he could, and talking was a trap. It led to intimacy, which led to affection, which led to attachments, which led to trouble, and he did not need more trouble. Other men's wives made the best lovers, because they already knew what they wanted and they always went home to someone else. And she'd just given him carte blanche to do as he pleased. Which meant he could drop a note to Lady Yardley after all.

Except that it felt all wrong.

Curse Treyford and his wretched bigamy. Had his bigamy never been discovered, had his marriage to Joshua's mother not been dissolved, had Joshua not been disinherited—well, Joshua would have become a fully-fledged aristocrat with all the morals of a dockside cat. As it was, by going off at fourteen to work in Birmingham, he had made middle-class friends and married a middle-class woman and developed inconvenient middle-class values. Like raising one's own children and being proud of hard work and staying faithful to one's spouse.

Mercifully, the hackney jerked to a stop, putting an end to this torture. The cabin swayed and men outside exchanged yells.

"Never mind," he muttered. "I hardly even remember it."

"You probably don't even remember my name."

"Of course I do. It's Clarissa, isn't it?"

"Oh, well done, Josiah."

The door opened and she allowed herself to be assisted gracefully to the footpath. Joshua jumped down and scowled at her. Blasted woman had to stop saying things like that, or he would find himself liking her rather more than was wise.

"Mrs. DeWitt," he said. "You will leave here tomorrow."

"I am willing to do whatever you ask, Mr. DeWitt."

"Good."

"So long as you do not ask anything that I am not willing to do."

With this astounding display of insubordination, she swept up the steps of his house and through the door without a backward glance.

JOSHUA PAID off the driver and bounded up the steps, through the door, and into his entrance hall, only to skid to a halt at the sight of Filby and Thomas, one holding the stupid bonnet and parasol, the other holding a green pelisse, both blinking at him with surprise. He went to fling his hat onto the hall table but—

He stopped short, staring at the table.

"What in blazes is that?"

The butler and footman exchanged a glance and did not answer. Joshua prowled around to study the alien object from a different angle. He sneezed and the two servants jumped.

Das appeared in the doorway. "Those colorful, fragrant things are known as 'flowers'," Das said. "The vessel that holds them is called a 'vase'."

"A vase? Why would I even own such a useless thing?"

He glared at the butler, who summed up the situation in two ominous words: "Mrs. DeWitt."

Joshua flicked the head of a fat pink flower—devil knew what it was called—and it bobbed cheerfully. The whole exuberant arrangement stood a good two feet tall and was nearly as wide.

"This is a colonization, Das. That woman is colonizing my house. Do you know what that means?"

"Years of bloodshed, oppression, and exploitation, perhaps?"

"I wouldn't be surprised." Joshua turned back to Filby, who had thankfully rid himself of the bonnet, and tossed the roll of paper at him. "Put that in the study. Is Newell here too?"

"Yes, sir. Mrs. DeWitt requested that he be treated like a guest."

"Guest? Ha! If I see him, I'll fire him. Tell him to make arrangements for that woman to go back home."

"You mean your wife?"

"That's the one."

"Mrs. DeWitt seems very charming," Das said.

"We are not discussing Mrs. DeWitt." Joshua glared at the table. *Flowers*. In a *vase*. All pretty and useless and taking up space, except the square occupied by the silver salver.

On which sat a letter. Addressed to him.

He couldn't put his hat there now, could he, so he put it back on his head.

"Das, we have work to do."

He pivoted again, made for the door, but Filby darted in front of him, brandishing that salver.

"Your brother Mr. Isaac called again, sir," the butler said. "He left another letter. We were going to send it after you to Liverpool."

"Send it wherever you please. Come along, Das. Not a moment to waste."

BACK OUTSIDE, Joshua headed toward St. James. Before long, Das was by his side, reading something as he walked.

Isaac's letter.

"Send him more money," Joshua said.

"He has not asked for money. He points out that he didn't ask for money last time either." Das's voice had taken on a provokingly judgmental tone. "He has made progress in his search for your mother and sister. He wants to see you."

The image of Isaac swam in his mind, as he had been the last time Joshua saw him. Ten years old—Fast legs—Scraped knees—Chattering faster than a magpie. Isaac, eyes bright at the thought of going to sea and not having to go back to school, pointing out that he was intended for the Navy anyway, so being demoted from the Earl of Treyford's legitimate third son to illegitimate third son made no difference, and he might as well go immediately if Lord Charles could find a position. And now—kicked out of the Navy with a bad leg, at a loose end, young enough to think finding their mother was the answer, but too young to understand that their mother didn't want to be found. A family reunion was a stupid idea; if they couldn't hold together fourteen years ago, they were not going to do it now.

"Tell him I'm busy. Send him some money or find him a job or...Tell him that..."

"Perhaps you should write to him yourself," Das said.

"I never write letters. I hire you and a dozen other secretaries to write letters. If I went around writing letters, I'd be wasting my time and you'd all be out of a job and nothing would get done and we'd all be miserable."

"But Mr. Isaac is your brother."

Joshua glared at his secretary, who didn't flinch. "Do I detect a tone of disapproval, Das?"

"Yes, sir."

"Do I pay you to disapprove of me, Das?"

"No, sir. I provide the disapproval for free."

"Remind me to bloody thank you some time."

He should have just gone to Liverpool, never mind that the trip promised to be dull. Or back home to Birmingham. No inconvenient family members ambushed him there.

"Mr. Isaac also warns you about Lord Bolderwood," Das added. "Apparently, his lordship is upset over the money lost on the Baltic investment."

"Everyone lost money on that one. I told him it was speculation."

"He reports that Bolderwood claims you swindled him and he is plotting revenge."

"If Isaac wants drama, he can go to Covent Garden," Joshua said. "Bolderwood is as frightening as a three-legged calf."

The young viscount was about as useful and sensible as one as well, curse him.

"Is his situation very bad?" he finally asked. "Bolderwood, I mean."

Das folded Isaac's letter. "Rumor is he borrowed the money for that investment. From a moneylender."

"What?" Joshua skidded to a stop. "I told him only to risk what he could afford to lose."

"I believe he remained optimistic."

"The devil save us from optimists. Idiots, the lot of them." He moved on again. "Send Cosway or someone to make discreet inquiries. Not that I want to bail that clown out. These young lords. Receive an estate as their birthright and they give it as much respect as they give their breakfast. To think that could have been me."

He twirled the signet ring on his little finger. Would he have been like that? If his father's first wife, Lady Susan Lightwell, had in fact died when Treyford said she had and hadn't turned out to be living in an Irish convent all those years—if Treyford's bigamous marriage to Joshua's mother hadn't been dissolved—if Joshua was still heir to the earldom as he had been for the first fourteen years of his life...Treyford was in excellent health, promising to be a blight on society for years yet, so would Joshua have been like Bolderwood? Fashionable, profligate, and utterly useless.

And also utterly bored.

What a waste.

"Bolderwood jilted Mrs. DeWitt, you know," he said, and enjoyed that he had surprised Das. "Three weeks before their wedding. Which is why her father asked me to marry her."

"Interesting."

"No, actually. Not interesting at all."

Das waved Isaac's letter. "In that, Lord Bolderwood also claims you flirted with *his* wife."

"I what?" Joshua's memory offered the image of a pale woman who kept tittering at him at Lady Featherstone's card party and ruined his enjoyment of the game. As he recalled, he'd been rude to her. Clearly not rude enough. "Wives," he said. "They disrupt everything. Never get one, Das."

"I already have one."

"You what? This a recent acquisition?"

"We've been married nearly five years."

"You've worked for me for four years." He considered this a moment. "Huh. Devoted woman. To follow you all the way to Britain."

"Coming here was Mrs. Das's idea, actually," Das said. "There was some family opposition to our marriage, and I had a, ah, disagreement with a senior official in the East India Company, so it seemed prudent to make a home elsewhere. Padma thought Britain would suit us well enough, as the British had been interfering with my family for generations. She has an odd sense of humor, my wife."

Joshua's brain buzzed with questions but he shut them down. He did not want to know about Das and his wife, and why they wanted to be married so badly they left their whole life behind, and how Das had annoyed the East India Company and, no, no, he did not want to know. He knew nothing about his secretaries. They did their jobs and went home so he could forget about them.

"Huh," was all Joshua said.

"Mr. Newell has a wife too, as well as six children."

"That many."

"Mr. Putney has a wife, as does Mr. Allan. And Mr. Cosway is courting Miss Sampson."

Joshua rubbed his neck, aghast. His secretaries had seemed so sensible and reliable, when the whole time they'd been going around getting married behind his back.

"Work, Das," he said, returning to more productive topics of conversation, as they strode into St. James Park. "We need a contract, patents, investors. We need to make the most of this finding. Electrical power!"

"It is exciting, but the inventor himself admits he sees no immediate practical application," Das said. "This will not make any money."

"I don't care."

Joshua stopped short, startled by his own words. He stared at Das, who stared back at him.

"I don't care," he said again, wonderingly. He looked away from Das, at the sky, at the gardens, at the horses and birds and people. "How would you say I make money, Das?"

"You observe what people will want in the near future and you act fast to invest in those things."

"When Dammerton blathers on about penal reform, he says

it's not about whether forgers should be hanged, but what the whole country will look like in fifty years. I have money, Das." He pivoted, saw the world anew. "If I stopped working now, the money would keep rolling in."

"Indeed." Das was watching him cautiously. "You could spend time in the countryside with your charming wife, start a family, and—"

"What the blazes? Have you taken leave of your senses?"

"Your life revolves around your work."

"Which is precisely how I like it."

"I think—"

"Do I pay you to think, Das?"

"Yes, sir. You do."

Joshua paced over to a tree, paced back to Das, back to the tree, back to Das. He had wanted to be rich; now he was rich. That had not been enough. He had wanted high society to receive him; now they did. That was not enough.

Now he wanted, he wanted...

He thought about his factories, turning out millions of metal objects a year: buckles and buttons and bobbins. His barges, carrying those metal objects through the canals he'd helped build. His ships, exporting them all over the world. His mines. His furnaces. His warehouses. His bank.

Every one of those made him money. And not one had ever excited him as much as new ideas like this.

"What about if I look beyond the near future?" he said. "Ideas that have potential, that might lead to something, even if it's not in our lifetime, but should continue simply because of their own worth? What do you think?"

"I think someone would still need to run your business."

Joshua waved a hand. "Oh, I could do that too. But everything could change. Get Buchanan to—"

"Buchanan resigned."

"What? He go off to get married too?"

"Said it was too much work."

"There is no such thing as too much work." Joshua rubbed his hands together. "The one thing we can be sure of in this life, Das, is that there is always more work. And isn't that grand?"

CHAPTER 4

M r. DeWitt could be as ill-mannered and unreasonable as he pleased, but he would *not* disrupt her plans to launch Lucy, Cassandra vowed the next morning, with strengthened resolve.

"Every marriage is different," Arabella had proclaimed at the theater the night before, with the wisdom of someone who had been married a whole five months. "We must each find what works for us."

And what worked for the DeWitts was to never see each other.

To this end, Cassandra timed her arrival at breakfast carefully. According to the housekeeper, Mr. DeWitt took a substantial breakfast at eight o'clock sharp before starting work, as was the practice of businessmen, so Cassandra made sure to be there at half past eight: late enough to avoid him, but not so late as to disrupt the staff.

She was highly satisfied, then, to sail into the breakfast parlor and find only Mr. Newell, a copy of *The Times* beside his plate.

"Today is going to be a marvelous day, Mr. Newell," she said, as she surveyed the spread of eggs, ham, pears, rolls, and cake: a far cry from her usual, much later breakfast of bread and jam. "I can feel it in every fiber of my being."

She helped herself to a pear and a generous serve of pound cake: fresh, spicy, and loaded with currants.

"You are in good spirits, Mrs. DeWitt," Mr. Newell observed. Always pleasant, was Mr. Newell, unlike *some* people she could name. "I trust you had a good time at the theater last night."

"Oh, it was splendid! And my grandmother has agreed to meet me today—at the British Museum, of all places—and I am certain she will take on Lucy."

She took a seat and smiled at the footman who brought her tea, in a fine china pot painted with gloriously fat cherries. The tea was hot and fragrant and just as it ought to be. Yes, everything was going to work out beautifully—ill-mannered, unreasonable husbands notwithstanding.

"What's more," she went on, breaking into her cake, "I have recovered from the shock of meeting my husband, and I am reconciled to the fact that he is dreadful. For better or for worse, after all." She ate a chunk of cake and considered the vows she had naively made. "Those are cunning vows, really," she added. "It sounds lovely if you don't think about it too hard, but what they're really saying is: Too late! No complaining now!"

Mr. Newell removed his spectacles, wiped them, then put them back on. "I fear Mr. DeWitt has ordered arrangements made for you to return home."

"Cancel them. We can both stay here. For my part, I shall not even notice him."

That sounded very sensible, and Cassandra would have been proud of herself, except that Mr. DeWitt chose that moment to enter, yawning, wiping a hand over his eyes, and generally making a mockery of her bold statement.

For she could not fail to notice him.

To notice, particularly, his state of undress.

He looked as though he had barely stumbled out of bed and down the stairs. His dark hair tumbled over his forehead, the stubble had grown into scruff, and a fresh purple bruise on one cheekbone suggested that his night had been rather more eventful than her own.

But worst of all: He had neglected to put on any clothes other than breeches and a loose-fitting wine-red banyan. That in itself might not have been horrific, except that the silk dressing gown whirled open around him, revealing an expanse of male chest. Very naked male chest.

"Oh dear, Mr. DeWitt," she said, staring in helpless fascination. "You forgot to get dressed."

Her husband stopped short, frowned those dark brows, and tilted his head as though trying to work out who she was. Then he rubbed both hands vigorously through his already disheveled hair. When he lifted his arms like that, the banyan fell back further and the muscles in his chest and abdomen shifted.

Good heavens.

He glared at her. "You would, wouldn't you?" he muttered nonsensically. "Well, of course you bloody well would."

"Please, Mr. DeWitt. Your language."

"If you don't like my language, don't sit at my breakfast table looking all..." He waved his hand at her in disgust. "Fresh and friendly and innocent as if you are unaware that you have thrown out my entire schedule."

"Your *entire schedule* involved you going to Liverpool, and even now you are not keeping to your own breakfast routine. In a house this size, we should be able to go days without seeing each other, with a little cooperation."

"Stop being so bloody reasonable," he grumbled. "Can't stand it when people go around being reasonable before I've had my coffee."

With another yawn, he tumbled into the chair across from her. She kept her eyes firmly on his face, but the memory of his naked chest danced in her mind. She thought it bore a smattering of dark hair. She thought it reminiscent of the gods and warriors in paintings.

She thought she had better not look again.

"Mr. DeWitt—"

He made a long rumbling sound. "Coffee before conversation."

As the footman poured his coffee from a silver pot, Mr. DeWitt stared at the cup with such fierce intent one might think he were filling it himself through the power of his will. The moment the cup was full, the aroma pervading the room, he wrapped both hands around it, sipped, and sighed, his eyes closed, his expression stirringly ecstatic.

That coffee so dark and hot...It reminded her of something. Then his eyes snapped open. He looked right at her.

Oh yes. That was what the coffee reminded her of. His eyes.

"Go home," he said. "If I'm running behind schedule today, it's your fault for making me stay out late last night."

"You amaze me, sir!" She spluttered with laughter despite herself. "It cannot possibly be my fault. By the look of you, perhaps the blame lies with drink."

"Perhaps you drove me to drink."

"Mr. DeWitt never drinks," Mr. Newell chimed in, and Cassandra started, for she had quite forgotten he was there.

Mr. DeWitt whipped his head around and scowled at the secretary, then he returned his attention to his coffee and took a hefty swallow. "Newell, you're fired."

"Yes, sir." Mr. Newell popped a forkful of ham into his mouth.

"Mr. Newell, you are not fired," Cassandra said. "You can't fire him. He's *my* secretary."

"I hired him as Secretary In Charge Of Matrimonial Affairs. That makes him *mine*."

"And I *am* the Matrimonial Affair, which makes him *mine*."

"That is specious logic. I refuse to entertain specious logic at the breakfast table." He waved his arms again, the footman by the wall watching the trajectory of the coffee cup nervously. "His job is to deal with you and your affairs, so I don't have to. He failed, because look, here we are."

"Which is your fault for changing your schedule."

"Which wouldn't have mattered if you hadn't disobeyed me."

"Which I wouldn't have done if you had been reasonable."

"I am *always* reasonable."

"You are...Oh! You will drive *me* to drink." She caught herself waving her arms around too—heavens, even Lucy never inspired her to such transgressions!—and brought them under control. "This is why we need Mr. Newell," she said. "We cannot possibly communicate with each other directly."

It seemed that Mr. DeWitt took this as a challenge.

In an exaggerated gesture better suited to the theater, he carefully put his cup to one side. In another slow, deliberate movement, he placed first one hand, then the other, flat on the table in front of him.

Then he half-rose and leaned toward her, that broad, naked chest drawing near.

"Newell," he said, not taking his eyes off her. "Tell my wife to go home."

Cassandra mirrored his pose. "Mr. Newell. Tell my husband that I mean to stay until I have satisfactorily arranged my sister's entry into society."

He leaned in closer, so she could see the thick lashes framing his eyes. "Newell, tell my wife that her sister can have a fat dowry, and then pack some desperate gentlemen off to Warwickshire to fight over her."

She leaned in further too. "Mr. Newell, tell my husband that not every problem can be solved with money and secretaries."

"Newell, tell my wife that I will not tolerate this pigheadedness."

"Mr. Newell, tell my husband that the only pigheaded one here is he."

"And Newell—" Mr. DeWitt stopped, frowned, and turned his head, giving her his strong, scruffy profile. "Where the blazes has he got to?"

Cassandra turned too. "Oh," she said, seeing the now-empty chair. "We frightened him off, the poor man."

She turned her head back, at the same moment Mr. DeWitt did; their eyes met and she realized that they were almost close enough to bump noses. Hurriedly, she plonked herself back down, but she found it hard to take her eyes off him, as he lounged back in his chair, all lazy grace and naked chest, and reclaimed his coffee. The sleeve of his dressing gown slid back to reveal a strong forearm. Cassandra quickly busied herself with her teacup.

"Poor Mr. Newell doesn't like arguments," she said. "He often has to run for cover at Sunne Park."

"Is your house such a battlefield?" He sounded amused now. "Pincushions flying through the air? Exploding bonnets? That sort of thing?"

"You're not far wrong. With Lucy..." She sighed. "I suppose you do not wish to know about Lucy."

"Not really. She's the sister you're trying to launch, I take it."

"Yes. And she's..." Never mind. He didn't want to know. Lucy was her problem, not his. She could not expect her husband to support her; she could only hope that he did not obstruct her. "I do not mean to be difficult or disruptive, Mr. DeWitt. I would not have come if it weren't important. I must do what is best for my family, and on that point I shall not be moved."

"You mean, I'm not going to get rid of you."

"Be grateful it's only me. It could be worse. Lucy could show up instead."

JOSHUA HAD SOMEHOW LOST their argument, but he found it hard to mind, as he settled back with his coffee, watching Cassandra drink her tea. Before she lifted her cup, she stroked the painted cherries on the china, and before she sipped, she inhaled the fragrance with obvious pleasure.

When she forgot to be polite, she was highly entertaining. When she was being polite, on the other hand, he could cheerfully consign her to hell.

"What happened to you last night?" she said. "It looks like someone punched you in the face."

"Someone did."

"Does that happen often?"

"Not very."

"Oh."

She took a knife and quartered her pear.

"Is that it?" he said.

"I don't know what you mean."

"That's all you have to say? 'Oh.'" She looked at him blankly. "Where's the love and sympathy, wife? You aren't wondering what happened? You aren't wondering if I'm in pain? You aren't wondering if your dear husband will be all right?"

"Mainly I'm wondering why you don't get punched in the face more often."

He couldn't help but laugh. She kept surprising him. "Because

I'm rich," he said.

Still laughing, he went to fetch his breakfast from the spread on the sideboard. When he turned back, loaded plate in hand, he caught her twisted around in her chair to watch him, although she quickly twisted back and pretended a fascination with her cake. Her head was bowed but her shoulders were tellingly tense: Her attention was on him, loitering behind her where she could not see. He was making her nervous, perhaps. It seemed an excellent notion to loiter a bit longer.

Her mass of brown hair was caught up in a simple bandeau, the morning sunlight picking up its red highlights and the fine hairs on the back of her neck, the bumps of her spine. Her hairstyle left her ears exposed, slightly pink if he wasn't mistaken, as well as the curve of her neck, down to where it met her shoulder. The edge of her gown rode just past the spot where he would place a lingering kiss if they were lovers.

It came to his attention that he was enjoying their conversation immensely, which was utterly irrelevant. It also came to his attention that her eyes looked more brown than green today, that she did everything with a fuss-free competence but betrayed her sensuality by inhaling aromas and caressing the china, and that she was not nearly as saintly as she pretended.

All of which was also utterly irrelevant.

What *was* relevant was that when she cared, she cared a lot, fiercely and firmly, and this made her more tenacious than he had anticipated.

"I shall ask Mr. Newell, as our Secretary In Charge Of Matrimonial Affairs, to hire a valet for you," she said, when he was back in his seat. "You need help with your grooming."

"I already have a valet. Somewhere."

"Then he will buy this valet a shaving kit and teach him how to use it."

"Shaving is a waste of time. Bloody beard just grows back again. You object to my whiskers, Cordelia?"

"*Cats* have whiskers, *Jonah*. Men have scruff. You look…"

"Disreputable? Do say I look disreputable. I adore looking disreputable."

She glared at him. He grinned at her. What a marvelous sport this was, being ridiculous and riling her up.

"Old-fashioned," she finished.

"I never."

"Men have not worn beards and earrings since Tudor times," she argued. "Why do you even wear an earring?"

"Because I have ears. We could get matching earrings."

"That's a silly idea."

"Got to have silly ideas to get to the good ones. Matching rings, then."

She held up her left hand with its slim gold band. "We already wear matching rings."

"So we do. How adorable we are."

He lifted his own left hand and they both looked at it. His ring finger was bare, and the bulky ring on his little finger was clearly a signet ring.

"That's not your wedding ring," she said. "What is that?"

He dropped his hand into his lap. "Nothing. I mustn't have a wedding ring then. Most men don't."

"Papa got matching rings for both of us, don't you recall? He always wore one to indicate his devotion and fidelity to my mother."

She lifted her chin, defiant and tense, challenging him to be cynical again, unwilling to entertain even the possibility of the truth. He could not mock her.

"It matters to you, doesn't it?" he said quietly.

"As I said, fidelity is the cornerstone of marriage, and a strong marriage is at the core of family, and family is everything."

But as she spoke, her gaze wavered and she looked impossibly young, lost, and vulnerable, like a newborn lamb just waiting for the foxes to tear her to shreds. If he were a different man, he would comfort her and keep her safe. But he was not a different man, she was not his lamb, and protecting her was not his job.

"Family is a nuisance," he said, and turned his attention to his food.

OF THE MANY difficulties Cassandra had with Mr. DeWitt—his bad language, his roguish grin, his insistence on baring his chest—one of the greatest was his rapid changes in mood. She had grasped that he was a man who was swift in thought and deed, but he was also quick to anger, to humor, to empathy, to indifference. She could not recall meeting anyone who was so quick at everything, and feared she would sprain her neck trying to keep up.

He also ate quickly, though she finished her cake and pear first, and it dawned on her that she would have precious little time to argue her case again, before he cleared his plate and strode out.

Besides, while he was eating, he was not talking. This seemed a rare and wonderful thing.

"I am seeing my grandmother the duchess today," she said. "It is important that I see her in person, because relations in my family have been a little strained since..." She considered. Since Papa married Mama. The duchess had not approved of her youngest son's choice of wife, although everyone was always polite and civil, of course. "Not too long. Only for the past quarter-century or so. My hope and expectation is that Her Grace will take Lucy to live with her, oversee her debut, and guide her through society. If we are fortunate, Lucy will make a good match and be happily married by the end of the year. I assure you, I shan't bother you at all. You will hardly know I'm here."

He shoved aside his empty plate and grinned.

"How is that amusing?" she asked.

"You excel at polite-speak," he said. "'I shan't bother you at all' means 'I don't want to talk to you any more than necessary.' 'You will hardly know I'm here' means 'I'm going to pretend you don't exist.' Am I right?"

"How marvelous that we understand each other."

"Which means, 'Of course you're bloody well right.'"

"Please, Mr. DeWitt. Your language."

"You like my language. It gives you an excuse to scold me instead of making an honest response."

"I don't…I wouldn't…You…Oh."

Words failing her, Cassandra folded her arms and eyed him mutinously. To suggest that she was not honest! She was simply being civil.

"You should not mock politeness," she said. "It's our best defense against killing each other."

"Our best defense against killing each other would be to return to our separate lives. We've gone a whole two years without even being tempted to kill each other, which is more than other married couples can claim. You ought to be ashamed of yourself, Mrs. DeWitt, trying to ruin our perfect marriage."

"I assure you our marriage will be just as perfect if we go about our business and ignore each other completely."

He heaved a sigh. "Have you ever heard of barnacles?"

"I beg your pardon?"

"Barnacles. They are horrid marine creatures that cling to the hull of ships and slow them down. They are damn near impossible to get rid of, and there are men whose sole job is to scrape them off. You, Mrs. DeWitt, are as tenacious as a barnacle."

"I shall take that as a compliment, Mr. DeWitt. I am glad you are beginning to be reasonable and understand that it would be a waste of your precious time to *scrape me off*."

Cassandra pushed back her chair and stood. He did not stand, of course, and it would be a waste of breath to point out that a gentleman never remained seated when a lady stood. Her husband was not a pure gentleman, but a strange, hybrid creature, one of the few who could cross between the opposing worlds of gentry and commerce, thanks to a rare combination of his breeding, business acumen, and, she suspected, sheer bloody-mindedness.

Those dark, intense eyes followed her as she rounded the table toward the door. She had to pass right by him and found herself pausing at his side. The bruise on his cheek caught her eye.

"It does look like it hurts," she said. "Although I daresay you deserved it. You are exceedingly infuriating."

Hardly aware of what she was doing, she lightly touched her thumb to the bruise. Her fingers brushed his cheek. The scruff was surprisingly soft, and she only barely resisted the urge to stroke it. She glanced down and there was his chest, still naked, still muscular, and yes, with a smattering of dark hair. She hastily withdrew her hand and tangled her fingers in her skirts.

There was something she had to say to him, but she couldn't think what it was.

"Are you going to kiss it better?" he said.

His tone was light and teasing and she carefully didn't meet his eyes. Instead, she concentrated on the wound. An angry purple mark, that sharp cheekbone, that hot skin, that soft stubble. She could do it. She could press her lips against his face, right there. She often gave her sisters a kiss on the cheek, and her mother too. It was easy enough. Bend down, draw closer to his heat and his energy, and press her lips...

She looked away from his cheek and accidentally met his eyes. Hot liquid brown.

He wasn't laughing now. He wasn't teasing anymore. His sudden seriousness vibrated through her and hummed over her skin. Suddenly she realized just how much of him there was, and how close he was. His hand was barely inches from her thigh. She would not even have to straighten her elbow if she wanted to flatten her palm on his chest.

Then—then—he stood. That is, he unfolded upward with a sinuous languor at odds with his usual swiftness. She arched back, and her bottom pressed against the arm of the neighboring chair. He made no move to touch her, but he seemed to loom; he seemed so much taller when they stood this close, and his chest so much broader when it was right before her eyes. Her skirts murmured against her legs, caressed by his robe. She became aware that her lips were parted, all the better to help her breathe, so she closed them. He glanced at her mouth, back at her eyes.

That body had lain on top of her own, their bodies had been joined—briefly, uncomfortably, but joined all the same. It seemed impossible and yet...

"I never kissed you," he said. "No wonder you haven't forgiven me for our wedding night."

"As you said." Her voice came out husky so she cleared her throat. "It's best that way."

"Yes. It's best that way."

He glanced back at her mouth, swayed slightly, then looked up and straightened away from her.

"You are highly disruptive. Camilla."

"Then we have that in common. Jeremiah."

She edged away from him and out the door, on knees that ought not be so weak, feeling breathless and confused and more than a little disrupted.

CHAPTER 5

The British Museum was laughing at her, for it turned out to be full of bare-chested, muscular men.

Cassandra hurried through the exhibition rooms, seeking her grandmother, but finding only near-naked gods and warriors. They adorned the ceiling of the entrance hall, soaring two stories above her head. They crowded the galleries, too busy flexing their marble muscles to notice they'd forgotten their breeches. They hung on the walls, etched in intricate detail, down to the last fascinatingly male curve and ridge.

She was staring at one such sketch—a muscular Saint Sebastian, naked but for a loincloth and pierced with arrows—when a clerk approached to offer his help.

As the clerk had considerately kept his clothes on, Cassandra was able to tell him that she sought the Duchess of Sherbourne. Fortunately, the duchess did not pass anywhere unnoticed, and he escorted Cassandra up a broad staircase lined with ornate wrought-iron rails and through a series of galleries housing antiquities and natural curiosities, before leaving her in a room overlooking the gardens, brightly lit thanks to a row of huge, arched windows.

In the room were a dozen or so large wooden crates, each as high as her elbows, their tops pried off and packing straw spilling out onto the floor. Her grandmother stood by one wall, surveying the space.

"There you are, Cassandra, my dear." The duchess waved her over. "Do come look at these."

The duchess, the same height as Cassandra but slimmer, wore a stylish olive-green gown with a matching turban over her thick white curls, fastened with a large circular silver pin. Her green eyes were bright and her face, lined in only the most dignified of ways, was alert.

"You're looking well, Grandmother," Cassandra said with a bob.

"So are you, my dear." Her grandmother favored Cassandra's russet morning gown with an approving nod. "You have more of your father in you than I recalled. I'm glad you could meet me here. Sir Arthur is planning the layout of his exhibition and he particularly asked for my advice. Are you familiar with the work of Sir Arthur Kenyon? He is a leader in his field." She stroked her chalcedony necklace, smiled, and stepped toward the nearest wooden crate. "Come. You will be astonished by this."

Cassandra most certainly would be astonished. She would be whatever her grandmother wanted her to be, if it helped Lucy.

So long as "this" was not any form of naked man.

With a smile, she obediently stepped up to the crate and peered over the edge at...

A rock.

It was big and square and white—impressively so, on all three counts—but still a rock.

On the other side of the crate, her grandmother stared at the stone, her hand pressed to her throat. "Isn't that simply marvelous?"

Cassandra kept smiling and looked harder at the rock. She noticed that its edges were chiseled with patterns: ridges and scrolls and possibly...a pig? Good. Pigs were fascinating; she could discuss them for hours. But, no. Not a pig. Just a pig-like chip in a scroll.

"Sir Arthur brought it from Greece himself," the duchess said breathily. "'Tis part of an ancient temple, he says. Sir Arthur maintains that classical statues and buildings were painted in bright colors, though most scholars insist he is wrong and that the unadorned marble is the most pleasing and authentic. A fierce dispute is brewing in the Society of Antiquaries."

Cassandra pictured a group of old men throwing big white rocks at each other. "That sounds fascinating," she said.

She followed the duchess to another crate and offered enthusiastic praise for an identical rock.

"I was never one of the bluestockings," the duchess said. "Sherbourne would not have stood for it, but even he agrees that a broad knowledge of the world prevents a lady from becoming dull." She smiled pleasantly. "Your mother was never interested in my advice on my granddaughters' education."

"Speaking of my mother—"

"Oh, look, there's Sir Arthur now."

Sir Arthur Kenyon was a robust gentleman in his fifties, who bore the hearty look of a man who reveled in outdoor activity. He strode into the room, quizzing glass fixed to his eye. Upon seeing the duchess, he performed a deep, gallant bow. The duchess responded with a gracious nod, her face touched by a girlish smile and an extra hint of color.

Now, *that* made the rocks more interesting!

"Well, Cassandra, my dear, it's been lovely to see you," her grandmother said, her eyes on Sir Arthur.

Cassandra's mirth faltered. That was polite-speak, as Mr. DeWitt would put it. Translation: "I don't want to talk to you anymore."

"I daresay we shall see each other again soon," the duchess went on. "You will attend your uncle Morecambe's rout this week, of course, and I shall send an invitation for my ball; it's in less than three weeks. I look forward to seeing you there."

With that, the duchess turned and started across the room, toward her beau and his big rocks, leaving Cassandra momentarily speechless.

"Grandmother! Your Grace!" she called, collecting herself and scurrying after her. "There was a particular matter..."

Her grandmother paused, her lips pursed. "Well, what is it?"

"It's Lucy, she's nineteen now, and it's past time for her to enter society and, since you are hosting a ball anyway, perhaps you might be so kind as to—"

"Oh dear, I feared it would be something like this." Her grandmother spared a quick glance at Sir Arthur before continuing. "Guiding a girl into society requires considerable time. You may think I sit around with nothing to do but wait for my granddaughters to rush in from the countryside and start demanding favors, but my schedule is full and I cannot simply abandon my other obligations to tend to your needs."

"I didn't mean..." Cassandra fumbled for a response. "There'll be no court presentation. Merely if Lucy made her debut at your ball..."

"I don't see why Lady Charles isn't seeing to it."

"Mama is unwell."

"I see. Well, your father did insist on marrying her. But that was decades ago and it does not signify now."

"Lucy is special," Cassandra rushed to say before her grandmother could turn away again.

"What are her interests?"

Making trouble. Breaking things. Getting drunk and singing bawdy songs in the middle of the night.

"She is a renowned beauty. She excels at dancing and singing and putting together outfits and—"

"And I am bored with her already." The duchess sighed. "Cassandra, my dear, I made my debut nearly fifty years ago. Back then, dancing and gowns were exciting for me too, but let me tell you, the faces change, the fashions change, but the conversations remain the same."

"If Lucy makes a good match, it will benefit all the family."

"A better match than yours, you mean? I advised strongly against your marriage to Mr. DeWitt—the son of the man who ruined my Susan!—but your father would not listen. Yet still you expect me to run to your aid, even while *you* are stirring up trouble too."

"I've never stirred up trouble in my life!"

"Oh? Then what do you call it when your husband and your former betrothed come to blows outside a club in St. James, as they did last night?"

That purple bruise on her husband's cheek. The feel of his skin under her thumb.

"Harry?" Cassandra said. "I mean, Lord Bolderwood was the one who punched him? Whatever for?"

"You'll have to ask your husband that, won't you?" The duchess gave a little shake of her head. "Dreadful man, your Mr. DeWitt, but my husband and my son do insist on receiving him." She shot another glance at Sir Arthur, as though he might sneak off to Greece if she did not keep an eye on him. "I see you are disappointed, Cassandra, but this has nothing to do with me. Your father made it plain that he neither valued nor needed my advice, when it came to his children. I don't know what he was thinking."

And you don't want to know, Cassandra thought. *If you knew, it would break your heart.*

Cassandra hadn't understood back then, either. "Here's what I'm thinking, Cassandra, my dear," Papa had said, barely a week after her wedding. Their prize sow Aphrodite had birthed a fine litter, and she and Papa were in the barn admiring the squirming, squealing piglets, while competing to think up the silliest names. Cassandra was daydreaming that her awful wedding night had resulted in a baby of her own, when Papa said, "Now that you're married, I'll have the lawyers transfer all my estate to you, which is to say, to Joshua. That'll save you trouble later on." She had asked what kind of trouble there could possibly be, and all he had said was, "You never know what will happen."

Except that he had known. He had known exactly what was going to happen.

But she couldn't say any of that, so instead she said, "Grandmother, please. Don't punish Lucy for Papa's decisions."

Her grandmother laughed, a jarringly pleasant sound. "How melodramatic you are, my dear. No one's punishing anyone." She placed a gentle hand on Cassandra's wrist. "I simply have too many other obligations. You do understand?"

"Yes. Thank you. I understand."

This time, Cassandra let her go. As she watched, the duchess tapped Sir Arthur playfully on the forearm and drew him into animated conversation, full of her suggestions for curating the exhibition. Sir Arthur nodded enthusiastically, a wise man who knew better than to dismiss the duchess's advice.

Cassandra left and roamed unseeingly through the exhibition rooms in search of the exit. Perhaps she *was* selfish, expecting her grandmother to leap to attention like a scullery maid, but to

Cassandra, it was the most obvious thing in the world: One put one's family first. Yet if she said that, the duchess would agree, smile pleasantly, and repeat that she was too busy.

"I'm too busy" was merely an acceptable way of saying "Everything else is more important than you."

How Mr. DeWitt would gloat when she confessed her failure. Worse: Going back to Sunne Park and telling Lucy and Emily that she had failed.

Again.

Finding herself nose-to-nipple with two muscular marble warriors, she folded her arms and scowled.

"I will look after my sisters. I *will*," she whispered to the warriors. "If you can go into battle with no clothes on, then I can find another way."

She knew nothing about big old rocks, painted or otherwise, but she knew how to make friends. Her marriage had lowered her social position, but she would rebuild it. She would make so many friends that Grandmother would change her mind and Lucy could blow up Parliament House and they would still be received.

"And don't you try to stop me," she said to the statues.

The statues did not try to stop her and Cassandra decided to claim that as a victory.

One day, she would follow her grandmother's example and lead an active life of her own. But for now, she would put her family first.

Family! With a sigh, she headed toward the gate and her waiting carriage. Her sisters hated her, her mother forgot her name, her grandmother thought her unimportant, and her husband wanted her gone.

If she'd known it would be like this, she would have brought her cat.

CHAPTER 6

Joshua was sprawled on the settee in his study, thinking hard, when a female voice outside the door sent his thoughts scattering like street urchins before the Watch. His eyes flew open, only to meet the provoking sight of the flowers on his desk, so he closed them again.

Curse that woman. In the three days since that breakfast, she had stayed out of his way, but her colonization continued ruthlessly. Vases of fresh flowers claimed territory throughout, the conquered staff smiled more, and pianoforte music invaded the air at odd moments, all the more odd because he hadn't known this house even possessed a pianoforte. Admittedly, the staff moved more quickly too, and the flowers were not unpleasant, and it turned out that music helped him think.

But none of that was the *point*.

Another voice outside the door: Filby. Good: The butler would not let Joshua be disturbed when he was thinking. Samuel used to sneak in, though; he'd snuggle up beside him, his dark little head pillowed on Joshua's arm. Sometimes he could still feel the pressure of that head, as though even his muscles remembered the boy.

But it seemed that even Filby could not withstand Cassandra's amiable invasion.

The door opened. A moment later, it clicked shut. Without looking, Joshua knew he was no longer alone.

He slitted his eyes open, took one look at the invader—as fresh as one of her roses in a pink-striped gown—and closed them again.

"Mr. DeWitt, we must talk."

"Go away. I'm busy."

"You are lying on the settee doing nothing."

"I never do nothing. I don't know how to do nothing. I'm a man on whom the art of doing nothing is entirely lost."

He kept his eyes closed, but he felt her presence, stirring the air.

"And why must you persist in this state of undress?" she said.

"Undress? I'm wearing a shirt, aren't I?"

He checked with one hand. Yes. He was wearing a shirt under his banyan. He opened his eyes, caught Cassandra watching his hand on his chest. Then she saw him watching her watching him, and hurriedly began rearranging the bunch of flowers, although they seemed adequately arranged to him. A faint blush rose in her cheeks, cheeks likely as soft as those petals she was fondling.

"But your cravat," she said, with a sideways glance.

"Don't like it. It restricts my movement."

"Your coat."

"Too tight. It restricts my movement."

She threw up her hands, which did interesting things to her bosom. "Heaven knows why you're so preoccupied with movement. You're not moving!"

In a single bound, he was on his feet. He arranged his banyan over his shoulders then glanced at her slyly, and yes, aha, caught her looking at him again. She was an unwelcome interruption, but at least she was an entertaining one.

He sauntered to her side, reached past her to fish some candied lemon from a bowl, and leaned one hip on the desk. As he chewed, she pulled a white flower out a few inches, turned it a few degrees, then pushed it back in one inch.

"What is the point of all these flowers anyway?" he said.

Her hands continued to move over the flowers, brisk, confident, competent. Whatever she was doing, the arrangement somehow became more harmonious. Clever, that. Pointless, but clever.

"Fresh flowers are pleasant."

"They're inefficient." He paced away from those devilishly competent hands. "You cut them, put them in a vase, and then they die."

"Everything dies. We cannot avoid loss, but we can compensate with pleasure and joy."

"Pleasure and joy?" He swung around. "Did you come here to philosophize at me? If I wanted philosophy, I would consult the works of someone more..." He sought the right word. "Dead."

"I shall keep that in mind."

"How long do you mean to plague me anyway? Newell says your efforts with the duchess failed."

"She merely feels neglected by her family. She'll change her mind."

"If the bloody woman doesn't want you, sod her. You have friends," he rushed on, before she could chide him for his language. "You're out at all hours and I can't take two steps without someone telling me how charming Mrs. DeWitt is, how agreeable, how amiable, how we must attend this tedious dinner or that ridiculous ball. Get some friend to dispose of Lucy for you." He paced over to the fireplace and back, the room smaller than usual today. "How about the woman you were with the other day—the tall, terrifying one?"

"Arabella, Lady Hardbury?"

"That's the one."

"She has offered, but she hinted that she might be, ah, in a delicate condition."

His legs froze, his heart raced with the fear that she might broach a conversation about delicate conditions. He risked a glance at her. Their eyes met briefly and then she hastily took to lining up the objects on his desk: a polished lump of iron ore, the bowl of candied lemon, a green glass paperweight filled with bubbles shaped like tears.

But all she said was, "Besides, it's the principle. The duchess is family."

"So you'll grovel to her."

"If that's what I must do for Lucy. I'd do anything for my mother and sisters and children. Oh—"

She pressed her lips tight shut, her hand frozen around the paperweight, but the word had snuck out. It wafted through the air with a stench more ripe than the Thames in summer. No doubt she was cursing her wayward tongue. He certainly was.

He breathed through the yawning ache of emptiness and the phantom sensation of his son's head on his arm. If she wanted children...

"There are plenty of children running around the streets of London," he snapped. "Help yourself."

"Of course, children would be too much of a nuisance for you, wouldn't they?" She dropped the paperweight with a clunk. "No wonder you didn't have any in your first marriage."

"Right," he said, not bothering to correct her. "A nuisance."

"And I hear your brother Isaac has called, but he's a nuisance too."

"You're all bloody nuisances. So if that's all you wanted to say, you can stuff your self-righteousness into your trunk and take it with you to hell." He strode to the door and yanked it open. "Now get out. I'm busy."

"Fine!" She marched two steps toward him, chin high, eyes fierce, but stopped. "Except…"

"What? What?"

"I'm afraid I got a little distracted," she said, sheepishly. "I meant to inform you that we are attending a rout at Lord and Lady Morecambe's house this evening."

He flung the door shut and leaned against it. "*We* are?"

"Yes. You and I."

"Lady Morecambe invited *us*?"

"She is my aunt by marriage. Of course she invited us."

That couldn't be right. Invite Cassandra, certainly. But Joshua too? Cassandra's uncle and grandfather—the Marquess of Morecambe and the Duke of Sherbourne—both received Joshua, but not to the more refined events, especially if Treyford would be there; society took care to avoid having Joshua and his father in the same room.

"Mr. Das and Mr. Newell have freed up your schedule tonight," she went on, cheerfully oblivious to her looming social faux pas.

He was too amused to mind that she had taken over his schedule too. He pushed off the door and paced back around the room, trying to hide his grin.

"I should be *delighted* to attend," he said.

"Good. It will be our first outing together as a married couple." She smiled. No wonder she was welcome everywhere, with a smile like that. "Mr. Newell has had a word with your valet, a Mr. Vickers, I believe, who will select an appropriate outfit and shave you. Please remove the earring and do try to sit still long enough for him to tie your cravat properly. And if you could submit to a more fashionable haircut..."

She eyed his hair, which was, admittedly, getting too long. He wondered how long her hair was, when she let it out, all those thick chocolate tresses tumbling down her back. He did not have a chance to wonder too long before she turned to leave, saying, "Just...make an effort."

Her skirts swayed about her as she marched to the door, graciously and purposefully, and he could almost make out the shape of her bottom and thighs beneath the layers of fabric.

"Is my hair so very terrible?" he called.

She stopped and turned back.

"It suits you, I suppose." She looked him over again. "Your bruise has faded to a fetching shade of yellow. Like a kingcup."

"Perhaps Vickers can find a matching waistcoat. I shall be the envy of every dandy in town."

She didn't seem to be listening. After a brief hesitation, she crossed back to him. "Why did Harry, I mean, Lord Bolderwood punch you anyway?"

"How the blazes did you know it was him?"

"You didn't hurt him, did you?"

"So *now* you have sympathy. For *Harry*."

"Well, you're bigger and more dynamic and..."

She fluttered her hands at him. It took him a moment to realize she was indicating the size of his shoulders and chest.

"He is a bit puny, isn't he?" he said. "Not all men can be as powerfully built as I am, you know. I trained as a blacksmith in my youth, and I worked as a stevedore. I'm still so strong I can balance a ton of steel on my little finger."

She gave an endearing huff. "You would need to be strong to carry your vanity, which must weigh more than a ton."

"Who said anything about vanity?" He feigned affront. "You're the one who started talking about how broad and muscular my chest and shoulders are."

"I never said a word about muscular shoulders!"

"So now you're saying I'm puny too. Well." He folded his arms over his chest, watched her eyes follow the movement. "That's a bit unkind."

"Of course you're not puny! You're shaped like a classical warrior and you know it. But that...Oh. You're impossible. Why...Oh."

Words having failed her, she closed her eyes and covered her face with one hand.

Faced with her charming embarrassment, Joshua could not maintain his act. He did enjoy teasing her, and her obvious curiosity about his body provided a marvelous source of entertainment. To strip away her polite facade and explore the real woman beneath would be...

Would be a very, very stupid thing to do.

"Baltic investment," he said.

She pulled her hand away from her face and peered at him with bright eyes. More green than brown today, they were. "I beg your pardon?"

"Bolderwood lost money on a Baltic investment scheme and blames me for it."

"Oh."

Her eyes glazed over, somewhere around "investment," which fortunately put an end to her questions. He would rather not mention Bolderwood's ridiculous accusation that Joshua had his eye on Bolderwood's wife. It was Joshua's frank declaration of Lady Bolderwood's *lack* of appeal that had earned him the punch.

"Anyway, please desist from any arguments tonight, and behave like a polite gentleman."

"Smug and idle, you mean? Wasting hours tying my cravat and composing stupid odes to women's eyes? Is that your notion of the ideal husband?"

She flashed a half-smile and he realized that, yes, that was her ideal. After all, useless, pretty Bolderwood had almost been her husband.

"Too bad," he said, irritated with her again. "I might have been a polite gentleman, but I'm not. And I'm glad of it. I'm a businessman, a Birmingham man. Everyone in Birmingham walks fast, did you know that? Because we all have purpose and activity. And as for these polite gentlemen of yours, strolling about with fancy cravats because they have nothing else to do with their time —bah! What a shame you didn't manage to marry one of them."

"Never mind that now. You are not the kind of husband I need, but you are the one I have. I don't mean to sound ungrateful," she added hastily. "I am immensely sensible of the sacrifice you made in marrying me."

He shrugged and wandered away from her. "No sacrifice," he said. "It means no one else can try to marry me. I don't want a wife, so one who hardly exists suits me well. The sooner you can go back to not existing, the better."

Silence filled the room, as if he had already gotten his wish. He resisted the urge to check that she was still there.

Until she came to his side and laid a hand on his arm, her expression soft and pleading.

"I know you are not that man, but could you not pretend?"

"Pretend to be someone I'm not?" He jerked his arm away from her. "Unlike you, I do not need everyone to like me. I have some pride."

"Some of us haven't the luxury of pride." Something hard flashed in her eyes. "I need everyone to like me because then they will invite me into society, speak well of me, and overlook the fact that I am married to the rudest man in England. They will be more likely to welcome my sister into society and less likely to object if someone wishes to marry her. And if Lucy does something dreadful, we are more likely to come out of it all right." She jabbed a finger at him. "And since your behavior reflects on me, the better you behave, the more likely I am to find a solution to Lucy. After which I shall go back to not existing, as you so charmingly put it, and you can go back to being as rude as you like."

She maintained her facade, but her little speech was edged with anger, tainted with frustration, searing with the hint that some part of her longed to scream the words and pummel his chest and hurl heavy objects at his head. Her sense of injustice, her lack of power, her subtle strength of character—he imagined them wrestling with each other like drunks in a brawl, wreaking havoc inside her, with only her politeness to keep them locked in.

A better man would help her fight her battles, so she could have some peace.

Well, he was not a better man, and he had battles of his own, and no one saw him going around pestering people for help. Start taking on each other's burdens and they'd never know when to stop.

Besides, he had agreed to a marriage in name only. Name only. Name. Only.

"What do I get in return?" he said. "For behaving properly and pretending to be someone I'm not?"

"Why would you need something in return?"

"When an employee performs well, I offer a reward. Or when a businessman hesitates on a deal, I throw in an inducement to make him agree."

"Helping your family should be inducement enough."

"And yet it is not."

She considered for a moment. "What do you want, then?"

What he wanted was for her to leave him be, to stop disrupting his life, to stop making him question who he was and how he got here and who he wanted to be.

So he did the obvious thing, really.

He stepped right up to her and pressed a hand to her waist to hold her steady, her body firm and warm under his palm. He lowered his head so his mouth was so close to her ear he could have nibbled it. A lock of her hair brushed his cheek. She was tense, and he could feel her breathe. Her warm, floral, womanly fragrance slid under his skin and into his blood.

He ignored it all and murmured in her ear. He explained clearly, descriptively, succinctly, what he wanted her to do to him, as reward and inducement for good behavior.

She responded exactly as he had intended: She gasped and stumbled away from him, hands pressed over her mouth, eyes wide.

"I will never do such a disgusting, depraved thing!" she cried. "That you would even think of it!"

Bull's-eye! He grinned, ignoring the void beside him where she had been.

"If you refuse to comply, I refuse to behave," he said.

"Oh, you..." Her lovely full mouth moved, helplessly seeking words to voice her outrage, then she gave up and stormed out, finally, mercifully leaving him alone, with his thoughts in disarray.

CHAPTER 7

Cassandra's infuriating, vexing, *depraved* husband neither shaved nor removed the infernal earring, and he met Cassandra's pointed look with raised eyebrows, which reminded her of his suggestion and her natural mortification. She carefully ignored him all the way to the rout at her aunt and uncle's house, where, fortunately, he went his own way, and she was able to enjoy herself, though she could not forget what he had said.

Routs were silly, really: a crowd speeding through a house, conversing in frantic, frivolous bursts, reveling in the crush even as they complained. But she loved talking to people and thinking up amusing conversation points and admiring other ladies' gowns.

She spied Arabella on the upper level and climbed the stairs to join her. Arabella made a haughty, cool island of stillness amid the social whirl, but her gentle smile suggested Lord Hardbury was nearby.

"Arabella, I must ask you something." Cassandra's hands were clammy in her gloves; she could not believe she was about to ask something so brazen, but she simply had to know. She started to speak but with this racket, she would have to nearly yell to be heard. "I need to whisper. Please stoop."

"How intriguing," Arabella said and complied.

"Do you ever..." Cassandra glanced around. No one could hear. "Kiss...your husband's...organ?"

A strange sound burst out of Arabella and she hastily covered her mouth with her fist. "Did you say what I think you said?"

Cassandra's cheeks burned. "Mr. DeWitt suggested that I...But I...Oh, stop laughing."

But Arabella only straightened, her shoulders shaking with the effort to repress her mirth. The astonishing sight of Lady Hardbury laughing drew unwanted attention. It also drew Lord Hardbury, bemusement replacing his usual scowl.

"Whatever are you two up to?" he asked. "Mrs. DeWitt, you look overheated. Do you need some air?"

Too embarrassed to look at him, Cassandra seized her first opportunity to escape. "Oh, there's Leo with Sir Gordon," she said brightly, and hurried away from her unhelpful friend.

If her color was still high when she reached the Duke of Dammerton and Sir Gordon Bell, they were too polite to comment. After some pleasant chatter, the heat mercifully subsided, and by the time Sir Gordon bowed and moved away, she felt like herself again.

"I see you brought that dreadful husband of yours," the duke said. "You remember what he looks like, then?"

She smiled at his good-natured teasing. "He is not really so dreadful, is he?"

"Good heart, bad manners. Better than the alternative, I always say," he said. "I never expected to see him here at Lord and Lady Morecambe's party, though."

"Lord Morecambe is my uncle."

"I know but...Lord Treyford is here, and DeWitt and his father do not get along."

"But he won't make a scene here."

His Grace's smile faltered. He started to speak, stopped, and then excused himself to talk to someone else.

Oh dear. Cassandra decided she had better go in search of her husband, although heaven knew what she was supposed to do when she found him. She nudged her way toward the balcony overlooking the main gallery, but before she could search for him, she came face to face with—

"Harry!"

"Cassandra!"

Harry Willoughby, Lord Bolderwood, looked as fair and handsome as the day they got engaged, three years ago now. His purse may be suffering, but his face, at least, betrayed no ill effects of his marriage to—

"Do introduce us, Harry, my sweet."

"My wife, Phyllis, Lady Bolderwood."

The tips of Harry's ears turned pink and he didn't meet Cassandra's eye. The two ladies subtly inspected each other. Lady Bolderwood's blue silk gown was elaborate and expensive, but her only adornment was a ribbon around her throat. Cassandra caught herself fingering the rubies at her own throat and hastily dropped her hand. She decided that, whatever Arabella said, Lady Bolderwood *was* pretty, and they made an ideal couple, and Cassandra was a big enough person to wish them well.

Besides, seeing Harry again confirmed that she hadn't a shred of feeling left for him. How odd love and romance were. Once, his attentions had left her giddy with delight and his kisses had thrilled her. Now, the idea of kissing him seemed ridiculous, whereas the idea of kissing her husband seemed...

Also ridiculous. For he was dreadful and she disliked him and he had made that depraved suggestion.

What about these two? Did they do that thing that Mr. DeWitt wanted? And how did they...Did she...Or did he...? Oh heavens, was she to spend all night wondering such things about her fellow guests?

The rout took on rather a different appearance.

"Such a pleasure to meet you, Lady Bolderwood," she said graciously.

"Everyone is thrilled to see you in town, Mrs. DeWitt," that lady said. "Rumor was your husband kept you hidden away so you could not curtail his...excesses."

Maybe Arabella was right, and Lady Bolderwood wasn't very pretty after all.

"The only excess I observe in my husband is his excessive generosity," Cassandra said.

Harry snorted. "He can afford to be generous. Just don't ask where he gets his money from."

"Do you refer to the Belgian investment, Lord Bolderwood?" Cassandra said. "I do hope you aren't going to punch him over it again."

"Baltic investment," Harry corrected her absently. "And that's not the half of it."

His expression was dark and clouded, as she had never seen on him, but before she could ask what he meant, his wife was hugging his arm, pressing her bosom against him, and gazing adoringly into his face.

"Now, now, Harry, my sweet," she said. "Mrs. DeWitt is right. This is neither the time nor place."

The couple exchanged an intimate look, shutting out the world. Harry ran his fingers down his wife's arm and she responded with a pinch of his chin.

Cassandra averted her eyes. Impoliteness took a variety of forms, she thought crossly, and curled her fingers around her fan.

She began to excuse herself, but Harry interrupted her, saying, "I always did admire your fortitude, Cassandra, that is, Mrs. DeWitt. I daresay you need it, with a husband like that."

"Some ladies will tolerate anything for the sake of luxury," his wife chimed in, oh-so-sweetly. "But why not, if one hasn't the fortune to find true love, like us."

No, Lady Bolderwood definitely was not pretty, Cassandra decided. She had sly eyes and nasty ears, and her teeth were too small.

Harry's ears turned pink again. "I trust you've put that whole matter behind us, Mrs. DeWitt."

"Oh, do say you've forgiven us for running away together." Lady Bolderwood's blue eyes were wide as she pressed her bosom more firmly against Harry's arm. "But love and passion overcame us so, we were powerless to resist."

Cassandra clenched her teeth and smiled, and somehow found enough air left in her tight chest to respond. "Of course I don't mind. I couldn't be more content. Obviously, it has turned out well for all of us."

"It *will* work out well," Lady Bolderwood said. "My darling Harry is seeing to that."

The couple exchanged another intimate look and secret smile. Cassandra willed herself to get away from them, but her feet didn't move.

"Whatever do you mean?" she said.

Harry glanced back at her, shrugged one shoulder. "Merely that one has a right to take control of one's affairs," he said. "Take justice into one's own hands, as it were."

"Heavens," Cassandra said. "If you are still angry with my husband—"

"Please!" Lady Bolderwood fairly shoved her face in Cassandra's. "We must not discuss Mr. DeWitt. You know what he's like."

"Yes, I do." Cassandra lifted her chin and refused to step back. "Joshua is brilliant, energetic, amusing, generous, and kind. You did me a favor, Lady Bolderwood. Joshua DeWitt is the best husband I could ever have."

She held the other woman's eye, determined not to look away first, but then came the loud sound of a glass smashing, and they both looked around at once.

A hush fell over the crowd. Angry male voices rose through the quiet.

Cassandra and a score of other guests peered over the balcony at the crowded gallery below. A small space had opened up around a spreading pool of orange, fruity punch.

And in that space stood two men, snarling at each other like a pair of fighting dogs. The older man, robust with thick gray hair, was her father-in-law, the Earl of Treyford.

The younger man was her husband.

Lady Bolderwood raised her plucked eyebrows at Cassandra. "You were saying?"

Joshua had not intended to start any trouble when he found himself face to face with his father and stepmother. Until that point, he had been enjoying the rout immensely and, as far as he could tell, had not offended anyone. Not much, anyway.

In fact, he had not intended even to talk to his father, but it would be rude to turn away now, and Cassandra did not like him being rude.

"Good evening, Father," Joshua said cheerfully. "And Lady Treyford. Fancy us all meeting like this. A little family reunion."

"What the hell are you doing here?" Treyford said.

Joshua planted his feet more firmly on the floor. "I was invited. Lord and Lady Morecambe are my wife's people, don't you know? Have you met my wife?"

"I don't give a damn about your wife."

"That's not very nice. My wife is lovely." He gave them both a broad smile. "Did you know that my wife's father, Lord Charles Lightwell, was the older brother of your first wife, Lady Susan Lightwell? Cozy, isn't it? All of us tangled up like the plot of a Gothic novel. Do you care for novels, Lady Treyford?"

"You will not address the countess."

And they called Joshua the rude one! Here he was, making pleasant and polite conversation, while his impulsive, hotheaded father said what he pleased. But as always, his father would get away with it and Joshua would be blamed.

He started peeling off his gloves as they talked. "Married again, are you, my lord? Only one wife this time?"

"Get out. You don't belong here."

"Now, now, Papa, that's no way to talk to your eldest son. I am a guest here too." He gathered both gloves in his right hand. "It's remarkable, isn't it, the way a huge fortune can give back what an invalid marriage license took away."

Joshua scratched his cheek, thoughtfully. As it happened, it was his left cheek that needed scratching. Which meant he had to use his left hand.

Which just happened to be the hand that bore the signet ring.

Which just happened to catch the earl's attention.

"That ring does not belong to you," the earl snapped, leaning toward him.

"Ring? What ring? Oh, *this* ring."

Joshua held his hand up high, made a show of admiring the ring. A voice in his head was yelling at him to stop, but he couldn't. And why in blazes should he? Let everyone watch. They had been content to shrug off his father's sins. Bigamy was usually considered a serious crime, yet Treyford had said, "But I didn't *mean* it," and all these people had nodded and said, "Well, then, if you didn't *mean* it, it's all right." As for the consequences of Treyford's perfidy, his selfishness, his lack of restraint, they all wanted to ignore those too, probably because the fatuous hypocrites wanted their own actions overlooked.

Then he met his father's eyes and grinned.

It was like waving a handkerchief at the start of a race.

Treyford lunged, fingers outstretched to grab at the ring, coming fast at Joshua, who knocked his father's hand away. Treyford's arm windmilled back and cuffed his wife's hand in turn, causing her to drop her glass of punch with a cry.

The glass smashed on the hard floor. Orange punch splattered nearby hems and stockings, and spread across the floor. The smell of alcohol and fruit rose in the air.

The crowd fell silent, but for the swishing of skirts as bodies turned. After the eerie hush, the tittering began. A space opened up around them, but no one intervened.

Let them watch. Let them stare. Let them see what happened when aristocrats tossed children away like the first draft of a letter.

"I rather like this ring," Joshua said into the silence.

"That ring belongs to my son and heir, curse you!"

The earl lunged again, but Joshua was taller. He held his hand out of reach, leaving his father to swipe at him like a thwarted cat.

"Speaking of sons, I hear your latest mistress is expecting," Joshua said. "What are your plans for her baby? Or is that not your concern? Making a child is much more diverting than dealing with it afterward, isn't it?"

The tittering swelled to a murmur, and then to a roar, rushing through Joshua's head along with his blood.

A pair of footmen slid in to clean up the glass and the punch. Orange splashes stained the embroidery on Lady Treyford's hem. Joshua had to stop this. He wished someone would stop him. Please, someone stop him. But no one ever would, just as no one would stop Treyford from discarding children.

The worst of it was that the earl wasn't even cruel, merely selfish and careless. He took what he wanted and never cared who might be hurt and what others might lose or what mess might be left behind.

No, the worst of it was that nobody condemned him for it, whatever Joshua said. It was like one of those nightmares, where he tried to yell but had no voice.

And then: A touch on his shoulder.

A moment later, two warm, feminine hands closed around his raised arm, gently lowering it, trapping his forearm against a pleasantly soft female body, holding it still. One of those hands slid up his forearm, and pressed into the crook of his elbow.

Cassandra, her shoulder pressing against his arm as she joined herself to him. Claimed him. Acknowledged him as her own.

He was so surprised that he let her do it. He breathed in her fragrance. His heart began to calm.

"Lady Treyford," his wife said. One would think from her tone that she had waited all year to meet this one woman. "How lovely to see you again. I believe we were introduced the last time I was in London."

The countess's expression suggested she had no recollection of meeting Cassandra, but she returned a greeting, as she had to do, given the audience. For all Joshua's complaints, he had to concede that Cassandra could wield politeness like a scimitar.

Then Cassandra looked up at him, her smile warm as if she

was happy to see him too, her eyes soft with something that might have been concern. Mostly likely concern for her precious sisters and her precious reputation and her extremely precious politeness. She stretched up, her body bumping against his, to speak in his ear.

"Joshua, please stop," she whispered. "I'll do it."

"Do what?"

She widened her eyes. The blush rose in her cheeks. "What you said. Your...inducement."

Oh. His *inducement*. Right. Ah. Well. Her fingers pressed into his arm, her eyes pleaded with him to behave. No surprise that she too was willing to ignore his father's perfidy for the sake of good manners, but strangely enough, he did not feel any annoyance at her.

So he patted her hand and enjoyed the way the blush deepened in her cheeks.

"Cassandra, my darling," he said loudly. "Allow me to introduce you to my father, the Earl of Treyford, and my dear stepmother, Lady Treyford."

The pair of them looked uncertain, his father's nostrils still flared, but Cassandra's calming, civilizing influence worked on them too, and they all rose above the seething pit of human emotion to remember they were genteel. They issued tense greetings. Politeness won again.

Then Cassandra addressed herself to Lady Treyford, blathering some nonsense about "the exquisite beadwork on your gown," and Lord Morecambe appeared and clapped Treyford on the shoulder and led him away under the pretense of discussing horses. The servants had cleaned everything up, and the guests resumed their chatter, and everything returned to normal. Like he had thrown a rock into a pond, and now the rock was gone and the ripples had passed.

Someone else came to claim Lady Treyford's attention, and Cassandra led him away. He breathed in her fragrance, enjoyed her warmth pressed to him in warning.

"Shall we go home, then?" he said.

She didn't look at him. "Not yet."

"We have a bargain."

She took a deep breath and smiled at someone behind him, still not meeting his eyes. "I will keep to my end of the bargain, but first you must keep to yours. We will stay another half-hour. We will circulate. We will make polite conversation—polite!—and you will make yourself agreeable to as many people as you can."

"How marvelous you are, my darling, how principled. What you are willing to do in the name of politeness! How delightful, that you will be so polite in public, yet in private—"

"Not here." Her tone was uncommonly sharp.

"These people—"

"They don't need to see that you're upset."

"I'm not upset."

She met his eyes then and her free hand covered his. "It's all right to be angry with him. But you cannot undo it now and you don't want these people to see that you're hurting."

Her eyes were big and concerned, their color neither green nor brown but something utterly new and irrelevant.

"I'm not hurting," he snapped. "I could not care less about the man. I simply dislike him."

"Then dislike him more quietly. You're making people uncomfortable."

"Heaven forbid anyone might feel uncomfortable."

"Joshua. Please."

She bumped against him again and brushed her lips over his cheek. The kiss was light and brief, yet the feel of it lingered long after her mouth was gone. Through the mess in his head, he was vaguely aware that she was soothing him like a skittish horse, but he could not summon up enough outrage to mind. She had a kind of courage and honor that put him to shame. He was curious to see how far she was willing to go with her "end of the bargain."

"You owe me," he said.

"I know."

"Half an hour."

"Yes." She led him a few more steps and then she glanced at him sideways, with a suddenly playful smile. "You got my name right," she said.

He'd forgotten that game. Never mind. He was running out of names anyway.

Besides, he had a new game now. Annoying his father was getting tedious. Teasing his wife would be much more diverting.

"You see?" he said. "You can achieve all manner of things with the right inducement."

CHAPTER 8

Later that night, after her maid had helped her dress for bed, Cassandra sat in her bedchamber and ignored the connecting door to Joshua's room. She ignored it so hard that it was a relief when his knock finally came.

She put aside the handkerchief she was pretending to embroider and moved forward to greet him. Really, this was like receiving a regular morning call in her drawing room.

Yet no morning call in her drawing room had left her so warm and nervous.

"Come in," she called, her voice too high.

In he blew, his red silk banyan flapping about his bare ankles as he charged toward her. He was halfway across the room when he pulled up, staring as if he had never seen such a creature as her in his life. She felt curiously exposed, even though nearly every inch of her skin was covered. Mercifully, his robe was tied shut, revealing only a triangle of skin below his throat.

"What *are* you wearing?" He prowled closer. "Are you dressed for bed or for a three-day hike in Scotland?"

Cassandra realized that she was cuddling herself. She straightened her shoulders and clasped her hands at her waist.

"This is warm and comfortable," she said.

"It would want to be, since there's so bloody much of it."

"Whatever do you mean? 'Tis only my nightshift, my bed jacket, and stockings."

He flicked the ruffled brim of her nightcap. "What the blazes is this thing?"

"It's a nightcap. It's warm and keeps my hair from getting tangled during the night. Which saves me time the next day. It is *efficient*."

"Oh well then, if it's *efficient*."

"If you wanted me dressed for—for—for seduction, you should have provided clearer instructions." A smile began to spread over his face. She folded her arms over her middle, remembered herself, and stood straight again. "For example, am I meant to be in the bed? Does this...activity take place there or..."

"This activity can take place wherever we please." His eyes flicked over her again. "I feel underdressed," he said cheerfully, and leaned forward confidentially to add, "As I am completely naked under this robe."

Good heavens.

He waggled his eyebrows and pivoted away. He ran at the bed, leaped, and, in a blur of wine-red silk, he wound up lounging on the far side like an emperor in a painting she had once seen. The robe stayed closed around his middle, although the lapels fell open to reveal that wretched chest again and the hem gathered around his knees.

He patted the mattress beside him meaningfully, and somehow she was standing by the bed, willing herself to climb on.

She had made a promise, and she was his wife, and as they were leaving the rout Arabella had winked and said, "The answer to your question is 'yes'," so it could not be that bad, but it would not make babies, and what was the point if it did not make babies?

But her husband did not like babies, so perhaps that was the point.

She hated him, then, wished him far, far away.

"You're looking fierce," he said, disarmingly gentle now. "Do you want me to go?"

Yes. Yes. Yes.

And yet...What if this led to other things? What if he did eventually bed her properly? What if she got with child? That would make this unpleasantness worth it. She had gone about this all wrong. She should have prepared for seduction. She surreptitiously wiped her palms on her bed jacket and tried to think of something seductive to say.

"Shall I...extinguish the candle?"

"Sweet mercy, no," Joshua said. "In fact, you should light a few more. You'll need them to see what you're doing."

"Oh."

"And I'll need the light to watch you too."

"You want to...Oh."

She didn't know what to do with her hands, which were fluttering this way and that. He, of course, was quite at his leisure.

"Should I be...on top of the covers, or underneath?"

"On top will make it easier. And I am trying to make this easy for you."

"Oh, is *that* what you're doing?" she muttered.

She crawled onto the bed near the pillows and sat with her knees hugged to her chest, her nightgown pulled tight over her feet. His powerful form in her peripheral vision teased her, dared her to look. She wriggled to dispel the peculiar sensations in her nervous body and kept her eyes straight ahead.

He made no move to touch her, but watched her, thoughtful and serious. It was as though there were two versions of him—one wicked and playful, the other gentle and caring—and the speed with which he switched between them made her head spin.

But there was also the ill-mannered hothead, the brash whirlwind, the intense idealist, the stubborn tyrant, the demanding employer...How confusing he was.

"You're being very brave," he said. "How far are you going to take this?"

"I am a gentleman's daughter and I honor my promises. You gave me half an hour of politeness so I can give you...Oh."

That wicked, playful glint returned. "Half an hour? Is that how long I get?"

"I don't know. How long does it take?"

The sound he made might have been a laugh, might have been a groan. He rolled onto his back and covered his face with his hands. She had no idea what version of him this was and was regarding him with some perplexity, when the ring on the smallest finger of his left hand caught her attention.

Right next to where his wedding ring would be if he hadn't lost it.

"What was it about anyway?" she asked. "The argument with your father." She shifted onto her knees and touched the ring lightly. "The two of you mentioned a ring. Was it this ring?"

When he rolled back onto his side, she took his ring hand in both of hers. He let it rest there, heavy and trusting, so much bigger and more powerful than her own. It was a busy hand, as she would expect from him: a network of veins and bones, with a long, thick scar near his thumb, a smaller one by his wrist. Not soft but not rough. His nails were clipped and clean. He said nothing when she ran a thumb over his knuckles, brushing against the fine black hairs, pausing at the ring. The band was ornate silver, with a large square bezel set with onyx, on which was engraved a coat of arms.

"It's a signet ring," she said. "Was this given to you when you were still Lord Treyford's heir?"

If this was the signet ring of Viscount Otham, the courtesy title for the heir to the Earl of Treyford, then Joshua had been entitled to wear it once. But now he was not: It claimed an identity—a very high social position—that was not his. Wearing it was a terrible thing to do.

Which was no doubt exactly why he wore it.

She glanced at him. His eyes were on their joined hands, and with his lashes lowered, he looked almost at peace. The candlelight softened his features, caressed the angles of his cheekbones, the curves of his lips. She could not recall ever noticing the shape of a man's lips before.

"It must have been difficult for you," she said. "To have lost everything at only fourteen."

"It was half a lifetime ago and of no interest whatsoever." His eyes flicked up to meet hers. "I can think of much more interesting things."

He tugged his hand free and set his palm on her thigh. Warmth and pressure coursed through her, sweeping up over her skin, pausing to swirl between her thighs. An odd sensation, intensifying, right there, where he...where they...where she...Oh dear.

His hand inched upward. She instinctively slapped both hands over it. She stopped his progress, but not her own body's persistent call.

And she should not try to stop him. She should encourage him. Seduce him, even. She would never get a child if she didn't.

"Backing out already?" he asked, rough and low.

"I will see this through." Her voice was unsteady and she tried to smile. She glanced at his...there...She thought she could see its shape beneath the robe but that was probably just the candlelight and her feverish imagination. "It would help if I knew why."

"Because it's splendid."

Wicked and playful again, but also sharp and intense, and his eyes, so heated, calling to her body, amplifying those sensations, uncomfortable and yet, well, almost splendid too.

"How can it be...Oh, never mind. I don't want...I mean." She took a deep breath, tried again. "Tonight. Your father. What..." She caught herself tracing the outline of his fingers on her thigh and stopped. "He did wrong, but he is still your father," she said. "And surely you owe some of your current success to whatever reparations he made you."

"Reparations? Oh, the innocence." He rolled onto his back again and folded his arms behind his head, staring at the pink canopy. The sleeves of the banyan fell back to reveal his forearms, incongruous against the pink silk brocade of the bedcover. "As soon as our parents' marriage was annulled—once it was proven that Father's first wife had died only the year before, so our mother was never legally his wife—Bram, Isaac, and I were hauled out of school like criminals and sent back to Treyford Hall. We expected our mother to be there, but she had run off somewhere with Miriam—that's my sister; she was four then. The house was shut up, no servants but a couple of old retainers, and all anyone told us is that solicitors were seeking some cousin or other to take us in."

"But your father?"

"We never heard from him again."

"Oh, Joshua."

He still seemed at ease, but his voice was flat and hard, and she fancied she could sense his tension.

"That first night in that big empty house...There was no fire, so I tried to light one, but I didn't know how to," he went on, still talking to the pink canopy. "I knew the theory, but had no practice. All my life to that point, other people had done everything for me. There we were, my two little brothers and me, with nothing, and I thought—if I can just light this fire..."

She pictured a dark-haired youth staring at the fireplace with such intensity it might have burst into flames from his glare alone.

"And did you?" she prompted.

He snorted. "Felt like hours before I even got any sparks from that blasted flint. Striking it over and over until my fingers were sore and numb. Until then, I had never realized how useless I was. But yes, I got it lit in the end."

The words sounded like the punchline to a bitter, humorless joke.

"I don't understand. If your father did not help you, how did you get from three disowned boys to wherever you all are now?"

"Another man came," he said quietly. "Another man, whom we had never met before, but who was disgusted by the whole business. He came to Treyford Hall, unannounced, uninvited, and he stayed and talked to us about it, when no one else would, and he vowed to help us carve out new lives. Isaac, he was only ten, he wanted to join the Navy and travel the world, and Bram, he was twelve, he wanted to go to India and catch tigers, and I wanted..." He paused. "I said I wanted to be rich. That man owed us nothing, but he came to help us anyway. The best man I ever knew."

Tears stung her eyes. She blinked them away. "Papa? He helped you? That was the debt you owed him?"

"Curse you. I didn't mean to make you cry."

"I'm not crying." She rested her cheek on her knees. "That's why you married me."

"I married you because he asked me to marry you and I'd have done anything for him. And speaking of marriage and debts—"

Oh dear. His mood had shifted again.

"You've delayed long enough, Mrs. DeWitt. It's time for my reward."

HE MOVED LIKE A CAT, all power, no effort, one moment lying on his back, the next kneeling down in front of her, hands resting on his thighs.

Cassandra mirrored his position, feeling a secret, unexpected thrill. He dwarfed her massive bed, through his physical size and sheer energy. She enjoyed looking at him, she realized. She enjoyed the long, lean shape of him, the contours of his broad shoulders draped in dark-red silk. She enjoyed the warmth that radiated off him. The quick flash of his smile. Those gleaming coffee eyes. His intensity. His focus. Even his discombobulating changeability. This was uncomfortable but surely it was good. Ladies never spoke of lust, were taught that it was shameful. But it must be good, she decided now, though she would die sooner than admit it.

Maybe he would hold her first. Or kiss her. That would be nice. It was so long since anyone had made her feel special.

She waited. He drummed his fingers on his thighs and looked about the room. If she didn't know better, she'd say he did not know how to proceed either.

"I'm sorry," she said. "I don't know what to do next."

"Perhaps I should go first. To show you."

Her imagination tried to picture that and rebelled. "How can you reach?"

He pulled back, eyes wide, and then laughed so richly the

mattress rocked below her knees. "On you, I mean," he said, still laughing.

"It's not fair to laugh at me. You men cannot demand that women be innocent and then mock us for being exactly what you say you want."

He wiped a hand over his face, his laughter subsiding to a groan. "I assure you I cannot reach. It is one of the tragedies of being human."

"Well, another tragedy of being human is that women aren't born knowing this kind of thing," she snapped irritably. "So if you want me to honor our agreement, you shall have to stop laughing at me and try communicating for once."

"You mean to go through with this, don't you?"

"We had a deal."

"You are adorable."

His tone was as languorous as a summer afternoon. He lifted one hand slowly, then rested his knuckles against her cheek, a touch warm enough to melt chocolate. He brushed his knuckles back and forth, back and forth, and she matched her breathing to his rhythm. His eyes searched hers, half puzzled, half...concerned? Then his gaze fell to her mouth. Back to her eyes. Back to her mouth.

And she thought: *My husband is going to kiss me now.*

She closed her eyes and waited. His lips would be as soft and warm as his caress. She would tangle her fingers in his hair. And run them down his neck, over his shoulders. Spread her palms over his chest. His skin would be hot to the touch, she was sure of it, and his body hard. She might feel his heartbeat. Feel his energy. And he would touch her too. That sultry caress would slide down from her cheek to her throat, perhaps even to her breasts, now clamoring for his touch. He was her husband. This was good. They would make babies. She heard her own breathing and shut her mouth to quiet it, but a moment later, her lips were parted again.

Waiting. Waiting. For him to—

"It is remarkably diverting to tease you," he said cheerfully.

She jerked back, her eyes flew open, and blood rushed through her head.

"You were *teasing* me?" She knocked his hand away from her face. "I'm trying to do the right thing, the honorable thing, and you're making *fun* of me?"

"'Fraid so."

He vaulted past her in a swirl of silk and landed on the floor with a thump. She spun around, her nightgown getting tangled up in her legs so she had to kick herself free. She gripped the bedcovers to keep from clawing at his wicked face.

"You never meant for me to do it?"

He grinned. "No."

"All this time I've been worried about it and wondering if other women did it with their husbands, and you...You... you fiend!"

"Mrs. DeWitt, you didn't!" He arranged his banyan around his shoulders, eyes wide and laughing. "Do you mean to tell me that while we were making polite conversation at the rout, you were imagining all the couples—"

"Not all of them! And I don't even know what to imagine but..."

"Oh, you are too adorable!"

The beastly man was laughing at her again.

She rose up on her knees, right at the edge of the bed, and swiped at him, but he danced sideways, out of the way.

"You horrid—" She swiped again. Again he dodged. And laughed.

"—Wicked—" Another swipe, another dodge, another laugh.

"—Awful—" Another swipe, harder, faster this time, and she

would have fallen off the bed if he hadn't darted forward and caught her forearms to hold her steady.

And kept holding her, gentle but firm, looking perplexed.

"I am all those things and more, but you already knew that," he said. "Why so upset?"

"I am only trying to do what is right. You ought not mock me for it." She pulled away from him. "That was not nice."

"Nice?!" He backed away. "Under what constellation did you ever imagine me to be *nice*?"

"Papa said you are a good man. And the Duke of Dammerton said you have a good heart. And Mr. Newell said—"

"Mercy. The naivety! Do you think I became rich by being *nice*? Do you think those fancy friends of yours court me because I'm *polite*?" He laughed, a bitter, mirthless sound. "Most of them cannot stand me, but they cannot stay away from me and that, my darling, has nothing to do with being *nice*. So forget any silly notion that I might ever be nice to you and, for mercy's sake, don't get any romantic ideas."

She gaped at him. "Are you so vain as to think I might fall in love with you?"

"You wanted me to kiss you just now."

"I did not!" she lied, cheeks burning. "You arrogant, insufferable fiend! I want nothing from you. You can go back to your...women and get them to do...that thing."

"Maybe I will. Because they never expect me to be nice, and when it's over—" His voice was tense and rising in volume with each word. "—I leave them and they leave me, and they bloody well don't nag me to behave or colonize my house or disrupt my life!"

"Well, *you* are disrupting *my* life." She borrowed a trick from Arabella: She raised her chin and looked into the distance. "You may leave now."

"Oh, I may leave, may I?"

"Don't let me keep you."

Of course, insufferable contrary beast that he was, he stepped closer. "I know that one," he growled. "That's polite-speak for 'Go away'."

"You must hear it a lot."

"So say it. Tell me to go away." He cradled her face, and she cursed his deceitful hands, for his touch was divine though he was a loathsome beast. "If I do kiss you, will you tell me to go away?"

He brushed a thumb over her lips, sending a frisson of pleasure down her spine. She fancied she saw his eyes darken. He would laugh at her again. He was not wrong; she was at risk of forming foolish notions, if only because she looked at couples like Arabella and Lord Hardbury, and Harry and Lady Bolderwood, and felt a terrible, futile yearning for what she could never have.

With a tentative hand, she grazed his hair, curled her fingers into it. It was ridiculously soft and she should never have touched him. But somewhere under that irascibility, that wild animation, that rudeness, hid a gentle, caring man.

"You are still so angry," she whispered.

His head jerked back, out of her reach. "I what?"

"With your father, with me, with all of us."

"What utter nonsense." He leaped back and paced about, waving his hands. "I don't care enough to be angry."

"Deep down angry."

"Stop telling me what I feel."

"It's all right. I understand."

"No. You do not understand." He advanced, loomed over her. "You do not understand a bloody thing."

"Joshua…"

She reached for him, to soothe him, comfort him, as she longed for someone to do for her, and she almost had a hold on him when he whirled away, fast and furious, and her hand snagged on his robe. He kept moving under the force of his own momentum, and she could not release her hand, and the ties came undone. The whirlwind stopped. He froze, facing toward her, his robe hanging open.

He was, as he had warned, completely naked underneath.

Oh, Saint Sebastian!

Cassandra stared, helpless to look away: that chest, flat nipples, ribs, lean waist, a trail of hair, and his...

His...what did she even call it?...manhood. It stood upright against his belly, darker than his skin, as big and angry and demanding as he. Through the pounding of her heart, she was aware of dark hair, lean hips, muscular thighs, and warmth, warmth flooding through her, robbing her of air, as her eyes sent an urgent message to her body and her body throbbed with a newly discovered need.

"Seen enough?" His voice seemed to come from far away, and she could not tell if he was angry or amused or something else altogether. "If you wanted to ogle my cock, wife, you should have just asked."

She shut her eyes, folded both hands over them. The darkness did not help: She could still see him, still feel him. After a year, a decade, a century, he muttered, "And I'm not angry, curse you," and the air moved and the door slammed and she was alone again.

Slowly, Cassandra lowered her hands and curled them into the bedclothes, resisting the sinful urge to touch those parts of her body that still clamored for the man. The room was too empty and the floor was a thousand miles away and she did not know herself anymore.

She scrambled off the bed and to the door, but froze with her hand on the latch. If she went into his room, she would—what? Put her arms around him, hold him, have him hold her.

If she went into his room, he would say something unkind, mock her, turn her away.

Instead, she stood and breathed herself calm, then went to her writing desk and composed a note: "Dear Lady Treyford," she wrote.

CHAPTER 9

It was not enough for the blasted woman to colonize his house. Now she'd colonized his mind too.

The next day, Joshua kept himself busy with meetings in the City and inspections at the dock—places he was sure not to encounter his wife—but his every moment was invaded by her image.

Stroking his hand. Gaping at his naked body.

Waiting for his kiss, eyes closed, lips parted.

So bloody tempting.

Stupid, stupid, *stupid* idea to go to her room last night. "Nothing but a bit of harmless entertainment," he had told himself, and was idiot enough to believe the lie.

Somehow he made it to the evening without losing his mind and settled down in his study with a report on sanitation, while Das scanned the day's correspondence before returning to his lodgings. Joshua should have been safe—Cassandra was out with her friends—but the words on the page turned to gibberish before they hit his brain.

Because his brain was occupied, by *her*: the hurt in her eyes, the tenderness in her hands, the softness of her cheek.

This never happened. Never. The one certainty in his life was that he could focus on his work and shut out the world. Yet Cassandra...She had infiltrated his brain by being so welcoming and honorable and courageous and caring and—Bloody self-righteous, is what she was. So smug, thinking she knew him, making him feel like an utter villainous blackguard. Well, he was a villainous blackguard, wasn't he, because he was human. He did stupid, unkind things. He made mistakes. Whereas she was so bloody perfect, wasn't she? She never did anything wrong, never lost control of her tongue or took leave of her senses or let emotion get the better of her.

He could have kissed her.

Kissed her, removed that silly nightcap and ugly bed jacket and everything else she seemed to need just to sleep. Kissed her, lain her down on that pink bedcover, under that pink canopy, and explored her pink—

"We need to go to Liverpool," he said to Das. He leaped out of his chair, paced to the fire, grabbed the poker, jabbed at the coals. "Still have to help Putney sort out the problem with the competitors. We can leave tomorrow."

Obvious solution, really.

If he'd taken that packet to Liverpool as planned, none of this would have happened. He simply had to put his life back to the way it was before, which was exactly the way he wanted it. Careless of him, to let her disrupt it. He could go on like this for years, traveling and trading and working. Years and years and years.

Years.

And years.

And years.

"Putney fixed it himself," Das said absently, not looking up from the papers he was studying.

"He what?"

"Letter's over there."

Das made no move to get it. Splendid. Even Das was acting oddly.

Joshua dumped the poker, grabbed the letter, scanned it. Curse it. Putney *had* found a solution. Good one, too.

"Why the blazes did he have to go and fix it?" he muttered.

"He *is* your Secretary In Charge Of Everything That Happens In Liverpool And Manchester."

"Huh."

Das still didn't look up. Joshua paced back to the fire, tossed on another log, enjoyed the shower of sparks, the leap of flames.

"Birmingham, then. Everything always makes sense in Birmingham. I haven't enough to do in London."

"This is not a good time to leave London, I'm afraid."

"Don't you tell me that I oughtn't leave Mrs. DeWitt. She is perfectly capable of looking after herself, and she has no more need of me than I have of her, and quite frankly, we have coexisted perfectly well for the past two years and everything was highly satisfactory until she came along and disrupted everything."

"A legal action has been brought against you. By Lord Bolderwood."

Joshua glanced at the papers in Das's hand. Das rose to his feet, lips pinched, unusually tense.

"This still about that stupid Baltic thing?"

"No, sir. Lord Bolderwood is suing you for criminal conversation."

DAS WAS an articulate fellow and he expressed himself well and it was not a particularly complicated sentence, but it was one of those sentences where the words made sense individually but the meaning of the whole eluded his brain. Joshua ran it back in his mind to see if he understood.

Criminal conversation. Adultery. Still his brain rebelled. Yes, he was no innocent. Yes, there were four gentlemen in London who could make that charge, if they cared to, but they didn't, because they had reached that stage of marriage where they allowed their wives to make a choice, and Joshua had made sure of that beforehand, because the forbidden held no lure for him, whereas efficiency and good planning did.

"Congress with Lord Bolderwood's wife?" he finally said.

Das shifted uncomfortably. "That's what makes the said 'conversation' criminal."

"This is ludicrous. He's suing me for sleeping with Lady Bolderwood?" Fair hair—Knowing smirk—Sly eyes—Unpleasant —Joyless. "I never touched the woman."

"He is seeking damages of fifty thousand pounds for the, ah..." Das consulted the wording. "The, and I quote, 'unauthorized use of his property'."

"Insolent pup. I wouldn't, quote, 'use' his, quote, 'property' even if I were, quote, 'authorized'. Even if I were *paid* fifty thousand."

Bolderwood had been much too prominent in his life recently. Punching him in St. James over some nonsense about his wife. That wife flitting about like a gnat at Featherstone's party. Isaac's warning of impending revenge.

Ah.

"They've been planning this a while," he said.

He paced, thinking properly now; Das, as always, the calm in his storm.

"This is..." He snapped his fingers, spun around, clapped his hands. "Yes, that's what this is. He lost the money, needed more, desperate to get it, blamed me—How bad is his situation, did you find out?"

"Bad. Debts somewhere in the area of thirty thousand, including honor debts and moneylenders."

"Awards in crim. con. cases have been getting higher. There was that case a couple of weeks ago."

"That chap Evans was ordered to pay damages of twenty thousand to Lord Oliver over his affair with Lady Oliver."

"Evans cannot afford that but I can. And I have a reputation. And I'm a wealthy upstart who doesn't stay where he belongs, and the jury could take offense at that."

The flowers on his desk eyed him accusingly. Only yesterday, Cassandra had rearranged them with those competent hands, while she spoke of pleasure and joy.

"This is disgusting," he said. "Disgusting, despicable, and distasteful."

"The court hearing is in two weeks."

"That soon." He paced again, thinking, calculating, disbelieving. "How does this idiot think he's going to get away with it? A trial means presenting evidence, and there will be no evidence because it never bloody well happened."

A sour taste filled his mouth. He had plenty of competitors and rivals. Enemies, even. They came with success. There was always something going wrong, someone trying to best him; that was part of what thrilled him and filled his days.

But this was so...personal.

Das did not say a word.

"I never touched the woman, Das."

Not that he cared what Das thought.

"I didn't," he said.

And Das nodded, once.

Joshua glanced at the clock. "Cassandra's at some ball and won't be home for hours. I'll tell her in the morning. You may as well head home. I'll deal with this tomorrow."

He followed Das into the entrance hall, watched him pull on his gloves and coat, seeing only Cassandra as she had been the night before, caring that he was upset, caring that he upset her. Waiting, lips parted, for his kiss.

"You don't think she might hear about it tonight, do you?" he said.

"Depends how discreet Bolderwood means to be."

"He's telling lies about his wife, he'd want to be discreet." Cassandra had been engaged to Bolderwood once. Oh, hell. What a mess. He should have kissed her when he had the chance. "But anyway, she already told me she doesn't care."

Das paused, turning his hat in his hands. He started to speak but stopped as a footman opened the front door.

The evening air rolled in, carrying the sound of a carriage approaching. Pulling up. The door opening. Closing. Voices. Footsteps.

"Well," Das said. "Now is your chance to find out."

A MOMENT LATER, Cassandra stepped through the doorway, heartwarming in a blue evening gown and velvet cloak. But his pleasure faded when she stopped short at the sight of him.

Their eyes met, held. Joshua felt as naked as he had the night before. Then her focus shifted so that she looked right through him and she swept into the hall.

"Good evening, Mr. Das." This with a pleasant nod and smile. "And Mr. DeWitt." This with a frigid tone and averted gaze.

"So you've heard then."

"I do not care," she said. Without looking at him, she reached for the clasp of her cloak at her throat. "Do you hear me, Mr. DeWitt? I do not care. Not a whit. Not a jot. Not one iota."

Her usually competent fingers were fumbling with the clasp. The cloak slipped back off her shoulders, revealing her smooth upper arms, the swell of her breasts.

"Let me do that," he said.

She flipped up both palms toward him, as if to ward off evil. He stayed away. She peeled off her gloves, gathered them in one hand. Perhaps she meant to slap him across the face with them. One did that in matters of honor. She would call him out. They would meet the next morning at dawn, walk their twenty paces, and she would shoot him.

Except, of course, that she did not care.

She slapped the gloves onto the table and attacked the clasp again viciously, with the fingers that had caressed his hand the night before.

"I care about my sisters and my mother. My friends, my house, my pigs, my roses, my cat." The clasp gave way. The cloak slipped from her shoulders and he reached for it, but she whirled it away from him, into the hands of the footman, who grabbed it and ran. "I do not care about you, or your activities."

"If I might explain."

She was already gliding toward the stairs and away from him. Her evening gown swirled around her legs, the legs he had never seen and never would. Her hair was in some complicated arrangement and tendrils escaped down the back of her neck. He would never see that hair loose; he had not realized until now how much he wanted to.

With one foot on the bottom step, she paused and looked back at him. The candle on the wall picked up the fire in her hair, at odds with her icy demeanor.

"I do not care if you bed every woman in England, France, and China."

"Cassandra, I swear I never—"

"Good night, Mr. DeWitt. Mr. Das."

She swept up the stairs and out of sight.

"You hear that, Das?" Joshua stared at the empty stairs, wondering that they weren't covered in frost. "She does not care. Not a whit, or a jot, or one iota."

"Ah...I'm going home now," Das said.

Joshua was still staring at the stairs and hardly heard him leave.

ALONE IN HER BEDCHAMBER, Cassandra turned and turned on the rug, her nightcap a twisted, rumpled mess in her hands. She had prepared for bed and sent away her maid, because she hadn't known what else to do. But it was too early to sleep, and her hands shook too much to sew, and her brain was too addled to read.

If only she were at Sunne Park now. In these hours after dinner, they'd all be in the drawing room. She and Lucy and Emily might act out one of Emily's plays, perhaps the one where Romeo and Ophelia eloped to the Forest of Arden. Or they would play games, like Musical Magic or Ribbons, and Lucy would insist upon the most dreadful forfeits. Or perhaps they would sing, try out the harmonies on a new song, and Mama would join in, and Mr. Twit would leap onto the pianoforte and stomp on the keys until he got a cuddle.

She didn't care. She did not care.

The bed loomed in the corner of her eye. Joshua had lain

there, and talked about his childhood. He'd laughed at her sleepwear and teased her mercilessly and cradled her face, and the whole time, he'd known that—

The fiend!

Cassandra flung aside the nightcap. She tore out of her room and down the stairs, and burst into his study.

The fiend sat by the fire, unusually still, so she made sure to slam the door. And what did he do but turn his head, raise his brows insolently, and lounge back in his chair.

A gentleman does not stay seated when a lady is standing, she could tell him, but why bother? A gentleman did not leave his coat and cravat lying around on the furniture. A gentleman did not curse in front of ladies. A gentleman did not bed the woman who had eloped with his wife's former betrothed.

The rising of her blood threatened to unlock her tongue. No: She was not one for dramatics or theatrics, tantrums or tirades. Her sisters were the lively, passionate ones. Cassandra was calm, sensible, practical.

She would be calm and sensible tonight.

"You will explain," she said, uttering each syllable with exaggerated clarity.

"You said you don't care."

"I would not care if you bedded half the women in the world, while the other half watched." Her voice rose. She took a shaking breath. Calm. Sensible. "But why her? Why *her*?"

He stretched out his long legs in front of him and crossed his ankles, the fire reflected in the gloss of his boots. How dare he be so leisurely? How dare he lie with that woman?

Harry, my sweet...Your husband's excesses...We must not speak of Mr. DeWitt...

"Why so bothered, madam?" he said. "Because of your

precious reputation? Or because you're still in love with Bolderwood?"

"Because she stole my life! I was going to have a real husband. Children. But she got that, and I got *you*!"

In a single movement, he stood. Loomed. Good: That would make it easier for her to kick him in the—the—the bollocks, and then he'd think twice before getting them out again.

"Has it occurred to you," he started, but she could not listen.

She advanced on strangely trembling limbs, her tormented mind filled with images of him kissing *Phyllis*, pressing his beautiful lips to *Phyllis's* poisonous mouth, and the rushing in her veins surged into her head and took control of her tongue.

"I had to stand there last night, and smile politely, while she made snide comments about how I only married you for your money—"

"She what?"

"And how she had true love with Harry—"

"So it's *Harry*, is it?"

"—And I'm saying that I'm perfectly content and the whole time she was laughing at me, because not only had she married my betrothed, she'd also gone to bed with my husband!"

"They're lying. I never touched her."

He stepped toward her but she circled around, out of his reach, behind the shield of his armchair. She gripped its ornate cresting rail in both hands. The words kept pouring out of her, and all she could do was hold on.

"Thought it was funny, did you? Poor little jilted bride, little charity case. Let's do her a favor and marry her because God knows no one else will. But why not have a joke at her expense? You do love to tease."

"I did not do this."

"Or maybe you thought to leave a little cuckoo in their nest?

What a jolly good laugh for the future: Let's see my wife's former betrothed raise my son!"

"Curse you!"

He sprang for her but she leaped backward, her fingers still hooked over the chair. It tumbled backward after her as she stumbled into the wall, and narrowly avoided crushing her stockinged feet as it thudded onto the rug.

"Get away from me! Don't touch me! I hate you!"

He froze, almost comical with arms still outstretched, and she thought she saw pain slice through his eyes. Then he pivoted away, strode across the room, and down one length and back again, like a caged animal. Cassandra pressed her shoulder blades into the wall, struggling for air, shivering at a trace of cold sweat down her back.

I hate you, she'd said. She never said things like that. Not her. She was always calm and sensible; her family needed her to be like that.

"I'm turning into Lucy," she muttered. "That's what you've done to me. You turned me into Lucy."

Across the room, he was watching her warily. Her skin prickled with unfamiliar shame.

"I'm sorry," she said. "I don't know what came over me."

"Don't apologize." He moved to the brandy decanter, poured out a measure with a loud clinking of glass. "You were upset, you let it out, and no one but the chair got hurt."

Poor chair. It did look pathetic on its solid back, its legs sticking helplessly in the air.

"Take a seat. I'll get it." He tossed back his brandy with a single swallow and started pouring some more.

Numbly, she perched on the small settee across from the upturned chair, the crackling fire heating her legs. She watched him carry two full snifters over to the small table. Then, with a single easy movement, he set the heavy chair back on its feet, threw himself into it, and jerked his chin at the brandy between them.

"Drink," he said.

"I thought you don't drink."

"I don't, usually. It interferes with my thinking."

"Other men don't seem to mind."

"Other men don't think that well to begin with. Drink it. It's meant to be good for shock or insanity or whatever the blazes is going on with you."

She lifted one glass, weighed it in her hand. "Do you think I have no right to be angry?"

"Be as angry as you bloody well like. But I've done nothing wrong this time."

She sniffed the brandy. The fumes tickled her nose. She remembered Lucy, how lively she was after drinking, how she had cut her foot on the glass but felt no pain.

"Better an aching head than an aching heart," she muttered.

"Cheers."

The first sip made her recoil, but she tried again. It was different from wine, the way it warmed her insides. Maybe it would warm her hands too. His hand when she held it had been so much warmer than hers. She wondered why that was. She sipped again.

"Lady Featherstone," he said abruptly. He was gazing into the fire, chin resting on his hand. The firelight caressed the contours of his profile. "Lady Peter Elton. Mrs. Westley. Lady Harrington. Almost Lady Yardley, but I put a stop to it when you arrived."

Oh no. Heavens, she didn't want to know. She sipped her brandy, and again. Three, four, five times. Once for each of the women named. She had claimed indifference. And she was indifferent. She was. It was just...*her.*

He turned his head to her, his chin still on his hand. In this light, his eyes were nearly black.

"Four women in three years. Not a bloody Bolderwood among them."

"And before that?"

"Before that I was married and faithful." He sighed and rested his head back against the chair. "I was nineteen when we married and Rachel was the first woman I ever bedded. We were married nearly six years and I was faithful that whole time and it never even occurred to me not to be. I mean...why would I want anyone else? I had Rachel. And then I didn't have Rachel, and sometimes I wanted..."

He stared at the ceiling, lost in a place she could never go. Perhaps staying busy was not always enough for him either.

"You were faithful to your first wife, but not to me."

"You're not my wife," he said. "We just happen to be married to each other."

"I see. Quite."

A marriage in name only. She could not complain: This man did not feel like her husband either. It was better they lived apart. It was one thing to want his kiss, or even his baby, but quite another to imagine him in her life. Her longing was not for him, but for what she had lost and could never have.

Another sip of brandy, then: for his wife. No. Six. One for each of the years he had been married to Rachel and loved her and was faithful to her. She had spoken of fidelity and he had mocked her, yet he had believed in it too, once.

"They all know: the husbands, the wives," he said, talking to the fire again, while she was taking the third of the six sips. He shifted his legs, his energy never staying dull for long. "They marry for family or property or a passing attraction, and courtship is so limited that they hardly know each other, and the men need someone to carry on the family line, and the women need someone to provide for them, and once you're in a marriage, it's near impossible to get out of it. So they do their duty and then...If two people are deeply committed to each other, that's one thing. But if not...People's lives don't end when they get married. Marriage doesn't turn people into little rag dolls who are miraculously released from the chaos of human feeling and desire."

She took the final sip. She should stop now. What a funny effect the brandy had. Like her knees were going to float away. She pictured herself rising knees first into the air, so she hung upside down, her nightgown slipping over her head, leaving her body exposed and her face covered.

Would he find her naked body as interesting as she found his? Probably not. He had already seen five other women. At least. She didn't want to know that. Ladies did not want to know these things and she was a lady. She would be interested in seeing his body again. How could that be? That she wanted to see his body but did not want him as her husband. How wicked and wanton she was. How he would laugh if he knew.

"My parents were so much in love," she said. "Always laughing and kissing. You could see that they enjoyed being together. They were always faithful to each other." Outside the window, a carriage passed, a man called out. Joshua was audibly silent. "You think me naive."

"We were all naive once. You'll grow out of it."

"I suppose that's what I'm doing now."

The glass was at her lips and she remembered she meant to stop. Two more sips: One each for Mama and Papa.

"I thought I would have that, one day," she said. Instead, she was married and had no husband. "My whole life stretched in front of me, and I was looking forward to living it. Then one day

Papa received a letter telling of Harry's elopement—and my future was gone. Can you imagine what that's like?"

No answer. He gazed at the crackling flames. She pulled her feet up onto the seat under her, tucked her nightclothes around her knees.

He was quiet so long that when he finally spoke, she jumped.

"I imagine it is like staring into blankness," he said. "Each day, you have to get up and face that blankness, and try to carve out another future even while you're grieving for the one you lost. I imagine that each day you remind yourself to concentrate on what you have and never hope for anything else, and in time, that becomes enough."

He knew.

Because of course: He had loved Rachel. Loved her and lost her. His loss was even worse than hers.

No sacrifice, he had said the day before. Marrying Cassandra and putting her out of sight made him safe. And made her the perfect wife for him. Because his idea of the perfect wife, was a wife who was no wife at all.

CHAPTER 10

The brandy had failed: Her heart ached for what they had both lost. Cassandra wanted to hate him, but that was not fair. She had agreed to a marriage in name only, back when she was too young to understand how long life could be when you had to live it alone.

Besides, she didn't want him either. If she could choose her husband, he would be nothing like Joshua DeWitt.

"I never had an affair with Bolderwood's wife," he said, stretching and reverting to his usual briskness. "I'm not much of a husband to you, but I can promise to be honest, and that is the truth."

The empty snifter was heavy in her hands, the reflected flames dancing in the cut glass. She replaced it next to the full one, saw how the flames swam in the rich color of the liquor too. She lifted the glass to admire it.

He had no reason to lie. What was the worst she could do to him? Go back to Sunne Park and never speak to him again? Take a lover so he could divorce her and cast them all out?

"Then why does Harry think you did?" she asked.

"I think this is a scheme to raise money and get revenge. I think they planned it."

"*They* planned it?"

"It's all I can think of." His gaze flickered to the glass in her hand and up again. "Assume that I'm innocent. Now, consider that they are in severe financial straits, they blame me, and I make an easy target."

"But to say that about his own wife! He must know that transcripts of crim. con. trials are published in full and sell in the tens of thousands. Her reputation..."

He shrugged, sighed. For a man who said he never got tired, he seemed weary tonight. "That's why I think she must be involved also. Other ladies have weathered worse, even emerged from such scandals with a certain cachet; she could brazen it out too, so long as he doesn't divorce her. The aristocracy is renowned for such behavior; people almost expect it now."

"They hardly seem on the brink of divorce. If you had seen them at the rout last night, all smiles and touches and looks and...Oh. Oh."

"What? What?"

"They said something about taking justice into their own hands. But this is...Heavens, Joshua, this is disgusting."

"Disgusting. Disgraceful. Distasteful. Despicable."

It was all of those things and more. She tried to comprehend it. How smug they had been last night, knowing they had planted a powder keg under Cassandra's family: not only Joshua, but Cassandra and her sisters by association.

"No," she said. "Harry would never do that."

"Perhaps your precious *Harry* is not the man you thought," Joshua said, irritably.

It was on the tip of her tongue to say that *Phyllis* must have been a bad influence, and she was ashamed of her willingness to blame the woman rather than the man. She recalled Harry's cozy triumph when he met his wife's eyes. He could not have been influenced if it was not already inside him.

"They told me they were swept away by passion," she said. "I don't know if we had much passion, Harry and I. I thought we were in love but I'm too sensible for passion."

"Not much passion?" He snorted. "You just hurled a chair across the room, woman."

It was so ridiculous she had to laugh. "You say the sweetest things."

He laughed too, and she thought that this was nice, chatting with him by the fire, curled up comfortably, warm inside and out. Maybe they could be friends some day.

"Harry and I were only engaged for a week before Charlie died, and I suppose I wasn't good company after that," she said. "He did visit me a few times, but I didn't have much to say."

Because her heart was so broken. Three years on, and still it hurt, the memory of the night when Charlie's friends brought him in, sweating and bleeding from the knife wound between his ribs, yet making jokes all the while. She was not long home from a ball, where she and Harry had danced twice, and Harry had kissed her and said he'd always hold her in his heart. Papa was up in Scotland, and Mama had to be sedated, and so Cassandra helped the doctor, her white ballgown smeared with her brother's blood, and she nursed Charlie for three days until he died.

"I liked Charlie. Everyone did," Joshua said. "And you were better off not marrying Bolderwood if he couldn't stand by you during a bad time."

"Did your marriage have bad times?"

A bleak look passed over his face. How he must miss his wife.

"Nothing in particular," he said, and added nothing more.

So THIS IS BRANDY, Cassandra mused, as the silence stretched between them. It put several thick panes of glass between her mind and the world. Her emotions were curled up in a little ball, like Mr. Twit sleeping at the end of her bed.

She missed Mr. Twit.

"You've drunk all my brandy," Joshua said.

She looked at the glass in her hand. It was empty. Oh.

"Lucy has taken to drinking brandy," she said.

"What? She's...how old?"

"Nineteen. I hide the bottles but she finds them. The first time, it was afternoon. Mama has this pet goat called Guinevere, and the goat gets into the roses. Lucy got the goat out and, under the influence of brandy, she brought the goat inside so it wouldn't attack the roses, and she tied a bonnet on its head."

"What for?"

"So no one would know it was a goat. It was a cunning disguise." She laughed. It had not been funny at the time, although Lucy had been laughing. But Lucy had been drinking brandy, and now Cassandra was drinking brandy, and really, the brandy did a marvelous job of making things funny. "So there was this poor goat, in this giant bonnet covered with fake cherries and grapes, running around the house, dodging the servants, and bleating and breaking things and eating the flowers. Finally, we chased her outside. Poor Guinevere. She wouldn't be caught again and wore the bonnet for an extra day until I could get it off her."

He laughed. She did like his laugh. It warmed her like brandy.

"Another time, Lucy dressed up in one of Mama's old gowns and a wig and sang bawdy songs."

"What bawdy songs?"

"I am not singing a bawdy song."

120

A slow, wicked smile spread over his face. "You know the words, don't you? Perfect, polite, prim Cassandra, singing bawdy songs."

"It was Miranda. She's my older sister. Half-sister, I mean. From Mama's first marriage."

"I don't care about Miranda. I want the song."

"I mean, Miranda found this old songbook and dared me to perform one, but then…"

She'd been twelve to Miranda's sixteen, and didn't understand the words. She had sat at the pianoforte, heart thumping, her breath so short she wasn't sure if she could sing, but she was determined to prove herself to Miranda, so she played the first two notes, and paused, and everyone was listening—the Bells and the Larkes were there too, as were the vicar and his wife and mother —and then—

"Miranda sang it instead," she said.

Miranda got into trouble, of course, and enjoyed every minute. Mama and Papa never learned the plan; they'd patted Cassandra on the shoulder and said they were glad they could rely on her to be good.

That time, Cassandra had complained, because Miranda and Lucy were naughty and got all the attention, whereas she was good and got none. So Mama took her to Leamington Spa, on a special trip just for her.

She missed Mama too.

"Sing it now," he said. "Shock me, Mrs. DeWitt. Besides, you have been drinking, and this nation has a proud tradition of using drink as an excuse to sing bawdy songs. It is your patriotic duty."

"Oh my. Well. If it's my patriotic duty." It did seem like an excellent idea, and she enjoyed the way he was looking at her. "It was called 'Oyster Nan'. Um…"

She gathered her hazy thoughts and sang:

As Oyster Nan stood by her Tub
To show her vicious Inclination;
She gave her noblest Parts a Scrub,
And sigh'd for want of Copulation.

He burst out laughing, his eyes dancing with delight, and she laughed too, enjoying herself more than she ought.

"What next?" he said. "Did Oyster Nan get her—"

"Don't say it." She pushed her hair from her forehead and tried to remember. "There was a vintner," she said. "And they...they sported."

"They *sported*, did they?"

"But they were interrupted, and then...I don't know. The words made no sense. Um..."

She sang again:

But being call'd by Company,
As he was taking pains to please her,
I'm coming, coming, Sir, says he,
My Dear, so am I, says she, Sir.

"Why are you laughing?" she asked. "It's not even funny."

But his hands covered his face and his shoulders were shaking. She imagined sliding her hand over those shoulders, his laughter rumbling beneath her palm, feeling the shape of his muscles and the warmth of his skin.

When his laughter subsided, he said, "You are a treasure."

His expression was soft, then. His smile mingled with the brandy and made her body feel odd and delicious, like it had the night before, on her bed, when she thought he would kiss her, and maybe he would kiss her now.

But he wouldn't kiss her. He had loved his wife. He didn't want her. And she didn't want him either. She kept forgetting that part.

She put the glass back on the table, and only realized she'd almost missed the edge when he lunged and caught it and moved it to the center. She could knock that glass off the table and it would break.

"She's broken," she said.

She glanced at Joshua. He was studying her with a slight frown.

"Lucy," she clarified. "She's broken inside and I don't know why. We've had our fair share of tragedies, but...I don't know how to fix it and it hurts to watch her breaking into pieces. You're a bit broken too."

His head jerked up. "Nobody's broken. That's just life."

"I think you are trying to stop life from happening, but life keeps on happening anyway."

She didn't know where that thought came from, but it seemed a very good and important thought. Brandy didn't interfere with her thinking. Her thinking was good. She understood now. She understood that...something.

But he didn't like it. Irritation flashed in his face. "Calling me broken because I don't paste a smug smile over everything and pretend I'm better than everyone else."

"Are you talking about me?"

"You have no idea what it's like to make mistakes," he said. "You can never understand human failings."

"How would you know what I do or don't understand?"

"When have you ever made a mistake? When have you made a bad decision? When have you even broken a single bloody rule? Huh? Name one thing you have done that you should be ashamed of."

The room tilted. This was what it meant to be drunk. Foxed, tipsy, bosky. *Was Papa bosky when he got himself killed?* The image of Papa swam before her eyes. Papa, hugging her after her wedding. Papa, explaining how the estate ran, telling her everything would be all right. Papa, lying motionless on the bloody straw in the stable. Even after his funeral, she didn't cry. She wrote to her husband, and when he couldn't be bothered to come, she took over running the estate, even though she didn't need to—they had a good land steward, and she was already busy with the household with Mama unwell—but she'd had to fill every moment from morning till bedtime.

"I bribed a public official," she said. "That's what I did. I lied to the law and I lied to the church."

Joshua had loved her father too. If she told him, she would hurt him. Good.

"Papa didn't fall off his horse and break his neck," she said. "He shot himself. And I bribed the coroner and the doctor and everyone else to cover it up so no one would know."

JOSHUA HAD ONLY HAD one glass of brandy, but his head was spinning as if he had drunk a whole bottle, and he had to grip the arms of the chair so he wouldn't fall off.

Then the world steadied itself. Cassandra sat staring at nothing, and everything was the same and would never be the same again.

Lord Charles had shot himself. No. Lord Charles was the most cheerful, warmest man he had ever known. He always had a kind word and a smile. He went out of his way to help others, and never let a penny rest in his pocket if someone else needed it more.

"Why?" The word hardly made it out of his choked throat.

"I don't know. He left no note. After he died, I learned he'd had financial problems, but you gave him enough money to fix that."

"Yes."

Money. What in blazes had the money been good for? For too long, Joshua had believed money could solve all problems, but every time he thought he was protected, life went and threw something else at him to prove, yet again, that he was wrong.

"Why didn't you tell me?" he said and immediately wished the question back.

She had written to tell him that her father had died in a riding accident. Invited him to visit the estate that he had inherited.

Instead, he sat alone in Scotland and mourned the best man he had ever known. He had sent money, Newell, and a cat. Bloody hell. He deserved to be pilloried.

"I didn't tell anyone," she said.

"Your mother?"

"She doesn't know. None of them know. You mustn't tell them."

She hugged her knees, her cheek laid on them so her hair listed to one side. She looked too young and innocent to carry this awful burden. Naive, he'd called her. Smug, he'd called her.

He moved to sit beside her on the settee. She lowered her legs and let him take her hand.

"What do you mean, none of them know? You carry this alone?"

She played with his fingers and spoke in bursts. "He did it in the second stable, the empty one. There was a storm, so I suppose the thunder masked the noise. A groom found him before dawn and told the housekeeper. She couldn't wake Mama because... Well. Because. So she woke me instead. I insisted on seeing him. I shouldn't have. Something tore inside me and I went empty. I sent the groom to fetch Sir Gordon Bell—he's the magistrate and Papa's dear friend—and I told him that no one must ever know the truth, and he agreed. If everyone knew, we would have...we would have had to bury him at a crossroads with a stake through his heart. My father. Buried like...I couldn't let that happen."

She was tracing the lines on his palm, but he doubted she saw a thing. He did not want to hear this but he had to.

"We paid the coroner five hundred pounds so there'd be no public inquest. That is, *you* paid him five hundred pounds." She sounded almost jolly. And he had accused her of pasting a smug smile over her emotions. Bloody hell. "The doctor refused payment, but you bought him a new carriage and horses anyway. You bought the groom a small cottage near Margate, and he moved away and married his sweetheart. The housekeeper Mrs. Greenway didn't want anything either, but you paid for her two nephews to go to Shrewsbury Grammar School. They're doing well. You are generous in your bribes."

"And your family?"

She had been twenty when she did all this. It had been a month after they married, and he couldn't even remember her face. Where in blazes was her mother?

"They don't need to know. By the time they woke up, it was all arranged. They had moved Papa, and Mrs. Greenway and the doctor washed him, and the doctor said his face was smashed in the fall so they had to keep the coffin closed."

A single tear fell onto his hand. She looked up at him. Her eyes were green and wet, the lashes clumped in little spikes.

"He knew, Joshua," she said. "He worried about dying before I could marry and keep everyone secure, and I laughed at him and said there was no reason he would die. But the whole time he was planning to do it, and that's why he wanted us to wed. He even transferred his property to you, so the Crown could not seize it. We killed him, you and I. If we never married, he would never have done it, and his demons would have gone away. And now he's buried in the churchyard, which is sacrilege, and we did this crime and I try to do the right thing but I can never atone for that. I get so angry at him sometimes."

Her logic was wrong, utterly wrong, but emotions had a way of making the worst logic seem right.

"Lord Charles said the same thing to me, when he asked me to marry you," he told her. "He said that Charlie's death left you all unprotected. I thought he was worrying unnecessarily."

Tears ran down her cheeks. He fumbled for a kerchief and wiped them away, trying to be gentle, but feeling rough and clumsy. She let him. Because she was taking care of everyone and no one took care of her. He pulled her against him and she slumped against his chest. He stroked her hair and wished he could take away her pain.

"It was his decision," he said. "He must have been hurting and you gave him peace."

She said nothing. He held her close and breathed in her fragrance, breathed through the tightness in his chest, the burning in the back of his throat. Cassandra had borne it all and he had mocked her. And Lord Charles: He would have done anything for Lord Charles, if only he had known. But Lord Charles was always so cheerful and congenial, even while he grieved for Charlie. Covering it all up with a pleasant, polite smile.

There was a woman who might know the full story, but he could never tell Cassandra about her. Cassandra still believed her father had been faithful to his wife. He would not take that from her too.

The poor thing. He had been so annoyed by her self-righteousness, her self-possession. It had been easier to think of her as a good, boring girl with polite smiles and petty concerns. He almost wished he didn't know this about her: That she was so much more.

THEY SAT TOGETHER A LONG TIME, Cassandra's weight warm and comforting against his side, until he realized she was falling asleep.

"Come on." He shifted out from under her and she protested, bleary and tipsy. "Let's get you to bed."

"I like it here," she said. "It's warm and you're comfortable."

"Your bed will be warm and comfortable too."

He banked the fire and went to pick her up. She was young and trusting and a little broken too. She was trying so hard to hold her family together. Sweet little fool. It was impossible. He knew better than anyone that families fell apart and there was nothing to be done.

"You're humoring me," she said. "That's what I do with Lucy when she's drunk. I agree with everything that she says."

"That's very wise. You should agree with me every chance you get."

He lifted her into his arms. She looped her hands around his neck and rested her head on his shoulder and tickled him with her hair. Her bosom pressed into his chest, her rounded hip against his belly. He had not been this close to a woman in months. He ignored his stupid body; she was upset, drunk, and his wife.

"One should never argue with a drunk person," she said, as he carried her out of the study and up the stairs. "This is something I have learned."

"I agree."

"One must be agreeable. You're not agreeable. You're disagreeable."

"No, I'm not. I'm lovely."

She laughed, her chest moving against his. She wasn't light, but she wasn't heavy. He liked the feel of her in his arms. The way her body moved with laughter and the laughter moved into him. Carrying her, as he ought to have done from the start.

"You're cantankerous."

"I'm charming."

"You're ill-mannered."

"I'm delightful."

She laughed again. Soft, gentle laughter. It was nice to see her laughing, but he worried about the pain that she had put away. The pain that had exploded out of her today. It had bewildered him at first, but he understood it now. How lonely it must have been, in her family, the only one knowing the truth, smiling pleasantly through it all.

And he...Selfish didn't even begin to cover it.

In her room, he lowered her onto her bed. Her eyes were big and dark in the light of the single candle, her brown hair wild against the pillow. He fingered the big bow of her bed jacket.

"Do you wear this thing to sleep in?"

"It's warm and comfortable. Like you."

He laughed despite himself, and helped her under the covers. She didn't need help, but he did it anyway. And he didn't need to lie down beside her, on top of the covers. Neither did he need to tangle his fingers in the silky tresses escaping from her bandeau. But he did those things too.

"What else do you need?" he asked. "Shall I fetch your nightcap?"

"You think my nightcap is silly."

"I think it is adorable."

He leaned over her, brushed his knuckles over her petal-soft cheek, and willed himself to get up. This was becoming torture. He had to pull away. He could not move.

"You never even kissed me," she said.

Leave the bed now, he yelled at himself. *Get out now*. But for once he was too slow.

She lifted her head and pressed her mouth to his.

The pure soft sweetness of her slid right through him, burning through his chest and emptying his head with the potency of a thousand brandies. His hand found its way behind her neck, sliding into her thick, soft hair, cradling her head so he could have more. Their lips moved together, exploring, opening, and when he tasted her with his tongue, she made a small sound in her throat that shot straight to his groin. She arched up into him, and he tasted her again. Deeper. More. And she—so generous and warm —welcomed him. She tasted like brandy and woman and hope and flowers, and he could not think how she might taste like flowers or why that might be a good thing, but she did and it was. He could melt into her, into her generous warmth, surrender to the thud of his heart and the urging of his cock, melt into her and have her melt into him, and all their heartache would melt away too.

He dragged his lips from hers, gently pushed her back onto the pillows. She smiled up at him and it took all his strength to keep his distance.

"There," he said. "Now we kissed."

"That was lovely."

"You're drunk. You think everything's lovely."

"Even your scruff is lovely."

Her palm rubbed his cheek and he resisted the urge to lean into her again. He lowered her hand, tucked it by her side. In the candlelight, he could not tell the current color of her eyes, but it didn't matter because her eyes made up their color as they went along, and that was only one of the delightful things about her to discover.

He needed her to fall asleep so he could escape this madness.

"Close your eyes," he said. She did. He stroked her hair back from her face, stroked her forehead, stroked her cheek. He longed to stroke every part of her. "Breathe in now," he said. "And breathe out. And in, and out."

She obeyed and then she was asleep.

Thank God. Now he could escape.

But not yet. That would not be right. She was upset, and he was sure it was wrong to leave someone who was upset. And it was the first time she was drunk, and she might be frightened, if she woke alone to a spinning room. So he should stay a little longer. Until he was sure she was calm. Until the feel of her lips had left his. Until his urge to weep had passed.

CASSANDRA AWOKE. There was almost no light in the room. She had a touch of nausea, a touch of headache. Her bed was warmer than usual. She was not alone. She was too sleepy to be frightened, and it was Joshua anyway. The weight over her waist was his arm. The heated wall at her back was his chest. She listened to him breathe: He was sleeping. She had kissed him. His lips had been warm too, and surprisingly soft. He had touched his tongue to hers. She should have been disgusted but instead a raw pleasure had shot straight down her center and all she had wanted was more. And the things she had said! She must never drink again. But he had not judged her. She did not move. She did not want to disturb him, or face him. Besides, it felt so lovely, to be wrapped up in this man. She closed her eyes and enjoyed it.

When she woke again, he was gone.

CHAPTER 11

The next afternoon, Mr. Cosway, who bore the cumbersome title of Secretary In Charge of Everything That Happens In London, showed Cassandra to the empty office that Joshua used when he was at the dockside warehouse. Dominating the small room was a desk crowded with dossiers and yard-long rolls of paper, as well as a globe and items of equipment she could not begin to name.

Also present: a cravat strewn over the chair, a coat tossed onto the table, a hat balanced on the globe. Joshua could not be far, as he had, yet again, left half his clothes behind.

Cassandra tucked away her rosewater-scented handkerchief as Mr. Cosway crossed to the window. The secretary was approximately the size of a carriage, with a shaved head, battered nose, and a peg where his left hand should be, but he spoke incongruously like a gentleman and treated her with every courtesy.

"He's on the dock with the children," he said, tapping the thick, greasy glass.

"The children?"

She hastened to the window. There was Joshua, clean-shaven today, in his shirtsleeves and a plain black waistcoat, crouching on the dock, talking to two boys and a girl. The children, who were no more than eleven or twelve, were simply but neatly dressed, and all were looking at him with enthralled faces. A woman who bore the air of a governess and whose features hinted at African heritage watched from nearby.

Cassandra pressed a hand against the window pane and leaned in. Her bonnet bumped the glass and she impatiently shoved it off her head so she could see.

Joshua's buckskins were pulled taut over his powerful thighs. The breeze ruffled his hair and toyed with the billowing sleeves of his shirt, teasing her with glimpses of the body within. Her palm recalled the tickling sensation of his scruff and she wondered at the smoothness of his cheek now.

One of the boys, the small, red-headed one, said something and Joshua nodded. He sketched a diagram on the wooden dock with his finger. The three children gathered closer, blocking her view.

For a man who declared children to be a nuisance, he seemed fond of these ones. For a man who claimed to be busy, he seemed to have time for them.

"What is going on?" she asked.

"The children are supposed to be working, but Mr. DeWitt, he likes to talk to them sometimes."

"What about?"

"Whatever's on his mind. Which could be anything. Always a thousand things on Mr. DeWitt's mind."

His expression was rueful, but he spoke with admiration also.

"He employs those children?"

"More like practical training, although they get some wages

too. There's some orphanages that work with him, where he pays for the children to learn things, reading and writing and arithmetic. Most children like that, if they get a job, it's in the factories or in service, but Mr. DeWitt says if they have the aptitude to do something different, then they ought to get to use it. Says aptitude matters more than birth. So some train here, and when they're ready, we help them find a job."

"Who is the woman?"

"That's Miss Sampson. The training was her idea, so now she's the Secretary In Charge Of Organizing The Training And Education. She's a good sort, Miss Sampson." His battered face broke into a smile and Cassandra couldn't help but smile too; perhaps Mr. Cosway thought Miss Sampson was more than just a good sort. "She taught me to speak prettily. Lots of people think that if you don't speak English the way they speak English, then you're not as bright as them. I don't mean Mr. DeWitt, though," he hastened to add. "Most people, they wouldn't give me a job, because some greedy pirate made off with my hand, but I said to Mr. DeWitt, 'I know shipping, and I don't need my left arm to think,' and he agreed."

Down on the dock, a clerk came to speak to Joshua. He looked up and their eyes met through the thick glass. He shook his head, then he nodded at the clerk, and gave her another look. She backed away.

Not so courageous now, was she?

She hardly noticed Mr. Cosway leaving, as she placed her bonnet on the table, folded her hands, and composed herself. She would not mention last night. She would not mention children.

She would not mention the dream that had blossomed overnight, delicate and pale, like a tiny wildflower poking up amid the ferns on the forest floor. She had thought she had buried the dream two years ago, given it up for lost along with so much else, but it had bloomed anew.

Children would bring pain, of course: She had lived long enough to know that whomever one loved would cause hurt, sooner or later. But they would also bring joy. Any pain could be borne if one had joy and love and laughter.

And her body was ready. That's why it turned so silly around him. It was the only explanation, given that he was so dreadful and infuriating and not at all what she wanted in a husband.

Except that he didn't want children, and he didn't want her.

Which is why she would not mention it.

"What the blazes are you doing here?" he said as he hurtled in, shrinking the room to half its size. "Docks are dangerous places."

"It's interesting to see where you work."

Their eyes met, and something shot through her, like a bolt of that lightning that bounced around inside him, like that jolt of pleasure when their mouths met last night.

She could have sworn he felt it too, that something leaped between them, a shared memory, a shared emotion, a shared desire, but he immediately bounded over to the window to check something outside. She remembered the moment when she thought they might be friends; even that seemed impossible in the light of day.

"Work being the operative word," he said. "Not chatting with my wife."

"You were chatting with those children."

"Which was work."

"You seemed fond of them."

"They're potential employees. So stop getting ideas."

"Ideas?" Her heart thudded. He knew. He knew what she wanted. "Whatever do you mean?"

He picked up a dossier, flicked through it, tossed it back on the desk. Papers slid wildly and he lunged to stop them falling to the floor. "I am busy, Cassandra. I don't have time for this."

"It will take less time for you to talk to me than it would for you to remove me. I am feeling particularly tenacious today. Barnacle, remember?"

He folded his arms. She lifted her chin. He narrowed his eyes. She raised her eyebrows. He scowled at her. She beamed at him.

He groaned and ran his hands through his hair, which she knew now was absurdly soft. "I liked you better when you were nice. So what is it? What? What?"

Cassandra dragged her eyes off his hair, pasted on her cheerful, sensible expression, and focused on the matter at hand.

"This issue of Lord and Lady Bolderwood," she said. "We must discuss what happens next."

"What happens next is this: I deal with Lord and Lady B. You go back to Warwickshire. Everything goes back to normal."

Disappointment flooded her and she smiled on. "But Joshua—"

"It's not your concern."

"It *is* my concern."

She took a step toward him, and another. But an invisible wall between them stopped her from taking a third.

"I must go out into society with everyone believing that my husband committed adultery with the wife of my former betrothed."

"So don't go out into society. Go back to Warwickshire. Problem solved."

"That will not do," she said. "We must stand united before society and discredit them in everyone's eyes. With society and public opinion on our side, they may feel pressure to drop this."

"You believe me."

"Yes. I do. And a wife stands by her husband."

He regarded her for a long moment, then he was moving again, prowling around the small space, poking and prodding things for no apparent reason at all.

"Others will too," she went on. "Lord and Lady Hardbury, of course, as well as Lord and Lady Luxborough. My aunt and uncle Lord and Lady Morecambe, and even my grandparents. We can also count on the support of the Duke of Dammerton. Of course, for the legal aspects, you will need a lawyer."

"I have a dozen lawyers."

"They are commercial lawyers. I suggest Sir Gordon Bell, whom I trust implicitly, as he had a long career as solicitor to many members of the aristocracy and is not without influence. Although I propose that our first step is to confront Lord and Lady Bolderwood ourselves and put an end to this today."

He regarded her a moment. "You sound as if you're planning a battle."

"They attacked my family."

"No, they attacked *me*."

"And you *are* my family."

"It doesn't work like that."

"Actually, it does."

He threw up his hands. "This has gotten completely out of control. Ours is a marriage in name only, remember."

"Last night—"

"Changed nothing. In name only!"

His roar was answered by the squawks of seagulls outside, and her own cries rose up inside her. Good heavens, what did this man do to her? He made her moods as wild as his own.

"Precisely," she snapped. "I now carry your name, which means my sisters do too and so your name affects my sisters' future."

"Your bloody sisters."

"And if you don't want my sisters to be your problem, then help me get them accepted by society and ultimately married, and the best way for you to do that is to agree to my plan."

He banged his forehead lightly against a map of London and then turned and lounged against the wall.

"You're talking sense again," he said. "Can't stand it when you talk sense."

As fast as her fury had come, it was gone, and she worked to keep herself from smiling. He had the most terrible effect on her equilibrium, and she would never understand why she found his beastly manner so charming.

"So do as I say and stop being obstreperous," she said.

"Obstreperous," he repeated, rolling the syllables around in his mouth. A playful half-smile brightened his face and his dark eyes fixed on hers. "But I like being obstreperous."

"And you're very good at it too," she managed to say, curiously breathy. "But perhaps, until this matter blows over, you could take a brief hiatus from insulting people and getting into fights and having affairs. I mean…That is…Oh no."

She pressed her fingertips to her traitorous lips and willed away the heat sliding up her cheeks. This was the trouble. She lost control of her tongue around him and expressed thoughts she didn't even know she had. All the restraint she was raised to show, the self-control that was meant to distinguish the rational, refined upper classes from the masses—a single conversation with him and twenty years of training went out the window.

And that look on his face: She knew that one. The playful, wicked one. The look that set her body clamoring for his touch.

He pushed off the wall and sauntered toward her.

She pressed a hand over her eyes, so she couldn't see him approach, but she could feel his presence, all that energy shooting through her, coiling and pulsing deep within. He came so close that his legs stirred her skirts and the faint spicy scent of him teased her nostrils, and part of her was back in that bed again.

"You do realize," he drawled softly, "that when you cover your eyes, I can still see you."

"No you can't."

He gently took her hand, his fingers warm and firm through her gloves, and she let him lower her arm. When he released her, she twisted her fingers into her skirts so she would not loop her arms around his neck. How silly her body was, wanting a baby so badly it overlooked the facts that she did not like him and he did not want her.

"Tell me true, now, Mrs. DeWitt. Are you jealous?"

Heaven help her, she was. How smug she had been, before, when he was a stranger and she cared nothing for him at all. And he was teasing her again, the fiend, but now she enjoyed it, because now she knew that he was kind under his brash facade, and this teasing was just for her, and that made her feel special.

"For appearance's sake, I mean," she said.

"So for *appearance's* sake, you would have me be a monk."

"No need to be a monk." Her heart performed a little quadrille and she had to swallow before she could speak again. "After all, we are married, and you know your way to my bed."

BLOODY HELL. He had walked right into that one, hadn't he? No longer could he use bedsport to frighten her away. It seemed she was no longer wary of the marriage bed.

And for the worst possible reason. It was not *him* that she wanted.

"I will do my duty, as your wife," she added, which words had the merciful effect of a bucket of ice water on his groin. Joshua backed away from her. Kept going until his back hit a wall.

"And?" he said.

A mistake to ask the question when he already knew the answer.

Her unspoken words filled the space between them, expanding like a giant balloon, taking up all the air in the room so there was none left to breathe. He needed her not to say those words. He understood what she wanted; she had given it away last night. He had to burst that balloon, burst it before she let it carry them both away.

Too late.

"And we might have children," she finished.

Her voice was so soft he almost didn't hear her, so loud he wanted to tell her not to yell.

"I can imagine them now, our children," she added, dreamily. "Running through Sunne Park, bright and energetic. Laughing. They'll have dark hair, I suppose, and be bright and mischievous. Little boys sliding down the bannister. Little girls running through the rose garden. Or the other way around. I don't mind." She laughed shortly, an unnaturally high-pitched sound. "If you saw Sunne Park, you'd know that it's a marvelous place to be a child."

She didn't know what she was asking. He could tell her— what? That she stood at the start of a path into a wood. There were terrible things in that wood: wolves and monsters and beloved, bright-eyed children. She would skip down the path anyway, picking flowers and singing. *Stay out of the wood*, he wanted to say. *It looks nice, but it isn't. It's full of things that will destroy you, like wolves and monsters and beloved, bright-eyed children.* But he could scream and yell and she would never listen.

Naive, optimistic fool that she was. They shared a kiss and a secret and she thought it changed things. Last night changed nothing. So he understood her better now, perceived the edge of worry underlying her smiles, saw that her pigheadedness was actually a breathtakingly fierce protectiveness, that she was trying so hard to be good when part of her longed to misbehave. Even knowing that, in the end, changed nothing.

She was a disruption, and this Bolderwood nonsense was a disruption, but they were small disruptions, and once he got back to his busy life in Birmingham, everything would go on as peacefully as it had before.

"Why don't you get a cat?" he said.

"You already gave me a cat."

"Then get a hobby. Something to keep you occupied."

"I run the estate and household at Sunne Park."

Sunne Park was, reportedly, a marvelous place to be a child. She would go back to that marvelous place and lavish all her affection on a child and never give him a second thought. And he would go back to his life in Birmingham, where he had no need of her at all, because there he had his work, which was all he had had for years now, and all he ever needed.

"Then you have no time for children too," he pointed out.

"Why are you so averse to having children?"

"Because they're troublesome."

"Then you needn't trouble yourself with them."

Her tone was sharper now. She was braver with him than she had been, or maybe she simply cared less, showing more of the true self that lay behind her polite, restrained facade.

"I will need your assistance with conception," she said swiftly, in a flat, tight voice. "The rest I can manage on my own. Our separate lives can continue as they were and your life need not change. You needn't even learn their names if that's too much *trouble* for you."

"*Their* names? So I'm to be your stud, am I? Your stallion."

"You can be involved if you want. Or not, as you want. But you...I don't know what you want."

I want to be wanted. I want to know I'll never again lose what I love. I want Samuel back, and I could have a hundred thousand children and that will never happen.

"I want everything to go back to normal," he said.

He turned and caught his own ghostly reflection in the window. He looked past it to the dock, to the three children. The girl had dark hair and rosy cheeks. The coloring they might expect if they had a daughter.

Cassandra joined him at the window. He studied her reflection in the glass; how beautiful she was, how warm her skin, how soft her body. It would be so easy, to pull her into his arms, kiss her breathless, touch his tongue to every inch of her, give her everything she wanted and more.

"What are their names?" she said.

"The girl is Sarah." His voice was hoarse so he cleared his throat to continue. "Miss Sampson says she is a mathematics prodigy. The tall boy is John and he writes perfect sentences. The red-headed boy is Martin. He wants to build a machine that can fly."

"You would be a good father," she said.

He didn't want to hurt her, but she was hurting him, and she didn't even know it. She assumed he had no children with Rachel and he never corrected her. If any of the London staff knew, they would never think to mention it, and Newell seemed harmless but he had the discretion of a spy. Joshua could tell her, but then she would become sympathetic and annoying and it wouldn't change a thing. And the longer he didn't tell her, the more impossible it was, and anyway, he needed to hold on to the memory. If he brought his memory out into the light, it would crumble into dust and he would lose that too.

"You don't know that," he said.

"You care about those children."

"They're potential employees. I care about all my employees. A happy employee is a productive employee."

"If you say so."

It was hopeless. She yearned and she would go on yearning, this brave, honorable, foolish woman who had sacrificed so much for others and asked only this one thing in return. And when she yearned, he yearned too, and it made him want to smash the glass with his fist.

"I am perfectly content with my life the way it is," he said.

"I see."

Then, watching her, he saw her perform her trick: She picked up her yearning and loneliness and disappointment and hope, and she packed them away, tied them up tight inside her, and sealed it all with an amiable smile.

He recognized the trick in her. He could see how well she did it.

Perhaps because he did it so well himself.

"And Lord and Lady Bolderwood?" she said. "Shall we call on them now?"

"It's a stupid idea."

"Indulge me."

"Fine. Fine."

She smiled brightly, too brightly. "We'd better get you dressed," she said. "Let me help you with your cravat."

JOSHUA WASN'T sure how it happened, but he found himself half-sitting on the desk, with Cassandra standing between his legs, coming at him with the length of fine muslin in those competent hands.

"How do you even know how to tie a cravat?" he asked.

"I know all sorts of things."

Her moss-green daywear covered her as fully as her nightwear did, with fabric to her throat and her wrists. But she had a very cunning dressmaker, for the black stripes on her front drew his eyes to the swell of her bosom, and her pelisse seemed to be fastened by a single cord under her bust, which ended in two fat, tempting tassels that teased him with the thought that it needed only one tug for the whole lot to fall away.

His hands found the edge of the desk and he curled his fingers around it.

"This is a bad idea," he said.

"Why do you say that?"

Her arms wide, she pushed the midpoint of the neckcloth against his throat, and then encircled his neck to cross the ends behind him and then drape them back over his front. She had to lean close to do it, with her stripes and her tassels and her scent and her hair, and she really didn't see why this was a bad idea?

"You might use the cravat to throttle me," he said.

"Not inconceivable." She crossed the cloth again at his throat, and her expression lightened. "I confess that half the time I cannot decide whether to kiss you or throttle you."

"What about the other half the time?"

"The other half I only want to throttle you."

His mouth started to form some stupid quip about kissing being better than throttling, but he stopped himself in time, and she went back to wrapping the cloth around his neck. Back and forth, swaying in, swaying out, brisk and competent, as if she had no idea. She called him wicked, but she was pure evil.

Then, sweet mercy, she was done with the layering, was tying the final knot, and still seemed unaware of her effect on him.

One would think he had no effect on her at all.

She pressed a warm hand to his cheek. "You shaved your scruff," she half-whispered.

"Damn stuff itches."

He could turn his head and plant a kiss on her palm. He could lean in and plant a kiss on her lips. She would let him, of course. She wanted a baby. She wanted to be dutiful. She gave no sign she wanted him. It shouldn't matter.

Yet perhaps she would genuinely enjoy it, if he kissed her now, without brandy. What if he nipped her earlobe? Would that make her moan, or squeal, or gasp? And what if he kissed her breasts? Or buried his face between her thighs?

"You do realize," he said slowly, "that we are in my office, in my warehouse, with my employees all around and docks crawling with sailors outside?"

As if to back him up, there came the pounding of little footsteps down the corridor. Small white fingers hooked around the doorframe, and then all of Martin swung around the corner and careened into the room.

"Mr. DeWitt! Mr. DeWitt!" Martin cried, then skidded to a halt at the sight of them, eyes wide. A tuft of red hair sat up at the crown of his head. "Are you two *kissing*?"

Cassandra leaped away, seized her bonnet, and used the window as a mirror to tie it. Joshua forced his tormented body upright, scooped up his coat, and thrust his arms into the sleeves.

"What is it, Martin? We're about to head out."

"I was watching the seagulls, and they always take off into the wind. I am sure that holds a lesson in how to fly!"

"Well done, lad." He grabbed his hat off the globe, twirled it around one finger. Cassandra was pulling on her gloves, her eyes flicking back and forth between the two of them. "You can tell me about it next time. Now, make sure you've done all your work for Miss Sampson."

"Yes, sir."

The boy darted off again. Joshua headed after him. He was already through the doorway when he remembered that he should let her go first, but if he started turning all polite, then she'd think she was reforming him, and the woman already had enough dangerous ideas.

CHAPTER 12

"This is the stupidest idea since Napoleon visited Russia in winter," Joshua grumbled as Cassandra joined him on the footpath outside Lord Bolderwood's house. She had visited here before, years ago, when the world thought this house might one day be hers.

She smoothed her skirts, straightened her bonnet, and packed up the last of her unruly emotions. They had made the carriage ride to Mayfair in silence, Joshua with his hat tipped over his eyes, while Cassandra gazed out the window and listed a thousand random things to quell all memory of what had passed.

"You should have helped me down from the carriage," she said, taking a shamefully petty pleasure in nagging.

He twisted around to frown at the carriage, and then at her. "You cannot manage by yourself?"

"The groom assisted me, but it should have been you."

"What for? Your legs seem to work properly."

"I'd like to see you jumping up and down from carriages while dressed in skirts and stays."

He blinked at her. "Mrs. DeWitt! Did you refer to your underwear in public? I am shocked!"

"You are nothing of the sort."

Despite everything, she could not help but be amused, her mood shifting with her enjoyment of his playful theatrics. She supposed he was enjoying himself too, for he extended his elbow in an exaggeratedly gallant gesture.

"Stop gossiping about your corset," he said. "Let's go give 'em a jolly good click in the muns."

She slipped her fingers around his arm. "I have no idea what a muns is, but please refrain from clicking anyone there. We are going to be polite, reasonable, and civilized, and persuade them to stop this nonsense."

"I still say this is a stupid idea."

"And I still say you should help me down from the carriage, but it seems neither of us will get what we want today."

At the door, she waited for him to knock. Rather than do so, however, he twiddled his thumbs and began to whistle. She looked at him. He looked at her.

"Are we going to stand here all day?" he asked.

"It is more appropriate for you to knock, as the gentleman."

He studied the brass lion head on the door. "Too heavy for you to lift, is it? Is this to do with your long skirts and corset? Or are your female fingers too delicate?"

"We should have brought Mr. Newell, to do this for you," she said, amusement warring with exasperation. She lifted the brass ring and knocked sharply. "Heaven forbid you should have to lift a finger."

He grinned. "I don't see why I should do everything around here, when you are perfectly capable of doing things yourself."

Before she could reply, the door swung open to reveal a

remarkably handsome man who was dressed like a butler, but who was much too young and unkempt for a butler in an aristocratic house. Perhaps it was Lord Bolderwood's financial situation, she mused, that meant he could not even afford proper servants.

The inappropriate butler ignored Cassandra and looked at Joshua.

"Yes, sir? How may I help you?"

Joshua made no reply. Cassandra gave him a pointed look.

"What?" he said to her. "Forgotten how to speak, have you? Must I do everything?"

"The conduct books would have it so."

"I've never read any."

"You astonish me."

She held out her card and finally the butler noticed her. "Mr. and Mrs. Joshua DeWitt to see Lord and Lady Bolderwood," she said.

He continued to block the doorway as he peered at the card. Taking advantage of his distraction and presumed inexperience, Cassandra moved straight at him. He instinctively stepped out of her way, thus granting them entrance. Joshua finally did something useful and kicked the door shut.

The handsome young butler did not even seem to notice that he had failed in his first duty of guarding the door. He looked from one to the other.

"Is this a business call or a social one?" he asked.

"Both," Joshua said with a laugh. "Does it matter?"

The butler scratched his cheek. "Well, do you wish to see Lord Bolderwood in the library, or Lady Bolderwood in the drawing room?"

"How about Lady Bolderwood in her bedchamber? I understand she entertains there."

"Joshua!" Cassandra elbowed him and fought her urge to laugh. "Behave!"

"What?" He turned to her with exaggerated affront. "He asked a stupid question. Why the blazes should I put up with incompetent butlers asking stupid questions?"

"He is merely trying to arrange us properly."

"You can take your 'properly' and put it in—"

"Hush."

The butler was rubbing his forehead, clearly unsure what to do next, and apparently unaware that he had revealed that both master and mistress were in the house.

Cassandra knew exactly how to proceed. "Ideally—Ah, what is your name?"

"Smith, madam."

"Smith." She repeated the word as if it were the best name in the world. "Now, ideally, Smith, my husband and I would meet with both the viscount and his wife simultaneously."

"That means at the same time," Joshua added helpfully.

"I'm sure a young man of your obvious talent could organize to have both of them in the same room."

"Herd them there, as it were."

"Herd them?" Cassandra turned on Joshua, eyes wide with mock outrage. "You must not speak of our hosts as if they were recalcitrant goats."

"Whyever not?"

"The conduct books are very clear on that point."

"Right. Do not call Bolderwood a goat. I shall endeavor to remember that."

"Please do."

He grinned and she felt peculiarly pleased with herself.

"Perhaps, Smith," she went on, "we could begin by seeing Lord Bolderwood in his library, and Lady Bolderwood could join us there." She recalled those sly, smirking eyes. "I am certain she would not want to miss this."

Smith did not look as certain, but she gave him no time to argue, as memory guided her steps straight toward the library. Smith scuttled past her and planted himself in front of the door.

His eyes swung wildly from one to the other. "I should check first, his lordship said."

"No need, Smith. You have done your job beautifully. Your mother must be very proud."

She advanced without hesitation, again forcing him to back away to avoid touching her. When she reached out a hand, he leaped aside, exposing the handle, which she gripped.

"My husband is teaching me to open doors all by myself," she said to the butler. "It is very liberating."

And enjoying the chuckle from behind, she pushed open the door to Lord Bolderwood's library and swept in.

JOSHUA TIPPED the hapless butler and sauntered after Cassandra, eager to see what she came up with next.

"Harry," Cassandra said warmly, as though she were happy to see him. Joshua glared at her back. That pushed politeness a bit too far.

Or maybe she *was* happy to see him.

Bolderwood leaped to his feet.

"Cassandra! And..." Bolderwood's face dropped when he saw Joshua. "What are you doing here?"

"I'm astonished you must ask, you insolent pup." Joshua sauntered to the middle of the room, enjoying the feeling of his wife by his side. He was used to fighting his battles alone; it was strangely warming to have an ally. "You seem to be making free with my name, putting it on legal documents and so forth."

"Joshua. Restrain yourself, please."

She was delightful when she became stern and he could be absurd. He was coming to enjoy her nagging. He suspected she was secretly coming to enjoy his teasing.

"What? You said I must not call him a goat. You never said I couldn't call him a dog."

"Please refrain from likening him to any animals." Mischief glinted in her eyes. "A man of your talents can find much better names."

"I did not wish to upset your delicate ears."

"Oh, *now* you're concerned about my delicate ears." She turned back to Bolderwood. "We have come to deal with this nonsense, Harry."

Bolderwood looked right at Joshua. "You bring your wife to do this? What kind of man hides behind his wife's skirts?"

"But they are such lovely skirts." He grinned at her. "Although generally I prefer to hide *under* them."

She slapped a hand to his chest, her eyes on his. "Behave, darling."

Darling? Ah, a game for Bolderwood's sake. For *Harry*.

"Anything for you, my little poppet," he said.

On impulse, he brushed his knuckles over her jaw. Her eyes darkened ever so slightly; perhaps she could be made to desire him after all.

Somewhere, a man cleared his throat and they jumped apart.

"Ah, Bolderwood, it's you, is it?" Joshua said. "Forgot you were there."

"We are in *my* library," Bolderwood said indignantly. "Of course I'm here."

"So easy to forget about you. My wife is so charming."

"Yes, I remember."

That smirk was going to earn the fellow a punch soon, despite Cassandra's rule against it. These two had probably kissed at some point. Maybe more than kisses. Not that Joshua was jealous, as such, because there was no way he could ever be jealous of an insipid idiot like Bolderwood. It was simply that Cassandra seemed to think that Bolderwood was what a gentleman ought to be, and if Joshua kissed her properly, she'd change her tune on that fast enough. But he wasn't going to kiss her. Go around kissing your lovely wife and the whole world could come crashing down.

"Harry, you will drop this lawsuit. We all know it's ludicrous."

Bolderwood took a painted enamel snuffbox from the desk and helped himself to a pinch. He snorted it and did not offer any to Joshua.

"I cannot do that, Cassandra," he said. "Justice must be served."

"Whatever financial trouble you have gotten yourself into, you must not solve it with such distasteful lies."

Bolderwood shut the snuffbox and studied it. Painted on each side were scenes of naked men and women, doing what naked men and women did best. Cassandra must have noticed the erotic artwork, but she ignored the insult of it beautifully. Joshua resisted the urge to shove the snuffbox down the insolent coxcomb's throat. He was fairly sure Cassandra would object to that.

Had she truly loved this despicable idiot? She had been nineteen, then. People could believe all sorts of stupid things at nineteen. That must be why they married women off so young. If they waited until women were old enough to get some common sense, they'd never get them married off at all.

"Lies?" Bolderwood said finally, rocking back on his heels, a faint, sneering smile playing around his lips. "But there's evidence of an affair. Lots of evidence."

Joshua grabbed the snuffbox, slammed it onto the desk. "There cannot be any evidence, because it never bloody well happened."

Cassandra was there at his side, her shoulder pressed to his arm. She looked Bolderwood in the eye. "Harry, you and I both know that this never happened."

The smile only broadened. "Doesn't matter what you and I *know*. Only matters what the jury believes." He folded his arms over his chest. "We don't expect the full fifty thousand, you know. We'll be content with twenty or thirty."

"We?" Cassandra repeated sharply. "You mean you and your wife."

Bolderwood's smile slipped: That was as good as a confession.

Cassandra sighed, the sound heavy with disappointment. "This is not like you, Harry. To drag your wife's name through the mud. Your respected title, your family name, the name of your children. And to do this to me, and Lucy and Emily."

Bolderwood's ears were turning pink and he picked up his snuffbox again, opening it and closing it, eyes on the box and not on the woman scolding him. Maybe this was not such a stupid idea, Joshua thought; Bolderwood's better nature might be regretting it, and if anyone could reach a person's better nature, it was Cassandra.

"You are better than this, Harry," she went on. "To disgrace your name and mine—for what? For the sake of money?"

"That's rich!" When Bolderwood looked up, his eyes were hard and flat, his better nature gone. "Judging *me* for what I'd do for money." He slammed down the box. "What about you, going out each evening dripping with jewels? You let your father sell you to *him*—" This with a wave of a hand at Joshua "Everyone knew Lord

Charles had money problems, and you don't mind where that money comes from."

Joshua was already pulling back his fist but Cassandra slapped a hand on his arm and stepped between him and Bolderwood with a stiffness unlike her usual grace. Society expected ladies to hide their emotions, especially the uglier ones like anger, but he saw it anyway, in the way she flattened those lovely lips, the sharp breath through her flared nostrils, the way her mouth worked before she spoke. He was glad she was angry, after what she had revealed last night.

"How dare you!" she hissed at Bolderwood. "You aren't good enough to mention my father's name, let alone judge what he did or did not do." She shook her head at him, disgust curling her lip. "This is not like you. The Harry Willoughby I knew was kind and honest."

"Maybe you never knew me."

She had said she was outgrowing her naivety, and Joshua fancied he saw her shed a bit of it there.

"If this is the kind of thing you do and say," she said, "then I don't want to know you at all." She whirled about and marched for the door, her color high, her head higher. She pulled open the door and Smith tumbled in.

"Take me to Lady Bolderwood," she said. "Now!"

The butler jumped to attention and obeyed.

THE MOMENT THE DOOR SHUT, Joshua turned back to Bolderwood and rubbed his hands together.

"Now she's gone, we can discuss this properly," he said.

"Properly!" Bolderwood spluttered. "You swindled me, you bastard. You had this coming."

"You beetle-brained, muttonheaded numbskull!" To keep from throwing any punches, Joshua paced. Dark, painting-shaped patches stained the wall, the bookshelves were mostly empty, and no ornaments adorned the mantelpiece. "I warned you it was speculation and not to risk what you cannot lose. And what do you do? You go to a bloody moneylender!"

"But you prime everyone first, don't you? We hear about how much you made here, or how much your friend Dammerton made there, until we're all begging you to take our money. You're like one of those gaming hells that plant people to say they always win big there, so off the bubble goes, expecting to win, only to get fleeced instead."

"No one else is complaining. You know why? Because they're not whining children."

"They're scared of you, but we are not. You bedded those other men's wives, and everyone will believe you bedded mine too. Everyone except naive, gullible Cassandra."

"You greedy, selfish p—poxed pizzle."

There was little point arguing. The muttonhead had convinced himself that he had been swindled. Probably easier than facing the fact that he had made some bad decisions.

Joshua shook his head, disgust unfurling in him. "You and your wife deserve each other. The worst part of this is that people might think I am so devoid of taste that I would ever look twice at that woman. No, the worst part is the insult to Cassandra. She deserves better." He picked up the snuffbox, examined the bawdy pictures on each side. "I'm amazed you haven't pawned this, along with everything else."

"That was a gift from my wife," Bolderwood said.

Joshua dropped the snuffbox as though it had bitten him.

"Women have desires too," Bolderwood added. "Sinful desires

to do sinful things, and if my wife finds her way into another man's bed every now and then..."

His voice trailed off. A hazy glint in his eye, a crooked twist to his parted lips, a hint of a flush. Bloody hell. Bolderwood was aroused by it! By the thought of his wife with another man. And if that was what they got up to...No wonder this adultery accusation made sense in their minds.

The presence of the extremely handsome, extremely unqualified butler took on a whole new meaning.

Joshua wiped his hand over his forehead as if he could wipe away the thought. Some things he did not need to know.

Meanwhile, Bolderwood was laughing softly, as if to himself. "And of course, I forgive her, because I love her."

"Did you ever think what this would do to Cassandra and her family?"

"She's an uptight prude, anyway, and boring. That's why you bed other men's wives, isn't it? Because your own wife is—Aargh," he finished on a gurgle, as Joshua buried his hand in the man's neckcloth and shoved him hard against the wall.

"You were saying?"

Bolderwood's face went red and he forgot the rest of his sentence.

"You will drop this lawsuit," Joshua said. "You end this now, or so help me, I'll make you sorry."

He loosened his grip to allow the man to speak. Unfortunately, Bolderwood had not grasped the lesson.

"By the time this is done, you'll be a laughing stock and we'll be rich," he rasped out. "We'll drop the lawsuit if you pay us now. Protect your sweet wife that way."

The door opened. Joshua turned his head, Bolderwood still pinned to the wall.

"What?" Joshua said to the butler. "What?"

Smith gulped, looking at his employer helplessly. Joshua hoped the lad made a good plaything, because he made a rotten butler.

"Mrs. DeWitt would like to go home now," Smith finally said.

Joshua dropped Bolderwood like a poisonous snake and adjusted his sleeves.

"We'll ruin you, Bolderwood," he said, while the younger man coughed and rubbed at his throat. He liked the "we," he decided, and went off to find his wife.

Cassandra stood by the front door, so tense she was almost quivering, her mouth pinched as she fiddled with the buttons on her glove.

"You were right," she said when she saw him. "This was a stupid idea."

"That's the smartest thing you've said all marriage."

She tried a smile, failed. Joshua was tempted to go back and pound Bolderwood to a pulp. But more than that, he wanted to restore her good mood. Those people had no right to take that from her, when she was worth a hundred thousand of them.

So he did what he could: He opened the door when Smith failed to appear, he proffered his elbow, he handed her up into the carriage before him.

He got his first reward when the carriage lurched off: She offered a hint of a genuine smile.

"Thank you for assisting me into the carriage," she said. "That was nicely done."

"I can behave," he said. "I behaved myself with Lord B. I didn't hit him. Not even once. I might have choked him a bit, but I didn't hit him."

A flicker of amusement. "How admirable you are."

"And I was going to call him a pig, but I remembered your ban on likening him to animals."

"Well done."

"So instead I called him a poxed pizzle."

She made an unladylike sound—repressed laughter, if he wasn't mistaken. He was succeeding. He would play the clown and make her laugh. It was bad enough that he hurt her so much, without letting scum like them do it too.

He beamed at her. "Are you proud of me?"

"Immensely."

"And how was Lady B.?"

"Lady B. is the most awful woman I have ever had the misfortune to encounter! She insisted it was true."

An odd chill shivered through him. If Cassandra believed the woman, if that was why she was upset...

"But she had this knowing smirk on her face the whole time," she continued, to his relief. "She even said it was romantic that her husband thought she was worth fifty thousand pounds! Heavens! Even *you* are more romantic than that."

"Romantic for a pimp, I suppose."

"For a what?"

"A man who procures customers for prostitutes. Did your governess teach you nothing?"

Half a smile. "I must have had a headache that day."

Their eyes met across the carriage. If he really wanted to improve her mood, he would go to her, hold her, kiss her. And then—what? Then what?

"What else did she say?" he said.

She huffed out. "That she could not help herself: She was overwhelmed by your charm and consideration. So I knew she had the wrong man."

"Indeed. What a shame women cannot give evidence in adultery trials. If she said that, they'd be laughed out of court."

"Then she mentioned your birthmark, as proof that she had seen you..." She waved a hand at him, looked away, her color rising again. "She said it is like a little horseshoe on your right thigh. Is that true?"

He would be on trial before all of London shortly, but this was the trial that mattered the most. He regretted, suddenly, ever sleeping with any other woman at all. It was hard to imagine wanting anyone else now.

"Other people would know of it too," he pointed out. "They could have told her."

"The old birthmark-as-proof-of-seduction ruse?" she said dismissively. "It shows up in Shakespeare and folk stories all the time. It was merely awkward that I had no idea either way. So I said that was no proof and I asked her to describe your..."

"My what?"

With a pointed glance, she indicated his groin, looked at him, blushed, and looked away.

"My dear Mrs. DeWitt! I am shocked! Also, I am very proud of you," he added.

Her eyes danced with mischievous glee. "I thought, 'What would Mr. DeWitt say in this situation?' and that is what I came up with. You are a terrible influence on me."

"I am an excellent influence. And?" he demanded. "What did she say? About my sugar stick."

"Your...? Oh. You are so vain."

"If ladies discuss me in such intimate terms, I have a right to know what they are saying."

She drew a breath to compose herself and gamely looked him in the eye. "She said it looked like all the others she'd ever seen."

"How many is she comparing it to?"

"I forbore to ask."

She was trying to look prim, and failing, for she had a glint in her eye and a smile playing around her lips.

"What did you say to that?" he asked.

"What could I say? Yours is the only one I've ever seen and that only fleetingly."

"Then let me tell you: She's wrong. Mine is better than all the others. It's bigger and stronger, and more handsome and more noble."

"All that!" She opened her eyes wide. "Magical too, I suppose?"

"It can do tricks."

"For example?"

"It can sit up and beg."

She groaned with what sounded like amused horror. A moment later, she broke: She covered her face with her hands and laughed, her shoulders shaking. He was half out of his seat to cross the carriage to pull her into his arms and kiss her until she had stopped laughing and was breathless with desire instead.

But he couldn't do that, so he settled back in his seat and enjoyed watching her. Enjoyed the way her laughter washed over him, rippled all the way to his groin. It took him by surprise, that desire could flare up, so hot and intense, simply from the pleasure of her company.

CHAPTER 13

By the time they were inside and peeling off their outerwear, Cassandra was once more the polite, well-behaved lady. Joshua could not decide if he was irritated that she hid her playful, bawdy side, or thrilled that he alone knew her secret.

Either way, it was irrelevant. It had been an entertaining interlude, and now he had work to do.

He turned to tell her precisely that, only to see her hand off her bonnet and gloves to the waiting footman and take hold of the fat tassels fastening her pelisse.

"You called me 'darling'," he said instead.

"He was annoying me."

"You kissed him, I suppose."

Her head jerked up. She glanced at the footman, who disappeared so quickly he almost sprained something.

"Bolderwood," he clarified.

"Not today I didn't."

"But before."

"We were engaged. So yes."

She tugged at the tassels, untied the bow. As he anticipated, the pelisse fell open and she briskly slid it off her shoulders.

As for kissing Bolderwood, she apparently felt no need to elaborate. Fair enough: Nothing to elaborate on. The whole matter was settled and of no interest whatsoever. He had work to do.

"Anyone else?" he asked.

Finally, he had her attention. "Are you jealous, Mr. DeWitt?"

"Be dreadful for me to be chatting with some fellow, and the whole time he knows he has kissed you and I do not. I did you the courtesy of telling you about my liaisons."

"That was a courtesy, was it?" she muttered, and stood before the small mirror to check her hair. "No one else. Except Hugh Hopefield, but I was only fifteen and he kissed everybody."

She looked at him then, and the entrance hall filled up with everything that lay between them: Her longing—His desire—Their new camaraderie—Her secrets—Their kiss. She had that look on her face, the one she got before she made an impossible request. He had to stop it now.

"Right, I've wasted enough time today." He clapped his hands once. "I have work to do."

Success! She did that trick again: She pasted a polite smile over whatever she had been about to say. He had seen her use politeness as a sword and as a warship; now she used it as a wall, and if he was shut out, it was all his fault.

"Quite," she said.

And as if he were already gone, she started shuffling through the cards and letters on the salver, sorting them into two piles. She paused at an unsealed note, unfolded it, and began to read.

"Right," he said again.

She did not look up, so he turned and headed for his study. But after only three steps—

"Joshua!"

He spun around. "Yes?"

"This note is from Sir Gordon Bell. He says he will learn what he can about Lord Bolderwood's case and call on us here tomorrow."

"You already wrote to him?"

She held out the piece of paper. "Before I went to the warehouse."

He ignored the note. "Before you asked me."

"I should not want to waste time," she said, an edge to her voice. "After all, you are always so busy."

She tossed the note onto one of the piles. It tumbled straight off but she ignored it. Instead, she picked up the other, smaller pile and brushed past him for the stairs.

Joshua stood where he was until her skirts had disappeared from view. Right. His study was straight down the hallway, with all the work that awaited him.

Yet somehow his legs took him up the stairs too.

JOSHUA LOOKED about the drawing room with mild curiosity. As he had no need for drawing rooms, he had never entered this room; Cosway had overseen its furnishings. Airy—Feminine—Blue walls and carpets—Useless ornaments—Pianoforte. Ah, so that's where the music came from.

It also had a writing desk, where Cassandra now stood, going through her correspondence.

"I thought you had work to do," she said.

"I do. Important decisions to make. That's what I do, you know. I make decisions all day."

Not that he could think of a single thing right now, but he had lists on his desk and Das would show up sooner or later. He crossed to the window, inspected the street and the park on its other side, and when he found nothing to complain about, turned back to face her.

Cassandra still stood expectantly, politely, letter in hand.

"So you've only ever kissed two men in your life," he said.

She dropped the letter onto the desk. "Three. I kissed you last night."

And he could still taste her, still feel her body curved against his as she slept. "You were drunk. It doesn't count."

Why in blazes had he started a discussion about kisses? Especially since she had declared her hand: She wanted him to kiss her, impregnate her, and go. Of course she would go. Everyone always did. Only his work was reliable.

If he went now, he would save them both a lot of heartache.

He did not move.

"If I kissed you now," she said, in a voice like rose petals, "would that count?"

The sensible part of his brain tried to wrest back control, to ward her off. Insult her, mock her, tease her, leave her.

But the sensible part of his brain was silenced by the sight of her, as she swallowed nervously, gripped her skirts, and then smoothed them down. Then she took one step toward him, two, three...

She moved slowly. He had time to escape. But suddenly she was right in front of him. Standing this close, in the daylight, he began to understand the trick of her eyes: They were a mix of golden-brown and green and he could look at them all day. Except that he also wanted to look at her cheeks, soft as petals and warm as life, and her mouth, those plump, curved lips that had caressed his last night.

Desire stirred with an eager savagery. Time to stop lying about why he had followed her up here.

"Are you trying to seduce me, Mrs. DeWitt?"

"I wouldn't even know where to start," she said with some asperity. "Although I should not need to seduce you. The door to my chamber is open. You may come in any time you like."

"You can start by making it sound more appealing than inviting the vicar's wife for tea."

"Oh."

She looked so sweetly uncertain that he almost relented. Then her face brightened.

"I'll wear my nightcap," she offered.

The laughter caught him unawares, as did the surge in desire. She looked so pleased with herself for making him laugh that he couldn't resist catching her face in his hands.

"It's working already," she said softly. "I'm making excellent progress."

He leaped away, clasped his hands behind his back. He roved around the room, aiming for the exit, the stairs, his study, yet somehow missing the door on each circuit.

"Would it be so dreadful?" Hurt threaded through her voice and sliced through his chest. "I *am* your wife."

"You didn't enjoy the wedding night."

"That doesn't matter. But if you need to enjoy it, tell me what to do. I am happy to do my duty."

Duty. He hated that word. Bloody polite-speak for "I'll suffer through it in the hope there's a child at the end."

He slumped against a wall. One way or another, he had to decide. He made decisions every day but he could not make this one.

What she wanted from him: A child. What he wanted from her: To lose himself in her welcoming warmth. End result: Cassandra lying still under the covers in the dark, gritting her teeth, thinking only of the children she would bear. And once she had what she wanted, sending him away and leaving him alone again. And if she did get with child...Oh sweet mercy, then what? Then what? Then what? That was the chant of his heart as it thumped in his chest.

Then everything would change, and he did not want anything to change.

Suddenly, he was irritated with her.

"You're difficult," he snapped.

She straightened and gaped at him. "I am the least difficult woman in the world. You know where the bedroom door is."

"Exactly." Unable to stand still, he resumed his pacing. "You are accessible, available, and compliant."

"Then I am easy, not difficult. You can take me as easily as—as —as a piece of candied lemon."

"You are not candied lemon. Candied lemon is not complicated. You are very complicated."

"Heavens, Joshua, you make as much sense as an Italian opera. I want children, I know how they are made, and I am aware of my duty as your wife. How is that complicated?"

"I am not one of those men who is aroused by a woman's obedience."

She was clearly puzzled, poor thing. "You want me to be disobedient?"

"I'm not aroused by disobedience either."

"By what are you...aroused?"

By passion, he wanted to say. *By knowing that you want me as much as I want you, not because it's your duty or because there's a baby at the end of it, but because you want to share pleasure with me and you will never leave.* But he couldn't say that, because the next thing he knew, she'd be acting that out for him, and that would only end in babies and tears.

He groped for an answer, for an end to this entire conversation.

He felt helpless, indecisive, unsure: He did not recognize this version of himself. From somewhere downstairs, he heard the front door, male voices. Das, most likely. He needed to decide. Put a stop to this, once and for all. Send her away. Get back to work. Find a lover, even. Anything to put his life back to how it was. Much more disruption and his life would fall apart. No, it wouldn't. He had forged something too solid, too strong. His world was his business, and his business would never fall apart.

But oh, sweet mercy, to put it all aside for a moment, just a moment, to forget the whole world except for this woman. He wanted to tear off her gown, release her hair. Stir her desire, make her want him so badly she forgot all about politeness and duty. He needed her wild, suddenly. He wanted her raw.

"Did you hate it when I kissed you last night?" she asked.

"No. But you might hate it if I kissed you."

"Why?"

"You are so nice and polite, my darling Cassandra."

He advanced on her, the curve of the pianoforte at her back. She made no attempt to escape, and he easily caged her in. *What the blazes are you doing?—No harm done—Get away from her—One time won't hurt.*

Then what? Then what? Then what? pounded out his heart.

"If I kissed you, it would not be nice," he said. "It would not be polite. It would be..."

He leaned in. She swayed back. He paused. She paused. Then he leaned in again, and this time she stayed still, though her breath came in warm, ragged puffs. When he took hold of her skirts, she yelped, then pressed her lips together. With wide eyes, she stared at him, as he inched up those skirts.

One inch...

Another inch...

Another inch—

Then the door crashed open and Joshua was clutching air, as she ducked under his arm and crossed the room.

"Bloody hell, what is it now?" he snapped and pivoted toward the doorway.

And everything stopped again.

The man who stood there was not one of the servants, nor one of his secretaries. Joshua did not recognize the man, but he knew him anyway.

A young man, a few years younger than him. A tall man, not as tall as Joshua, but wiry and strong, with similar coloring and similar features. Longer hair, tied in a queue, the way some sailors wore it. Weathered skin, as if he spent a lot of time outside, in the Navy perhaps. A walking stick, as if he had sustained an injury in the Navy and been discharged.

Joshua's overworked heart skipped, stopped, thudded, and he tried to tell himself it had nothing to do with this man, because this man was not a man he knew. He did not want to know him. It had been too long.

"What the blazes do you want?" he said.

"It's me. Isaac," the man said. "Your brother."

IT TOOK Cassandra a few moments to catch up with what was happening, as her dazed mind and heated, pulsing body tried to recover from Joshua's closeness. She even felt a flash of uncharacteristic irritation with the newcomer, until she looked at him properly and realized what he had said.

This was Isaac! Joshua's brother! She started forward, already smiling in welcome, when she realized that Joshua was still. Very, very still.

She paused, looking from one brother to the other.

"And?" Joshua said abruptly. "I sent you money. If you want more, tell Das."

Then he was moving again, toward the door. He brushed past Isaac, at full whirlwind stride. Hurt flashed over Isaac's face, and Cassandra stared in confusion. As far as she knew, Isaac was ten years old when Joshua had seen him last. How could he possibly bear him any animosity?

"I don't need money," Isaac called to Joshua's retreating back as he reached the top of the stairs. "As I wrote, I wanted to—"

"I'm busy." Joshua whirled around. "I cannot see what else we have to say to each other. I don't have time for this."

Cassandra rushed forward. "Joshua! Please. This is your brother."

"Barely. I've not seen the boy in fourteen years."

"We can't—"

"Not more nagging," he snapped. He barely looked at her. "I've wasted enough time this morning on your idiotic notions."

She recoiled, stung. A moment ago, they had been about to kiss. An hour ago, they had been friends and allies. And now—

Now he was leaping down the stairs, taking them two at a time in his haste to get away.

Isaac stared after him. He was a couple of years older than her, and was no doubt confident in his own domain, but now he seemed lost and alone.

Curse her husband.

She dashed down the stairs, just in time to see Joshua barge past Mr. Das with a terse "Das, we're going out," scoop up his outerwear, and charge out the door.

Mr. Das, still in his coat and hat, bowed easily to Cassandra, apparently inured to Joshua's ways after all these years. Perhaps in a few years, she would be inured to him too. A few years? He would not even give her a few hours. And he called *her* complicated!

"I invited Mr. Isaac to stay here," Mr. Das said. "I apologize. It was not my place."

Isaac was coming down the stairs swiftly, despite having to place both feet on each step, supported by his stick, before he could tackle the next one.

"You did the right thing," she said, loudly enough for Isaac to hear too. "Isaac will be staying here, and if Joshua does not like it, then he can either explain to me why, or find somewhere else to sleep. You will tell him that, Mr. Das."

"With pleasure, Mrs. DeWitt," Mr. Das said with a bow, and left.

Cassandra turned to Isaac.

"Never mind Joshua," she said. "He is not polite at the best of times. I, for one, am very happy to meet you."

Isaac looked at the door and back at her. "You are his wife, I gather. I apologize for the intrusion, Mrs. DeWitt."

"Nonsense," she said. "You must call me Cassandra and I will call you Isaac, for we are brother and sister now."

"It was a mistake to come," he said stiffly. "I'll not go where I'm not wanted."

"Whyever not? Joshua does it all the time. Besides, you *are* wanted, and never mind him."

Filby the butler was hovering, awaiting instructions, and so she gave them: a room for their guest, and tea in the drawing room.

"Now," she said briskly to Isaac, "I have had a rather astonishing day so far, and I mean to refresh myself by drinking tea and eating too many cakes. I insist that you join me and entertain me with exciting stories about life at sea."

She waited. After a moment, his face broke into a shy smile

and his lost look faded away. At least she had accomplished one thing today.

And perhaps he would also tell her more about their family. Perhaps something he said would help her understand her husband, and why he needed to push everyone away.

CHAPTER 14

That night, Cassandra lay in bed, watching the candle burn down, tensing at every sound.

Until finally she heard footsteps, the door of the next bedroom opening and shutting, and her body came alert like a cat.

She tugged off her nightcap, eased out of bed, and pressed her ear to the connecting door, listening to the sounds of Joshua moving around. A thunk—a boot hitting the floor?—and a second thunk. The clang of the poker as he tended the fire. And then—silence. No movement. No footsteps. Nothing.

He was not coming to her.

No surprise, really. After all, her day had been marked by failure—failure to persuade Lord Bolderwood to drop the case, failure to persuade Joshua to make love to her, have children, accept Isaac. Yet amid the day's disappointments had been a world of delight: seeing him with the children, tying his cravat, their intoxicating camaraderie, the thrill of misbehaving, of laughing together, of their near kiss.

We are husband and wife, she reminded herself, *however he tries to deny it*. Their marriage was not what either of them wanted but it was what they had.

She tapped lightly, opened the door, and slipped into his room. He stood by the fire, his banyan tossed over breeches and shirt, staring at nothing. His hair tumbled over his forehead and the firelight licked at his features and the shadow of his next day's beard.

"What?" he said without looking at her. "I'm busy."

"Yes, I can see that."

She felt like an intruder, but went to his side anyway. Perhaps he would send her away, but her longing to recapture that day's closeness made her stubborn. Besides, if she hesitated every time she risked failure, she would be like Mama and stay in bed all day.

Finally, he shifted and inspected her with narrowed eyes. Her body responded to his gaze and she tried to ignore it. That was not what she was here for, not this time.

"That is an ugly bed jacket," he said. "What possessed you to buy such a thing?"

"Notions of warmth and practicality, mainly."

From Joshua, she decided, that was almost an invitation to stay. So she adjusted the lapels of his banyan, her fingertips sliding over the warm silk as her knuckles bumped against his hard chest.

"How was your day?" she said.

"You're using polite-speak on me now?" he said. "If you've come to seduce me, just bloody well say so."

Yet he did not move away. His eyes dipped to look at her mouth, before fixing on some point over her shoulder. She resisted the urge to slide her arms around his neck, to inhale his clean, spicy scent, taste his mouth again, press her body to his.

"I came to talk about Isaac," she said.

At that, he pulled away, but she gripped his lapels and he came back to her. It felt like a prize. She flattened her palms over his chest. The heat of his skin radiated into hers and there—there— the beating of his heart. Her own heart beat faster in response and she reminded herself to breathe.

"I don't want to talk about Isaac," he said. "I want to talk about your bed jacket."

"My bed jacket is not important. Your brother is."

"No." He frowned at her bed jacket, as though it were a puzzle he had to solve. "You have your priorities all wrong."

"He told me he is looking for your mother and sister. I had not realized you never heard from them after they left."

"Everyone left," he muttered. "I think it is the bow that makes it ugly." He fingered the offending bow and his knuckles brushed the underside of her chin. A frisson danced down her spine and rested below her belly. "It must scratch your chin. That is entirely ridiculous."

"The fabric is soft. It doesn't bother me at all."

"It bothers me."

He tugged at the bow, and she felt it loosen. He was undressing her! Oh heavens. She dragged her attention back to his family; it was more important than seduction. For now.

"It must have been difficult for you," she managed to say. "For your mother to leave without saying goodbye."

All his energy was directed toward untying that bow. "She had just been demoted from countess to mistress. Funny how women get upset about that kind of thing. There, much better without that bow." He smoothed open the top of her bed jacket. His hands briefly rested on her chest, an inch above her breasts. Yet if he noticed that, or her ragged breathing, he gave no sign.

"Bloody hell," he went on. "There are more ties."

"Yes, they hold the jacket closed. They're very useful that way."

"No, they are entirely unsatisfactory."

His nimble fingers plucked at another tie, and another, and another. Each time he tugged on a bow, he tugged at her breath, tugged a little more desire to the surface of her skin. She hauled back her wayward mind.

"And to think your sister was only four the last time you saw her," she went on. "Miriam—that's such a pretty name."

"You do realize I am aware of all this information."

"You might have forgotten it. You have a selective memory."

"There."

His hands slid over her shoulders to part the bed jacket, and lingered, heavy and warm. His eyes burned as he looked her over, with a heat that had nothing to do with the fire, a heat that coursed through her body. She shifted uncomfortably and glanced down, uncertain. Her nightgown was not immodest, but its upper edge rested on the swell of her bosom and the fabric was thin, which meant...Oh dear. She moved to fold her arms over her chest, but, swift as always, he captured her wrists, holding them loosely at her side.

"No, no," he said, his eyes roaming wickedly over her. "I've decided I like your bed jacket a lot better when it is undone."

When his eyes met hers again, they were playful and intense all at once. She licked her suddenly dry lips and tried to speak again.

"Um. As I was saying..."

"Were you saying something? I didn't notice."

"I think Isaac is feeling lost and alone."

He released her wrists and dropped his eyes again. "Actually, no, your bed jacket still offends me."

"He was in the Navy for more than half his life and he is only twenty-four."

"I think it would look better on the floor."

Oh heaven help her. "And now that he has been discharged, he does not know what to do with himself."

"Definitely needs to be on the floor."

He used only his fingertips to chase the bed jacket down her arms and over her hands, a touch so slow and delicate and tantalizing that she bit her lip to avoid crying out.

He knew what he was doing to her, curse him. But what she had gleaned from Isaac mattered too.

"I know what you're doing, Joshua."

"Rescuing you from this ugly garment. I am very heroic."

"You're avoiding talking about your brother."

The bed jacket slithered down her body, pooled at her toes. His fingertips rested on her hands like butterfly feet.

"I am alone with my wife in my bedchamber," he said. "Of course I don't want to talk about my brother. You know, your nightshift is ugly too."

"He said you tried to keep them all together."

Her words hit a mark that she did not know was there. His expression turned cold and hard, like steel; his shoulders tensed and he dropped his hands. Already she missed him, missed his teasing and his sensuality, but she had to say this. She had to understand. She had to make him understand.

"That when Papa came to help you, you wanted you and your brothers to stay together but they wanted to leave. You tried to stop them from going, you said your family had to stay together, but it was what they wanted, the Navy and India, but that's no reason to turn your back on him now."

A tick of a clock, a beat of her heart, a pop from the fire—then he moved so quickly she did not know his intention until she was already tossed over his shoulder like a sack of potatoes, her chin bumping his back, his arm an iron band around her knees.

In only a few strides, he was back in her room. He hauled her off him and she flew through the air and landed on her mattress with a bounce. Her nightshift was tangled up around her thighs and she automatically tried to smooth it down.

"Stop it," he ordered harshly.

She froze. But he was not looking at her legs.

"Stop trying to fix my family," he said. "You're trying to fix your sisters and my brothers and me and—whatever it is you're trying to do, stop it. It is very tedious and extremely unwanted."

She lifted her chin mutinously. "He's going to stay here. I've invited him."

"Of course. Why shouldn't everyone move into my house?"

"It's my house too."

He glowered at her. "And stop being so right all the time. Now, I'm going back through that door and you will not bother me again."

She scrambled up onto her knees. "But what about the other thing?"

"What other thing?"

"My bed jacket. And my wifely duty."

He buried his fingers in his hair and made a sound like a growl. "You're trying to seduce me again. You and your wifely duty and your empty womb and your ugly bed jacket. I don't have time for this. I have some very important work to do."

"It's two o'clock in the morning."

"Then I have some very important sleeping to do."

No, he would not leave! She would not let him.

Cassandra grabbed the hem of her nightshift and pulled it up over her head. And then it—Oh no! It caught on her hair and she yanked at it, yanked harder, feverishly aware that her whole body was exposed to him—she should never have done this, it was so brazen, and now she felt a fool—and she yanked again, and the shift came free, half her hair tumbling down her back after it.

But his eyes burned as they roamed wildly over her nakedness, and she basked in the heat, unable to move.

Not an inch of him moved but his eyes. Her ragged breaths were too loud in the silent night and her heart performed a drunken quadrille. She swallowed away her nervousness, and the sound of her gulp, so embarrassingly loud, made her unfreeze. She whipped the shift in front of her and clutched it over her breasts.

"Perhaps I should not have done that," she said, her voice strange, uneven.

She watched, mesmerized, as he extended one arm, with slow, deliberate care, and flicked the door shut. His eyes were dark and liquid in the candlelight, and a matching liquid heat pooled in her belly.

"Done what?" His voice was rough velvet caressing her anguished skin. "Taken off your shift, or tried to cover up again?"

"Um."

He eased closer. The height of the bed brought their faces level. If she leaned forward, her covetous breasts would graze his chest. She pressed her arms more urgently over her breasts, not for modesty now, heaven help her, but because they needed to be touched and pressing them like this felt good.

A gleam in his eye suggested he knew, or maybe that was her imagination, because how could he know, and why did he have to be so wicked, and why did she long for his teasing to continue even as she longed for it to stop?

"I think you'll find, my lovely wife, that both of those were a mistake."

He tugged at her nightshift. She clutched it more tightly. He raised an eyebrow, wicked playfulness mingling with heated promise.

"It's only fair," he murmured. "You saw me naked."

He tugged again, and this time she let him take the shift and drop it onto the floor.

CHAPTER 15

Joshua caught barely another glimpse of Cassandra's exquisite breasts before she crossed her forearms over them, her hands on her shoulders. A thrillingly inadequate effort. Her hair was tumbling down around her face, her eyes were wide and dark, and she breathed in short, shuddering breaths that echoed his own.

She was sheer perfection, and he was lost. What a fool he was to have started this. But he had, and here they were, and now he was nothing but need for her. Need and a faint clanging, somewhere in his brain, saying that he must not touch her. Because...Because...Something.

Ah, yes, because if he touched her, the world would collapse.

What utter nonsense.

"I thought you didn't want this," she said.

"I can stop any time I want."

"So why don't you stop now?"

"Because I don't want to yet." He hooked his fingers around her wrists. The world did not collapse. "Because first I want to look at my wife."

She allowed him to lift her hands away from her body, to rest them back by her sides. Her full breasts, rising and falling. The round curve of her stomach. The softness of her hips and thighs. The promise of the dark curls at that sweet juncture.

His hands yearned to caress every inch of her. His tongue to taste her. His cock to fill her. Something of his thoughts must have shown in his face, for she gasped and covered her eyes with her palms.

He chuckled unevenly. "I can still see you."

"Cannot."

"What a shame, because I so like looking at you."

He came as close as he dared, let his lips find her ear. Her hair tickled his cheek and he resisted the urge to bury his face in it. She kept her eyes firmly covered.

"Do you like me looking at you?" he whispered, breathing in her scent, feeling it fill his veins. "Be honest now."

With a long shuddering breath, she said, "Yes."

Oh sweet mercy. "Would you like me to touch you?"

"I...It's my...I mean...Must you consult me at every step?"

She did not even know what she wanted, still less how to express it. Could she imagine what he wanted? To trail his mouth and hands over every soft, fragrant inch of her, from those luscious breasts down to her belly. To part her thighs and touch her and kiss her until she lost all coherent thought. Until she forgot everything that she wanted except his touch.

He had started this stupid game, and she had upped the ante, and now she did not know the next play. His turn then: He would tease her and taunt her, torment her with her own desire, until she understood its power and would think twice before playing with him again. Risky? He took risks every day. And he could stop any time he wanted. He could always walk away.

He retreated to a moderately safer distance. "The trouble with touching you is that you have no idea where it leads."

"I have some idea." Her tone was dry beneath the breathiness. "Our wedding night, if you recall."

"Which you did not enjoy."

"I will do my—"

"If you mention your bloody wifely duty one more time…"

He trailed off. She needed to understand that playing with desire was like playing with fire. It wasn't the only problem, it wasn't the biggest problem, but it was still a problem.

"I should not touch you, but if I do not touch you, you will never understand." He dragged his eyes off her, looking around. A vase of roses sat on the table by her bed. Three roses, pink and half-opened. "What a conundrum. It's a good thing your husband is an inventive problem-solver."

He eased a rosebud from the vase and turned back to her. With a yelp, she uncovered her eyes. Oops: Cold water had dripped down the stem and splashed onto her skin. A droplet of water, right there on the softest, roundest part of her thigh.

"My apologies," he said.

"Now you find your manners?" she muttered. "*Now*?"

He couldn't help grinning as he used the heel of his hand to wipe away the drop, taking longer than he needed. She gasped, and he mustered all his will to haul his hand off.

He wiped the stem dry on his clothes, then tilted the rosebud toward her, enjoying her confusion. He was a devil for teasing her, but how he loved this part too.

"I shall touch you without touching you," he said. "Aren't I clever?"

He brushed the rose over her parted lips, his eyes not leaving hers. Beyond the flower's fragrance lay another scent, headier, more potent: the scent of her. He trailed the rose up over her cheek, back to her lips, over her chin, over her jaw. She arched her neck, offering her throat, and he accepted her invitation, dragging the petals down over her rapid pulse, the dip of her collarbone, down, down to one hard nipple. He sketched a circle around it, then brushed back and forth, his attention torn between the sight of her body and the sight of her face, and he wondered if he had gone mad.

She made a little whimper and covered her eyes again, and a new thrill of pleasure shot through him.

Yes, he had gone mad.

"Here, hold this," he said, briskly.

She opened her eyes, blinked at him dazedly, then took the rose. Trying to ignore her nudity and his own arousal, Joshua lit a second candle and plucked a freshly laundered kerchief from his pocket. He smoothed it open on the bedcovers beside her and began to fold it again, with uncommonly clumsy hands.

"A blindfold?" Her confusion was palpable. "That's how we fold them for blindman's buff."

"You said it: If you can't see me, I can't see you. You will have no need to be shy."

She laughed breathily and said, "You're as silly as I am," but she did not resist as he tied the lemon-scented linen over her eyes, knotting it behind her head. When he gently tipped her onto her back, she fell easily and lay with her legs outstretched.

There: He had touched her again, and the world still had not collapsed.

"Are you all right?" he asked, his eyes trying to take in all of her at once, laid out for him, her skin warm in the candlelight, her body soft with trust.

"I think so." She fumbled for him, caught the edge of his robe. "This is very…"

"Depraved? Do say depraved. I adore the way you say depraved."

"Perhaps. But we are married," she added, as if to reassure herself. "So this must be all quite proper."

"Proper!"

He climbed onto the bed, knelt beside her hips, and plucked the rose from her trembling hands. She fumbled for him again, found his knee, spread her fingers over his thigh. Her searing touch streaked through him, but he ignored it. He feasted his eyes on her, and lowered the rose to her lips.

"I will strip away your proper," he promised darkly. "I will strip away your nice and polite. I will strip away everything until you are nothing but raw, savage, aching need."

CASSANDRA DID FEEL DEPRAVED, and she had never dreamed that depravity could feel so good, that anticipation could make her quiver. How wickedly delicious it was to lie naked before him like a sacrifice, enclosed in a dark, secret world of promise. And how fierce this craving to pull him on top of her and revel in his weight and strength. She could hardly believe this was her, and was relieved he had taken control.

She did not understand his game but, to her own shock, she enjoyed playing it and basked in his teasing. If he could make her feel like this, she would do whatever he asked.

The soft, fragrant petals tickled her lips, tracing their shape, and she was breathing in rose and, beyond that, him.

"The petals are not quite the color of your lips." His voice smoldered like hot jagged coals. "But ah, your cheeks...Your blush, here, where you blush for me."

The feathery touch trailed up over her cheek, circled lazily, then slid down and grazed her jaw. She tilted back her head in a silent command. He obeyed, and the rose quivered over the sensitive skin of her throat.

"There is just enough light for me to see your pulse, racing in your throat," he murmured.

Yes, it raced, and her blood did too, rushing madly through her like a river in a storm. She tried to breathe, tried to stop breathing. She dug her fingers into his thigh. Her world narrowed down to the sensations: his hard muscles under her fingers, the mattress heating her back, the silk of his robe tickling her, and that rose, tormenting her with lazy zigzags over her chest. Fluttering between her breasts, circling first one and then the other. She arched her back, in another demand; the obedient petals grazed her nipple, oh, so pleasurable, but not enough, oh heavens, never enough. A mewling sound escaped her lips and he answered with a rough, breathy groan. He swept the rose across the valley between her breasts to continue his torment on the other side. How was it that he touched her in only one place and she felt it everywhere?

"Your nipples are darker than the rosebud," he whispered. "And I bet they have a sweeter taste."

She caught herself rolling her hips and forced herself to stop. One hand still anchored her to his iron-hard thigh, and she realized that her other hand was on her own thigh, tracing shapes in her own skin, and she tried to make herself stop that too.

"I bet your skin right here is as soft as these rose petals." Those rose petals caressed the underside of her breasts. "What a shame you won't let me touch you."

She tried to tell him that he could touch her, she never said he couldn't, he was the one who had made that silly rule, so of course he could, and he should, please, he should, but he did not want to hear, he had his game, and she had no breath to speak and craved so much more.

The rose skated over her ribs, tracing the curve of her belly. She wanted it back on her breasts and between her legs, but no, not the rose, it was too feathery, too delicious, too much, she needed more.

"If you let me touch you, I would touch you here too. And down here."

The rose swept over the curve of her hip and she squeezed her thighs against the madness throbbing between them. It skimmed over her thigh to her knees, then crawled, slow and desperate like a sleepless night, up the valley where her legs met, right up over her inner thighs, brushing the curls at their juncture.

"If only you would let me," he whispered.

She whimpered, letting her thighs fall apart, and she realized how close her own fingers had crept to the insistent molten ache. Dimly, she was ashamed of her sinful brazenness, but not enough to stop.

Yet he cruelly ignored her invitation, her need, and the rose danced inexorably away, feathering up over her belly, across her ribcage, finding again the undersides of her breasts.

She lost her patience, gripped his arm, so strong and sure beneath her hungry hand.

"Joshua, please."

"What a shame you won't let me touch you, and kiss you."

"I will. I do. Stop teasing. Yes."

The rose stilled. "Why?"

"I don't understand."

Then the rose was gone altogether. Their only connection was her hand on his arm, and she slid her palm up to his shoulder, rising up to him, clutching at him, tugging him closer.

This time he did not obey. He pushed her gently back down onto the bed but leaned over her. Even blindfolded, she sensed his tension. She let her hands roam over his back, kneading the muscles.

"Why do you want this?" he asked softly.

"Because I want...what...I..." Something to do with husband and wife and duty and babies and she couldn't think, not with this coiling and tightening and throbbing in her body, not with him so close, and his shoulder under her hand, and her legs, moving, curling around his. "It's too much."

A mutter. A curse. What had she done wrong now? Why did he have to be so complex?

"What do you feel?" he asked.

"I feel...everywhere...and it's...It's so..."

"Do you like it?"

"I want more. But I need it to stop too."

She curled her arm around his neck, sinking her fingers into his hair, trying to pull him down to her, but he did not yield.

"The only way to stop it is to touch you more," he said.

"Then I need you to touch me."

"That's what you want?"

"That's all I want. Please, Joshua. Nothing else matters but that you touch me."

"Oh, Cassandra," he groaned.

His hand landed on her hip, firm and warm, and he slid it up her side, commanding a tide of heat beneath her skin. His breath and cheek were on her throat, his hair tickling her, and her own moan filled the room as he cupped her breast and burned her pulse with his lips.

She yanked off the blindfold, blinked in the half light, drank in the sight of that strong hand around her breast. His eyes were questioning, heated, and they imprisoned her own as he lowered his head and licked her nipple. Pleasure shot through her and she arched her back, digging her fingers into his neck.

"You will drive me mad," she whimpered.

"That makes two of us."

She tangled her fingers in his hair and hauled his face over hers.

"Are you going to kiss me now?" she asked.

"You have a preoccupation with being kissed."

"Only by you."

No sooner had she uttered the words than their lips met in a heated fury. He plundered her mouth with a hunger that ignited a passion so deep within her that it felt as strange as it felt right. His tongue tangled with hers, and she rose up into him, holding him against her, her hands newly wild. She fought with his robe and his shirt to get to his skin, and he did not help her, feasting on her mouth as though it was all he needed to live.

Until he abandoned her lips and kissed his escape over her jaw.

"More." She grabbed his head. "I need you to kiss me."

And this time she feasted hungrily on his mouth, not letting him leave her again. She wanted more and more—and his hand, oh heavens, his hand, jilting her needy breast in favor of her hip, her outer thigh, her inner thigh, and she parted her legs, hardly knowing what she craved, until he pressed against the persistent ache, right where she most needed his touch.

She fell away from him with a cry, struggling for breath, their eyes locked, his fingers stroking.

Stroking. Stoking the fire within her. Like a magician commanding the tides of pleasure.

He brushed his lips over hers. "I'm going to kiss you," he

whispered against her mouth. "As you never imagined being kissed."

He slid away from her, and she tried to hold him, but he had his own plans, as relentless as those stroking fingers, changing her world. He dragged his hot mouth down her throat, to her breasts, attending to her nipples until she kicked with impossible pleasure. And then—Oh heavens! He slid his fingers inside her. Her senses began to crumble.

"Joshua! You...I...Oh."

"Hush, sweetheart." He breathed the words over her skin. "I haven't finished kissing you yet."

Unyielding, he burned a trail of kisses down her body, branding her with his warm mouth and soft-rough stubble, and she watched, dazed, as he parted her thighs with demanding hands, positioned himself between them. No, he wouldn't. Not there, he couldn't kiss her...

He did.

Pleasure spiraled through her. She arched off the bed. Her head fell back on the pillows. One strong hand pinned down her hips and still she writhed, seeking an escape from these exquisite sensations that must never, ever stop. His tongue was hot and strong and insistent, and his cheeks on her thighs were rough and soft, and her ache intensified, curling and swirling within her. She tried to move but he wouldn't let her and she wanted it to stop and he wouldn't stop and she wanted it to go on forever and it did, it did, and then the pressure was too much and bliss rippled over her, all the way to her eyeballs, all the way to her toes. He released her, as she arched and shuddered and cried out.

And even when the sensations had passed, her thudding heartbeat was echoed by a sweet, hot pulse between her legs.

Her breathing had barely steadied when she felt him climbing off the bed. She opened her eyes and smiled at him, waiting for the next part, waiting until he gave her all of him. He stood by the bed, looking at her, and she was not at all shy about her nakedness now. Soon she would have his body too.

"So that's why," she said.

"Yes. That's why."

His voice was hoarse. She reached for him but he eased away. He swayed toward her, swayed back. He seemed unsure, indecisive. That was odd. He was always so decisive. Even when he knew he was wrong, he was very decisive about it.

His uncertainty infected her. She shivered, though she was not cold.

"Joshua?"

"What?" he snapped.

She recoiled, confused. "I don't think that was all. We..." She did not have the words to say what she wanted. "That...that won't make babies."

"That was enough. I told you I could stop."

He scooped up her nightshift and tossed it at her. She caught it instinctively and twisted the cool fabric in her hands as the door closed.

A click.

He had locked the door.

Leaving her naked and alone in the candlelight, with a wilting rose and that sweet, smug pulse fading between her thighs.

No sooner had Joshua fumbled with the key than his shaking hands were in his breeches. He stumbled across the room, fell to his knees, sought his own release with one hand, the other hand stuffed between his teeth to muffle his groans.

First was the utter pleasure, his mind still in the next room:

Cassandra, oh sweet mercy, Cassandra, succumbing to the impolite desire, sweet and savage in her need. Her skin beneath his palms, her scent fogging his brain, her taste filling his mouth, her mewls of pleasure caressing his ears, and oh, sweet mercy, the sight of her. The intense quivers of her flesh as she came on his tongue.

But when his pleasure had passed, then came the self-loathing over the seed he had spilled, the sting of the toothmarks in his hand, and the hollow in his chest.

He had only meant to tease her, to taunt her. How had it gotten so out of hand?

But she wants me too, now. I have no doubt of that.

Yet he'd denied her that also. The most generous woman he had ever known, and he kept denying her, and himself. And what, exactly, had he achieved? All he had done was hurt her again, break the fragile bonds forming between them, and leave a mess on the floor.

Congratulations were in order. He had achieved exactly what he intended, except, perhaps, the mess on the floor. How stoic he was, how heroic and clever and strong. What a champion. What a genius. What a man.

He cleaned up, stripped off, washed in blessedly cold water, and crawled into his empty bed.

He had not slept here last night, he realized. Last night he had slept with her. It felt like a year had passed, packed into one day: Cassandra and Bolderwood and Isaac and Cassandra.

Bloody hell, I'm stupid. I should never have started that. I should never have walked away.

He punched the pillow, lay back down.

I could bed her without getting her with child. There are ways. I know.

He tossed over onto his side.

No, not fair. I promised to be honest; that would be the worst lie.

He flipped onto his back.

One time wouldn't hurt. What are the odds she falls pregnant the first and only time? One time would be plenty and no harm done at all.

He tried his other side, bunched his fists up under the pillow.

I could have lost myself in her, let her lose herself in me. Yet I walked away. What an idiot.

I walked away.

He tossed himself onto his back and stared into the darkness, and a peculiar peace settled over him.

I did it. I walked away. I said I could stop, and I stopped.

He had nothing to worry about, then. Nothing to fear at all.

CHAPTER 16

The following day, Cassandra sat with Sir Gordon Bell and Mr. Das around the large table in Joshua's study, waiting for Joshua, who was rumored to be somewhere in the house. She had not seen him since he left her room the night before, and she would be happy if she never saw him again. How could she look him in the eye, after her shameless behavior and his chastening departure?

Then in he charged, kicking the door shut behind him, creating a whirlwind that made the papers on the table flutter. Cassandra stared at the wall of books, as hot humiliation slithered over her skin.

"Sir Gordon, excellent," Joshua said. "Let's get this nonsense over with."

This moment will pass, she thought. She would ignore him and he would ignore her.

Except that he didn't.

He stopped beside her chair. A sideways glance proved he was facing her. A light touch on her shoulder: She flinched away, horribly aware of their audience.

"Are you well?" he said softly.

She had to look at him then. He had not shaven this morning either and was without his coat, with his cravat tied in a simple knot over the throat she had tasted the night before. She bit back her scold over his appearance, for she was wise enough now to understand that her scold was not about that at all; besides, she did not look much better, for she had slept poorly and risen late, and pulled on a loose old morning gown because her maid was busy with other chores. What with housekeeping matters and correspondence, she had no time to change before Sir Gordon was announced. But Sir Gordon was a family friend, and Mr. Das was easygoing, and Joshua was a fiend, so his opinion mattered nothing at all.

Yet his expression was gentle for a fiend, and she caught herself reliving the thrill of his mouth. Under the cover of the table, she squeezed her thighs shut, feeling the tenderness of the faint pink rash his unshaven cheeks had raised.

"Thank you," she replied. "I am quite well."

"Good."

The heavy clock ticked—once, twice, three times—and then he was moving again, pacing up and down the room, claiming the attention with his sheer dynamism.

"Scandal and debauchery require a special kind of lawyer, it appears, Sir Gordon," Joshua said. "My regular lawyers excel at commerce, but for expertise in adultery, one must turn to the upper class."

Sir Gordon could not be shocked. He steepled his fingers, regarded Joshua steadily with his clear blue eyes, and said nothing. Mr. Das fiddled with his pen and hid a smile.

"My husband has difficulty expressing himself, Sir Gordon,"

Cassandra said. "I assure you, we are grateful that you are leading his defense."

"I'll be grateful when he can make this case go away so I can get my life back to normal."

Oh, how thoughtful of him to remind her of his *normal* life without her. He had made that clear last night, leaving her, yet again. He was very talented at leaving her.

He was very talented at kissing her too.

She squeezed her thighs together and wondered how she could want to be near him, yet hate him all the while. Of course, she would have to be near him to throttle him, so perhaps it did make sense.

"First, we must deal with the rather substantial evidence," Sir Gordon said.

"Evidence!" Joshua stopped pacing. "What bloody evidence?"

"If you'll be quiet, Joshua, Sir Gordon will have a chance to tell us."

With a snort, Joshua paced over to the sideboard and poked inside the ceramic bowl that held his candied lemon. Sir Gordon opened his dossier and his mouth to speak when—

"What the blazes is this?" Joshua said. "This isn't candied lemon."

"Heavens!" Cassandra slapped her palms on the table. "How can you worry about candied lemon when your family's future is at risk?"

"I have no use for family. What I need is candied lemon. Das?"

"We ran out. That's *rahat lokum*."

"Which is?"

"The English call it 'Turkish delight.' Sounds less foreign that way."

"Turkish delight." Joshua picked up a small cube and studied it critically. "It's pink," he said, sounding appalled. He sniffed it warily. "It's sweet," he added, and his eyes found Cassandra's.

A faint smile touched his lips. Last night's heat glinted in his eyes and kindled an answering spark inside her. He popped the sweet into his mouth, licked his fingers, chewed slowly, swallowed, his eyes on hers the whole time.

"And it tastes like roses," he said. "I like things that are pink, sweet, and taste like roses."

Heat coiled in her cheeks and pooled in her belly. Heavens, even here, in a room with Sir Gordon Bell—her father's friend, whom she had known all her life!—and Mr. Das, that insistent pulse started up between her legs.

And he knew, the fiend!

Oh, how she wanted to throttle him! Tear out his hair! How dare he tease her like that after what he did last night!

Smiling broadly now, he placed the bowl by her elbow and lounged against the table beside her, because, of course, he could not simply sit in a chair like a normal human being.

"Try some," he said. "You might like it."

"Thank you, I won't. Please continue, Sir Gordon," she said. "There will be no further interruptions."

Sir Gordon cleared his throat in a suitably lawyer-like manner. He smoothed his hands over the dossier in front of him and looked at each of them in turn.

"It turns out that Lord Bolderwood's solicitor began his career as one of my clerks at Lincoln's Inn," Sir Gordon said. "He found it, ah, advisable to share the details of the case for the benefit of all concerned."

"As I said," Joshua muttered.

"Cassandra—Mrs. DeWitt, I should say." Sir Gordon turned the dossier on the table, turned it again. "You may prefer to withdraw while we discuss this. Mr. DeWitt can tell you the pertinent parts later."

Polite-speak for "This is going to be bad."

"My husband is a very busy man, Sir Gordon," she said. "It would be an inefficient use of his time to repeat the information in a separate interview."

"You might not like what you hear."

"Then I shall pretend it is not there. That seems to be the preferred approach in this household." She looked at Joshua. "Where is Isaac today?" she asked pointedly.

Joshua narrowed his eyes and was about to speak when Mr. Das coughed, which had the miraculous effect of causing her husband to say only "Carry on, Sir Gordon."

"There are eyewitnesses." Sir Gordon pulled two pages from the dossier. He slid one page toward Cassandra and the other to Mr. Das. "Three servants and two innkeepers who claim to have clearly seen the, ah, events."

"*In flagrante delicto*, I presume?" Joshua said. "I do hope they have exciting, explicit details in their testimony, keep the masses enthralled."

He seemed to be enjoying himself, but Cassandra suspected that his attitude served to cover his anger. He did not realize how he betrayed his vulnerability when he did that. No wonder he disdained politeness: He had never learned that a polite smile was the most effective armor of all. It made it harder for her to be angry. Absurdly, it made her want to protect him.

"I wonder who scripted their testimony," he went on. "Do you think Lord and Lady B. sat together one night over the sherry, giggling away while they wrote it down?..."

Cassandra silently pulled the bowl of Turkish delight closer. Joshua did not notice, talking on as he was.

"...Or do you think Lady B. came up with it all herself, based on her fantasies? Or Lord B. based on *his* fantasies?..."

Stealthily, she scooped up all the Turkish delight in one hand.

"...If they want money, they should consider publishing their stories. With illustrations, naturally. *Fanny Hill* was banned but still sells well, and if they—ooff."

She shoved the sweets into his open mouth, then pressed her fingers over his lips. His lips were warm and soft, and his eyes heated and amused. He made a noise and she gave him a warning look.

"Don't talk with your mouth full, darling," she said. "It's not polite."

He had no choice but to chew and say nothing. Sir Gordon and Mr. Das were fighting smiles. Cassandra sat and tapped the list of names.

"Perhaps Isaac could talk to them?" she suggested.

"Wah gish oh," Joshua said. "Osh ak aw."

"Yes, this *is* a matter for family. So glad you agree with me." She smiled at Mr. Das. "In accordance with Mr. DeWitt's wishes, please ask Mr. Isaac to help out with this."

Finally, Joshua cleared his mouth. "I don't want Is—"

"Hush, now. We've dealt with that item. No time to waste," Cassandra hurriedly said. "Next, Sir Gordon?"

To her relief, Joshua did not protest, but sat in the chair beside her and shook his head at her, amused in his defeat. Under the table, his leg nudged hers and she moved away. Whatever his game, she would not let him tease her today.

"The next piece of evidence comprises a set of four letters." Sir Gordon pulled out a few more pages. "These letters were allegedly written by Mr. DeWitt to Lady Bolderwood, expressing, ah, affection and, ah, longing."

Affection. Longing. Cassandra had never received a letter like that. Like the love letters Sir Gordon was sliding across the table toward them. The letters were short. Efficient, her husband.

And angry again, but this time his face was hard and cold, his lip curled in disgust.

"Most of the pages are copies," Sir Gordon explained. "The one on top is said to be an original, to verify your handwriting."

She did not want to look, but the uppermost page called to her like a siren. She did not know Joshua's handwriting—Mr. Newell penned all their communications—but she could believe it was his. The writing was nearly illegible, as if he wrote too fast and energetically for his quill to keep up, so that words were smudged and the page was splattered with ink.

Yet she made out the opening salutation: "*My dearest one.*"

She averted her eyes, ignored the sick chill shivering through her chest. Longing. Affection. None of her business.

Clearly Joshua thought so too, for he did not spare her a glance as he gathered up all the pages.

"I wrote those letters," he said in a tone like steel. "But not to Lady Bolderwood. Someone stole them from my personal belongings. Last I heard, that's a crime."

Sir Gordon regarded him over his spectacles. "The privilege of peerage—"

"Sod their bloody privilege!" Joshua slammed a fist on the table. "They will return the original letters in full or so help me I will shoot them both where they stand. Next."

Nobody said a word.

"Next!" Joshua repeated.

He shoved back his chair and paced around the room. Cassandra turned back to Sir Gordon, pleading with him silently.

Sir Gordon lifted the next page from his file. "Third, and finally, these are the dates and times that Mr. DeWitt was reportedly, ah, having a tryst with Lady Bolderwood. It would help if Mr. DeWitt can account for his whereabouts at these times."

Mr. Das took the page and opened his own dossier. "I can check this against Mr. DeWitt's work schedule," he explained. "I keep a record of all his business meetings and movements."

They waited in awkward silence as Mr. Das worked. Cassandra traced the whorls of the woodgrain with her finger. She glanced up to see Joshua watching her. Then he pivoted away and went to the window. Cassandra returned to her tracing.

When Mr. Das shuffled the papers together, he looked uncomfortable. "These are all periods that are unaccounted for in your official schedule. Sir."

Joshua stared out the window. "Isn't it interesting," he said with dangerous calm, "that every so-called tryst fits with a gap, and they have letters taken from my rooms. Now, who would have that access? Who is highly familiar with my work schedule?"

He turned like a clockwork doll and looked right at Mr. Das, who looked right back at him. The air in the room prickled and hissed.

"No." Cassandra looked from one to the other. "There must be a perfectly reasonable explanation that has nothing to do with... anyone in this room."

"Perhaps that's another matter Mr. Isaac can look into," Mr. Das said coolly.

"Perhaps that would be for the best," Joshua said. "Is he here?"

Without another word, Mr. Das left the room.

"No," Cassandra said again. "Joshua, you cannot possibly believe that." She shot an apologetic look at Sir Gordon and went to Joshua's side. "There must be another explanation. Mr. Das would not let you down like this."

"How do I know if I can trust him? He was married for years and never said a word."

"Whose fault was that?" She turned his face to look at her, ignoring the apparent irrelevance of his statement. "Did you ever ask him? Did you ever take an interest in his personal life?"

"No. He has no personal life. He doesn't exist outside work."

"Then how can you...Never mind. Think. Who else could it be?" She held his face in both hands, ignoring Sir Gordon, who was making a point of arranging his papers. "Someone else who could come and go freely in your house. Who might find your private letters and know what they were. Who also had access to your schedule."

He looked troubled, and she wanted to smooth away that trouble, and hated herself for her weakness.

"You can work it out." She recalled his words from the night before, when he chose the rose. "I have heard it said you are an inventive problem-solver."

A new gleam mixed with the trouble in his eyes. "You have heard that, have you?"

His look was so warm she could feel herself melting. Longing for his touch.

His touch. Her longing. His departure. Her humiliation.

She yanked herself away from him and was halfway across the room when, from somewhere else in the house, came a sound that froze her in her tracks.

"Did you hear that?" she said.

"Hear what? What?"

She cocked her head to listen, dread clawing at her stomach. There it was again: a woman's laugh, bright like crystal.

"No," she said. "It can't be."

But it was. A moment later, the butler was at the door, announcing Miss Lucy Lightwell and Miss Emily Lightwell.

"She brought Emily?" she said faintly, as another burst of laughter hit her ears, heading up the stairs, if she wasn't mistaken.

She turned to Sir Gordon, who was gathering his papers. "Sir Gordon! Mama is at home alone!"

He nodded, understanding as few did. "I'll send an express to have someone check on her." He tucked his dossiers under his arm. "I'll see myself out. Mr. DeWitt and I will communicate regarding the next steps. Let me know if I can assist you further."

"I may require your services again very soon," Cassandra said, marching past him. "As I'm about to murder my sister."

CHAPTER 17

J oshua bounded up the stairs after Cassandra, who was already talking as she entered the drawing room.

"Lucy, how could you!" Cassandra was saying. "Have you no idea how dangerous it is, to travel alone from London?"

"Spare me, Mother Cassandra," drawled a melodious female voice. "I did not come all this way for your nagging."

The voice belonged to a young woman with glossy dark hair, big green eyes, and delicate features arranged so artfully that parts of Joshua's brain crashed into each other and he almost forgot how to walk. A red-haired girl with a sickly, anxious air stood by the table, her hand resting on a large, covered basket.

"I like Cassandra's nagging," Joshua said. He stopped next to his wife, pressed a hand to the small of her back. This time, at least, she did not pull away. "You must be the legendary Lucy."

Lucy inspected him from top to toe. "And you must be—Oh my," she said, looking past him.

He twisted to see Isaac, leaning nonchalantly on his cane with an easy, rakish charm.

Lucy's eyes flicked between Joshua and Isaac. "Which one of you handsome devils is Mr. DeWitt?"

"We both are," Joshua said, his mood beginning to lift.

"Two Misters DeWitt!" Lucy stepped forward, all grace and coquetry. "No wonder Cassandra has kept her husband secret these past two years—she had two of you! You greedy thing, Cassandra. And you scold me when I so much as look at the baker's son."

"The baker's son hasn't the constitution to handle your looks, Lucy," Cassandra said. "It upsets him and he crushes the bread."

"Do tell how it works," Lucy said. "One woman with two men."

"I could draw you a picture," Joshua offered, which earned him a wifely elbow in his ribs. He was starting to enjoy himself, despite everything, but before he could tease Cassandra some more, Das sauntered in.

Joshua's enjoyment faded. No, not Das. Please, not Das.

"Look at you," Lucy crooned to Das. "You're brown!"

"Lucy!" Cassandra scolded, but Joshua was curious to see what happened next.

"And you're pink," Das said.

"No, I'm not. I'm white."

"Definitely pink." Das jerked his chin at the other girl. Emily. "And your sister there is looking rather green."

Confusion flickered in Lucy's eyes, and then a slow smile spread over her face. A genuine smile this time, Joshua realized.

"I'm pink, she's green, and we're both feeling blue!" Apparently delighted, Lucy danced toward Das. "I like you. Do you know how to waltz?"

"My wife has been teaching me."

"How sweet." Her tone turned saucy. "You won't remember your wife's name once you've waltzed with me."

"If you think that, then you know nothing of love and a good marriage."

Lucy's expression faltered, revealing a vulnerable, lost girl beneath that brain-shatteringly beautiful facade. "Lucy is broken," Cassandra had said, and he began to understand what she meant.

But then Lucy laughed again and danced back to the basket, which she opened, saying, "I have a gift for you, Mother Cassandra!"

Out leaped something fierce and gray that streaked straight for Joshua. He had barely identified it as a cat when it climbed him like a tree, finally coming to perch on his shoulders, its tail swishing wildly against his face.

Joshua twisted up and around to grab the cat. With a growl, it dug in its claws, pricking his skin through his shirt.

"No, Mr. Twit!" cried Lucy. "Don't do that!"

"*What* did you call me?" Joshua asked through a mouthful of fluffy tail.

Lucy laughed and started toward him, hands raised. He instinctively stepped away and, to his relief, Cassandra came to his rescue, nimbly inserting herself between him and her sister. She reached up and patted the cat. He fancied he felt it relax. That is, it unhooked its claws and stopped whipping his cheek.

"Mr. Twit," Cassandra said softly. "That's what I named the cat you sent me." Mischief danced in her eyes and his desire stirred, despite his current indignity. "Apt, really. He tends to be willful and poorly behaved at times, but he is lovely if you rub his belly the right way."

His own belly tightened at the thought of her rubbing it, any way at all. Of him rubbing her belly. Of their bellies rubbing each other.

"And you claim to be so good," he said.

"I never claimed anything of the sort."

Then began what could only be his punishment for his idiocy of the night before.

She reached up both arms, bumping against him. He rested his hands on her hips, to steady them both, and suffered through it, her floral fragrance softening his brain even as his body hardened, as she crooned to the cat and coaxed it off his shoulders and into her arms.

Where the wretched beast was enviously content. It rubbed its head against her throat, batted at her chin, and settled against her, purring, its paw resting right on the edge of her bodice. He watched her fingers scratch the cat's throat, and cursed himself for a fool all over again.

He had only meant to tease her a little, and now he was the one tormented.

He looked up to see everyone watching, with varying degrees of curiosity, and then, mercifully, Newell arrived.

The red-headed girl stirred to life. "Mr. Newell!" she cried. She ran across the room and threw herself into the secretary's arms. "I missed you. I have so much to tell you."

Joshua looked back at Cassandra in time to see hurt flash across her face before she ducked her head and crooned to the cat. He realized that Emily had not even spoken to Cassandra, whereas Lucy had displayed open animosity. After all that Cassandra had done for them! Had they no idea what she had given up for them? That she always put them first?

He would throw the wretches onto the street for treating her like that, except she would likely object. Besides, he'd have to throw himself out after them, for treating her even worse.

NEWELL PROVED worth his weight in gold, for he ushered the two sisters upstairs, putting an end to the drama. Das and Isaac talked quietly in the doorway, and Cassandra sought solace in her cat.

Two weeks ago, Joshua had been perfectly content, alone in this huge empty house. Now it was overrun with a wife, a secretary, a brother, two sisters, and a cat. An infestation, after all. He tried to work up some irritation, but all he could see was the hurt on Cassandra's face when Emily ignored her and ran to someone else.

"I'm sorry," Cassandra said, jogging the cat on her bosom. "I never dreamed they would come."

"They seem fond of Newell."

"He has become like an uncle to them. It's terribly inappropriate, I know, but I am busy and we cannot keep a governess."

"Why not? It cannot be a case of money."

"It's more a case of Lucy." She sighed. "I'll take them home. Maybe between us, Mr. Newell and I will be able to herd them into a carriage."

Take them home. Which meant she would leave too, and finally, finally, his life would be back to normal.

Excellent.

"They may as well stay, now they're here," he said. "And you do need to marry her off. Let's launch her right away."

She glanced up, surprised. "Surely even you recognize that she said shocking things. She is not ready for society."

"She is *perfectly* ready for society. The question is whether society is ready for her."

She groaned. "You want to make trouble. That's why you're suddenly so amenable."

"My dear Mrs. DeWitt! When did you become so cynical? I am merely offering you my support in finding her a husband." He enjoyed her skeptical, exasperated look. "What a shame the

Regent needs no wife, for your Lucy would make a magnificent queen and lead the kingdom into chaos in no time."

She gave a wan smile. "If only she could find someone who... understands her and loves her and makes her happy. She is not bad, only..." She sighed again. "It's the least that she deserves."

It was the least that Cassandra deserved too. But, instead, all she had was him.

Yet even after what he had done to her last night, she had stood by him today, teasing him, flirting with him, comforting him over Das's betrayal.

"Buchanan," he said abruptly, his mind leaping into action. "You were right."

She looked confused. "Who or what is Buchanan?"

"Former junior secretary. Smart, but lazy. He had access to that information—and he resigned recently. All fits." He planted a kiss on her forehead and grinned at her. "You're a treasure. Das!"

He whipped away from her, to where Das and Isaac stood outside the door, regarding him warily.

"It's Buchanan!" he said to Das. "Let's go cut off his kneecaps."

It wasn't much of an apology, but Das seemed to understand. "With pleasure," he said.

"And Isaac. Make yourself useful, won't you? Find these witnesses and get the truth out of them. Money, fists, charm: Use whatever works."

Joshua handed the list of names to Isaac and twisted the letters in his hand. Cassandra stood in the doorway, cat still in her arms, eyes on the letters. Then she pasted on that cursed oh-so-nice-and-polite smile, averted her eyes, and swept off toward the stairs.

"Excuse me," she said, brushing past him. "I must get Mr. Twit settled and fed."

He watched her go, up to her bedroom, he supposed. He should tell her about the letters. She would understand. The world would not end. The memories would not crumble into dust. She had a right to know.

He turned back to Das.

"Cassandra's grandfather, the Duke of Sherbourne—he makes a pretty penny from his investments with me, doesn't he?"

Das cast him a thoughtful look. "Indeed. You have helped swell his coffers considerably."

"Yet when my wife sought help from his wife, the duchess was not helpful. Not sure I can continue partnering with a man whose wife treats my wife so shabbily. I shall have to call on him and let him know that. Let's arrange that."

"Good idea."

Joshua looked up the stairs, to where Cassandra had gone.

He looked down the stairs, to where his business lay.

"Your wife is really teaching you to waltz, Das?"

"Yes. She has joined me here in London." Das considered his fingers a moment. "She is keen to meet Mrs. DeWitt and suggested you might both join us for dinner one night."

Well. There was a surprise. Joshua never met his secretaries' families. And a duchess's granddaughter was not likely to visit the home of an employee. But Cassandra did seem to like meeting new people, and she would argue that Das was more than an employee, and Joshua was curious.

"Have her write," he said. "It's probably some shocking breach of etiquette but Cassandra can decide."

He considered the letters in his hand, considered the stairs leading up, the stairs leading down.

"Mr. Isaac and I can deal with Buchanan," Das said. "If you have other matters to address."

"Right," Joshua said. "I just have to...Right."

He went to the stairs. He went up.

JOSHUA FOUND Cassandra alone in her room, fussing about with a gown. As he loitered in the doorway, she offered that polite smile and didn't quite meet his eyes. How intolerable was her politeness when she wore it like armor! He had stripped it away last night, only to force her to don it again.

Nobody's fault but his own.

"Where's the cat?" he asked.

"My maid is seeing to him."

"Where will he sleep?"

"With me, usually. Unless he, too, runs away in the middle of the night."

"Ah."

He let himself look at her bed. His kerchief was folded neatly on the bedside table. Three roses sat in the vase, one slightly the worse for wear.

He whipped his head back to look at Cassandra, who hastily ducked and made a show of inspecting the hem of the gown.

"She's very beautiful, isn't she?" Cassandra said, rubbing at a spot that he suspected did not exist. "Lucy, I mean."

"Astonishingly so." Yet he knew which of the sisters he would rather look at. "The other one, the redhead—"

"Emily."

"She'll be a beauty, too, one day."

"Yes. And Miranda was called an Incomparable."

"I've heard rumors."

"They are all great beauties, my sisters."

"Indeed."

He looked at the letters in his hand. From somewhere down the hallway came the laugh. He closed the door against marauding sisters and, after a brief hesitation, locked it. Again he caught her watching him; again she returned to the gown.

"So." He strode across the room and tossed the letters onto the little table. "If you've finished fishing for compliments..."

"I was not fishing for compliments," she snapped, her color rising. "I was making conversation. That's what polite people do. But I suppose you don't want to talk about my sisters."

"Not really. Do you want to talk about the letters I wrote my wife?"

"I'm your—" She stopped short and smiled that infuriating smile. "It's none of my business."

She grabbed a clothesbrush and attacked the hem, fiercely enough to scare away any lingering mud.

"And you say *I'm* impossible," he muttered. "Can you *be* more infuriating?"

She stopped brushing. "What on earth have I done now?"

"Try a bit of honesty. You might find it refreshing. I certainly would."

"Are you saying I'm dishonest?"

"The only time you are not dishonest is when you are drunk or lustful. You think politeness is a virtue, but mostly it's annoying."

"Then it's jolly good you feel comfortable saying what you think."

"Try it."

She dropped the gown and leaped toward him. "Fine! Yes! I want to know about your first wife. Why she was so marvelous that the thought of bedding me sends you fleeing like I'm some repulsive monster." She brandished the clothesbrush at him. "And don't you dare call me dishonest for hiding behind politeness when you hide behind busy-ness. It's a wonder you found time in your schedule to call on me at all."

She turned away, snatched up the gown, and resumed her assault.

"I *am* busy," he snarled, stalking closer. "I am not one of your fine gentlemen who has nothing to do all day. I have multiple businesses to run. It's who I am, it's what I enjoy, and I like my life like that."

"Then go back to it. You know where the door is. Be sure to lock it again so I don't come ravish you."

"Oh for mercy's sake, stop taking it out on your gown."

He snatched the brush out of her hand. She grabbed for it but he held it out of reach.

"Give me that," she demanded. "So I can get dressed and get out of this house and away from you!"

"I don't find you repulsive," he said.

"Splendid. Then you won't be averse to catching me when I swoon over your compliments."

"Bloody hell." He hurled the brush across the room. "Cassandra—"

"Are you still here? Don't let me keep you." She glared at him. "You know that one. It means *Go away*."

She spun away from him, a crazed creature in a crazed dance. He must be hearing the same music, for he spun her back toward him, all the way back, into his arms, against his chest. He did not know this dance, but he knew the next step: He caught her head with one hand and sealed his mouth over hers.

CHAPTER 18

The meeting of their lips brought back the passion of the night before. Joshua was so hungry for Cassandra that one taste would never be enough.

But he forced himself to lift his head.

"Not repulsive," he said.

"You are impossible."

"You are perfect."

Her eyes were dark with fury and something else, and his heart was wild with longing and something else, and he had no words, so he used his wordless mouth to cover hers.

This time, she welcomed him, pushing up into him, her mouth as fierce and demanding as his. He kissed her with the force of all the words he did not have, and she was telling him something too, yelling at him with her kiss, with her tongue. Her hands gripped his waistcoat, twisting and fisting the silk, pulling it tight over his shoulders, drawing him into her softness, and he drew her into his hardness, needing her closer, closer, closer. He could not deny his need. He could not deny her anything.

They broke off, gasped for air, and she tore at his shirt, his shirt that was too long, the hem inching up his thighs and buttocks and hips, and why in blazes did they need so much blasted fabric restricting them all the time? His desperate hands found the bodice of her gown, hauled it down. Eagerly, he freed her breasts, covered them with caresses and kisses, but it wasn't enough, not enough, dear sweet mercy, it was never enough.

She whimpered and growled and slapped his side. "Joshua, I can't...I can't...Give me..."

He jolted away, scared and wild, only to see that she protested not him but her gown, for he'd inadvertently pinned her arms. He yanked it over her elbows and hands, and she freed herself, the gown falling about her waist.

He had hardly a moment to enjoy the sight before she hooked her arms around his neck, her eyes bright, her mouth swollen, her hair wild, her cheeks flushed. She claimed his mouth and pulled at his hair and kneaded his muscles with those competent hands. He hauled her back against him, but—

Too much. Never enough.

He carried her to the bed, climbed on, laid her down, while she held onto him as if she feared she might fall.

"Joshua," she whispered. "What are you doing?"

"Tupping my wife, I hope."

"It's the middle of the day."

"Your conduct books say a man can't tup his wife in the middle of the day?"

"They don't mention the matter at all."

"You read the wrong books."

She laughed breathily and tumbled back on the pillows, lifting her hips to help him as he shoved up her skirts, up over her stockinged knees, her bare parted thighs, her quim warm and ready. He pressed his hand against her and she bucked and moaned, so he fell between her thighs, kissed her perfect lips, and sighed as she found his skin under his shirt.

"I need you," he heard himself say, cursing his own inelegance, fumbling with his falls. "I need…"

His cock sprang free and he shoved his breeches down his thighs. Her hands were warm and eager, wandering over his hips, gripping his buttocks, as she arched into him.

"What you do to me," he growled in her ear. "I need…Oh mercy, you drive me mad."

"I do that?" She sounded surprised and smug.

"You do. It's you, it's all you. Only you."

Her wandering hands slid around his hips, to his front, bumping his cock. She gasped and stilled, and he nipped her ear and told her everything was all right. She touched him then, gently, tentatively, torturously.

He pushed her thighs wider, lifted her, and she let him. She tipped back. His eyes didn't leave hers, so deep, so dark, so drunk with desire, and oh yes, she did want him, as he wanted her, and he pushed deep inside her, as deep as he could go, reveling in the sensation of her heat enveloping him, holding him tight.

Her fingers dug into his spine and he froze. Held himself over her. Cursed himself. He'd gone too hard, too much, too soon.

"Cassandra, sweetheart? Are you all right?"

Her eyes were on him but he had no idea what she saw. Then her lashes fluttered and her lids closed.

"Oh," she said.

She rolled her hips and clenched her muscles tight around him.

Oh mercy. Sweet, sweet mercy.

"Oh," she said again, and again she rolled her hips and squeezed.

Inflamed, encouraged, he dipped his head to the soft skin of her breasts, tasted and nuzzled, tugged a nipple between his lips.

"Oh," she said, and did it again.

He withdrew slightly, sank back in, and she welcomed him, and when he thrust an awkward hand between them, she rocked against him, squeezing him, finding her rhythm, taking her pleasure. She knew now what she wanted; she was discovering how to get it.

"Take it," he murmured in her ear. "Take your pleasure on me. Use me. Have me. Take it all, love, take it. Take me. Take everything you want."

He pleasured her breasts, gave her his cock, and watched her, awed, like he was viewing a miracle: Her head was thrown back, a flush stained her throat, and then she froze, her eyes widened, and he felt the soft cry build inside her. He captured her orgasm with his mouth as the pleasure shuddered through her and through him and he felt more pleased with himself and the world than he remembered feeling in years.

She reared up, locking strong thighs around him, her hands searing his skin—he could forgive the miles of blasted fabric in their way so long as he felt her hands on his skin—and he took his pleasure, feeling every inch of her with every inch of him, over and over and over, enveloped in her generous heat, in her limbs, in her. In all of her and only her. And when he came, deep inside her, he buried his face in her neck and surrendered to the waves of pure bliss.

Even after he relieved her of his weight, he stayed deep inside her. He had nothing else to do, and nowhere better to be.

His heart still pounded and, yes, hers did too. He felt the cool sheen of sweat over his back where her hands still caressed him, and he was still inside her, softer now, warm and content. Contentment was all he found in his heart, too, when he searched it. He raised his head and looked at her: her eyes closed, lashes dark on her cheeks, the flush mottling her throat, so warm, so beautiful, bathed in daylight.

Daylight.

Gradually, he became aware of other things. Small things. Approximately six miles of fabric was bunched up between them, what with her gown and his shirt, and his buckskins dug into his thighs and his boots—Bloody hell, he still wore his boots! She deserved better, and surely even he had more finesse than that!

And slowly he became aware of the rattling of carriages, yells from the street, servants exchanging a word in the hallway, footsteps pounding overhead.

"Bloody hell," he said.

Her eyes opened, a mesmerizing amber-green.

"What's wrong?" she asked.

"It's the middle of the day."

"Oh. I forgot." Her soft laugh stirred as she lay and listened to the noises of the world they had left. Her face fell. "Oh no," she said. "I made noise. What noise did I make? I forgot. How could I forget? What if they heard? What if they know that we...Oh."

She was so adorable, as she tried reconciling her public self with her private self, and he was inordinately pleased with himself for finding this part of her. Grinning, he pulled out of her and off her, let her legs fall. He stroked her hair, kissed her. He picked up her scent on his fingers and his body stirred again.

"We're married," he reminded her. "It's all quite proper."

"Proper!" she repeated. "Oh you fiend!"

She slapped him lightly, so he kissed her, long and slow, and reveled in the way she kissed him back.

"That was rather inelegant," he said. "I should have made love to you properly last night."

"Yes."

"I wanted to. I…"

He had no words and she did not push him. "That was not like our wedding night," she said instead. "I worried but it was…lovely."

He said nothing. There was no point wondering if anything might ever have been different.

From somewhere came a laugh, *that* laugh, and a singsong call of "Mother Cassandra!" and another voice, Newell perhaps, moving the speaker along.

"Oh heavens," Cassandra said. "I completely forgot she was here."

And he felt proud of himself for that, at least.

THEY HELPED each other tidy up and dress. Cassandra went through the motions, and was grateful to have motions to go through. How comforting to have something sensible and practical to do. The world felt strange, yet normal. Her body felt unfamiliar, yet natural. And to dress with a man felt completely new and ages old.

Yet somewhere amid this new familiarity, awkwardness sprouted and grew.

The letters, of course.

They still sat on the table, taking up too much room. She picked them up and held them out.

"It's all right," she said. "I already knew you loved her."

He took the letters, considered them. "It wasn't a love match, but we were friends." He glanced up. "I wrote these to her after she died. I missed her."

His dark eyes were tinged with anguish, an old sorrow, a new anger, and she belatedly grasped the full horror of their theft.

"And they stole them! I swear, Joshua, if you don't shoot them, I will."

He brushed a finger over her cheek. "Don't bother. They're not worth it. We'll finish them easily enough."

She had made a royal mess of his cravat, and he went to the mirror to retie it without seeking her help, so she did not offer it. Instead, she watched him peering at his reflection as though tying his cravat was the only thing on his mind. How curious people were: that they could experience something like that—that lovemaking that made the world splinter and dance—and then settle into domestic routines as though nothing at all had passed.

Although she was not sure what had passed. Certainly, she did not know what happened next. The world outside that door was demanding her attention and she wanted to be alone.

"How did you meet her? Rachel."

"Her father was John Watkins, who owned the manufactories where your father found me a job as an errand boy," he said, looping the cloth efficiently around his neck. "I worked my way up, and by the time I was nineteen, I was a senior clerk and Watkins was grooming me to take over. He had no succession plan because Rachel was his only child, and she was twenty-seven and unwed, and until me he had not found anyone suitable. She wanted to manage the business but Watkins didn't take her seriously, and she felt the men who courted her didn't either. She offered to marry me if I let her run the factories with me."

"And did you? Let her run them?"

"I'd have been a fool not to. She excelled at it, knew every inch of the business. Watkins never realized how much she had to offer. Even when we were doing well, he thought it was all me." He finished up the imperfect knot, patted it, and shrugged. "It still stuns me," he added, turning back to her. "How much is wasted when men decide that certain babies are worth nothing because of their birth or class or sex or skin? How much do we all lose, as a nation, as humans, by dismissing people simply because they are not like us?"

"Like what happened to you."

"What the blazes are you on about now?"

"I mean, you were a lord and then overnight the world decided you were worth nothing, but you proved them wrong. You could have given up, or become bitter. But you learned and now you want to make the world a fairer place for others too."

"You think that I...But I'm just..." He made a frustrated sound and scrubbed his hands through his hair. "I'd better go."

"Will you..." She paused. "I suppose I shall have to cancel my evening plans, spend the evening with Lucy and Emily and figure out what to do about them. Will you join us for dinner? I mean..."

"I don't know about dinner," he said. "But I'll come to you tonight. If you'll have me. Once is not enough."

JOSHUA WENT about the rest of his day with renewed vigor, until finally it was night, and time to go to her. He made love to her properly, with no fabric between them—with nothing between them but the candlelight.

And when the candles were out and he held her against him, their skin so close he could not find the edges, he listened to her breathe and stared into the darkness and said, "Rachel and I had a son."

She jerked out of his arms. It was too dark to see her expression, which is why he'd told her in the night.

"I didn't know," she said. "Papa never said. *You* never said."

"It never came up in the conversation."

"Oh, maybe when I expressed my desire to have a child? You might have said, 'I already had a child and I lost him'."

He pulled her back against him. She gave him her weight and did not argue anymore.

"He was barely five when..." He closed his eyes in the darkness. "One day he was fine, then he was sick, and then he was gone. There was nothing we could have done differently. Just one of those things. One of the ways the world likes to laugh at us, to remind us that we are never in control."

"I'm so sorry."

"I don't want your sympathy."

"Too bad. You have it anyway."

His heart beat too fast, and he was too hot, suddenly, but if she noticed, she didn't say a word. She stroked his chest, soothing him, and soon he calmed.

"What was his name?" she asked softly.

"Samuel."

He focused on her hand, the warm pressure skating over his ribcage, resting familiarly on his belly.

"What was he like?"

He had pictures, no words. She moved, her hair feathering him, her mouth finding a spot just above his collarbone.

"He was a little whirlwind," he said. "He wouldn't walk if he could run or jump or skip. He wanted to know everything about everything. I never realized how much I didn't know, until I had to answer his questions." He stared at the dark, seeing those images of the past, fearing he would lose them. "Bram sent this tiger-skin rug from India: his idea of a joke. Rachel thought it was horrific, so of course I used to put it out on the floor to annoy her. Samuel loved it. He'd have long conversations with it, and we'd find him asleep on it, hugging the tiger's head. We called him our little tiger."

When he stopped, she did not ask him anything more, but waited patiently for him to speak again.

"After he died, Rachel...She needed something to do. We had housing for all our workers—following Robert Owen, you see— but she became obsessed with providing decent housing for everyone in Birmingham, fixing up derelict buildings. One of those buildings collapsed."

"Oh heavens. Joshua."

"I razed them all. Built them anew. It didn't bring either of them back."

Here in the dark, with her, the world receded and he felt he could tell her anything at all. She stroked his hair, and he let her comfort him.

And as he drifted off to sleep, he had the odd thought that maybe the void inside him had nothing to do with the loved ones he had lost.

CHAPTER 19

J oshua came to her the next three nights too, sliding naked under the sheets with wicked words and teasing hands. She marveled at his passionate response to her, and her fevered response to him, at the way their lovemaking left her feeling at home in her own body as she never had before.

Afterward, they chatted quietly. He spoke of his businesses and associates and ideas; she spoke of her friends and garden and Sunne Park's famous pigs. Fearful of breaking their fragile accord, she never mentioned their families, their past, or their future; neither did he.

Most of all, they never spoke of children, and though she dared not mention it, she secretly wondered if she might already be with child, for they made love two or three times each night, sometimes him on top, and one time he turned her over, and other times he pulled her on top of him. "Riding rantipole," he called that, and teased her for being lazy, and demanded to know why he had to do all the work, and urged her to ride him faster, which she found difficult when she was laughing.

"Be greedy with me," he whispered to her. "Be greedy and selfish and rude. Do as you please, take what you want, and for mercy's sake tell me if I do something you don't like."

They slept wrapped around each other, but he awoke early and she awoke alone. During the day, they went their separate ways, but at odd moments—usually highly inappropriate moments—a memory of their lovemaking would flash across her mind and heat her insides, and she would think that she did not recognize herself. Which she also knew was a lie.

It made her feel stronger, somehow. She felt more equal to dealing with the swollen household and to waging their social war.

And to putting up with her sisters' ceaseless complaints. About how London was boring, and Cassandra was selfish, and how, Lucy grumbled on the fourth day after their arrival, as the three sisters sat in the drawing room, "it is utterly stupid that we came all the way to London and we cannot even go to Vauxhall Gardens."

Lucy stopped tearing through the pages of a magazine and threw it across the room. Apparently, she found that diverting, for she immediately threw another.

"Or the theater," Emily chimed in, her tone sounding more like Lucy's every day. "It's stupid not to go to the theater."

"You're not meant to be in London at all," Cassandra pointed out for the thousandth time, as she sorted through the gratifyingly large number of invitations, deciding which would be of most use. "Letting you go out would be like rewarding you for misbehaving."

"So we must stay locked up like scullery maids while *you* go out all the time," Lucy said.

"Not at all," Cassandra said. "I would never lock up a scullery maid."

"No wonder you do not want us here. You want to enjoy town without us."

Enjoy? This social whirl, and the effort of making herself popular, was exhausting.

But her social campaign seemed to be working. The impending trial was earning her hundreds of hours of gossip, as society and the press debated which party was telling the truth, and battle lines had emerged between Bolderwood supporters and DeWitt supporters.

The Bolderwood camp spun a story of a naive wife and wicked seducer, with the noble husband willing to forgive his wife for her foolishness but determined to punish the seducer for his crime. It was a fine and convincing tale, but Arabella, who had appointed herself general of the campaign, reported that the DeWitt army was stronger, for Cassandra was well-liked, her parents had been adored, and everybody disapproved of Lord Bolderwood's elopement in the first place. Furthermore, gentlemen wished to remain on Joshua's good side, as he was their connection to industry and the new money that it promised, and when Joshua joined her at evening events, the consensus was that Mr. and Mrs. DeWitt were fond of each other.

Unfortunately, their grandmother had not changed her mind about taking Lucy, but she supported Cassandra by loudly discrediting Lord Bolderwood and rallying her own allies. Privately, the duchess had opined that Mr. DeWitt should settle the dispute outside of court; Cassandra had politely but firmly replied that her husband would not do that, as the allegations were false.

It would be a waste of breath to point out to her sister now that Cassandra's primary aim was to smooth Lucy's entry into society. For reasons Cassandra could not fathom, Lucy had decided that Cassandra was a villain.

"I can go out freely because I'm a married woman," Cassandra said. "If I could trust you to behave, Lucy, you could make your debut and get married too."

"Married woman, my foot!" Lucy sneered. "Do you two even talk to each other?"

"Why don't you get a marriage of your own before you comment on mine?"

"I like Joshua," Emily volunteered.

Good," said Cassandra. "So do I."

It was perplexing how much she liked him now. It had seemed so simple when she first suggested children: He would bed her, it would be unpleasant but she would get with child, and then they would return to their separate lives. That they would part was still inevitable, but she feared she would miss him. Perhaps he would visit her at Sunne Park. Perhaps they could meet in London each spring, and she could have a passionate affair with her own husband.

But he was giving her what she asked for; she had no right to ask for more. When the time came for them to part, she vowed, she would not say a word.

"Mr. Newell knows a clerk at Drury Lane," Emily said abruptly. "He offered to take me backstage, and I could meet the actors and actresses and playwrights, and show someone my plays."

Cassandra stared at her. "Meet actresses? Please wait a few years before you destroy your reputation. For now, stick to amateur dramatics and remember you are the granddaughter of a duchess."

"Which does us no good at all," Lucy said and sent another magazine skittering across the floor. "Where is this precious duchess anyway?"

Before Cassandra could find an answer, the butler appeared at the door.

"A caller, madam," he said. "Her Grace, the Duchess of Sherbourne."

"Good morning, Cassandra, my dear," their grandmother said as she breezed in, stylish in a sky-blue gown and matching turban. She ignored Lucy and Emily, standing prettily, and immediately launched into a speech.

"You have gotten what you wanted: Congratulations," the duchess said, with her pleasant smile. "Setting your husband on mine, so now Sherbourne says that I must abandon my own interests for you, for it's only thanks to his investments with Mr. DeWitt that he can pay for them. I abhor this vulgar emphasis on money, but such are the times in which we live."

"I don't understand, Grandmother."

"Oh, don't feign ignorance, dear. You know what I'm talking about: Your husband demanded that I do your bidding or Sherbourne will be cut off. You are more cunning than I realized, and I concede it was well played, but I would rather you did not exercise such ploys against me."

A sweet pleasure radiated through her as she understood: Joshua had secretly intervened to help her, and now, it seemed, her grandmother would take Lucy after all.

And Cassandra had promised to return to Sunne Park when that was done.

The pleasure faded, replaced by a hollow disappointment. By helping her, Joshua ensured that she and her sisters would be gone sooner and his life would go back to normal.

Well. This was what they had agreed. This was what she had wanted. She could not blame him if she kept changing what she wanted.

"My schedule is less busy anyway," the duchess went on. "For now Sherbourne says I spend too much time with Sir Arthur. Where is she, then?" Her eyes fell on Emily. "Not that one, she's too young."

"I'm fourteen!" Emily protested.

"Hush, Em," Cassandra said.

"You don't look a day over eleven and ought to be in the schoolroom. Really, Cassandra, you should..." The duchess spread her fingers in a gesture of defeat. "No concern of mine. If I take an interest, you'll expect me to drop everything for that one too. Do send the child away, though."

Emily looked stricken and Cassandra silently cursed their grandmother. But this was Lucy's moment. One sister at a time.

"Emily, dear," she said. "Perhaps you can talk with Grandmother another time."

"Why can't I stay?" Emily looked around, hurt. "Lucy! Tell them I can stay."

But Lucy was feasting her eyes on the duchess and said nothing.

"Fine." Emily stalked to the door. "I shall be in the *nursery* playing with my *dolls*. Off with their heads!" she yelled and marched out.

Cassandra resisted the urge to go after her. She dared not leave Lucy alone with the duchess.

"You must be Lucy. I see you are a beauty, indeed." With uncharacteristic demureness, Lucy sank into a deep, graceful curtsy. "With those looks, men will not notice if you speak gibberish. Is it too much to hope that you have some interest in the classical world?"

"Old Greek and Roman things?" Lucy said, with an eye-roll. "So boring."

The duchess's mouth tightened, and Cassandra repressed a

sigh. Why, oh why, did Lucy have to break things? She had told Lucy of their grandmother's fascination.

But Lucy had not finished.

"All those Greek temples and Roman statues and so forth," she said. "They are all so bland and boring and white. Imagine living in a world where every building, every statue, and every item of clothing is the same color. It would be like a nightmare."

"Go on," said the duchess, her head cocked with interest.

Cassandra looked back and forth between them. She could not tell if Lucy was expressing a genuine opinion, or if she was being cunning, and it occurred to her, yet again, that she did not know her younger sister at all.

Lucy smiled, all earnest innocence. "I have always thought it would be marvelous if they were painted bright colors. But, of course, everyone would say that is vulgar, wouldn't they?"

"'Everyone' should not talk about things they don't understand," Her Grace said, her eyes bright and sharp. "My dear friend Sir Arthur Kenyon maintains that the ancients did paint their temples and statues in bright colors, but that the paint has come off over the centuries. Others say he is full of nonsense, but time will show he is right."

The duchess beamed at Lucy, who briefly met Cassandra's eyes and did not give away a thing.

"I shall launch you at my ball next week," the duchess announced. She turned back to Cassandra, her mouth pinched. "If that meets your demands, madam?"

"We are grateful, Grandmother," Cassandra said, ignoring her tone. "When this matter with Lord Bolderwood has passed, I shall return to Sunne Park. Would Lucy be able to remain with you?"

"If she comports herself well at the ball, then yes, I shall see her through the Season. You know my view on the matter of Lord Bolderwood, but like your father, you refuse my advice. I suppose you will come running for my help again when you need it."

"I shan't come running and I shan't seek your advice, so you need not concern yourself with that," Cassandra said, more sharply than she had ever spoken to her grandmother before. Perhaps she was tired. Perhaps she had allowed Joshua to influence her more than she realized. She opened her mouth to apologize, but her grandmother had already turned back to Lucy.

"Then I shall concern myself with you. Come along, Lucy, my dear. We shall have to turn London upside down to get you ready in time. Good day, Cassandra."

The duchess swept out, with Lucy at her heels. At the door, Lucy twisted around and poked out her tongue, before she flounced out.

CASSANDRA FOUND EMILY in the upstairs parlor she shared with Lucy, in quiet conversation with Mr. Newell, a Shakespeare volume on her lap. When Cassandra came in, Emily fell silent, looking sulkily at her book. Mr. Newell hovered awkwardly.

"Emily," Cassandra said. "I know you're—"

"A is for Apple. B is for Ball. C is for Can't Hear You."

"Emily, please listen."

"Not now. I'm learning how to read. As I am only a *child*. In the *schoolroom*."

"We must keep the duchess happy, for Lucy's sake. I am sorry she was rude to you."

"D is for Door. E is for Exit. F is for Find Your Own Way Out, Now, Dear."

"It's Lucy's turn, and in a few years—"

"You'll get rid of me too, the same way you're trying to get rid of

Lucy. You want us both gone so you can lord it over Sunne Park all by yourself."

Cassandra slapped the book in Emily's lap. Emily's chin jerked up. "You can't have it both ways," Cassandra snapped. "One day you say I'm locking you both in, the next that I'm kicking you both out."

"G is for Go To. H is for Hell."

"Emily!"

"It's all right, Mrs. DeWitt." Emily yanked the book away and shuffled back. "I shall stay locked up in the nursery, while Lucy goes out with the duchess to get a ballgown, and Lucy goes out with Isaac to talk to witnesses, and Lucy, Lucy, Lucy."

"It used to be like that for me, too, with Miranda, always taking the attention. But you can—"

"I don't care. I'm not like you."

Then the full meaning of Emily's words hit her. "What do you mean, Lucy went out with Isaac to talk to witnesses?"

"I is for I Don't Care. J is for Jump Off A Bridge."

Cassandra sighed. "Em. Listen. Maybe later we can go somewhere, perhaps to Astley's Amphitheatre."

"Mr. Newell can take me. You're too busy, always so busy, running the household or fighting with Lucy or going off with your friends. K is for Killjoy. L is for Leave Me Alone."

"If you want to be treated like an adult, Emily, start behaving like one."

"N is for No I Don't Want To Talk To You Right Now."

"You forgot M," Cassandra said, giving up. She had no idea what else to say or what she was doing wrong.

She looked at Mr. Newell, who wore the pained "please let me turn into a chair now" expression he often wore when caught in their arguments. "If we might have a word outside?" she said.

Out in the hallway, Cassandra closed the door to the parlor.

Immediately came a sound that was suspiciously like a book hitting the door.

"I'm sorry, Mrs. DeWitt," Mr. Newell said. "I know Miss Lucy ought not have gone out with Mr. Isaac, but she insisted and she can be...willful."

Cassandra sighed. She would have to talk with Isaac. And he might be with Joshua, for at least Joshua was talking to him now, and she would very much like to be with Joshua. Oh, for night time to come faster. To be in the dark, in that warm bed with their bodies wrapped around each other and the rest of the world forgotten.

"It's not your fault, it's mine," she said. "You are my secretary, not their governess. But I can hire a governess for Emily now that Lucy will stay with our grandmother and cannot drive anyone away. If you could place some advertisements and speak to the agencies, I shall ask the other ladies if they can recommend someone."

"Of course," he said. "I shall start today."

"Poor Mr. Newell. I have embroiled you in our family matters, while taking you from your own family for too long."

"Mrs. Newell understands. She has hopes of a holiday by the seaside in summer...but perhaps this is not the best time to mention that."

"This is the perfect time to mention that. For I need your help desperately and would grant you any wish at all. Take your family to the seaside for a month, and Mr. DeWitt will give you a bonus."

Mr. Newell smiled. "Thank you, Mrs. DeWitt. I apologize also for mentioning my friend at the theater. But Emily does so love drama, and she writes such witty plays. Perhaps someone—not an actress, mind you—but someone who understands theater could also make a good governess. Merely a suggestion."

What was the right thing to do? Whatever she did, she always ended up getting it wrong. Joshua would say that respectability did not matter, that he would buy respectability for Emily. Cassandra was more interested in buying her little sister happiness, before Emily turned bitter and faded away.

"A good suggestion," she conceded. "So long as Emily doesn't actually mean to be an actress. She is too young and anxious for her age and..."

"If you don't mind my saying, Mrs. DeWitt, I think Emily is frightened of losing everyone."

Oh my dear Em, that's what I fear too. Cassandra swallowed away the lump in her throat. Why did she not know how to talk to Emily? Every day she conversed with scores of people, but she could not talk to her own sister. But since Papa had died, Cassandra had been so busy, running the estate and the household and changing the garden and naming the pigs and a thousand other things.

Busy? Heavens, now she sounded like Joshua or her grandmother. But she had been busy. And the busier the better, so she would not think about Papa and Mama and Charlie and all that had been lost. Perhaps that was why Lucy and Emily resented her.

She patted Mr. Newell's arm. "I shall find a way to fix this, and I apologize for upsetting you," she said. "So far this morning, I have upset two sisters, one grandmother, and a secretary. Now I shall scold Isaac, which will upset him, and if Joshua is there, I will no doubt end up upsetting him too, after which I can congratulate myself on a day well spent."

CHAPTER 20

Joshua sat at his desk, meaningless numbers dancing before his eyes, and cursed himself for not doing business outside the house again today. His uncharacteristically wayward mind was too aware that Cassandra was at home too, and kept returning to the interesting question of whether he could talk her into bed.

He had just reached the conclusion that he must try or he would get nothing done—and really, in this state, tupping his wife was a matter of efficiency—when she opened the door and came in.

"No wonder you keep running off to the City," she said, leaning against his chair and threading her fingers through his hair. He slipped an arm around her waist. "It's a wonder you can hear yourself think in this noise. And here I am, interrupting you again."

"I might be able to find some use for you." He let his hand wander meaningfully over her bottom. She giggled and half-heartedly slapped him away.

"Not now," she said. "I need to find Isaac."

"You do not need to find Isaac. You need to lock the door and get onto my desk so I can have my way with you."

"Hush. I will not."

"Fine. Leave the door unlocked, but don't complain to me when the servants see you with your skirts—"

"Hush." She covered his mouth with her hand, and he grinned and nipped at her fingers. "You must not make such indecent proposals."

"My proposal was perfectly decent," he protested. "You're the one who proposed we make love in broad daylight with the doors unlocked."

"I never...Oh, you are terrible," she said, but she kissed him anyway, then pulled away and sat against the desk. "Isaac took Lucy out to meet the witnesses."

"And? He was probably only trying to keep her out of trouble."

"By taking her to rough parts of London to meet liars and engage in threats and bribery? How is that keeping her out of trouble?"

"Ah, good point. I'll talk to him. And as for you, now that you have interrupted me..."

He slid her sideways, caged her against the desk, and kissed her.

"Joshua. We cannot do that here, and I must go out. You will have to wait."

"No. Can't wait. I want you too much to concentrate, so if you leave me wanting, my businesses will fail, and then I would have no money and no work."

"But you would have plenty of time to...to..."

"What? What?"

"To...You know."

"Say it." He lowered his head, slid a hand up her thigh, and whispered in her ear. "Be wicked and say it and maybe I'll let you go."

"You're teasing me again. Behave."

"If you want me to behave, what is my inducement?"

The moment he said the word, he remembered her promise from the night of the rout, and saw in her face that she remembered it too. It seemed a lifetime ago now, but the memory rose between them, and sweet mercy, he wasn't going to get any work done. He had never asked that of her again, and had not intended to. But he could still tease her; she did not seem to mind his teasing now.

"You owe me," he reminded her. "Time to settle your debt, Mrs. DeWitt."

Her blush deepened. "Maybe I will. Later."

Sweet mercy. Let later be now.

"Although," she added, "that doesn't make babies."

And whoosh. His desire washed away, leaving bitter disappointment in its wake. Because it was still all about babies for her. There was no mistaking her desire for him, but in the end, she would leave him as cheerfully as he would leave her.

Good. That was what they had agreed. She would make no fuss. Excellent.

"Of course." He stood and pulled away, turning his back on her to adjust his clothing and his face. "You need all the seed you can get before this nonsense ends and you go back to Warwickshire."

He risked a glance at her, and scowled at her small, polite smile. He did not know what it meant and he could not ask her, because some things he did not want to know.

"I'll talk to Isaac," he said and made for the door. At the door, he stopped and turned back to say something more, but he didn't know what that was, so he left.

How irritating that he was now Cassandra's messenger boy, as well as her stud, Joshua grumbled to himself as he went in search of Isaac. Good to see he was so bloody useful to his wife.

He found his brother in the stables, saddling a horse, apparently under instruction from one of the grooms.

"What in blazes are you doing?" Joshua asked him.

"Re-learning horses," Isaac said. "Last time I rode, I was nine, and now I've forgotten half of it and have a gammy leg besides. You don't mind, do you?"

"Be my guest." He glanced at the groom, who melted away. "Cassandra doesn't like that you took Lucy to visit the witnesses."

"Why?"

"Because Lucy is a genteel lady, and genteel ladies are meant to be accomplished at dancing and watercolors, not bribery and intimidation."

"Shame, because she is very good at them," Isaac said. "You did say to use whatever works, and they would have said anything to make her happy."

"Bloody hell, I don't have to worry about *you* with her, do I?"

"Never fear." Isaac laughed. "My sense of self-preservation is far too strong for that. But I had to do something with her. She gets that look in her eye, like she's planning to burn down the house."

"I know the look. But listen. Isaac. Society: It has rules. Lots of them. Stupid rules, but if you get them wrong, you can upset everything."

By "everything" he meant "Cassandra." He had never cared about the stupid rules before she came along.

"Have you managed to locate Buchanan yet?" he asked, changing the subject.

Isaac brightened. "Yes. The muttonhead confessed. Said he stole your documents because Lord B. offered him a piece of the winnings." His mouth twisted. "And a piece of Lady B., too, if I understood correctly. For a man who's suing you for adultery...but maybe it's not adultery if the husband watches." Isaac let out a long, low whistle. "I saw some things in the Navy, but I tell you, it's nothing to what the fancy folk get up to."

Joshua snorted. "Lord and Lady B. can do whatever they want with whomever they want, but I wish they'd bloody well leave me out of it."

"And you can bloody well leave me out of it too," came the voice of a third man.

The horse threw up its head and whinnied, and Isaac and Joshua turned to see their father, the Earl of Treyford, marching into the stable yard, brandishing a walking stick at them like a sword.

"What in blazes are you doing here?" Joshua said.

"I demand that you stop your wife from writing to my wife," Treyford said. "Whatever trouble you're in, it's not my business."

"Make it your business, you selfish shuffler," Joshua snapped. "And if my wife writes to your wife, your wife should bloody well have the courtesy to write back."

"Is that him?" Isaac said.

"That's him."

Treyford glared at Isaac. "Whoever you are, get out of my conversation with my son."

Isaac's head jerked back. "I'm your son too. Isaac."

Their father looked momentarily perplexed, but quickly recovered. "Get away with you. I don't need another one hanging around."

"You wouldn't," Isaac said. "Each time you see us, you're reminded of your own shame."

"Well said, brother," Joshua said, his anger fading. His mood lifted further when Lord Hothead's color rose.

"It was a mistake," Treyford snapped. "And the two of you have turned out all right, so I hardly see what you have to complain about."

"Three," said Isaac.

"Three what?"

"You have three sons from your not-marriage to our mother," Joshua explained. "No wonder you have difficulty keeping track of your wives, when you can't even keep track of your children."

"Maybe you should hire a secretary to help him," Isaac suggested. "Secretary In Charge of Reminding The Earl How Many Children And Wives He Has."

"Excellent idea. Each morning at breakfast, the fellow will walk in and say, 'This is your daily reminder that you are married and must not get married again.'"

"And that you have this number of children and please do not make any more unwanted children."

"Pair of bloody wits, aren't you?" Treyford said. "And I know there were three of you and the other one is in India, doing well for himself, and he cannot complain either."

"What about Miriam?" asked Isaac. Again, Treyford looked blank. "You don't even who that is, do you?" Isaac's own color rose and he twirled his stick in the air. Tempers ran in the family, it seemed. "Our sister, your daughter. She'd be eighteen now and not one of us would recognize her on the street. If she's even alive."

Treyford twirled his own stick. "It was her mother's decision to take her away. I had nothing to do with that."

"Where are they, our mother and sister?"

"Isaac, let it rest," Joshua said.

Too late.

"How the hell am I supposed to know?" the earl ranted.

"Deborah was upset, she took the girl and left. She had money and all her jewels. What was I to do? The mistake had been made and the most important thing was to protect the title."

"'The mistake had been made'," Isaac repeated, his face screwed up in disgust.

Money, bloody money. Joshua had more of his father in him than he realized, and certainly more than he wanted.

"You'll never change, will you?" Joshua said quietly. "You'll never understand what it was that you did."

"You're judging me? Me, your own father, and you with this sordid matter with Bolderwood."

"Pack of lies," Joshua said. "The witnesses have admitted to being paid for false testimony, a former secretary has confessed to stealing my personal letters, and over the next few days, I'll secure alibis for all the so-called trysts. After which, Bolderwood will be laughed out of court and out of town. And everyone will know that he's a liar, and they'll also know that my own father would not speak in my defense."

"Why should I? You don't deserve that."

"But my wife does. So why don't you do something decent for once in your life and show the world where you stand?"

Treyford scowled at him, paced around, then came back and nudged Joshua's chest with his walking stick. "If I speak up for you, tell all my circle that Bolderwood is lying to get money out of you—you and your wife will stay away from the countess and me. We want nothing to do with either of you."

"My pleasure."

"And get back to Birmingham where you belong. Good day."

With that, the earl marched off.

Isaac stared after him. "He would have preferred to put us in a sack and drown us like kittens, wouldn't he?" he said. "So much for family. Well, when I find Mother and Miriam, we'll have a family again."

Joshua winced. Poor, hopeful Isaac. "Forget about them," he said. "Our family finished years ago. We have no mother, we have no sister—"

"And no brothers either."

For a long moment, neither spoke, then Isaac turned back to the horse. "I guess I'll go too. Get my own rooms. Get a horse and ride around Britain."

Fine. Let him go again. Isaac had left before, he would leave again, and Joshua had lived happily without his brothers for half his life so he had no use for them now. Cassandra and her sisters would go back to Warwickshire, and Isaac would go off to wherever he wanted, and Joshua could get back to Birmingham where he belonged.

"As you wish," he said. "Now I have work to do. Lots and lots of work."

WHEN JOSHUA LEARNED from Newell that Cassandra was staying in that night, he joined them at dinner for the first time. Isaac entertained them all with tales of re-learning to ride, Lucy entertained them with tales of shopping with the duchess, and Emily told tales of the theater. Cassandra said little, sitting at the other end of the table from him, with a gentle smile that slipped when their eyes met.

After dinner, he went back to work, ignoring the look Cassandra gave him. But their music and laughter invaded his study, cheerfully disrupting his peace. That must be what it was like at Warwickshire. What was the place called?

Sunne Park. Stupid name.

Long after their noise had stopped, he went to his bedchamber and undressed. He pulled on his dressing gown, under the baleful glare of Cassandra's cat. The cat had taken to sleeping in his bed, as he had taken to sleeping with Cassandra. And now he would do it again: Go through that door to where she awaited him, hold her, love her, forget himself in her, until his whole world narrowed down to her and the way they made each other feel.

He did it because he wanted to be with her. She did it because she wanted children. And once she had what she wanted, she would leave.

He tumbled onto the settee, not moving even when Cassandra rapped on the door and came in, wearing her stupid bed jacket with its ugly bow.

"Are you all right?" she asked.

"Just thinking."

"I do that. Staring at the fire, thinking. I've learned it does not help at all."

He grunted. She waited.

"Shall I leave you?" she finally asked.

"No."

By the time he thought to retract the word, she was already seated at his side.

"Will you tell me what's wrong?" she said. "You've been quiet all evening."

"Nothing's wrong."

"Are you coming to bed?"

"I might…"

He waved a hand at his own bed. Her smile faltered.

"You're tired of me?"

"No. No. I just…"

He just wanted to spite her, petty, selfish bastard that he was. No reason to be confused. It was all very simple: They were enjoying each other for now, and then they would go back to their normal lives. Him amid the noise and industry of Birmingham; her amid the noise and warmth of family.

She tucked her feet up under her, pressed against him, and curled her fingers in his hair. He had become too used to her.

"I forgot to thank you earlier," she said. "For intervening with the duchess. Although she is unhappy about it."

"Treyford is unhappy with your intervention too. He still wants nothing to do with us. All your amiability cannot fix that. He will never change, and he thinks you are annoying."

"I don't much care what Lord Treyford thinks, to be honest."

"Mrs. DeWitt! I am shocked!"

She eyed him defiantly. "You were right and I was wrong. I am disgusted at the way he and Lady Treyford have not said a word in your defense. You are a hundred thousand times better than he is, and he can claim no credit for that at all."

He couldn't help grinning. "I say, Mrs. DeWitt. I think you might be starting to like me."

"I still want to throttle you half the time."

"All part of my charm."

The noise she made—a little snort like one of the pigs she was so fond of—was adorable. He did not tell her this, and congratulated himself on his restraint. He also did not tell her how beautiful she was, or how he longed to bask in her joy, or how the world was lovelier with her in it.

"The duchess will bring Lucy out at her ball," she said, more quietly. "And if Lucy behaves herself, she can stay with her for the Season. That will be the problem of Lucy solved for now."

"And in a few more days, after I secure my alibis, the problem of Bolderwood will be solved too," he said. "Then it will all be over."

"Yes. It will all be over."

He found nothing to say to that, so nothing was what he said. She shifted, spread her hand over his chest as though seeking comfort, and rested her head on his shoulder. Even like that, she enveloped him. Even more so when she leaned into him, slid her lips over his jaw and down his throat, and he knew it had been futile to think he could stay away.

And why should he, anyway? Just this little touch made him ready for her. His cock was more than happy to service her, to give her all the seed she wanted. That should be enough. It was enough. He wanted nothing more from her anyway.

He closed his eyes, let his head fall back, let his world narrow down to her explorative caresses, the press of her softness against him. Her very essence seemed to coil about him like a warm, fragrant mist. She parted his robe, letting in the evening air then chasing it away with her touch, as she feathered an exquisite trail downward until her hand bumped against his erection.

"Won't you tell me why you're upset?" she whispered.

"I'm not upset."

"My dear, sensitive husband."

"Sensitive?" Outrage had him opening his eyes, trying to ignore her teasing hand. "I am not sensitive. I am never sensitive. I am strong and tough and fierce and...Oh." The wondrous woman curled her fingers firmly around his shaft. "And hard," he finished on a rough breath.

"Very hard. And *very* sensitive." Her grip was both firm and gentle, her eyes watchful. "Do you like it when I do that?"

"Now you're teasing me."

She held on tight, stroked up his length, did it again.

"Oh dear. Do you not like to be teased?" Her eyes glinted mischievously. "Shall I stop?"

He laughed, all breathy and groaning, which made her laugh too. She shifted onto her knees beside him, never letting him go, and he turned his face to her as helplessly as a sunflower to the sun. She kissed him, slow and sensuous, tugging his lower lip between hers, flicking him with her tongue.

"You should visit me at Sunne Park," she whispered against his mouth.

Through the fog of his desire, he thought: *Yes*, and then he thought, *Why does she want me there?*

"What for?" he managed to say.

"I'd like you to see it. It's a beautiful old house, and the gardens are spectacular. It's not even a day from Birmingham. You could bring some work. You can have Papa's study. I'll show you my secret arbor."

"I've seen your secret 'arbor," he said. "I dock my boat there every night."

She squeezed him and he yelped, but grinned anyway. His whole body was grinning.

"I could still throttle you," she warned.

"I'm almost looking forward to it."

But this—this was even better. He closed his eyes, soaking up the sensations, her hand stroking his cock, her mouth nipping at his jawline and sliding down his throat. Then down his chest, his ribcage working overtime as his body demanded more air, her tongue flicking over his nipples, her hair teasing him, her nose bumping him, her mouth gliding down, down, toward his belly.

He fought with himself, and did not know if he had won or lost when he opened his eyes and caught her face in his hands.

"Cassandra, love, you don't have to. I was teasing."

Her playful smile stirred his blood to a new level of heat. "But I do owe you."

No, not as a debt. It had to be freely given or not at all. She only wanted babies; this did not make babies. He needed her to want it for herself. If she wanted it for herself, then she wouldn't want to leave.

"You told me you like it," she said.

She freed her head from his hand and returned her mouth to his skin, murmuring at him between kisses that he was helpless to stop.

"You do it for me, and it feels good, and I want to make you feel good. And you won't tell me why you're upset, so I must find another way to make you feel better, because when I'm upset, you make me feel better, and I like that we do that for each other."

Yes, yes, but...He could not bear for her to feel obliged.

"Besides, I'm curious," she added. "I want to try it and it has taken me this long to work up the courage. So frankly, it would be churlish of you to refuse me now."

She won. He surrendered.

"I wouldn't want to be churlish," he said. "My wife is teaching me to be polite, you know."

"And my husband is teaching me to be wicked."

Threading his fingers in her hair, he watched through heavy-lidded eyes as she took him in her mouth. She experimented first, with nibbles and licks and kisses that would kill him. He heard his own breathing, ragged and shallow through his tight, tortured chest.

"I don't know..." She looked up at him. "Tell me what to do. If you don't tell me, I won't know."

Somehow, he managed to wrap her hand around the shaft and tell her how to take him, and soon she found what he liked. Oh, sweet mercy, that felt good. Because she was sensitive too, and she cared about getting it right, and that was her, wasn't it? Seeing people, caring about them, and giving, always bloody giving, always wanting to right the world. He should stop her but he liked her taking care of him, and he was selfish enough to believe that she enjoyed it, because he enjoyed taking care of her, and she liked that they did that for each other and he liked it too, and he couldn't think, he only knew that this felt splendid and she was his wife and he must not come in her mouth, but oh sweet mercy her mouth was wonderful, and she was wonderful and—

She released him. Cold air hit his wet cock. He bit back a scream.

Freeing his fingers from her hair, he fought for breath and patience. He opened his eyes to see her bathed in firelight and breathing raggedly too.

"Are you all right?" he asked, all on a breath.

"Yes. I'm...It's quite...That is...Don't you think?"

"I wouldn't know."

She laughed and he cradled her cheek and marveled at her soft eyes and plump lips.

"Say you'll visit me at Sunne Park."

"You keep doing this to me, I'll promise you the world."

"I didn't ask for the world."

She lowered her head but it was no use. She had already defeated him.

Ignoring her confused protests, he pulled her up and shoved up her annoying nightwear. Once she understood, she eagerly straddled him and guided him inside her, sinking down on him with a high-pitched moan that almost broke him.

She buried her face in his neck and he gripped her buttocks, thrust his hips, wanting to savor her but needing to be deep inside her, deeper, deeper, desperate now, fearing that he could never be deep enough. He willed himself not to lose control, not yet, but then she put her lips to his ear and whispered, "I love the feel of you inside me," and he did lose control, coming hard with a shudder that shook them both.

Yet she had no shudder of her own.

He wrapped his arms around her, their bodies breathing together. He felt marvelous and guilty.

"You didn't come," he said.

"So I win."

He laughed and breathed her in. "I am as weak as a kitten now, but when I get my strength back, I will carry you to that bed and pleasure you mercilessly, and then we'll see who wins."

CHAPTER 21

Of the seven alleged "trysts" with Lady Bolderwood, Joshua could recall his whereabouts for five. So he, Sir Gordon, and Isaac tramped across London, getting sworn, verified statements from the people he had been with at the time: A trio of scientists—A pair of bankers—Head of the girls' orphanage—Head of the boys' orphanage—Mrs. O'Dea.

Hardly an odyssey, but this was London at its busiest, and by the third day, they were still only on the fourth call.

"This will be the final nail in Bolderwood's coffin," Sir Gordon said as they approached the heavy doors of the boys' home. Sir Gordon had been excellent throughout: another good suggestion from Cassandra.

Sir Gordon lifted the door knocker and rapped sharply.

"We've dismantled Bolderwood's case so effectively that I expect the court will refuse even to hear it," he said. "By next week, this will be over."

By next week, it would all be over. The court case. The

Duchess of Sherbourne's ball. Joshua's stay in London. His relationship with Cassandra.

Then life would go back to normal. It had been so thoroughly disrupted that Joshua hardly recalled what normal looked like. He'd done almost no work recently, but Das seemed to be managing everything in his stead and said the other secretaries were making decisions without him too. Perhaps he would visit Cassandra after all. Sunne Park was almost on the way to Birmingham. He could travel with her and Emily, stay there a few days, admire her roses, meet her pigs, and be on his way.

The door swung open to reveal Mr. Clopstow, who ran the home, blinking earnestly in his black suit. Clopstow's mouth fell open at the sight of Joshua, and he pulled his chin back into his neck.

"I fear you did not receive our note, Mr. DeWitt," said Clopstow. "This is not a good time to visit."

"Too bad if my visit is inconvenient," Joshua said. "Get out the guestbook so Sir Gordon can verify my presence here on... whatever day it was. Sir Gordon has the details." He looked past him, into the dark hallway. "Where is young Martin? I'd like a chat with him. I've not been at the warehouse for a week."

Clopstow blinked some more. "Sir, we intended to inform you of the details once it had passed."

A cold breeze slithered out of the hallway and under his coat. "Once what had passed?"

"I'm sorry to say, sir, that Martin was one of the boys who died."

The chill spread over his shoulders, stiffening his neck, disrupting his pulse. "Died? What do you mean, died? I saw him a week ago. He was perfectly healthy. How do perfectly healthy little boys go about dying?"

A hand landed on his shoulder. Isaac. He jerked away. He was not upset. He had a valid point. Of course, Clopstow could make a valid point too, which was that perfectly healthy little boys did go about dying on a daily basis. It was their chief design flaw.

"There was an outbreak of fever, in the neighborhood," Clopstow blathered on, wringing his hands. "And with all the boys here..."

Martin. Bright-eyed Martin, with his red cowlick and clever mind. Martin, who observed seagulls to learn how they flew. Who studied Italian so he could read DaVinci. Who designed his own kite and cried tears of joy when Joshua took him to see a hot air balloon.

Martin couldn't be dead. He was going to invent a flying machine. Now who would invent a flying machine?

"How many?" His voice sounded hoarse. Dust from the house, perhaps. So much dust. In their lungs, their little-boy lungs.

"Six died, sir. The worst has passed, we believe."

Six little boys, just up and died, all unnoticed. What the blazes was the point of it all, anyway? At least Clopstow didn't feed him all that claptrap that people fed him when Samuel died. Not that this was the same. Samuel was his son and these were orphans to whom he gave training and jobs. He wasn't grieving for them, not personally, because he wasn't attached to them, not personally, because only a fool would get attached to little boys who would just up and die.

"What kind of bloody incompetence led to that?" He welcomed the anger, for it chased away his chill. "Thought you were competent and decent, Clopstow, but you're a blinking muttonheaded nincompoop, to let half a dozen children die."

"Sir, we did what we could."

"Clearly not enough."

He spun and marched away from that blasted door, that blasted house. He glanced back to see Sir Gordon enter the home with Clopstow, while Isaac came after him and leaned on his cane while Joshua paced.

It wasn't easy to pace. April was doing a good impression of November today and his boots sank into thick, cold mud. A band of ragged children raced by, calling good-natured gibes at each other as if they weren't half-starved and half-frozen and halfway to being dead too.

"It never gets easy, does it?" Isaac said quietly. "I was eleven when I lost my first friend in a battle, and the other one to illness a few months after that. I didn't have a lot of friends."

"I don't know what you're blathering on about," Joshua snapped. "And you should cut your hair."

"You got attached to the boy."

"Did you fall off a horse and get a blow to the head?" He had to stop. He needed someone to stop him. Cassandra would stop him. "I did not get attached," he said, through clenched teeth.

"Good. Because if you were attached, you might have been grieving and upset."

"I'm not grieving and I'm not upset. I'm angry because of their bleeding incompetence. They should have been able to prevent it. Why can we not bloody well prevent it?"

He kicked the wall. Pain shot through his toe. Stupid wall. Stupid boots. Stupid boys who went around dying. Stupid him. Stupid, stupid, stupid.

His jaw ached. His toe throbbed. His stomach churned. If only Cassandra were here. She would not stop the pain but she would make it easier to bear.

Cassandra, who might be with child even now.

He slumped against the wall, watched a peddler push his barrow through the mud.

What the blazes had he been doing, bedding her? Night after night, he'd made love to her, carefully avoiding telling himself what that meant. And if he did think of it, he thought, *it doesn't always happen*, or *the damage is done*, or *it means nothing to me, I'm going back to Birmingham.*

What clever tricks he played on his own mind.

And now his mind had its revenge and played tricks on him. It showed him a picture of Cassandra, with a swollen belly and beatific smile. Of Cassandra, glowing with love, a pink, squalling baby in her arms.

Of Samuel. His little body cold and still and unnaturally white. For hours, Joshua had watched over him, his own body growing still and cold too, but never still or cold enough.

How could he have forgotten? But he hadn't forgotten, had he? He had simply ignored those thoughts so they would not interfere with his lust. How clever he was. How very bloody clever.

Behind him, the door opened and shut, and then Sir Gordon was with them, a fresh piece of paper in his hand.

"As expected, your name appeared in the guestbook at the time," he said quietly.

Joshua hefted himself off the wall without looking at either of them. "Right. Let's go."

"Perhaps our visit to Mrs. O'Dea can wait for another day," Sir Gordon suggested, still with that irritating hushed tone that people used to convey sympathy. Sir Gordon had four or five adult children and had likely also lost at least one child. Everyone had, one way or another, though no one spoke of it. Lord Charles had been the Duchess of Sherbourne's son, and she still got up and put on a stylish turban each day. So why did Joshua feel so alone?

"Yes," he said numbly, heading for the carriage. "That can wait for another day."

INSTEAD OF GOING home or back to work, Joshua dragged Isaac around a dozen coffee houses, salons, and taverns, until Isaac was complaining and Joshua had run out of reasons to delay. He felt hollow and bruised, and he hated that he felt like that; he wanted to be with Cassandra, and feared he could not bear to look at her.

Yet when they arrived home and were informed that Mrs. DeWitt and her sisters were in the drawing room, he followed Isaac up the stairs.

"Do you think we are walking into a rose garden or a battlefield?" Isaac whispered to him. "I never know which it will be with these three. Then it changes in the blink of an eye and I never understand why."

A detente, at least, it seemed: The three sisters and Newell were playing cards. If Joshua was not mistaken, Cassandra and Lucy were partnered together, and Lucy had a glass of sherry by her elbow. If there had been a battle, then Cassandra had either lost or elected not to fight.

She met his eyes and smiled, a smile that crept into the hollowness inside him. He crossed the room and jabbed at the fire with the poker.

"Lucy had a wonderful time with her grandmother again today," Cassandra told nobody in particular.

"She let me try on one of her old court gowns," Lucy said. "From when she was lady-in-waiting to the queen about two hundred years ago. It weighs more than a calf, and I had to walk sideways through doors. It turns out that I am extremely talented at walking sideways through doors."

Isaac was over at the drinks. "Why would you want to walk sideways through doors?" he asked. "Why not go backward like the rest of us?"

Lucy laughed. "It's the style of gown, silly. It has huge panniers out the side."

"Ah." Isaac, having run out of conversation about gowns, poured himself a drink. Joshua, who had never had any conversation about gowns, joined him at the sideboard and studied the bowls of sweets and nuts.

"The skirts are so big, a couple of children could hide under them," Lucy went on. "Why, I suspect I could hide even a grown man under there."

All saucy innocence, she waited for a reaction. Joshua looked to Cassandra for guidance. He noticed that Isaac, Newell, and Emily also looked to Cassandra for guidance. Cassandra breathed in, breathed out, and played a card.

"Your turn, Mr. Newell," she said calmly.

Newell played his card. Cassandra considered her own hand. Isaac poured a drink. Joshua chewed on a piece of candied lemon. Emily hunched her shoulders and whispered, "Your turn, Lu."

Lucy did not even look at her cards.

"I spent hours practicing my curtsy and waltz today," Lucy said brightly. "My poor legs are *so* tired. A lotion would relieve them, if I could find someone to rub it in."

Isaac coughed and tossed back his drink. Joshua poked through the nuts in search of one he liked. No one said a word.

Until Lucy started to talk again, and Cassandra cut her off.

"How was your visit to the boys' home?" Cassandra asked. "Did you see Martin? Has he learned how to fly?"

Joshua did not turn around, because he still had not found a suitable nut, and he could not answer questions about dead boys if he did not have a suitable nut.

Isaac stepped in to fill the silence, talking as he poured another drink. "We have four alibis now, which Sir G. has verified. Tomorrow we'll get a statement from the woman whom Joshua visits, and then it is all done."

Oh hell. Oh bloody, bloody hell.

Isaac's words ricocheted around the room like an echo in a tomb, and left a cold, still silence in their wake.

Moving so slowly that he almost creaked, Joshua turned around.

Cassandra was studying her cards intently, tapping a finger on her lips as though she faced a life-or-death decision. Newell wore a pained smile, and Emily, who was so sensitive to atmosphere the Navy could hire her as a barometer, looked ready to shatter.

Only Lucy seemed happy.

"The woman whom Joshua visits?" she repeated. "What woman?"

"Did I say 'woman'?" Isaac said hurriedly. "I meant 'wombat', which is an odd badger-like animal found in the colony of New South Wales. There's a specimen at the Royal Society, did you know? Dead, of course, but most things at the Royal Society are. So, wombat. Only a wombat. Ignore what I say. I'm just a drunken sailor." He gulped his brandy. "See? Drunken sailor." He poured and gulped another.

"Do tell us about this woman," Lucy said. "She sounds most intriguing. Joshua, is this woman—"

"Lucy! Enough!" Cassandra slapped the card table, which was not sturdy enough to withstand a battle between the Lightwell sisters, for it shook and shuddered and Lucy's sherry tumbled over. Newell rushed to clean up the spill; Cassandra and Lucy, eyes locked on each other, did not even notice. "For one blessed moment in your life, can you have enough regard for others to quell your need to be the center of attention."

The two sisters stared at each other like hissing cats. No one else moved, but for Newell mopping up the sherry.

Then Cassandra sat back in her chair, considered her cards, and said, "It's your turn, Lucy."

Lucy rolled her eyes and sat back too. "Marriage changed you,

Mother Cassandra." She tossed a card onto the pile. "You're no fun any more."

"I was never much fun. You and Miranda were always the fun ones, making trouble and taking attention."

"So you're jealous."

"I am not jealous."

All the while, she had not looked at him. She did not look at him now.

Joshua tossed a walnut from hand to hand and Cassandra kept on not looking at him.

They played on in silence, without Lucy trying to provoke a scandal, or Isaac talking about Joshua visiting women, or anyone asking awkward questions about dead boys or fathers' mistresses.

As soon as the last card hit the pile, Lucy rose and shook out her skirts.

"I need my rest," she said. "It's such hard work, being the center of attention." She glared at Cassandra. "I shall be spectacular at the ball, you'll see, and the day I go to live with Grandmother will be the best day of my life."

"Mine too. I shall hold my own ball to celebrate the fact that you are gone."

Lucy tossed her head and stalked out.

Cassandra stood, smiled brightly, and looked at everyone but Joshua.

"I shall turn in too," she said and headed for the door.

Behind her, Emily leaped to her feet, looking panicked and alone. Impossible to believe the girl was fourteen. In the doorway, Cassandra turned back and held out her hand. Emily dashed over to her and they left together. Well, at least one sisterly relationship had been salvaged.

Newell hovered awkwardly for a moment, then edged toward the door. "I shall retire too," he said.

"Newell," Joshua said, yanking off his coat. "I understand you have an uncommonly large number of children."

"Six, sir. It's not that uncommon."

"We've taken you away from them. If you need to go home…"

"Mrs. DeWitt has raised this matter," Newell said. Of course she had. "I can stay longer, if you need me."

"It'll be over soon. But for now, you are the official Sister Herd."

"Ah, 'Sister Herd,' sir?"

"Like a goatherd, but for sisters. Keep them fed and watered, make sure they stay in the yard, and don't let any foxes near."

"Oh. Ah. Thank you, sir. I think."

Newell wisely made a run for the door before he could be awarded any more impossible jobs.

CHAPTER 22

Isaac took his drink to the card table, where he sat and shuffled the cards.

"I should not have mentioned Mrs. O'Dea, should I?" he said.

Joshua snorted. "If you don't learn to keep your foot out of your mouth, you're going to break your other leg too."

Grabbing the bowl of nuts and the nutcracker, he joined Isaac. He sat where Cassandra had been, Cassandra smiling brightly and not looking at him. He felt a little ill, a little hot, a little cold, and his fingers found the knot of his cravat. She thought the woman was his lover, of course, and never dreamed that the truth was worse.

My parents were so much in love...My father's devotion and fidelity...Fidelity was a cornerstone of their relationship and of our family.

"I never know the right thing to say with them," Isaac said. "It's growing up in the Navy. Not a lot of women. You know we—"

"Spare me the details."

"Details spared."

Having cast aside his cravat, Joshua settled a walnut inside the nutcracker. He looked up when Isaac made a scornful sound.

"What? What?"

"Nutcracker!" Isaac scoffed. "Can't you crack it with your bare hands?"

"Is that what you do in the Navy? Crack nuts?"

"I thought you didn't want the details."

Joshua flung the nut at Isaac, who snatched it easily out of the air. With a cheeky grin, he positioned the walnut between the heels of his hands, laced his fingers, and squeezed. A moment later, the shell cracked.

"Bet you can't do that, big brother," he crowed, peeling the shell off the kernel. "Gone soft pushing a pen around."

"Ha." Joshua took another walnut. "I'll have you know, little brother, that I hauled crates and worked a forge."

"Our uniforms had buckles made by your factory," Isaac said. "I remember the insignia. There I was, on the other side of the world, wearing a buckle my brother had made. I wonder if Bram has anything you made, or Mother and Miriam."

Instead of answering, Joshua focused on the walnut between the heels of his hands. It seemed a stupid, inefficient thing to do when he had a perfectly good nutcracker—also made by his factory—but he was not about to be outdone by his little brother, even if his little brother had spent fourteen years hauling ropes and rowing boats or whatever it was sailors did. Fortunately, he did manage to crack it, and grinned to pretend the red indentations in his skin did not sting.

With a derisive snort, Isaac went back to shuffling. Joshua plucked out fragments of kernel and tossed them into his mouth.

"Just tell her who Mrs. O'Dea is," Isaac said, dealing the cards.

"It will upset her. It's a betrayal."

"The woman has nothing to do with you."

"That's not the point. If Cassandra learns the truth, she'll be devastated."

But neither did he want her to think Mrs. O'Dea was his lover. She had not cared before, back when they were strangers, but shared nakedness tended to change things. Heaven knew, he could not imagine even looking at another woman now, and the thought of her looking at another man...

If only he had told Cassandra that earlier.

When Isaac had dealt out the whole pack, they picked up their hands. Joshua had no idea what game they were playing, but he sorted the cards anyway.

Isaac put down a card. "You might think you are protecting her, but she'll be hurt one way or another," he said. "I think she's strong enough to take the truth."

"When did you become an expert on my wife?"

Joshua still had no idea what game they were playing. He tossed down a random card. Isaac didn't object, so he must have done something right.

"Lucy says Cassandra works all day," Isaac went on. "Running the estate, the household, visiting neighbors, looking after everyone in the parish, by the sound of it. She hardly has a moment for herself, or for them. Always busy, apparently."

He had not known that about Cassandra. And yet—she had told him. How did he know things and yet not know them? What tricks his mind played.

"She need not do that," Joshua said. "She has enough money to hire others."

"Maybe that's not what she needs."

"Maybe you should shut up about things you don't understand."

Isaac tossed down another card. Joshua was good at seeing

patterns but he had no idea what all these cards were about, so he chose another one at random.

"What's the problem with their mother, anyway?" Isaac asked. "Lady Charles."

"She's unwell."

"With what?"

Joshua didn't know that either. He didn't want to know. Go around asking people questions about their mothers and who knew what could happen. But he should know. He should be up there now, telling her about Mrs. O'Dea, breaking her heart. She would be upset, and he would comfort her, and she would expect to make love. He could not bear to make love to her tonight, and he could not bear to stay away.

Selfish coward. He hated himself, but his heart had already been broken today, and that was enough for them both.

Isaac didn't press for an answer and they kept throwing down random cards until their hands were empty and Isaac shuffled again. It was not an exciting game, but it suited his mood perfectly.

"I found Mother and Miriam," Joshua said abruptly.

Isaac's hands jerked and cards flew everywhere. "You what? Where are they?"

"They don't want to be found. I looked for them some years ago. After Rachel died."

"And?"

"The investigator passed on a message from Mother. She said she and Miriam were well and did not want any contact with any of us."

"Why would she? What about us? I only wanted...Damn." Isaac shoved back his chair so roughly the table shook. He limped over to the sideboard and got another drink. Isaac drank a lot, now Joshua thought of it, and he wondered if he should say something. Cassandra would know.

"Miriam is eighteen and I would not recognize her, or even my own mother," Isaac said. "What a bastard."

"Who? Me or you?"

With a short, joyless laugh, Isaac shook his head. "Why didn't you tell me?"

"You seemed hopeful. I didn't want to disappoint you." Isaac was staring at nothing. "Do you still think I should tell Cassandra about Mrs. O'Dea?"

"You don't want her thinking badly of you?"

And there it was. Joshua would break Cassandra's heart and sully her memories of her father because he could not bear that she thought badly of him.

"Right. That's that, then," Isaac said, after a long silence. "This matter with Lord B. is almost over and no family to look for...I guess it's time to move on."

"What will you do?"

"I don't know anymore."

"Stay, then. There's plenty of room and if you want a job or anything..." He didn't know what to say. "Cassandra likes having you around."

It was rubbish, but Isaac seemed to understand. He nodded, perhaps he even smiled, and that was settled.

Joshua willed himself to stand on legs that were too heavy. Too many memories and dreams haunted him and a hollow dread churned in the pit of his stomach. He could sit here all night, but for Cassandra, alone in her room, thinking badly of him.

He pushed back his chair. "I must have a conversation with my wife."

CASSANDRA TRIED TO GET COMFORTABLE, but the bed jacket tangled about her legs, and the nightcap twisted on her head, and the bed was too big and empty. Well, she had better get used to it again, because tonight she would sleep alone. Not even with Mr. Twit, who still preferred Joshua's bed.

Another traitor.

It is not a wife's place to mind. Ha! Her own words rang mockingly in her ears. What a smug, naive fool she had been. Easy to spout such nonsense when one is not truly a wife. Her mistake had been to believe anything had changed. Everything had changed for her; nothing had changed for him.

She lay still only when she heard Joshua enter his own room, her ears straining at every sound, and when the connecting door eased open, she feigned sleep. The mattress sank as he sat on the side of the bed. He said nothing and she dared not breathe.

Which is probably why he knew she was awake.

"I've a ship leaving for New York tomorrow," he said quietly. "We can put Lucy on it, if you'd like."

A reluctant laugh slid out of her and she flopped over onto her back. "Britain's last war with the Americans ended only recently. Send her there and we'll start another one."

In the faint light coming from his room, she could make out his shape, but not his expression. He made no move to touch her, and she sensed an uncharacteristic lack of energy about him that frightened her. She pressed her hands against her stomach, as if she could massage away the dread.

"I know I said I did not mind." Her voice sounded small in the darkness. "And when I said it, it was true. We were strangers then. But I do mind. I don't want to mind, but I do."

He shifted on the bed, but said nothing.

"You never promised to be faithful." She hated that her tongue tripped on that word, hated that he heard that, that now he knew. "But you did promise to be honest."

"You are the only woman I have touched in nearly a year. You have disrupted my life so thoroughly that I would never have space for anyone else."

She studied his dark shape. "You visit another woman."

"Her name is Mrs. O'Dea. She has nothing to do with me. She was..." He leaped to his feet, but even though he roamed restlessly about the room, she sensed a flatness about him, a reflection of the odd bleakness she had noticed earlier in his eyes. It made her want to comfort him and she hated them both for that.

He stopped at the foot of the bed, like a visiting angel of doom.

"She was the mistress of..." He paused and continued hesitantly. "A friend of mine...He...It turns out that he...ah...he gave her my details before he died, and last month, she wrote to say she was unwell and needed money. So I called on her."

He had hesitated. Joshua never hesitated.

"He must have been a very good friend," she ventured.

His only response was to resume his pacing.

"You're not telling me the full story." She hauled herself up against the pillows. "There's more. Who is she? Who was the man?"

With her eyes, she followed his prowling shadow. The silence grew and grew; it grew so thick that it squeezed her shoulders and choked up her throat and ate up all her air.

"No," she whispered. "You're lying."

In two strides he was back on the bed. She curled into the pillows and realized he could not have lied when he had not spoken.

But she had heard him say it all the same. Papa.

Mama and Papa, flirting with each other on the night of Charlie's twenty-first birthday, joking about how Charlie was "born early," only eight months after their wedding, getting so bawdy that Miranda and Charlie fell to their knees and begged them to stop, but Mama and Papa only laughed and waltzed around the room.

Mama and Papa, the one sure thing in her world. They were so solid, so strong. Their family was built around them, and that's why her family was strong. Why it would always endure. Why it was worth fighting for.

"No," she said again. "Papa never had a mistress. Other men do, but not Papa. He was faithful to Mama. Always. They were devoted to each other. Why are you lying? You're trying to cover for yourself, aren't you? That's why you're lying."

"It's the truth, Cassandra."

"I don't care what you do." How shrill she sounded! She hated that, hated him, hated them all. "But how dare you tell lies about my father. Our family...He would never..." Her breath failed her, taking her words along with it. "He would never."

She fell back against the pillows, lips trembling. Briefly, he loomed over her, as if he might hold her; she hated him and longed for him to hold her close.

But he sat back and did not touch her at all.

"I'm sorry," he said. "I never meant to tell you."

How he had scoffed, when she first boasted about her parents' fidelity and devotion. He had already known then. Perhaps she had known too, and pretended to herself that she did not.

She hugged herself, as if that might hold her world together, but it had already fallen apart.

And it was still falling apart, faster and faster, Papa with his mistress, and Mama with her cordial, and Miranda with her silence, and Lucy with their grandmother, and Emily with her theater, and Joshua with his work, unraveling, unwinding, all of them spinning further and further away from each other, and in the end there would be nobody left, just silly, naive Cassandra, sitting alone in the dark.

What a fool she had been, trying to hold them together. It had been futile from the start.

"I want to meet her," she said. "Will you take me to her?"

He would leave her, but not yet, not today. She wanted his weight on her, to keep her from floating away.

"If that's what you want," he said.

"It is."

"Very well."

"No, not really."

"Very well."

"No. Yes. I do. Really."

"Very well."

Another silence. This one grew too, expanding between them and pushing them apart. Even while he sat there, he was getting further and further away.

"Are you...are you coming to bed?" she asked.

He stood. "You should sleep."

Yet again, he was running from her. Yet again, she did not know why or how to stop him. A week of weaving their secret world of two and it needed only an hour to crumble.

Holding them together would prove futile too.

"There's something else," she said. "You are not yourself tonight."

"I'm tired."

He was never tired. She searched for something to say.

"Did you see Martin? You said you would see him today."

"He's dead."

His flat tone sent a chill rippling to her bones. A bright life gone, the little boy who careened into the office, appalled that they might be kissing. And Joshua on the dock, laughing with that boy, giving him his time and insisting he did not care. Oh, the darling fool.

"I'm so sorry," she whispered. "What happened?"

"Sickness. It doesn't matter. London is full of children. What do six more or less matter?"

"It's all right to say you loved him."

"There you go again," he snapped, catching the door with one hand. "I'm going to bed."

She fought with her clothing to clamber to her knees. "You have so much love to give. You ought not deny it. Love always comes with the risk of loss, but we must love all the same."

"For mercy's sake, Cassandra. You speak of yourself, not me."

"If we have..."

The words withered in her throat, but he heard them anyway.

"If we have a child, it is your child, not mine," he said, hard, distant, chilling. "I want nothing to do with any of it. That part of my life is finished."

And this time he truly was walking away.

Again.

"You will not leave," she ordered, scrambling out of the bed. He ignored her. "Do not leave again, Joshua. Not again, not this time."

The door slammed in her face. The grind of the key, the click of the lock.

Curse him.

She ran out into the hallway, to his other door—only to hear him turn the key in that one too. She hammered on the wood, yelled his name, not caring if she woke the family or the servants or all the demons in hell. Then—the sound of the connecting door opening. She dashed back into her room in time to see Mr. Twit come hurtling through the slit before the door was closed and locked again.

"Curse you, Joshua," she called through the door. "You cannot keep walking away."

Silence.

Mr. Twit shook off the indignity of his eviction, plonked himself on the rug, and started cleaning a leg.

"It's back to you and me, Mr. Twit," she said.

The cat gave her a dubious look and went back to licking his fur.

And here she was again, alone in the dark. She slid her hand over her belly, closed her eyes, and said a silent prayer.

CHAPTER 23

It was Mr. Newell who informed Cassandra the following day that Mr. DeWitt had ordered the carriage to be ready in fifteen minutes, if Mrs. DeWitt still wished to call on Mrs. O'Dea. Cassandra sighed and told Mr. Newell to thank Mr. DeWitt and inform him that Mrs. DeWitt did still wish to call on Mrs. O'Dea, and she would be ready.

Joshua seemed to be his normal energetic self, bounding down the steps and leaping into the carriage, the sun glinting on his earring. He was unshaven again, and she wanted to catch that bristly face in her hands and kiss him until he laughed.

Instead, she said, "How is your work today?"

"Must you bore me with your polite small talk?"

"Would you prefer that I bore you with rude, big talk?"

"I would prefer silence."

At which he leaned back and tipped his hat over his eyes. They did not speak again until the carriage reached their destination and they stood side by side at the door of a simple but respectable house.

"This was another of your stupid ideas," he said, as she knocked. "For a smart woman, you come up with the stupidest ideas."

"I have to know. You don't have to come in, if you don't want."

"Of course I'm coming in."

She smiled to hide her relief. He would abandon her, sooner or later, but it would not be today.

The maid who opened the door recognized Joshua and led them to a clean, sparse sitting room, where a woman sat sewing by the window, in which hung a cage with two chattering songbirds. She was perhaps in her mid-thirties and wore a plain brown house dress. Sandy curls poked out from under her lace cap, her face was thin and colorless, and when she put aside her sewing to greet them, she revealed eyes of pale blue.

Cassandra knew a horrid disappointment at Mrs. O'Dea's appearance. She realized, to her shame, that she had been hoping to meet a painted butterfly, so she could tell herself that Papa had been attracted only by the costume. But Papa's former mistress was no actress performing a role to entertain a lord's passing fancy. Somehow, that made Papa's betrayal worse.

Mrs. O'Dea greeted them both politely, but her inspection of Cassandra was frank.

"Charles spoke of you fondly, Mrs. DeWitt," she said.

Cassandra's last, lingering hope dissolved like smoke. But she still had her politeness and a lifetime's training in hiding her emotions.

"I must own, Mrs. O'Dea, that my father never spoke of you at all."

"As is right. There are things that children, whatever their age, ought not know about their parents."

"And yet there is much I feel I need to know."

Mrs. O'Dea met her eyes steadily. She had a solemn air that

was far removed from Mama's former vivacity. Cassandra could picture her as wife to a vicar, not mistress to a popular lord.

Her father's mistress! Oh heavens, what was she doing? When had sensible, well-behaved Cassandra become someone who visited her late father's mistress?

But when Mrs. O'Dea indicated a seat and offered refreshments, Cassandra sat and politely refused tea. Mrs. O'Dea sat too, while Joshua paced to the window and poked his fingers through the cage at the birds. He was a few yards from her and a thousand miles away.

"I fear this conversation is necessarily going to be indelicate," Cassandra said. "I apologize for the intrusion, but it was a shock to me to learn of your existence. I always believed that Papa was faithful to Mama."

Mrs. O'Dea's mouth tightened, but she inclined her head graciously. "He was. Until me. He told me that for more than twenty years, he'd known no woman but his wife."

"You do not mean to tell me he loved you."

The words were unkind and Cassandra was immediately ashamed, but Mrs. O'Dea did not seem to mind.

"He needed me," she said. "We met after your mother left him."

"She never left him!"

Over by the window, Joshua turned sharply, but she ignored him.

"Charles said that Emmaline left him," Mrs. O'Dea said, frowning in obvious confusion.

"Why would he say that? She never...Oh. Oh."

She could feel Joshua's gaze piercing her, and she stared past Mrs. O'Dea's questioning look, at the wall. On it hung a framed silhouette portrait of a man who was not Papa.

In a way, Mama had left Papa, hadn't she? She had left them

all. Cassandra had never realized it might have felt like that to her father. A fortnight ago, she would not have understood; she could not have forgiven him.

But now she knew the intense loneliness of having one's beloved near but impossible to reach.

"After Charlie died," Cassandra said.

"Yes." Mrs. O'Dea smoothed her skirt over her knees. "He wanted to talk about Charlie. That's how it started."

"You knew Charlie?"

"My husband knew Charlie from Oxford. He was a professor, my husband." Mrs. O'Dea followed Cassandra's gaze to the silhouette and nodded. "He used to invite students to our rooms and we'd talk about everything, late into the night. We liked Charlie."

"Everyone liked Charlie," Cassandra said.

Yet someone had shoved a knife between his ribs, and so Papa, like Joshua, lost a son. But unlike Joshua, Papa had not raged or locked his doors against the world. No: Papa had smiled. Smiled and smiled and kept on smiling.

Much like Cassandra did.

"Your father wanted to talk about Charlie, so he came looking for Charlie's friends," Mrs. O'Dea went on. "He said no one would talk about him. His friends would change the subject and avoid him. So we talked. At first, it was only talking. But I was newly a widow then, and I missed my husband too."

The small room filled with the echoes of a hundred thousand heartaches. How did they do it, these frail, proud humans? How did they get up, day after day? By thinking about other things, and lying to themselves, and finding love and joy and comfort where they could.

To her surprise, Mrs. O'Dea smiled at her. "He spoke of you too, Mrs. DeWitt. His Cassandra. He said you were his rock. But you were too young and had borne too much, and he didn't want to burden you anymore."

Tears pricked at her eyes. "But it wasn't enough, was it? It was never enough to save him."

Then Joshua somehow was right behind her, hands on her shoulders, giving to her what he would not let her give to him.

"'Save him'? It was an accident." But Mrs. O'Dea sounded unsure. Perhaps she already knew the truth, somewhere deep inside. Perhaps she held the key to why Papa had done what he'd done.

And so Cassandra said, "He shot himself."

The words were hardly out of her mouth when Joshua said, "Cassandra, no!" His hands were firm and sure on her shoulders, but his tone was unusually menacing when he added, to Mrs. O'Dea, "You will tell no one that. No one must know."

Mrs. O'Dea nodded, but her mind was elsewhere, her eyes focused on some place that she alone could see.

"Have you ever experienced a London fog?" she asked. "That's what Charles said it was like in his head. A thick, cold, soupy fog filling his head and choking his heart and his stomach. He said he felt as though he would never see through it or feel sunlight again."

That, then, was the answer. Cassandra still did not fully understand, but it was probably the best answer she would ever get.

Charlie had died, and both Papa and Mama fell apart, each in their own way, and their family fell apart too. There never was anything she could have done.

Joshua had tried to warn her, in his way. He had had two families and they both fell apart, which was why he did not want a third. He cared for her, but he would leave her too, and even a child would not hold them together. Brilliant, efficient Joshua: He knew that nothing would ever hold together, and it was a waste of time to even try.

It was hopeless and futile, and it always had been. She would return to her life and be right back where she started.

Cassandra stood. Joshua's hands slipped away. She wrapped politeness around her like a cloak. "I apologize for this interruption, Mrs. O'Dea. I thank you for your kindness, both to myself and to my father. If ever you have need of anything, please do not hesitate to contact my husband or me."

Mrs. O'Dea stood too and looked from one to the other. "At the very least, it is wonderful to see you two together. Your match was the one thing that made Charles happy." Cassandra did not dare look at Joshua. She could feel him not looking at her. Oblivious, Mrs. O'Dea smiled. "He said you would make each other happy and give each other what you truly need. He would be pleased to see that that, at least, has come to pass."

Another way Cassandra had been in error. When Papa asked her to marry Joshua, he had meant it not as a burden, but as a gift. Papa never intended for Cassandra to sacrifice happiness for her family, but rather to find happiness for herself.

Oh, Papa, she thought. *Dear, dear Papa. You were so very right, and you were so very wrong.*

LORD CHARLES'S misguided matchmaking hopes were still bouncing around Joshua's mind when their carriage trundled back into the traffic. For the first time since Mrs. O'Dea had exploded that particular powder keg, he looked at Cassandra, who finished arranging herself and offered a wan smile.

He should tell her how he could look at her all day. That she did bring him happiness. That she made him stronger and calmer and he was every kind of fool.

Lord Charles had meant well, the poor, broken man, lost in a fog and smiling all the while.

"Don't smile at me if you don't mean it," he snapped. "You don't have to hide everything under a bloody smile."

The smile disappeared. "I smiled at you because looking at you makes me smile. Except when it makes me want to throttle you or slap you or kiss you or all of those at once. I can smile at you and still be upset at others, because I am capable of feeling more than one thing at a time, and if that is too much for you to comprehend, let me tell you I jolly well don't care." Like a soldier, she straightened her gloves and her shoulders and tormented him with her politest face. "It seems I shall have time to help Lady Morecambe pick out some new china after all. She is wavering between the Delft and the Wedgwood. If you would be so kind as to let me down at Bond Street."

Polite small talk. That was cruel and unusual punishment, and she knew it. What was the alternative? Rude big talk. Very well then.

"Tell me about your mother," he said. "She left, she didn't leave, she's unwell, she's not unwell. Do you have a mother or not?"

"I do and I don't." Her look seemed to challenge him to argue, so he stayed quiet. "When Charlie was dying, the doctor gave Mama something to help her sleep. She's been taking it ever since. She is not always sure what is real."

She lifted her chin and stared out the window, but not before he saw the shine in her eyes. Finally, he understood: Lady Charles was an opium eater and had retreated into her own world.

"All this time?" he said.

"On and off. I've discovered she takes less if she has something to occupy her mind. She used to have an interest in herbs and cordials, so last autumn, Mrs. Greenway and I fixed up the distillery, with new equipment and recipe books. Now she potters about in there most mornings, devising new cordials for us to sample. Her orange and sage wine is...interesting, shall we say. At least she is in the world for half the day."

She looked as calm as if she had nothing on her mind but her aunt's choice of porcelain, yet still she was turning herself inside out trying to fix her family, and not one of them seemed to know or care.

He was the worst of the lot, because he knew and he cared, and still he hurt her, time and time again. Yet somehow he couldn't stop himself, because whenever being with her started to feel right, another part of him insisted that it was very, very wrong.

Then her face was soft and gentle, the face he usually saw by candlelight. His legs jiggled with the urge to hurl open the carriage door and throw himself out.

"What Papa wanted," she said quietly. "For us."

"No. Do not go getting romantic ideas simply because your father wanted it."

"I was going to say I knew nothing of his matchmaking. I thought I was marrying you only to secure the inheritance."

"And I told him I had no wish to marry again and would accept a marriage in name only."

"Which is why we agreed to return to our separate lives."

"Exactly," he snapped, more irritated by her than he could ever recall being. "It means nothing that our bedsport is highly satisfactory—" He stopped. "It is satisfactory for you?"

"I have no complaints but I feel no need to discuss it. Heavens, what was Papa thinking? That I might be married to a man who discusses the most inappropriate things."

"That I'm married to a woman who cares more about what is appropriate than about expressing her own needs."

"A man so devoted to expressing himself that he cares not if he upsets others."

"A woman so concerned with not upsetting others that she makes herself miserable."

"A man who has learned only to run away from loss."

"A woman who has never learned to fight for what is hers."

The carriage lurched into a hole and their noses nearly bumped. As one, they realized that they were leaning across the carriage toward each other. As one, they threw themselves back against the squabs.

"You are talking utter nonsense again," she said.

"As are you. Just as well this is nearly over, then, isn't it?"

"Quite."

He scowled at her. She glared at him. He folded his arms so he would not pull her onto his lap and shove up her skirts and make her cling to him while he clung to her.

"You said you would visit Sunne Park," she said into the silence.

"When you need me to impregnate you?"

"Oh, I shouldn't like to put you to any trouble. Perhaps I'll take a lover. Save you the inconvenience."

Like blazes she would. "Better get someone with stamina. You're demanding in bed, once you forget to be polite."

"Perhaps you could use your expertise to hire someone suitable. You could call him the Secretary In Charge Of Impregnating My Wife Because I'm Too Selfish And Busy To Do It Myself."

"That's a stupid job title."

"They're all stupid job titles!" she yelled.

He recoiled, stunned. What the blazes was wrong with his

secretaries' job titles? And what did any of it have to do with her womb? And where had their camaraderie gone and why did she not want him and why was it so hard to breathe?

She gathered herself after her outburst.

"Do you know, Joshua, I shall be glad to return to the peace and quiet of Sunne Park without you."

"And I'll be glad to return to Birmingham. Birmingham is the noisiest place on Earth and it is still more peaceful than putting up with you."

"We need put up with each other for only three more days. If Lucy pleases Grandmother at the ball, Lucy will live with her, and Emily and I will leave. You will aid in that by behaving *properly* at the ball." She eyed him bitterly. "I trust that getting rid of me will be all the *inducement* you need to behave."

"Getting rid of you is all I want," he lied. "My behavior will be *impeccable*."

CHAPTER 24

I t was with rue that Cassandra recalled her claim at the first breakfast she shared with Joshua: that they could coexist in the same house and never see each other.

Well, clever them! They had done exactly that! In the three days since their quarrel in the carriage, she did not see Joshua at all. She heard him sometimes, moving about his room at night, while she lay alone in the too-big bed longing for the oblivion of sleep. Once she heard his voice, when he called to a servant; her heart beat faster and her breath snagged—but all she heard next was the slam of a door.

Only thanks to Mr. Newell did she have confirmation that Joshua would join her and Lucy at her grandmother's ball.

While dressing for the ball, she was grateful for her maid's brisk competence, for Cassandra was useless, her body jittery with dread and excitement, her mind repeating a futile scold. *This is just another ball and he is just another man,* she told herself, as Ruth shoved her toward the stairs and darted off to help Lucy. *It was always going to end, and now it has.*

Yet halfway down the staircase, she had to pause and grip the bannister, for her legs stopped working and the world emptied of everything but the tall, dark-haired man in the hall.

He was pacing, of course, and flicking his white evening gloves against his thigh. His black evening coat hugged his broad shoulders, and her lonely palms ached to slide across those shoulders, down his chest, over his thighs, to feel his power, the heat of his skin through the silk.

Joshua turned his head toward her then and went still, mid pace, mid flick, watching her with dark, unreadable eyes.

Unfreezing her feet, Cassandra concentrated carefully on each step, for her knees had trouble remembering what to do. Heavens, she was behaving like a giddy debutante in the throes of her first infatuation! Yet no debutante knew this searing desire to press her naked, aching body to a man, or this hollow yearning to disappear with him into their secret world of two, or this chilling fear of their unscalable, invisible wall.

She missed him. Even when she stood right in front of him, she missed him.

"What the blazes is that on your head?" he said. "Is some poor pink bird flapping about London with half its feathers missing?"

"This is the part where you tell me I look lovely."

"Why should I? You just did that yourself."

That wicked, teasing smile still affected her. She fought her own smile and curled her fingers around her fan so she would not throttle him, for his cravat was tied too exquisitely to mangle. He was freshly shaven, and oh, how she longed to rub her cheek against his and inhale his spicy scent. The earring was gone, and finally, finally, he had submitted to a haircut, fashionable and flattering.

"You clean up nicely," she said.

"I aim to please."

"You do nothing of the sort."

Yet he did please her, looking so dynamic and handsome and strong.

Looking so...impeccable.

I trust that getting rid of me will be all the inducement you need to behave, she had said during their quarrel.

Getting rid of you is all I want. My behavior will be impeccable.

She swallowed her hurt—who knew victory could hurt?—while something like confusion crossed his face. She was grateful when the footman brought her evening cloak, as it gave her a reason to hide. But it was Joshua who settled the velvet cloak over her shoulders, his hands lingering. Joshua who fastened the clasp at her throat. His knuckles brushed her skin, and she held her breath and studied the full lips she was no longer allowed to kiss.

When he glanced up, everything stopped. She drowned in the hot coffee of his eyes, his mouth so close their breaths mingled, his chest barely inches from her own. The candlelight flickered and she fancied he looked puzzled, lost, seeking. Hope speared her reeling heart.

Then he whirled away, snatched up his gloves, and resumed flicking them against his thigh.

"Is this ball meant to be tonight?" he said. "Or will they move it to tomorrow so our Miss Lucy can get there in time?"

Cassandra smoothed out her cloak and her tangled thoughts. "She is waiting to make an entrance." She sighed. "It would have been better had she dressed at Grandmother's house, but the duchess has not quite forgiven me."

Then skittering footsteps sounded above and Emily came racing down the stairs, her face bright with excitement.

"She's coming, she's coming!" she cried, and turned at the bottom of the stairs to look up. Staff members clustered around, and Mr. Newell and Isaac too, all watching the staircase. Everyone liked Lucy, for she was agreeable to everyone but Cassandra.

When Lucy appeared on the landing and paused for effect, basking in the hushed admiration from below, Cassandra forgot all of it. She forgot their fights, their resentment, their pain, their loss. She saw only her beloved little sister, radiant in her white ballgown, pearls in her glossy dark hair and a blissful smile curving her lips. Lucy, alive with spirit and wit, floating down the stairs, advancing relentlessly toward her new life without them.

Cassandra tried to etch every detail on her memory; she did not know when she would see Lucy again after tonight. She pressed her lips together against the tears and hoped, prayed, that tonight marked the start of Lucy finding happiness again.

"She's so beautiful," she whispered. She glanced at Joshua, but he was looking at her, not Lucy. She released a high, shaky laugh and did not know why. "Society will be astonished."

"Society will never recover."

He sidled closer, until his chest almost brushed her shoulder and his legs teased her skirts. His closeness slid under her skin, swirled through her body, heating her with need for his touch. His warmth, his scent, enveloped her, and her gown felt so tight it was a wonder she could breathe.

"*You're* beautiful," he murmured. The caress of his breath sent shivers down her spine. She thought his hand brushed her hip but she could not be sure.

Nearby, the servants and Emily fussed about with Lucy, bringing her cloak and gloves and fan like she was a princess. Cassandra turned her head, caught a glimpse of Joshua over her shoulder, and fought a peculiar urge to weep. They were only words, uttered easily and too late. He was being kind—his kindness was one of the things she loved about him—but kindness was not what she wanted from him now.

"You've never complimented me before," she managed to say.

"What?" He sounded indignant. Acting. Playing. Teasing her again. "Surely I've blathered some nonsense about your hair or your gown or your eyes."

She half-turned, calmer now they stood on familiar ground. "You probably don't even know what color my eyes are."

"Of course I don't," he admitted cheerfully.

Yes, back on familiar ground, and no reason to be disappointed. Such a silly thing to care about. As if her eye color mattered at all!

"Your eyes are impossible," he explained. "They can be greenish, or brownish, or greenish-brown, or brownish-green. In the sunlight, they even seem golden. When you weep, they turn green. When you are lustful, they turn brown. When you laugh, they get lighter. When you are angry, they get darker. So how in blazes am I supposed to know what color your eyes are when they keep changing all the time?"

Oh. Oh. The familiar ground disappeared again and there was nothing under her feet, and all she could think to say was, "You noticed."

In the silence, his own eyes were heavy and shadowed. She could not guess what he was thinking and lacked the courage to ask.

"You needn't spout such nonsense," she said briskly, turning her fan in her hands. "I am satisfied with my looks and always have been. I simply get silly when I compare myself to my sisters."

"Here's the comparison: Lucy is beautiful like a diamond. You are beautiful like a rose." He glanced at her fancy headdress. "A rose that has pink feathers sticking out of its head, that is."

Finally, she laughed, for he was being absurd and she was being a fool. It was she who loved roses; he thought them a frivolous waste of time. Had he said she was beautiful like iron ore or a factory or a pile of work, well, then she could be pleased. Instead, she felt lonelier than she ever had before.

A cool breeze caressed them: A footman had opened the door. Cassandra met Joshua's eyes and reminded herself that she had achieved what she came for, and everything was exactly as it ought to be. He had made her no promises and told her no lies.

If her heart was breaking, it was nobody's fault but her own.

"Excuse me, love birds," Lucy called from the doorway. "Is this ball tonight? Or shall we ask them to move it to tomorrow so you can finish canoodling?"

THE FIRST DANCE was underway by the time they arrived. Cassandra deposited Lucy with the duke and duchess and went her own way. Of course she did, Joshua thought, watching her pink feathers bob through the crush. That was what they did now, and a few clumsy, belated compliments would do nothing to change that. Joshua felt at odds with his own body. He wanted to blame the cravat, the coat, the ridiculous breeches, but he knew it was not that. He seemed to have developed a talent for doing everything wrong.

He wandered around the ballroom aimlessly, sending people scattering with his scowl. Every now and then he caught a glimpse of her. Saw Dammerton approach her; saw her smile. Someone blocked Joshua's view and when it cleared, the duke was writing on her dance card.

Bloody Dammerton, flirting with his wife, asking her to dance. She liked dancing, Joshua knew, and she was good at it too. Dancing had always seemed such a waste of time, but now he wished he had learned. She would like that. Or not. Dancing did not make babies either.

What an idiot he was, staying away from her. They only had a few more days until Sir Gordon got Bolderwood's case quashed: Was he going to waste the time sulking? He remembered her philosophy about cut flowers: They did not last but one could enjoy them while they bloomed.

The dance ended and the guests milled about in the echoing chatter of a room suddenly bereft of music.

"What the hell are you doing here?" came a familiar snarl by his shoulder.

Joshua almost groaned at the tedium of another fight with his father.

"Good evening, Father."

"You promised to stay away from us," Treyford said.

"This ball is hosted by my wife's grandmother, and my wife's sister is making her debut. You knew I would be here, so *you* ought to have stayed away."

"You ought not be in London at all."

Isaac had been right: Treyford hated him because he was a reminder of his shame. Which meant that, under his bluster, the man was ashamed.

Joshua opened his mouth to answer but stopped when a new, excited hush claimed the crowd.

The Duke of Sherbourne, nigh on seventy but spry and alert, claimed the middle of the empty dance floor, Lucy by his side, her fingers resting on his. The sight of the young lady, graceful beyond measure and beautiful beyond words, sent a murmur of admiration through the guests. Joshua felt a broad smile break over his face, his chest swollen with undeserved pride. He scanned the crowd for Cassandra—this was her moment as much as Lucy's —but his seeking eyes could not find her. His smile faded, his pride deflated, his eyes searched. What a selfish fool he was; he should be at her side.

The duke released Lucy, raised his hands for silence, and then filled it as only an experienced orator could.

"My lords, ladies, and gentlemen. It is my great honor and delight to present to you—my granddaughter, Miss Lucy Lightwell."

The crowd applauded politely, murmuring to each other, eating the newcomer up, as the orchestra struck up the rich strains of a slow waltz. The duke bowed, Lucy curtsied, and together they danced across the floor.

Joshua searched fruitlessly for Cassandra again, an odd panic edging through his limbs, and was about to go looking for her when Treyford spoke again.

"Is that the girl?" Treyford said, his eyes on Lucy, a pensive faraway look on his face. "She looks a bit like Susan."

Lady Susan Lightwell, the youngest daughter of the Duke and Duchess of Sherbourne, Treyford's first wife, and Lucy and Cassandra's aunt. Perhaps Treyford had gone to that time, thirty-odd years ago now, when he was eighteen and Lady Susan sixteen, and the pair had eloped and then—What?

Joshua knew nothing more. He did not know why the pair had eloped or why they had parted; how Lady Susan, the Protestant daughter of an English duke, had wound up in an Irish Catholic convent for another sixteen years; or whether Treyford had truly believed Lady Susan was dead when he married Joshua's mother. The reason Joshua did not know was that he had never asked. He had been too angry to so much as wonder.

Cassandra had seen that he was angry, and he had denied it, but she had been right. Again.

More couples joined the waltz, and he finally spotted his wife, watching Lucy with a mix of pride and sorrow, exchanging the occasional comment with her tall, haughty friend, Lady Hardbury.

As if he had called her name, she turned.

Their eyes met.

The orchestra roared, and then it faded away, and she was the only one in the room.

Then someone jostled her and she looked away. The crush returned, the discordant music, the stuffy air, the tightness of his cravat.

He would go to her, now. He glanced at his father, who had returned from the past and was bestowing his usual scowl, the scowl that always triggered Joshua's ire, and now—

Nothing.

Joshua studied his father's face, as if seeing it for the first time and—Nothing. No rage, no fury. Indifference—Distaste— Nostalgia for what had never been—Irritation over the time he had lost. This was all he felt for his father now.

Joshua was not angry anymore.

"I apologize, sir, for any unnecessary trouble I've caused you," he said.

The earl's scowl faded into surprise. "You what?"

"That does not mean I condone or forgive what you have done. It mainly means I don't care anymore."

Treyford stared, bemused. But he quickly recovered. "That's not much of an apology."

"Better than your apology."

"What apology?"

"Precisely." Joshua tugged off his left glove, twisted the signet ring off his finger, and held it out to his father. "I believe this belongs to your heir."

His father's eyes narrowed and he extended his hand tentatively, as though he feared this were a trick. Joshua dropped the ring onto his palm.

His hand felt naked without it and he massaged the empty spot. He had worn that ring since he was twelve, moving it from finger to finger as he grew, and now it was gone. It had never been his; he had held onto it too long. Treyford turned it in his hands, inspecting it with a frown, then he slid it onto his own little finger for safekeeping.

Joshua put his glove back on, and once more held out his hand. This time, Treyford did not hesitate to shake it. He bowed. His father bowed. Then Joshua turned and headed for his wife.

CHAPTER 25

At first, Cassandra had eyes only for Lucy, whose dancing was perfection and behavior exemplary, and with each dance step more of Cassandra's worry melted. If the whispers she overheard were any guide, London was already smitten.

But then her eyes were scanning the sea of dark coats, moving over them quickly, for the men inside them were tepid and dull. Only one was dynamic and alive, and when their eyes met, the music faded and he was the only man in the room.

For a beat of her heart—two beats, three—she was the only woman.

If they were the only couple in the room, why, he would cross the floor and sweep her into his arms, and they would waltz—

Waltz? Joshua? Not likely. And what need had she of a waltz, anyway? What need had she of a man who knew the right time to sit and the right time to stand and could say the right things while saying nothing at all?

None of that mattered. It was *this* man she needed: strong and true, caring and vulnerable. He lived by his values, he was buffeted by his emotions, he changed things for the better, and he had so much love to give that he did not know what to do and drove himself mad trying to hide it.

She almost shook with the intensity of her yearning. If only she could tell him: "It's you. It's only you. Don't leave me. I need you."

And he would laugh and say, "Been in the brandy again, Mrs. DeWitt?" and then he'd run as fast as he could.

Someone jostled her. She had to turn and when she looked back at him, couples blocked her view.

"With looks like that, your sister might survive your family's shame." The sly female voice slithered over Cassandra's spine. "Then again, she might become a courtesan."

Lady Bolderwood.

Disbelieving, Cassandra took in the fair curls, the extravagant gown, the nasty little smirk. No surprise that Lady Bolderwood was being insulting. No surprise, even, that she had addressed Cassandra when they had ignored each other for a week.

But a great surprise that the woman even attended the duchess's ball.

Others were watching. Cassandra lifted her chin and, without a word, gave Lady Bolderwood her back: the cut direct.

She spied her grandmother three potted palms away and marched right to her.

"There you are, Cassandra, my dear," the duchess said. "Shall we declare Lucy a success?"

"Why is Lady Bolderwood here?" Cassandra demanded.

The duchess cocked an eyebrow. "The invitations went out long before your little dramas came to town."

"Grandmother, you should have revoked her invitation. This is my sister's debut!"

"And my ball. I do not live to do your bidding, Cassandra."

"We are family," Cassandra said. "I thought I could count on your support."

The duchess's lips tightened. "You ignore my advice, you manipulate my husband, you force me to shelve my interests for the sake of your own, and then you have the impertinence to address me thus at my own ball?"

Cassandra struggled under the weight of the accusations. Put like that, she sounded awful. No wonder her grandmother resented her.

Habit had her ready to apologize, and yet—No, she decided. She had not manipulated or forced anybody. She was entitled to her own decisions and opinions, and she would never be ashamed of supporting her sister.

But before she could tell her grandmother exactly that, the music ended, closing the waltz with a smattering of applause. The crowd began to mill and the orchestra launched into a bright, fast reel, but they were too eager, it was too soon, and they stopped again abruptly, creating an unexpected silence, into which rose the voice of Lady Bolderwood.

"...but the old duchess has life in her yet. At least, she has Sir Arthur Kenyon in her. Indeed, I hear he's in her most afternoons."

THE CRUDE BARB rose into the silence and exploded like a firework. A million scandalized faces turned their way. The duchess gasped. Her hand flew to her throat and the ugly color of humiliation mottled her cheeks. Her mouth opened, closed, worked, and she glanced about, wide-eyed and panicked. Titters rippled outward, and the proud duchess looked ready to faint.

With quick steps, Cassandra planted herself in front of her

grandmother and indicated for her grandmother's friends to join her in making a human wall.

"Oops," came Lady Bolderwood's giggle. "I ought not have spoken so loudly. Still, 'tis not as though everyone did not already know."

Too much. Cassandra's head spun, her elbows floated, and it vaguely occurred to her that rage acted upon her like a potent brandy. She seemed to grow to twice her height and her mind was clear and sharp. She pivoted slowly, dimly noting the audience, Joshua striding toward her, but ignoring them all. She was a fierce falcon now, and her prey was a rodent with sly eyes. She was hardly aware her legs moved and, when she spoke, she did not know her own voice.

"You disgusting, despicable viper!" Cassandra hissed in Lady Bolderwood's smirking face. "Have you become so grubby that you must sully everything else too?"

Lady Bolderwood tossed her head. "You are so naive, Mrs. DeWitt."

"The games you and your husband play in your bedchamber have distorted your view, Lady Bolderwood, and now you cannot tell what is real and what is not." She stepped closer. The viscountess stepped back, so Cassandra stepped closer again. "How *dare* you mock and judge, you malicious, vile asp? How *dare* you let your own corruption pollute someone else's honor? How *dare* you insult *my grandmother*?"

Lady Bolderwood screwed up her face, as Harry stumbled up to them. A strong presence warmed her side: Joshua.

"How dare you speak to me like that?" Lady Bolderwood snarled. "I am a viscountess and your better."

"My better?" Cassandra scoffed. "You are not the better of the lowliest, filthiest worm crawling on its belly through the muck."

"Here, don't speak to her like that," Harry broke in. "DeWitt, control your wife."

Joshua pressed a firm hand to her waist. "Not a chance," he said cheerfully. "She's splendid when she loses control."

"Leave," Cassandra said. "Both of you. Now."

"You are nobody, Mrs. DeWitt," sneered the viper. "You cannot make us leave."

"But I can."

The Duke of Sherbourne.

Her grandfather was not a tall man, but as one of the most senior men of the age, he did not need to be. Harry, at least, was smart enough to duck his head in deference.

Also joining them were Arabella and Lord Hardbury, the Duke of Dammerton, and...was that the Earl of Treyford? Heavens. Arabella caught her eye and winked. Behold the vanguard of the DeWitt army.

The duke looked down his nose at Harry. "You are not welcome here, Bolderwood. Years ago, I told my son he should have called you out for your treatment of Cassandra, but Charles said he wearied of bloodshed and was glad you had cleared the way for her to marry a good man. I did not understand what he meant until now. You disgust me." He looked the younger man over coldly. "Do not think I am too old to call you out myself."

"Nor I," proclaimed Treyford, causing a dozen heads to swivel in surprise. "I used to love a good duel. Something about the smell of gunpowder in the morning."

Cassandra was starting to wonder if she had hit her head and this was a dream.

"No duels, please," drawled the Duke of Dammerton. "Much better sport will be watching Bolderwood's face on Monday when the court hears the full story of how he stole Mr. DeWitt's personal letters, bribed witnesses to provide false testimony, and prepared to perjure himself. All in a feeble plot to defraud Mr. DeWitt of money, because Bolderwood is too feckless to pay his own debts."

Bolderwood looked around wildly like a cornered fox, edging closer to his wife, his sole remaining ally. He saw Joshua and prepared to attack—Joshua raised an eyebrow and he fell silent.

But the one thing an aristocrat always had was his composure, and Harry's did not let him down.

"Come along, Phyllis," he said. "I grow tired of this ball. Let us seek more diverting entertainment."

With a sharp look at Cassandra, Lady Bolderwood took her husband's arm and they swept out through the hostile crowd.

Cassandra could not applaud, but she did clap her hands together once as she turned to check on her grandmother. The duchess stood still and straight, her eyes locked with those of the duke, the couple engaged in the kind of silent conversation that was possible after a marriage of more than four decades. Then Her Grace inclined her head and swept out of the ballroom, two friends and her husband in her wake.

With the drama passed, the audience dispersed.

Joshua still had his arm around her waist. "Well done, Mrs. DeWitt! I am very impressed."

Giggles bubbled up in her. "I think your father offered to fight a duel over my honor. What on earth is going on?"

"Don't tell anyone, but I suspect your grandmother put something in the punch."

"That would explain why everything tonight is topsy-turvy. This is the exact opposite of the first night we went out together." She began to soften into him, then remembered where they were. "When you argued with your father and I tried to calm you down."

"You mean the rout when you spent the whole time imagining women putting their mouths—?"

"I didn't!" she protested. "Well, not the whole time."

His laughter warmed her as no fire could, and all she wanted was more of him. To retreat to their own world and forget everyone else.

Which was difficult, when everyone else was in the same room and giving them little looks.

"Lucy is like an angel tonight," she said. "I keep waiting for her to set fire to something, but she has not put a toe wrong since we left our house. Everyone already adores her and she will be a great success if..." She searched his eyes. "Do you think it will last?"

"I think you should stop worrying about her. Let her do the worrying for once. A wise woman told me we should enjoy things while we can."

Cassandra felt odd, for as she opened her mouth to answer, she was sure that somewhere inside her lay the right words to fix everything.

If only she could find them.

But she did not. Because first the music started, and then the music stopped.

And then came the laugh.

Lucy's laugh, washing over the crowd like a shower of stars, a laugh calculated to turn heads, a charm that turned thinking humans into automatons.

A laugh Cassandra knew too well.

"Oh no," she muttered. "What has she done now?"

WHAT LUCY HAD DONE, Joshua saw as they pushed closer through the crush, was commandeer a footman bearing a silver tray loaded with glasses of champagne. Most were full, a couple were empty; he suspected from Lucy's color that they had been emptied into her. She had also gathered a small band of spellbound young men who feasted their eyes on her every move.

Lucy selected a full glass from the tray and raised it as if making a toast.

"Whoever catches this glass," she announced, "that man shall have a waltz."

She tossed back the champagne in a few neat gulps and then hurled the glass into the air. A scramble ensued and the men leaped high, displaying skills honed on the cricket fields of Eton and Harrow. One proud victor caught the glass with a "hurrah!". His rivals sportingly slapped his back and they all turned back to Lucy, like so many panting puppy dogs eager to fetch a stick.

"I'm going to kill her," Cassandra muttered. "This time, I'm truly going to kill her."

Fair enough. Even Joshua could see that this was bad. He shouldered through the resistant crush toward Lucy.

Lucy raised another glass. "Whoever catches this glass, that man shall have a kiss."

A cheer met this announcement. She drained the drink and sent the glass flying. The scrambling halted Joshua's progress, until a victor flourished the glass to a fresh round of cheers. "A kiss! A kiss! A kiss!"

Lucy laughed again, raised another full glass, in an unsteady hand, champagne sloshing over the rim.

"Whoever catches this glass, that man I shall marry!"

The puppy dogs howled.

Joshua shoved closer, not taking his eyes off Lucy's hand, the hand lifting the glass, the glass that must not fly, the glass that was almost at her lips, the glass that was almost in his grasp when—

She spied him from the corner of her eye. Guessed his purpose.

And with a graceful swing of her arm, Lucy sent the still-full glass arcing through the air.

It tumbled end on end, dumping a shower of champagne on squealing ladies and hollering men, yet still arcing up, up over the reaching, grasping fingers, headed straight for the massive chandelier. In horror, he imagined it smashing into an iron arm and showering glass upon skin and eyes. But by the luck of Lucy's devil, the glass lodged precariously between two branches. A few candles puttered out. The chandelier rocked. The glass slipped, the crowd gasped, the glass stuck again.

The young men jostled around under it. At the center, Joshua saw to his relief, was Lord Hardbury, tall, fierce, and safely married, scowling and ready to spring.

But one young man proved to be enterprising: He pulled off one of his shoes and threw it hard at the chandelier. The chandelier rocked. The glass slipped. Another shoe followed and the glass slid from its perch. The young men surged, arms outstretched, knocking even Hardbury off balance as they wrestled, jostled, forming a forest of seeking fingers. The glass bounced against those fingers, jumped, bounced further, jumped, bounced, jumped, and the best hope now was that it fell and smashed.

Until one hand broke through the others, a large gloved hand attached to the black sleeve of a tall, dark-haired gentleman, who plucked the glass out of the air.

Then hand and glass disappeared into the crowd.

Everyone froze. Silence fell. Joshua could not see the man's face. A moment later, he could not see the man at all.

"Him!" Lucy bellowed, pointing. "I shall marry that man! Stand aside, London. That man is mine!"

Obediently, slowly, the scandalized, titillated crowd parted, murmuring, shuffling, craning their necks, to reveal—

A footman.

Everyone gasped.

The footman was short. He wore red livery and an expression of sheer terror.

"It wasn't me," the footman stammered, holding the glass away from him as though it were poisoned. "Please. I'm sorry. It wasn't me."

"Who was it, then?" someone yelled.

"I believe it was a, ah, a Scottish gentleman."

Heads turned, but the tall, nimble-fingered Scotsman had wisely made his escape.

"A Scotsman!" Lucy cried. "I'm going to marry a Scotsman."

Most of the ladies looked suitably scandalized. Most of the gentlemen looked faintly bemused. But Lucy's new circle of fervent admirers, a quartet of wild young bucks, clapped and cheered.

Which is possibly why Lucy flung her arms wide, tilted back her head, and broke into song.

"*Should auld acquaintance be forgot—*" Off-key, and more of a bellow than a tune; usually, she sang angelically, but usually, she was not drunk. "*And never brought to mine—*"

Hand flung out like an Italian soprano, she wobbled the last awful note, sounding increasingly like a sick cow as she ran out of air. The sounds faded into the hush of a crowd that did not know what to do next.

Then the young bucks slung their arms around each other's shoulders and bellowed in response:

"*Should auld acquaintance be forgot, And days of auld lang syne.*"

Joshua gripped Lucy's elbow.

"Time to go," he said.

"I just need to—"

"You are not leaving my sight until you are locked in your room."

"Are you pleased with yourself, Lucy dearest?" Cassandra had joined them. She looked frighteningly calm, but for the color staining her cheeks and the shrillness of her tone. This did not bode well. The last time Joshua saw her like that, she had overturned a chair. "Did you get sufficient attention? Have you ruined us enough or have you something else in mind?"

"Oh Mother Cassandra, isn't this fun?" Somehow, Lucy had another full glass of champagne. "You should drink more."

She lifted the glass to her lips, smiled angelically, and with a flick of her wrist, threw the contents straight at Cassandra.

Cassandra gasped, stepped back. She was quick, but not quick enough: The champagne missed her face and hit her square on the bodice. The bodice of her white, silk dress, pressing the thin fabric to her skin and—

Joshua nearly sprained something getting his coat off; certainly, he heard seams tear. Lucy was laughing, London was watching, as he wrapped his coat around his wife, who hugged it tightly over her chest.

The pink feathers in her hair quivered, but otherwise she seemed calm and dignified. For once, it was Lucy who appeared unsettled, fearing retribution.

Yet Cassandra merely smiled. "You're right. I should drink more," she said.

Holding the coat together with one hand, she took the last full glass of champagne from the idiotic footman's tray.

"A toast to my dear sister Lucy, for her unforgettable debut."

She took a sip, Lucy laughed, and Cassandra tossed the drink in her face.

CHAPTER 26

W ith a wild screech, Lucy pounced. She tore the pink feathers from Cassandra's head and waved them triumphantly. Cassandra, one hand clutching the coat, the other at her hair, had no chance to retaliate before Joshua tossed Lucy over his shoulder and marched for the nearest door.

Then Arabella was holding Cassandra's right arm and Lord Hardbury held her left, and they guided her outside and packed her into their carriage to take her the few blocks home. She buried her face in Joshua's coat and inhaled him, her mind still on the shambles of the ball and social debris left in their wake.

When she stumbled through the front door, Joshua and Lucy were nowhere to be seen. Arabella offered to stay with her, but Cassandra wanted to be by herself.

Whoever that self might be.

Numbly, she dumped her outerwear in the entrance and climbed the stairs to her room, listening to the sounds from the floor above. She needed a maid to help her undress but had no will to call. She had no will to do anything but press her forearm to the wall, and rest her forehead on her forearm, and wait for the world to end.

She felt rather than heard Joshua come in and lock the door. She didn't move, but every one of her senses tracked his presence.

Three glissades of her dancing heart later, he enveloped her in his solid heat. His arms were strong and sure around her waist, and his chest made a safe, sturdy wall against her back. How lovely to be wrapped up in him like this. If someone attacked her, he would shield her. If her legs gave way, he would catch her before she fell.

His lips brushed over her jaw. "You outdid yourself tonight, my sweet," he murmured.

"Are you laughing?"

"Only on the inside."

He nuzzled her again, half caress, half tickle, and she tilted her neck for more. His scent filled her senses and his caress rippled out over her body, cascading over her skin like warm water.

"Are you planning to stand against the wall all night?" he asked.

"For the rest of my life, I think."

Oh, how she loved his soft chuckle. It belonged to her alone, to their intimate moments together.

When he detached himself, she kept her face to the wall and mourned his absence, but he did not go far: He tugged the pins from her hair and let them fall. His fingers combed through her hair, lifting its weight, letting it tumble down over her shoulders and back, languidly as if he had all the time in the world and nothing better to do than play with her curls.

"Where is Ruth?" she managed to say.

"With Lucy. I shall be your lady's maid tonight."

He gathered her hair over one shoulder and, with nimble fingers, unbuttoned her gown. She lowered her arms long enough for him slide the sleeves over her shoulders. He chased the gown down her body with his fingers, his hands grazing her waist, her hips, her legs, all the way to the floor. Every touch injected new vigor into her body, as though she were a doll in a story and he the magician bringing her to life. Doll-like, she lifted one foot and then the other so he could pull the gown away.

Still she had not looked at him. Hope shimmered through her but it tangled with the dark fear that if she looked at him, this would end and he would leave her again. She replaced her arm on the wall and rested her forehead on it again.

A few tugs of his nimble fingers and her corset also fell away.

"I make a good lady's maid, don't I?" he said.

Once more, his body enfolded her. His nibbling lips at her throat sent new invitations to pleasure that her body was eager to accept.

"My lady's maid never did that," she whispered.

He responded by cupping her breasts and teasing her nipples with his thumbs.

She leaned back into him. "She never did that either."

"What would you do if she did?"

"Give her a raise, probably."

Another intimate chuckle. How she loved the way she could feel his laugh with her body. She arched her back and rested her head against his shoulder, and enjoyed his enticements.

"Will you dress me in all my nightclothes now?" she asked. "My shift and bed jacket and nightcap?"

"I shall dress you in your nightcap and absolutely nothing else."

"Oh, you are wicked."

"*I'm* wicked? You're the one who'll be running around in nothing but your nightcap."

Desire and joy spiraled through her. And his teasing! If only this moment were a solid thing that she could embrace and keep forever. His desire, his kindness: She did not know if they were enough. But she needed him now, and he was there, and that would have to do.

"I want to feel you everywhere," she whispered. "I want my world to be nothing but you."

All at once his caresses stopped and she thought: *There, now I've done it, now he will go.* But he did not move away. He drew a deep, shuddering breath and rested his lips on her shoulder.

"Joshua?"

"I'm here."

He was less leisurely this time as he tugged up her shift and she helped him pull it over her head. When he came back to her, he had removed his clothes too, and his hot skin melded to hers, the promising length of his erection pressed against her. He squeezed her inner thighs and she whimpered.

"Hold on to the wall, sweetheart," he growled in her ear. "Let me take care of you."

"You can do it here?"

"I can do anything you want. Inventive problem-solver, remember?"

Without warning, he quickened his fingers in her neediest part, and she pressed into the wall and pushed back against him and tried to stay upright as he stroked her with such relentless ferocity that she gasped and pounded at the wall with her fists. He pulled back her hips, plunged deep inside her, filled her completely, and did not let her go, and she was nothing, nothing but sensation and love and him, woman and man and pleasure and hope. When bliss rippled over her, melting her limbs, those strong arms held her up and did not let her fall. He held her up and thrust into her, demanding and powerful, dynamic and rude, and she held on, she held on, and wished she could hold on forever and never let him go.

ONCE HE HAD CARRIED Cassandra to bed, Joshua climbed in beside her, because it would be ludicrous to go when he would only leave half of himself here. She snuggled up against him, her hand spread over his chest as if to hold him down, and he surrendered to the contentment.

Then she laughed warm puffs of air and traced little swirls on his skin.

"What?" he asked.

"Lady B.'s face. Oh, I've never been so angry in my life."

"How did you know about their games in the bedroom?"

"I'm not as naive as I was."

"You never breathed a word."

"One does not speak of such things," she said primly.

"Clearly one does," he retorted. "Never tell me you reached that conclusion alone."

Caught out, she squirmed, and he savored the movement of her softness.

"I confess that Arabella and I discussed it. One time. But it's all right," she hastened to add. "We are married women."

"I swear, you make up these rules as you go along."

Her fingertips traced careless circles around his nipples. "It's over for Lord and Lady Bolderwood, I think."

"They overestimated themselves."

"And for Lucy too. Her Season is over."

"On the upside, if we can track down that Scotsman, we can pack her off to the Highlands. Shame it wasn't an American, though. Or a Brazilian. Brazil might be almost far enough."

"I don't know what to do," she said. "Where did I go so wrong?"

He pressed his lips to her hair, breathed her in. "You did what you could. She's nineteen and old enough to make her own choices. And for some reason, she chose to ruin herself."

"I suppose tomorrow we might as well head straight back to Sunne Park."

Just like that, this was their last night. He lay too still and listened to her breathe. Her fingers had stopped teasing and she was too still too.

A few more nights would not hurt. His life was in Birmingham, hers at her estate, but they could still have a few more nights.

"You're here now," he said, sounding stupid and strained. "No need to go rushing back. If you can still show your face here."

"I'll keep my eyes closed, so they don't see me."

Oh sweet mercy, the sheer delight of her!

"I heard of a physician who specializes in weaning people off drugs," he said quietly. "Perhaps you'd like to meet him."

She lifted herself up and stared at him, but the dim light masked her expression.

"To discuss your mother," he clarified.

Her fingertips pressed into his chest and she brushed her lips over his cheek. Lingered. "Thank you. Yes." She dropped back against him. "You will go back to Birmingham soon?"

"Soon. That's where my life is." He tangled his fingers in her hair, and his heart kicked up too hard. She would feel that. She would know. "We could all travel together," he suggested. "I could break my journey at Sunne Park. Meet these famous pigs you're always blathering on about."

"That would be nice."

His heart settled. The silence and the darkness mingled with her presence and bathed him in contentment. She shifted off him and turned over, and he curled himself around her.

The house had almost settled for the night; no sounds but the uneven footsteps of Isaac heading up to his room. Cassandra was soft and her breathing was even, and it was only because he thought she slept that he spoke.

"Are you with child?" he whispered into the night.

She stirred. He ought not have asked. "It's too soon to tell."

"When will you know? I want to know."

"Hush. We must be patient."

He caught himself tensing his muscles and willed them to relax. "It seems like an inefficient system to me."

"And yet babies keep on getting born."

"That's human ingenuity, that is."

"Oh, is *that* what you call it?"

He fancied she sounded strained too, but he could hardly tell what was real anymore.

"I could stay until you know, before I go home to Birmingham," he said. "If that's what you want."

She said nothing, and nothing, until her nothing grew so heavy it almost crushed him.

I want you, he wanted her to say. *I want you, with or without a child.* But that was merely his vanity talking, his selfishness. His life was in Birmingham and everything he wanted now was there. It was just that sometimes he got confused, because Cassandra felt so good, and there was no shame in caring about her, and they'd had an odd night, and everything had been topsy-turvy since she arrived.

But he had made the promise now.

"About the child, I mean," he clarified.

"Yes."

"So that's settled then."

She was still. Stiff. She did not move, but a gap opened up

between them anyway, and he did not know what he had done wrong or how he had misunderstood.

But then she spun in his arms and threw herself onto him, her hands and mouth attacking him with a startling hunger and passion. He had no time to wonder, as his desire flamed and burned everything else to ash. She climbed on top of him and he welcomed her. Urged her, breathlessly, to take him and hungrily, greedily, took as much of her as he could. He knew her passion was fired by her longing for a child, he knew that, but if he focused on the sensations, he could almost believe it was her longing for him, because if she longed hard enough, and loved him hard enough, then it would be safe to hold onto her, for they would never fall apart.

CHAPTER 27

The next day, Cassandra woke late, and alone. She stretched with contentment in the warm bed, until she remembered the detritus of her life. The thought of facing her sisters at breakfast made her feel faint, and perhaps Joshua had anticipated that, for he had sent up a pot of tea and a slice of pound cake, along with a rose, and she wondered if that was his idea or if he'd simply told the servants to send what she liked, and she decided it didn't matter, because he would leave in the end anyway.

She looked at the tea and cake, and remembered his words, and felt nauseous. *This is regret making me ill*, she thought. She had never imagined she was betraying herself, when she agreed that when it was over with Lucy and the Bolderwoods, it would be over with them. She had *agreed*. She had even *wanted* it.

His own position was plain: He would leave her as soon as she confirmed that she was with child. The child he intended to ignore. It was a victory, of sorts: At least she was getting a baby out of it. Oh, yes, a triumph indeed. She almost wished she could never get pregnant, because then he could never leave.

But it didn't work like that. One way or another, he would go. She must take what she could and be glad for it.

She was composing letters in her mind when music drifted up from the drawing room. At first, she simply sat and listened before she decided to be brave and headed downstairs.

It was a cozy scene: Lucy at the pianoforte, Isaac hovering near her, Emily flipping through a book, making idle comments, and Mr. Newell perusing a newspaper.

One by one, they became aware of her in the doorway, stopped what they were doing, and turned. They all stared at her, like actors in a play where no one knew the next line. They were all waiting. For her. Whatever happened next in her little family, it was up to her.

Cassandra turned to Lucy. The room grew so big she might as well be on a stage before a breathless audience of four thousand rather than four.

"What's that music you're playing, Lucy?" she asked, amiably. "I don't think I know that tune."

Three heads swiveled to look at Lucy, for the next line was hers.

Lucy stroked the keys and adjusted the sheet of music unnecessarily. "Isaac bought a bunch of songs yesterday, and I'm trying them out," she said. "This one is my favorite so far."

"Oh dear, Isaac." Cassandra tried to stay cheerful and amiable. "I hope they aren't, ah, sailors' songs."

He looked a bit sheepish. "They *seem* all right to me, but to be honest, I find it hard to tell. Perhaps I'll learn what's proper as I keep better company."

"Better company? You won't find that around here," Cassandra said dryly.

Inadvertently, she met Lucy's eyes, and she thought she saw the glint of a conspiratorial smile.

"Mrs. DeWitt?" Mr. Newell waved his hand in the air. "I checked all the songs, Mrs. DeWitt. I assure you they are not unsuitable."

"Mr. Newell, you are a godsend."

Another pause. A thousand different futures lay before them.

Cassandra said, "Very well, Lucy. Let's hear you sing this one."

She looked at Lucy, and Lucy looked at her, and everyone looked at both of them, and then Lucy said, "It's called 'The Skylark's Dream'."

Lucy began to play the pretty tune, and sing the pretty words, in her not-drunk, pure mezzo alto. Isaac prepared to turn the pages, the others returned to their reading, and Cassandra sat at the writing desk. No one asked what they would do next, and if they were to ask, Cassandra would say that they were staying in London a few more days, after which they would return to Sunne Park and carry on as if nothing had ever happened at all.

CASSANDRA WAS on her seventh attempt at a letter to their grandmother, when the butler announced Lady Hardbury.

Arabella swept in, elegant in a blue-and-white promenade gown. She paused and looked imperiously down her nose at them, but ruined her own effect when a wry smile curved her lips.

"What a disappointment," she drawled. "I had hoped for more blood and bruises. I was even prepared to help hide a body; Hardbury and I were placing bets on whose it would be."

"We are being very civilized," Lucy said. "We are singing nice songs and saying nice things."

"And now you can put on your nice gowns so we can take a nice stroll in Hyde Park."

"Oh, *can* we?" said Emily, throwing an imploring look at Cassandra. "It is such a lovely day for a walk."

"A walk, before all of society?" That thought made her feel faint too. "I cannot face them, Arabella. They'll give me the cut."

"Don't be absurd," Arabella said. "They'll be too busy gawking and pointing to give you the cut."

Cassandra laughed despite herself. "Was that supposed to make me feel better?"

"We can go in disguise," Emily suggested.

"Stop worrying, Cassandra, it will not be as bad as you fear," Arabella said. "You will be happy to learn that Lord and Lady Bolderwood absconded for the Continent last night, and everyone agrees they behaved disgracefully. Furthermore, you are widely liked, which makes it easier for others to overlook your transgressions. The best part—and I am exceedingly proud of this —is that Hardbury, Dammerton, Sir Gordon Bell, and I have put it about that throwing glasses is an ancient Warwickshire tradition performed for luck, and that perfectly respectable people do it all the time. And can you imagine? Most seem willing to believe it, and some even claim to have already *known* that." She shook her head slightly. "It makes me wonder what other nonsense society will believe if the right people say it. Oh, and at least six gentlemen wish to court Lucy, and they hesitate only because they are unsure whether to seek permission from the Duke of Sherbourne or Mr. DeWitt."

"Six?" Lucy said faintly. She didn't look pleased. "Oh."

"And this evening, you will accompany Hardbury and me to the theater, where you will wear your finest jewels and wink at everyone while you sip champagne."

"Champagne? After last night?" Cassandra said. "Lucy and I were *wearing* champagne."

"Exactly. It will be more entertaining that way, and you do know how I like to be entertained."

"Oh, please, can we?" Emily said again. "But I suppose you'll just say I'm too young to go out."

Again, everyone looked at Cassandra, waiting for her decision. She truly had ended up the head of their family, regardless of whether she could do it. She tried to figure out what was right, but she had no idea and was tired of doing the right thing anyway. Doing the right thing had not made anyone happy.

"You *are* too young, so we shall simply have to dress you up," Cassandra said. "If anyone asks, we shall say you are our seventeen-year-old third cousin Georgiana from York."

Emily clapped her hands with delight. "Or Rosalind. I should rather be called Rosalind. And I am a French emigrée who is spying—"

"No." Cassandra held up a silencing hand. "I am willing to bend the rules, but I draw the line at treason."

As it was Sunday afternoon, Hyde Park was at its most full. Which meant, Cassandra thought, feeling faint again, there were tens of thousands of people to stare at her. But on the upside, it also made it easier to hide.

Arabella was not wrong. No one gave Cassandra the cut, but neither did they rush to approach, waiting to see what others did first. But she did receive cordial nods to go with the speculative looks.

Lucy, Emily, and Isaac stayed apart but within sight. Lucy was also getting speculative looks, especially of the male variety, but Isaac's scowls and threatening manner with his cane kept them all at bay.

And of the ladies who did approach, not all were friendly. One lady, Mrs. Peale, a former Bolderwood supporter, was almost belligerent.

"What is this absurd story that throwing glasses is a Warwickshire tradition?" Mrs. Peale said. "I never heard of such a thing."

Arabella's look was cool. "And? The tradition has existed happily for centuries without your knowledge or approval."

"But Miss Lightwell said she wished that man to marry her!"

"Really! The depth of ignorance among the so-called educated classes," Arabella muttered. "How tedious to explain yet again." She sighed impatiently. "The young woman flings the glass and makes a wish *for the future*. But each wish will come true only if the glass is caught. Miss Lightwell wished that she would get married, not that that particular man would marry her. Good grief, Mrs. Peale, is Hampshire so dull that you have no traditions of your own? Or is it that *you* are so dull that you cannot comprehend them?"

"Of course I understand traditions, my lady," Mrs. Peale protested, fairly quivering with indignation. "But it seems to me that Miss Lightwell was...That is, she appeared..."

Arabella's eyebrows rose.

"I mean to say, she looked..."

Arabella's eyebrows climbed higher.

"Everyone thought she was..."

"Beautiful," Arabella finished. "Miss Lightwell is uncommonly beautiful. A curse of such beauty is that it inspires petty jealousy in certain women and leads to spiteful gossip. I have no time for such women. Don't you agree, Mrs. Peale?"

At which point, Mrs. Peale apparently remembered who Arabella was and realized that, upon reflection, she truly did agree.

"Terrible thing, petty jealousy, spiteful gossip," she said. "Not me! Ha ha. And such a lovely tradition, this wishing on flying glasses. Perhaps my Frances can do that at her come-out."

Arabella widened her eyes. "That would be *marvelous*."

Somehow, Cassandra managed not to speak until she was sure they were out of earshot. "Arabella, you are wicked. You are deliberately distorting the truth."

Amusement lit Arabella's face. "Hardbury has bought me a publishing house. He says I must not use it for mischief, but it is so tempting to fill volumes with arrant nonsense and see how much people believe." She pursed her lips thoughtfully. "I don't see why that's wrong. Men have been doing that for centuries, the only difference being that they won't acknowledge that it's nonsense."

"The idea of you owning a publishing house is terrifying."

"Isn't it, though?" Arabella smiled with satisfaction. "What do you mean to do about Lucy? Give her a thousand pounds and put her on a boat to Brazil?"

"As tempting as that is, I agree with Joshua that she must make her own decisions. I still do not understand what she wants, or why she is determined to ruin herself, but all we can do is try to stop her from putting herself in any real danger. For now, I suppose she'll return to Sunne Park with Emily and me."

"And Mr. DeWitt?"

"Will return to his life in Birmingham."

She heard her own clipped tone and avoided Arabella's look.

"One of the many things people are saying," Arabella said after a lengthy pause, "is that Mr. and Mrs. DeWitt are devoted to each other."

"Clearly, that is not so," Cassandra said briskly. "Or if it is, we are about to be devoted to each other from a distance." She stopped short, her legs suddenly not working any more, her lungs suddenly short of air. "It is as though...My whole life was a simple five-note tune and he has turned it into a symphony. This is what knowing him has done to me, and now I cannot imagine experiencing the world any other way. And to think…" She shook her head bitterly at the fine people swirling around them. "A few weeks ago, we strolled in this park and I wished I could be married to any of these other gentlemen and now—I would rather have no one if I cannot have him, while he counts the days till we part."

"He cares about you, Cassandra." Arabella placed a hand on her arm. "No one who saw you together last night could doubt it."

"I know that he cares, but not only for me," she said quietly. "He cares for everyone and everything. He cares so much that he hurts himself, and so he denies that he cares, and gets himself into such a tangle over it! If I were to tell him I love him and want him to stay, he'll say it's because I want a baby or because I'm doing my duty. He insists on being alone, and why should he be alone when I am here to love him?"

Arabella sighed. "For a man who claims to love honesty, he tells himself a lot of lies."

"Maybe they're not all lies. He can care about me, and still prefer to live separately, because there are so many other things he cares about more." She stared at the brown waters of the Serpentine. "I was lonely before and I thought that was awful. But to be with him and yet not be with him—this is the loneliest, most awful thing in the world."

A light breeze rippled the surface of the water. A duck glided past, followed by a line of ducklings. Before Cassandra could count them, they had disappeared into the reeds.

"I wish I had answers," Arabella said. "But my own experience has shown me that the most important things in life cannot be taught; we must learn them on our own."

"Sometimes I think there are the right words, if only I could find them. To prove to him that if we share pain, it gets smaller, and if we share joy, it gets bigger. But he doesn't want to know. He's going to leave me, Arabella. He's going to leave me and I don't know how to stop him."

CASSANDRA COULD HAVE EASILY INDULGED her misery longer, but Arabella gently reminded her that London was watching, so she put away her feelings and sealed them with a smile.

A quick look confirmed that Lucy still trailed behind, guarded by Isaac and Emily, and, marvel of marvels, she had not yet incited a single riot, duel, or brawl.

Another look revealed the Duke and Duchess of Sherbourne, strolling arm in arm, the duke telling the world that he stood by his wife and cared nothing for vicious rumors started by an unpleasant woman who had been forced to flee.

In tacit agreement, Cassandra and Arabella drifted closer, feigning unawareness, hoping to be seen. A delicate dance: Cassandra could not approach the duchess, but must hope that the duchess approached her.

The alternative was the cut direct, which would ruin her forever.

The duchess saw Cassandra. Looked right at her. Met her eyes. Held them.

Cassandra waited, like a prisoner awaiting a verdict.

Then the duchess said a word to her husband, who followed her gaze, nodded graciously at Cassandra, and released his wife's arm. She took a few steps toward Cassandra and stopped. Cassandra left Arabella and closed the gap, so they met each other like duelists, their seconds watching on.

"You are looking well rested, Cassandra, my dear."

"The spring air agrees with you, Grandmother."

"It is beneficial to one's health to take a turn."

"I daresay that is what keeps you looking young."

In fact, her grandmother looked tired. Cassandra knew she did too. But that was not the point.

"I must apologize," Cassandra said. "I have struggled all morning to find the words. My sister and I..."

The duchess's mouth tightened. She looked into the distance. "I must apologize too," she said, with quiet dignity. "I should never have allowed Lord and Lady Bolderwood to attend the ball and not only because...Well, you know why. But you spoke in my defense anyway. That was...admirable and gracious. And I...I thank you."

The duchess was proud. Cassandra knew the words had cost her.

"We are family," Cassandra said.

"Yes."

Her grandmother sighed. She glanced at her husband, who was in conversation with the Duke of Dammerton, and looked back at Cassandra.

"Sherbourne and I have been married for more than forty years," she said. "That is highly unusual, and I consider myself blessed. Last night, my husband told me that he feels the same. You young people cannot imagine what it means to have shared a life as we have. One can never understand the workings of another's marriage; at times, one cannot even understand the workings of one's own." She began to walk, and Cassandra fell into step beside her. "Sherbourne says that we must not turn our backs on you, not when you stood by me. Last night demonstrates that we have a duty to step in as grandparents, as clearly you are not coping. He says that Lucy needs guidance and a firm hand, which I can provide better than you can. I cannot take her now, you understand, but perhaps she can stay with us in the autumn, when I do not have as many obligations."

"Thank you, Grandmother. Lucy is not bad or unkind, she simply…" What? The truth was, Cassandra had no idea what went on in Lucy's mind.

"My Susan was lively too," Her Grace said. "She was only sixteen when she ran away with Treyford. It was not a bad match but I…I told her I wanted nothing more to do with her, and so she never came back to tell me she was alive. And your father too…" She breathed in sharply through her nose. "Charles and I often argued, for he never wanted my counsel. Perhaps that is one of life's tragedies: We are all doomed to make mistakes, regardless of the advice we receive, and we are all doomed to watch those we love ignore our advice in turn. I have regrets, Cassandra. One cannot reach my age without them. But life goes on, and we must carry on too."

"And your…interests, Grandmother?"

Her look was sharp. "Sherbourne permits me to continue my work with Sir Arthur, if that is your meaning."

"Lady Hardbury has acquired an interest in a publishing house," Cassandra said. "Just now, she was telling me of her aspiration to publish Sir Arthur's theories about his big old rocks, I mean, his belief that classical temples and statues were once painted."

It was a rotten fib, of course, but only what Arabella deserved.

A gleam lit the duchess's eye. "That would be greatly in the public interest. I shall mention it to Sir Arthur. I have some ideas for how he might best organize his thoughts." Then, with a quick, pleasant smile, she was detaching herself and nodding her farewell. "Anyway, Cassandra, my dear, don't let me keep you. I have a very full schedule, and I daresay you do too. I shall write you about the girl."

No sooner were their grandparents out of earshot, than Lucy bounded over.

"Well?" Lucy demanded. "Am I to be transported to Botany Bay?"

"We did consider it," Cassandra replied. "But as Governor Macquarie has only recently restored order to the colony, we hesitate to incite another rebellion by sending you. She may invite you somewhere in the autumn, and for now we must call this London trip a failure, for we did not get you a husband."

"We got you one, though."

For the briefest moment, Cassandra entertained the possibility that Lucy had devised this whole drama for the sole purpose of bringing Cassandra and Joshua together—and then dismissed it. Lucy lived from moment to moment, along with whatever demon was driving her, and knew little of strategy.

Besides, if that were her plan, she had failed as miserably as Cassandra had.

"I like Joshua," Lucy went on. "So does Emily. Will he live with us at Sunne Park?"

"He will return to his life in Birmingham."

Lucy's mouth fell open in a melodramatic show of shock. "Mother Cassandra! Can you not do anything right?"

She flounced back to Isaac and Emily, leaving Cassandra alone to sigh.

"Apparently not," she said to no one.

Then, finally taking her grandmother's advice, she smiled and carried on.

CHAPTER 28

It was nearly two weeks before Joshua and Cassandra packed her sisters and cat into a carriage and, accompanied by Isaac, servants, and the contents of half the shops in London, started on the journey home.

During those two weeks, they shied away from society, leaving the gossips unsatisfied and Lucy's would-be suitors heartbroken. Instead, they visited every place in London worth visiting and, Joshua had been pleased to note, Cassandra also insisted that her sisters spend time at orphanages, under instruction from Miss Sampson.

Despite his ongoing neglect of business, it struck Joshua that he ought to accompany them around town, and not only because he felt odd if Cassandra was not near.

"It would be irresponsible not to come with you," he said. "Let Lucy run around London unattended and next thing we know, there'll be another Great Fire or Revolution."

Cassandra and Joshua dined with the physician who offered advice for helping Lady Charles, and with another physician who proposed the new and disparaged theory that disease was carried by water and that cleaner water in cities could save lives, a notion that Joshua found fascinating.

They also joined Das and his wife for an enjoyable dinner, and when Cassandra referred to the two men as friends, rather than as employer and employee, Joshua found no reason to object. After that, Das returned to headquarters to temporarily take over the reins of the business, and perhaps, Joshua suggested in passing, Das might devise new job titles for the secretaries, as *someone* had declared the existing titles to be "stupid." Newell rejoined his family in Birmingham, from where he continued his hunt for a governess.

And on a sunny afternoon in May, the convoy of carriages trundled through the gates to Sunne Park.

Lord Charles had always spoken of his estate with pride and love, as did Cassandra, and when the carriage swung around the drive, with the afternoon sunlight falling on the sprawling red-brick manse, Joshua understood.

"Well?" Cassandra said, hugging his arm after he helped her down from the carriage. "Is it not splendid?"

Joshua would not call it "splendid" so much as "jumbled." The house boasted gables of various shapes and roofs of various pitches, with a profusion of pepper-pot chimneys and mullioned windows. Surrounding it were a moat—a moat!—and a line of fruit trees dressed in a riot of pink and white blossoms.

It was full of character and life and, despite its size, had an air of welcome. One could be lulled into thinking of a place like this as home. The warm spring air washed over him and filled him with something suspiciously like hope.

Nonsense. Nothing more than the effect of the sunlight, too much fresh air in his lungs, that sort of thing. The day was too bright, and the fragrant country air hummed with life, and such things did tend to give places a dreamy feel.

And he did have a tendency to get confused sometimes, these days.

Odd to think that legally, he owned this house, when he had not earned it. It was a gift bestowed upon him, along with his wife, by a man who hoped to make them happy when his own hope of happiness was gone. *Lord Charles, you fool,* he thought. *It was a valiant attempt, but you had it wrong. This is not my house, and I am not that man.*

The fact was, this was all very pleasant and idyllic, but none of it would last. He had forged a life in Birmingham, he had forged *himself* in Birmingham. What he had built there was who he was and that, at least, could never be taken from him. That, at least, could never fall apart.

Cassandra was looking at him expectantly, wanting him to be pleased, and he was pleased. Ridiculously so. But that didn't feel real either.

"It has a moat!" he said. "When are you expecting the invading hordes?"

She gave him a pointed look. "Today, apparently."

"Mrs. DeWitt! Did you just call me an invading horde?"

She laughed and led him over the bridge, her face bright with excitement.

"It has more to do with drainage than defense," she said. "Newer places have great ornamental lakes instead. But it is well stocked, if you like fishing, and I do like having somewhere to throw Lucy."

At the stone archway marking the entrance, Joshua paused to read the inscription: The year 1533 and the words "*The sunne is new each day.*"

"That's from Heraclitus," Cassandra said.

The name stirred a memory from schoolbooks at Eton. One of those Greek fellows, the sort who had nothing to do all day but sit around and state the bleeding obvious, for no apparent purpose other than the torture of English schoolboys two thousand years later.

"Fellow couldn't spell 'sun'," he said. "It's inefficient, to have all those extra letters."

"It was built in Tudor times. They didn't have spelling back then. Come on."

He allowed himself to be led inside, to greet the butler and housekeeper, the sense of unreality growing stronger as his boot heels rang out on the flagstones. He half-listened to Cassandra and Mrs. Greenway discuss Lady Charles and housekeeping matters, as he let his eyes bounce over the paintings and paneling to the staircase with its glossy bannister.

Bannister. Children. Cassandra saying: *I can imagine them now, our children, running through Sunne Park, sliding down the bannisters, dashing through the roses.* Dark-haired, bright-eyed children, and he could imagine them now too. He blinked away the images and took to making inane comments to keep them at bay, as she led him through the great hall, a formal dining room, a stylish drawing room, and into a large, book-lined room.

He should not have come. He should never, ever have come.

"This is Papa's study," Cassandra said.

Yet it had the air of a room in use.

"Your *father's* study?"

"I've been using it. That is, it was convenient. When I started looking after the estate. But it's yours, really. I mean, it's your house. And we must discuss the bedrooms. Mama still uses the suite connected to the master suite, so you—"

"Mercy, no. I cannot sleep connected to her. Where do you sleep?"

"In the room I always used. If you don't want Papa's room, where...?"

"You choose. I won't be here long before I go to Birmingham."

"Of course." They stood looking at the study and not at each other. "How long do you think you'll stay?" she finally asked, trailing a finger down the doorjamb.

Ah, he knew that question. When he showed up at a gentleman's country house, his host's wife would ask it, and later he'd hear them arguing. Polite-speak for "I don't want you here." He never minded. He always had somewhere else to be anyway.

But this was Cassandra, and she did not seem averse to having him around. Maybe she actually meant "I want you to stay," or maybe she merely needed to know his plans so she could manage the housekeeping, and how did it happen that they spoke daily and he still didn't know what she was saying and still didn't know how to ask?

It was a simple enough question. He wasn't usually too stupid to answer simple questions but all he managed was silence.

So she answered it for him. "You said that you would stay until I...conceived. That was the agreement."

"Right. Well. If that was the agreement." It came out brusquely, loudly, despite the wood paneling and thick carpets. "Still too soon to know?"

"Yes."

"Right. Well. What else have you to show me?"

She guided him through the rest of the house, but she skipped the upper floors, and since upper floors things like nurseries and schoolrooms, he was happy with the omission.

WHEN THE TOUR of the house was done, Cassandra offered to show him the garden.

"I mean, not all of it today," she added hastily. "But perhaps you'd like to see my private garden..."

Joshua was about to make a bawdy joke about her private garden, but she looked very shy all of a sudden, and so instead he said, "Why not?"

Still looking shy, she rushed him through the main flower garden without comment, even though the crowded beds were spectacular to his city eyes. They bloomed in a profusion of colors, and chattered and buzzed with bees, butterflies, and birds.

The breeze ruffled his hair and his shirt—he had, of course, shucked off his coat and cravat, enjoying Cassandra's teasing about his difficulty in keeping his clothes on—and he sneezed only three or four times.

"This is all your doing?" he asked.

"It was begun more than a century ago," she said. "I merely add to it, and I have a small army of gardeners to follow my every command. Oh, look, the Goat's Beard is in bloom!"

"The what?"

She pointed out a purple flower with long, spiky petals. "Goat's Beard."

"What kind of name for a flower is that?"

"A perfectly good name," she said stoutly, walking on. "Lots of flowers have names like that. There is Goosefoot, Fat Hen, Busy Lizzie. Ah, Devil's Shoestring, Sneezewort, Nipplewort—"

He burst out laughing. "You're just making these up now."

But she wasn't laughing. She led him around a hedge and into a secluded garden the size of a spacious parlor, and she stood nervously with her fingers tangled together.

This mattered, he realized. So he strolled into the middle and looked around properly. The garden was hidden by high hedges, and a stone path wound through islands of colorful flowerbeds to a small folly with an embroidered seat. Another path led to a fountain: It featured a statue of a curvy, mostly naked woman, standing in a large shell and pouring water from a jug.

"I mean," she rushed on, "it's only a little garden and it's not much compared to the rest, but..."

"How long have you had it?"

"Mama gave us all a garden plot when we were children, but I was the only one who took to it," she said. "So over time I annexed them all and turned it into my private garden. I started when I was about ten, I think, and I kept adding to it."

He wandered along the path, letting his hand trail over the flowers as he passed, soaking up the chatter of the birds and the gurgling of the fountain. The beds were generously planted, and carefully nurtured, and were so full of variety and color and life that he could look at them all day. The hedges kept out the world, even kept out time, and teased him with the idea that they were alone in the world.

"Is this meant to be you?" he asked, studying the statue. "She's rather indecent, don't you think?"

She whacked his belly. "Stop being puerile. She's lovely." A distant look entered her eyes as she wiggled her fingers under the flow of the water. "She's inspired by Arethusa, the waterer. Mama bought it for me in Leamington Spa. I complained that I never got any attention, and so Mama took me on a special trip, just her and me, and when she bought this, she told me that love was like an endless spring, where the water flowed and flowed and flowed. It will never run out, she said, and no matter how much love you need, there will always be more."

Suddenly, Joshua understood.

Cassandra's sisters were so beautiful and lively that she felt plain and dull in comparison, for all that she was pretty and witty and well-liked. So she had carved out her own space in the garden, where she did not have to compete. Even now, when she was de facto head of the household, she did not claim what was hers. Here, and here alone, she felt fully herself.

The dream-like sensation faded. His thoughts were as sharp and clear as ever, and he was fiercely, ferociously, glad he had come.

"Do you like it?" she asked shyly.

He pulled her into his arms. "Very much. It is just like you."

"And the house? Do you like your house?"

He ignored the "your," looking at the garden with new eyes. "I suppose we must see someone in their own home to understand them," he said.

"Perhaps if I saw your home in Birmingham, I'd understand you. Your devotion to your work, your love of metal."

She would not see a home. She would see an empty house, the place where he slept and changed his clothes. His real home was the space in his head where he kept his work, the one thing no one could ever take from him.

She had shown him an important piece of her; he owed her something in return.

"I never had a particular love of metal," he said. "That is simply where I landed. But I came to admire the alchemy of the blacksmith, the way a man can bend iron to his will. With heat and pressure, one can transform the very nature of things. A lump of ore or a piece of scrap can be forged into something powerful or useful or beautiful. Something strong, solid, lasting. I like the idea of that."

"And that is Birmingham," she said.

"Yes."

She pulled away from him and went into the folly and leaned back on the seat. She took off her bonnet and placed it beside her, then closed her eyes and turned up her face. The afternoon light caressed her soft complexion and the hint of red in her hair, and he wished he could hold the sight forever.

Then she opened her eyes and smiled, and he joined her on the seat.

"It's *your* house," he said.

"It's yours."

"Forget what the law says. You *earned* this house." Sudden fury at her family coursed through him. "You love it. You run it. You make it work. Your family are too stupid to see it, but they need you. And you do not see it either. Your sisters followed you to London."

"They went to London to be naughty."

"No. They went because they do not know how to live without you. You are at the center of this family. You hold them together. You are the head of this family *and* its heart, and this house is *yours*. Claim it. Stop giving up your space. Fight for what is yours. Kick your mother out of that room and claim that study as your own."

She stared at him, eyes startled, lost and searching. She looked distressed, and he never meant to cause her distress. He brushed his hand over her cheek and had barely said her name when she cried, "Kiss me."

He kissed her. Sweetly and sensuously, they explored each other, and yes, she still tasted like flowers, but he could not taste her well enough like that, so he tugged at her greedily. She clambered astride him and proceeded to twist his hair and rain soft kisses over his face and throat. He would never know which of them it was who hoisted up her skirts and opened his falls, but soon he was inside her again. The birds chattered, the fountain flowed, his wife tugged his bottom lip between her teeth, and then said, "I bet you can't do this in Birmingham."

He had no breath to laugh, still less to talk, so he took his breath from her, and drove deeper inside her as she fell harder on him, until she sank her teeth into his shoulder, and they came.

Afterward, he felt the moment when her awareness returned, for she shifted and buried her face in his neck.

"I'm sorry," she said. "I don't know what came over me."

"It's all the birds and the bees. Don't apologize to me. I enjoy a good ravishing in the garden."

"I used to be so well behaved and now, I...It's your fault."

He grinned. "And I am very proud of myself."

Even after they tidied themselves up, he felt lazily warm and content, so he encouraged her to lie back against him and he closed his eyes.

"We should go," she said. She didn't move. "We have things to do."

"Not yet. It's still warm enough and it's peaceful here with you. Let's stay a little bit longer."

He did have things to do. Lots. But the sun was warm, and the bees were buzzing, and her weight was comforting, and his limbs and eyes were heavy. He was suddenly more weary than he had ever been in his life, and it wouldn't do any harm, if for a moment, for the first time in fourteen years, he stopped and took a rest.

CHAPTER 29

For a man who claimed to have a lot of work, Cassandra thought several times over the following days, Joshua did not seem to do much, although he still bounded about with more than the usual amount of energy, firing off ideas and getting excited at the slightest thing. Every day he had some part of the household in an uproar, and they all adored him anyway.

He barged into the dairy and frightened the dairy maids, until they realized he simply wanted to know what they were doing and how it all worked, this business of turning milk into butter and cheese. On laundry day, too, he interrogated the laundry maids; the poor things blushed and giggled as they stammered out answers, for the whole time they were holding his drawers. He spent a day fascinated by the pigs, strode out to meet tenants, quizzing them until they were dizzy, and hatched a scheme with Mr. Ridley at End Farm to rebuild a rickety bridge using a new design. He even invaded Mama's distillery and delighted her by rating her wines. Messengers and letters came from Birmingham every day, and Mr. Das sent a new secretary too, but Joshua grumbled that he could not concentrate, though Cassandra didn't know what he meant, for surely he was seeking the distractions; the distractions did not seek him.

Days passed. One week. Two. He joined the family for dinner, and after dinner too, and passed each night with her. They made love and chatted quietly, and she went to sleep with hope in her heart.

Only to wake up alone.

The sunne is new each day: Oh, how those words mocked her! She used to consider the inscription to be a message of optimism —a reminder that at any moment one could start anew—but now she understood it as a message in futility. As each day stretched on, her husband drew closer, yet when the new sun came, it started all over again, and she was no closer to keeping him than she had been the day before.

Because he was always leaving.

When she dared to comment that he worked less than before, he waved a hand and said, "Das is coping. I'll get back to it in Birmingham." When she mentioned the midsummer festival, he said, "Yes, but by then I'll be back in Birmingham." And when she suggested he get a pair of dogs to accompany him on his long walks, he looked interested and then said, "What's the point? I can't take them with me to Birmingham."

Birmingham, Birmingham, Birmingham. How she hated it, that noisy, dirty, fast-paced city that called to her husband. She hated it even though she understood now: Birmingham was where he had forged his life and himself. It was where he had transformed himself from an unwanted illegitimate boy to a wealthy, powerful industrialist. To become a country gentleman would be a betrayal of himself. Birmingham was not a place: It was his identity, his heart and mind.

Trying to make him stay with her would be like trying to stop the sun from rising.

And so she lied to him.

She said nothing about her missing monthly courses, or the nausea, fatigue, and sore breasts, and he did not seem to notice. She told herself it was not a lie, not really: It *was* too soon to be sure. Even after she spoke of it to Mama and to the midwife and to a friend, she did not mention it to him. To think she had once believed that if she had a child, she could dispense with the husband! Now guilt mixed with dread, and her tongue was tied, for as soon as she uttered the words, he would leap to his feet and say, "Excellent. My work here is done."

Yet he had made her a promise, and she had to tell him. How cruel this was: To have the child she longed for meant losing the husband she loved. She had never felt so torn in her life.

But maybe, just maybe, if she asked him to stay with her, maybe, just maybe, he would. Maybe this child would hold them together.

If we have a child, it is your child, not mine. I want nothing to do with any of it.

Or maybe not.

In her darker moments, she thought it would be better once he was gone. At least then she would be free of this dread, which was worse than nausea and fatigue, for the dread fought with hope and their tussles clawed at her. At least then her heart would be broken all at once, rather than breaking a little more each day.

ON A SUNNY MORNING, nearly a week after her conversation with the midwife, Cassandra was sitting in the bay window of her ground-floor parlor, sewing her secret and arguing with herself, when she glanced up to see Joshua striding through the garden toward her window, his coat hooked over one shoulder.

Every part of her stilled, except her pounding heart and shaking hands. *Today*, she resolved. *Today*.

Of course, she had made that resolution every morning for several days, and each evening when she saw him, the words did not come.

But I must, she thought, her eyes eating up the sight of him, fearful it would be the last. *If I cannot hold him, then I shall hold this*: His face tilted up to the sun, a smile playing over his lips, a whirlwind of energy as he moved in easy, powerful strides.

Suddenly, she couldn't bear it, but before she could hide, he spotted her sitting at the huge, open window, merely feet above him.

"Ah, fair princess!" he called, stopping and doffing his hat. "Are you occupied?"

"Nothing important."

Clumsily, she shoved her sewing into her workbasket and forced a smile.

"Stay there, I'll come in," he said, turning away.

"I don't see why you should waste time going around to the door," she called back. "It would be more efficient simply to climb through the window."

He grinned. This might be the last time she saw him grin. "Mrs. DeWitt, you are a genius."

In a single bound, he leaped onto the sill, and balanced there, framed by daylight. An image of virility and strength to hold onto, to remember once he was gone.

"Oh my," she said.

"Did I impress you? Do say I impressed you. I adore impressing you."

"I am immensely impressed."

She slid off the window seat, her mind on her workbasket and the papers on the table, watching as he leaped down and tossed his coat onto a chair.

"I have had the most exciting conversation with Mr. Ridley," he said, spinning back to face her. "Together, we have been utterly brilliant. Our bridge is going to be stronger and more durable than any bridge in the history of Warwickshire. Oh, and I met Mrs. King—do you know her?"

"She's the midwife."

"That's the one. I told her about that chap we met in London who thinks disease is carried by water and she says it sounds right to her, whatever the fancy doctors say. Indeed, she says she's sick of fancy doctors telling her about things they know nothing about, like women's bodies—I tell you, I blushed so hard."

"You did nothing of the sort."

"So I think I should invite this doctor down and see what he needs, because if he's right, we could save all those people's lives. What do you think?"

He whirled her around in a mad, improvised waltz. She twined her arms around his neck and held on tight. Maybe before she told him, they could make love one more time. One last time.

"I think you make the world a better place," she said, and kissed him.

It was only meant to be a simple kiss but he turned it into something longer, and when they broke it off, she was breathless. He smiled against her lips.

"I like it when you kiss me first," he said.

"I like it when you leap through windows."

"I'd leap through any window in the world if it got me one of your kisses."

Then she was smiling too. He *did* care for her. She *was* important to him. He enjoyed himself here. He had sought her out. He was learning to see Sunne Park as his home, and her as his wife.

She was worrying unnecessarily. Everything was going to be all right.

"Do you remember that first day we met—I mean, that day in Hyde Park," Cassandra said. "Do you know what I thought of you?"

"That I was unutterably rude and needed to shave?"

"That too. But you had so much energy, I imagined you had been hit by lightning and the lightning was still bouncing around inside you. And the best part is that when I am with you, that lightning slides inside me too."

He stilled, for too many beats of her racing heart, and then he cupped her bottom and pulled her against him. "Well, Cassandra, if you want me inside you..."

"Oh! You!"

He feigned innocence. "What? Why do I get the blame when you're the one saying shocking things?"

His touch and teasing ignited her desire, the potency surprising her given that she was already with child. Yet that desire was maddening too, because she knew what he was doing: He was using it to hide.

He was already running away.

"I have something to show you," she whispered, reluctantly dragging herself from his arms.

"Mrs. DeWitt! And us in broad daylight too."

"Hush!"

She led him to the table, where she had left the house plans. Her hands were clumsy as she smoothed them out, and her mouth was dry and confused. To think that when they first met, she did not care what he thought and said whatever she pleased!

Somehow, she untangled her tongue to speak.

"I am proposing a few changes to the house to reflect the changes to the family." She pointed with one finger and hoped he did not notice it shaking. "This wing here; we don't use it much. I thought to convert a few of the rooms into an apartment for Mama. It is near the kitchen garden and her distillery, so she can grow herbs and have a patch of garden all of her own. We have no dower house, but this way she can have her own privacy and space, but also be part of us."

He said nothing, studying the paper, his lips pursed in thought.

"And here, well, I'm doing less with the estate now, so Papa's study—I mean, the main study—it's not being used, I mean, except...So..."

No need to say it. He could read the label she had written: "Mr. DeWitt's study," with the room next to it designated "Mrs. DeWitt's workroom," and she liked the idea that they would be working side by side.

She glanced at him.

He said nothing.

She slid away the top page to reveal the plans for the bedchambers on the first floor.

"With Mama in her own apartments, we can move into the main suites."

She smoothed her hand over the plans: "Mr. DeWitt's bedchamber," and, next to it, "Mrs. DeWitt's bedchamber." Not that they ever slept apart now; he used his own room for washing and dressing only. She curled her fingers into her skirts. Still he said nothing. He had gone horribly still.

"Of course, I shall redecorate them extensively, to make them our own, so you must let me know what colors you prefer, or let me choose and..."

Her words trailed away as he touched a finger to the ink.

"Why?" he said, so quietly she barely heard. "Why did you do this?"

She could not understand his question, and his profile gave no clues. "You said I should claim the space, so this is what I'm doing. But our marriage gave you this house too, whatever you say, and you should feel comfortable. "

"Ever the dutiful wife."

"I'm trying to do what's right."

And we are right, she wanted to scream. *We are right. Together, here or Birmingham or anywhere, I'm stronger and happier for knowing you, you're calmer and happier for knowing me.*

And then she recalled his words in London, when he said he wanted her to be honest, not dutiful and polite. Honest was hard, because if he didn't like her honesty, she had nowhere to hide.

Besides, she was nursing a much bigger lie than this.

She waited, hoping that he would burst out with something like "No, this is how I want it" or "Yes, that'll work," and Birmingham would be gone.

Instead, he said nothing. He picked up the pages and leaned back against the table, staring at them, although she did not know what he saw.

"I want you here," she said unsteadily, to his profile. "I know your life is in Birmingham, and I'll go there with you happily if you want. But this is your home too."

Every inch of him was as taut as a rope about to snap. She had no breath and she had no skin and she still had to tell him the rest.

But then he shuffled to the third page. The one she hadn't been brave enough to reveal: the upper floors, with the nursery and schoolroom. And the little sketches of animals and flowers drawn by her friend and neighbor Juno Bell, as ideas for painting the walls.

He lowered the plans and stared across the room, at nothing, perhaps, or at the window through which he had leaped. He understood; of course he did.

She waited, her hands clammy, her mouth dry.

His brows drew into a frown, and she realized his gaze had sharpened on something: her workbasket, with its jumble of fabric. His eyes hardened. Whatever he was feeling, it was not joy.

It is your child, not mine, he had said. *I want nothing to do with it.*

Her heart fell and shattered.

He had seen, he had understood, and now he would leave.

CHAPTER 30

J oshua had been staring unseeingly ahead for what seemed like hours until he realized what he was staring at. The shadows in the folds of the white fabric in Cassandra's workbasket began to form themselves into shapes. Shapes that danced before his eyes, like the little animals she meant to have painted on the nursery walls.

But how like him, these days, to look at something and not see it. How adept he had become at not noticing everything beneath his nose.

He put aside the pages, the plans she had made to bring him into her house. Perhaps she wanted a father for her child. Perhaps she was merely doing what she believed was right. It was so appealing, but it wasn't real. His real life was in Birmingham.

The floor was as unsteady as a ship in a storm as he crossed to that workbasket, with its taunting pieces of fabric. He pulled out the first piece and almost laughed at himself. It was merely her nightcap, and the jokes they had enjoyed, oh, how he would tease her and—

It was a nightcap, but it was not hers. He made a fist with one hand and settled the little bonnet on it. Pins and needles poked out here and there, for she had not finished making it. It would not take her long; the bonnet was very small.

"It's too small for you," he said, and wondered when he had become so stupid. All that country air and domestic bliss had addled his brain. There was comfort in being obtuse, freedom from making decisions.

She didn't respond, though he could feel her hovering somewhere behind him. Her every move stirred the air, it was so still and thick and warm.

He laid the little bonnet on the window seat and tied its little yellow ribbons in a bow. Samuel had had one just like it, covering the dark fuzz on his pink head. The ruffles used to wobble furiously when he screwed up his face and cried.

Joshua reached into the workbasket again. Another piece of fabric. Also unfinished. A little white dress or petticoat or whatever it was called. Samuel had worn these too, his chubby baby legs kicking around in them. Until the day when he was four, and Rachel had taken him out of skirts and put him in breeches for the first time. How proud of himself he had been, running and stomping and jumping, as if discovering his legs anew.

This, too, Joshua laid out on the seat, below the bonnet. This, too, was not finished: She was embroidering it with masses of little flowers. *Waste of time, the baby won't care*, he wanted to tell her. But he knew why she did it: She was impatient too, and this eased the waiting. *The baby will only break your heart*, he wanted to say, but she wouldn't listen to him. She was as unwilling to listen as he was to see.

And back into the basket, wool this time: another bonnet, half knitted. He did some arithmetic—he learned enough from Rachel to perform that count—and calculated that the baby would be born in winter, so yes, they needed a warm hat. And warm, woolen stockings, their ends still hooked around needles. Tiny little stockings, to warm those precious little legs. Only partly made, like the baby.

He arranged them below the dress.

A baby. A half-made shadow baby.

This is what she wanted to tell him, although behind his willful stupidity, he already knew. He could have looked at a calendar and counted the days. He could have wondered why in the past month she had never needed a few nights alone. Or why she rested most afternoons now, when she never had in London. Or why he saw her eating at odd hours and sometimes not eating at all. He could have wondered any of those things, but he had not, because he had not wanted to know. He who wanted to know everything did not want to know this.

"I thought Charles for a boy," she said, in a voice too thin to be hers. "Maybe Charlotte for a girl, or something else. If you agree."

"So you are sure?"

"It is still early but the signs are there and—"

"Are you sure or are you not sure?" His voice sounded harsh to his own ears.

"I'm sure," she said in half a voice. She swallowed and coughed and tried again. "I'm sure."

This was his. It could be. All of it. This lovely woman, who made his heart swell and brought him peace. This baby. This house. This family. All of it—laid out for him on a silver platter. His to have, his to hold, his to love, his to lose.

All he had to do was take it. Turn around, take three steps, pull her into his arms, and say yes.

He didn't move.

"You got what you wanted," he said.

"I want a husband." Her voice was harder than usual, and

sharp and trembling. He turned to face her. He could be that husband. He could stay. He simply had to pull her into his arms and say yes. "A whole one. Not one who is always leaving me."

But his feet didn't move. His arms didn't move. He opened his mouth to say, "I am your husband," but what came out was, "I need to go to Birmingham."

And he saw it then: He saw the moment he lost her.

Loving, warm, welcoming, steadfast Cassandra, who had taught him how to use his heart again, who had brought joy to his days and hope to his plans: She turned on him before his very eyes. Withdrew inside herself, pulled away.

She had felt him like lightning. He had felt her like a fire in winter.

And now her warm welcome was gone.

"Then go," she said. "Go and stay gone. I'm not keeping you here."

She pushed past him, gathered up the shadow baby, her movements rough and awkward as she shoved the fabric back into the basket. And when she straightened and looked at him, a stranger lay behind those changeable eyes.

"You're right: You aren't my husband. We just happen to be married. So if you're going to leave, you may as well leave now. You've had one foot out the door since you arrived anyway."

She was sending him away. Of course she was. She had never needed him; she had only wanted a child. Those plans—yes, the dutiful wife. What a hypocrite she was: accusing him of always leaving her, when she had been leaving him too. Once the baby came, she would have no time for him and whatever they had would have crumbled. She didn't mean to be cruel, but she had never truly loved him. It was his own fault, for being so hard to love.

No matter. They had what they wanted. This is what they had

agreed. Separate lives: him with his work in Birmingham, her with her baby. This had been nothing but a foolish interlude. Real life called. Five minutes in his factory, in the life he had forged from nothing, and he'd know himself again and forget this nonsense.

"If you have no further need for me, then, madam," he said.

"What I need from you is something you cannot give. Go. Go to your home in Birmingham."

She turned away, her shoulders straight and cold. He could go to her, put his arms around her, join them again as they were meant to be joined.

But he didn't.

He picked up his coat and went. He went and went and kept on going until he reached his house in Birmingham.

THE HOUSEKEEPER LOOKED PUT out when Joshua came barreling into his house without warning, and he suspected it had something to do with the dust sheets over the furniture and the piles of clutter throughout the main rooms.

"We didn't realize you'd be here, Mr. DeWitt," Mrs. White said. "We pulled everything out of storage to clean and make sure there was no damage. There were rats, you see. All gone now—the rat catcher came—but I thought it best to do a right thorough spring clean anyway."

Rats. Worse than sisters, were rats.

Go and stay gone. I'm not keeping you here.

"Carry on," he said. "Get my rooms ready and put out a meal. I want to be alone tonight."

The housekeeper looked around helplessly, more embarrassed than the clutter merited. A closer look revealed why.

These were not Joshua's things.

He had had them take away all Rachel's and Samuel's clothes, her books, his toys, but here were the things he had kept. Rachel's blasted clock collection, a dozen of the things, mercifully silent. He had never understood her fascination with clocks, the way they ticked ticked ticked all the time. And there was the horrid tiger-skin rug. Blazes knew why he had kept that.

The clutter took up too much space and made him fidget.

You aren't my husband. We just happen to be married.

"Will you be traveling again soon, sir?" Mrs. White asked. "We've not got a full staff on, but I can have them back here by morning."

He waved a hand, seeing not clocks and clutter but a private garden, alive with flowers and bees, with a fountain and a woman.

What I need from you is something you cannot give. Go. Go to your home in Birmingham.

"I have to get back to—" He stopped in time. If he had finished, she would think he had taken leave of his senses. Because he'd been about to say "Birmingham." It had been his refrain for so long that it was all his brain seemed to know.

What he sought wasn't here. Because—

Of course not. He only used this house for dressing and sleeping.

"Never mind," he said. "I don't need much. I'll spend most of my time at work."

OUT IN THE STREETS, he headed for the factory on foot, surprised by how fast everyone walked. Of course they walked fast—this was Birmingham; it was he who had turned slow. He quickened his pace and soaked it all up, the noise, the bustle, the surge of effort and victory and loss. The smoke from the factories, the stench of the canals, the yells of canal men, and some factory workers singing. Yes, Birmingham, where money was king and hard work was his queen.

By the time he reached his headquarters, he was walking at a decent speed again, his head was used to the clanging, and he had mostly stopped coughing. Yes, Birmingham. Everywhere everyone was working, producing, making useless stuff useful.

Das looked only mildly surprised to see him, rising from the desk, where dossiers were neatly stacked and everything appeared to be in order. And, of course, when he quizzed Das, he learned that everything was in order. He let Das talk, while he paced around the office, and tried to find it interesting, but most of what the man said was gibberish, which was odd, as Das was usually focused and clear.

I want a husband. A whole one. Not one who is always leaving me.

Everything felt odd, not only Das's gibberish. Everything was meant to come together once he got back here. But Das had everything under control, and the secretaries had taken to making decisions themselves, and it seemed that they made good decisions. They weren't secretaries, now, though, were they? They were managers, and those were the new titles that Das proposed. Joshua had made himself redundant. They didn't need him either.

I want you here. This is your home too.

No. No. His home was here, in Birmingham. This was who he was. He had just...forgotten.

"Well, I'm back now," he said, cutting Das off mid-sentence, ignoring his raised eyebrows. "All looks good. But you know, we need to make changes."

"One more thing, then." Das straightened an already-straight dossier. "You know that I have immense respect for you, Mr. DeWitt, and I am grateful for the opportunities you have given me."

Oh no. Bloody hell. No.

"I have learned a lot these past years and enjoyed myself immensely. These past weeks at the helm have been the best weeks of my career."

No. Hell, no. Not Das too.

"The experience has firmed my resolve to run an enterprise of my own. I do not intend to be your secretary forever."

"Now? You're leaving right now?"

Das looked puzzled. "No," he said slowly. "But if you are making changes, you should be aware."

"Right. Changes. I'm aware."

JOSHUA LEFT SOON AFTERWARD. They would all carry on fine without him. Just as they would at Sunne Park.

What he sought was not there either.

He headed into the streets, not sure where his legs were taking him. He had a vision of himself, wandering around the streets of Birmingham for years and years, stopping passersby to say, "I need to get to Birmingham" and not understanding when they told him he was already there. They'd call him the Lost Man of Birmingham. "He used to be someone," they'd say when they saw him stumbling past, along the canals, amid the warehouses and factories, down High St. and Moor St. and Mercer St., asking for directions to the city where he was. "He used to be someone, but then his wife kicked him out and his friend left and his business fell to pieces and he lost everything he had."

Bloody hell. He was starting by losing his mind.

He shook off the odd vision and made his way home, to find a house full of clutter, with his bed prepared, meal laid out, and the staff gone.

I know your life is in Birmingham, and I'll go there with you happily if you want. But this is your home too.

He picked up one of Rachel's clocks. The day he came home, when she was heavily pregnant and thoroughly bored, and he found her in the dining room up to her elbows in cogs and screws and blazes knew what, having pulled apart three clocks and not yet put them back together.

And Samuel's tiger-skin rug, with its great heavy head and yellowing claws. The little boy cuddling the tiger's head and telling it his stories, and looking up at him with a solemn frown to ask, "Papa, do tigers dance?"

Then Joshua looked in the tiger's big glass eyes and he laughed.

He laughed until he wanted to weep, but he could not weep so he laughed some more.

He had been right: He *had* needed to come back to Birmingham. He needed to come back so he could see that his life was not here anymore. To understand how completely everything had changed, that he was no longer the man he'd been. To understand how thoroughly Cassandra had disrupted his life and colonized his heart.

Ah, Samuel, my boy. And Rachel, my friend. Birmingham, my past. Cassandra, my love.

He would not undo it. Even knowing what he knew, he would not accept any version of his life or his past that did not have Samuel in it. He had tried to block out the pain, but all he had done was also block out the love and joy.

That's what Cassandra had been trying to tell him from the start.

He would never find the answer in Birmingham, or Sunne Park, or London or any place on Earth. The answer lay not in metal or roses or baby bonnets or even in a tiger-skin rug.

The answer lay in her, and him, and in their secret world of two.

For a smart man, he could be very bloody stupid.

He dropped the tiger skin, and with the energy borne of excitement, a new excitement powered not by fear or anger, but by joy and love, he left the house and went back to find Das. They had work to do.

CHAPTER 31

By the third day, Cassandra had accepted that Joshua wasn't coming back.

The first day had been easy; rage had given her resolve and his departure had given relief.

The second day had been awful; she twitched at every sound, hoping it was him, and hurting every time it wasn't.

The third day, she was useless. Her body was lethargic, her mind agitated. She blamed the rain, though it had never bothered her before; but Lucy and Emily were in a mood, what with Joshua's disappearance and her news of an imminent governess, so when the rain eased, she escaped to her garden, to find peace.

No peace. Not here, not for her. She had vowed not to succumb to heartbreak, but heartbreak, it seemed, was a physical thing. Her limbs were tired, her middle heavy and aching, and although she had been mercifully free of nausea today, she had a hollow where her heart should be.

The rain began again. Softly, but enough to trap her here, in her folly, with her flowers and her fountain and her regret.

Good. She could not move anyway. It seemed very important that she did not move.

She closed her eyes and listened to the soft rain falling on the roof. From the bushes came the chattering of birds, indignant about the weather. In this spot, she and Joshua had made love, when she had no words and had tried to hold him with her body.

Stop giving up your space. Fight for what is yours.

Perhaps she should have fought harder for him, but it had been hopeless from the start.

"Cassandra."

How she loved the way he said her name, his voice rough and husky over the rain, a soft lilt on the middle syllable like he was chanting a refrain.

"Cassandra."

That hint of urgency, as though she mattered, as though he loved her too. As though any moment now he would scoop her up into his arms and hold her tight and never let her go.

"Cassandra?"

A confused note too. Worried even. She did not like him to be worried. Even a dream could wound her heart, so she opened her eyes to dispel it.

It was not a dream.

Joshua stood on the edge of the folly, the rain falling behind him, watching her with his hot-coffee eyes. She let herself look at him, his whole dynamic length. Hers, yet not hers, and so very real. Droplets of rain clung to his hair and to the wool of his coat, and his beloved face was gentle and told her nothing.

He came back!

He came back?

The horrid fiend left her and then dared to *come back*? Did he so enjoy breaking her heart that he wished to do it again?

"No," she said. "You left me, so you can stay left."

He took one step toward her. Two. Her body wanted to move, but she must not move. Instead, she began to shiver.

"Please, Cassandra. I have so much to tell you."

She hugged her heavy, aching middle. "You cannot come and go and come and go, and play with me like this."

"First, know that I do love our child," he said. "I want and love our baby."

"No. No!"

Her agitation was too much. It overcame the lethargy and the ache, and she hauled herself to her feet.

Wetness gushed between her legs. Her belly cramped. Her legs failed her.

He caught her before she fell.

Every muscle in her body clenched and she grabbed onto him hard. His face was pale and no longer gentle. His eyes held her: He held her up with the power of his gaze. If he looked away now, they would all fall down.

"There's blood." He spoke with no voice. She watched his lips move. "On your skirts."

Her head began to float away. Then her arms and her torso. Floating away and dissolving into the rain. She felt so light. She had no weight. No, his arms took her weight. Her legs were no use to her now. She could not move. She could not speak. How could she move or speak when she could not even breathe?

I want and love our baby too. He had been afraid to love the baby and now she had lost the baby and he would hurt so much that he would turn away from her and she would lose him too, all over again.

She was losing both of them. She was losing everything. She had to stop this. She had to stop the blood. She had to stop time. She had to stop the sun from setting and the rain from falling and the flowers from growing.

"I can't stop it," she said.

Her hand ached. She looked at it, puzzled: a white claw gripping his arm. The arm that held her up. The arm that was all she had left in the world and that would leave her again too.

He scooped her up in his arms and, before she had gotten her bearings, he was striding out into the rain, away from her flowers and her fountain and her peace. She curled up into him and fisted her hands in his coat, while the rain slid down her neck in cold rivulets.

"It's raining," she said. "We can't go in the rain. You'll get wet."

But all he did was hold her more tightly and walk more quickly. He looked straight ahead, the rain flattening his hair, sliding over his jaw. She buried her face in his neck so she did not have to watch any of this happening.

It was not good to walk in the rain. They'd get wet. He might slip and they'd all fall down. Or he might catch a chill. She would not like him to catch a chill. Her hair must be a mess and she had only washed it that morning. Because that morning she had not felt nauseous. Because the baby was not making her nauseous any more. They should not go in the rain. The rain would ruin her gown.

Never mind. The blood had already ruined it.

He held her so tightly. He walked so fast. She risked a glance at his face; it was hard and set and angry. She buried her face in his neck again. She did not want to remember him like this. She did not want to remember his face as it looked the day she truly lost him, lost him and their baby, and her hope and her love, lost everything all at once, all over again.

HE CARRIED HER. His arms ached. His legs ached. No load had ever been this heavy or this precious. No walk had ever been so long.

It was so far. It had never been this far. How did it get so far? Another nightmare then: walking and walking and never getting closer, his shattered wife growing heavier in his arms, clinging to him, and him, helpless, no idea what to do for her, how to help her, only walking, walking, walking.

Then suddenly he was there, in the kitchen garden, muscling through the nearest door into the kitchen, where it was hot and fragrant and abruptly still.

"Get the doctor," he barked at the first face he saw. "No, the midwife. Get the midwife." He didn't stop walking. He could carry her forever. "No, the doctor. The midwife. Get them both. Get everyone you can find."

And then there was Mrs. Greenway, stoic and sure, and he came to a stop. Cassandra kept pulling on his coat, her eyes closed so no one could see her. Mrs. Greenway touched a light hand to Cassandra's cheek. A benediction. The housekeeper had been there to help with Lord Charles. She knew what Cassandra had done that day. She knew Cassandra. She would know what to do.

"She's bleeding," he said. And then: "I don't know what to do." His voice cracked, but she understood. She put together "midwife" and "bleeding" and understood.

"You take her up to her chamber and put her on the bed and we'll look after her," she said. "This is women's business. We know what to do."

He turned, relieved. Cassandra would get the help she needed and it wouldn't come from him. He wanted to help her. To do something. But what did he know of this? How had he grown up to be so useless?

Behind him came a barrage of calm, urgent commands: "Sally, get that hot water for Lady Charles's bath and send it up for Miss

Cassandra instead. Mary, get clean linens. Joseph, go now for Mrs. King," and there was more, but he didn't hear the rest, because he was heading up the stairs. Still she clutched him, pressing her face to his neck and making a small sound, a keening sound, like a wounded animal.

That was the sound of her heart breaking.

He shouldered into her room and lowered her onto the bed, bloody skirts and all. She kept her eyes closed. He pulled off her half-boots and wrapped a hand around her foot, and he couldn't ignore the blood. He knew nothing about that kind of blood. He passed right over it to her chin, to fumble with the buttons on her pelisse but she pushed his hand away.

"No." She kept her eyes closed. "Not you. Not you."

The words winded him like a kick in the gut. His legs almost collapsed. That's how severely he had broken them—even now, in her greatest need, she wanted him gone.

Well, too bad for her. He was her husband and he wasn't leaving.

"You need to get undressed," he said. "You've blood..."

His voice failed him. He didn't know what to say; it wasn't blood and they both knew it. He tried again to unbutton her pelisse, but the buttons shrank down and away, too small and slippery for his clumsy, shaking fingers.

And again she pushed his useless hands away. This time she did look at him: stared at him with wild eyes.

"No." Her voice was forceful now. She raised her head, pushed him away. "Not you. You can't. You mustn't. No."

"Cassandra. I need to help you. Tell me what to do. Oh, sweet mercy, just tell me what to do."

"I want my mother." She closed her eyes, dropped her head back on the pillow. Fat tears slid out from under her eyelids and ran down her cheeks. "I want my mother."

He wiped away her tears with his useless, shaking hands, kissed her forehead, and left the room. He took three steps, stopped, unsure. It was wrong to leave her alone. She should not be alone. But she did not want him. She wanted her mother.

And somehow Lady Charles must have heard, for a moment later, she was there.

"Cassandra," he said to her. She came forward. Stopped. Wavered. "She's bleeding," he said. What a stupid word. Bleeding was what happened when you cut yourself. "Our baby. The baby is..."

"Oh, the dear child."

She surged forward, toward her daughter's room, and then stopped. And wavered. He saw it then: her fear. The pain of losing her son was too much; she had let it break her. So she had left her husband and her family and retreated into a world where she was free of pain. He could not judge her; he had used a different method but he had done the same.

No more.

To turn away from his own pain was to turn away from Cassandra: This was what he had discovered in Birmingham. And the one thing he knew, with every inch of his miserable, useless being, was that he would never turn away from Cassandra again.

He wrapped his hands around his mother-in-law's upper arms, held her steady, and studied her eyes. She was fully aware and present. She looked longingly toward her bedroom, toward the place she hid from her own failures, her shame, her guilt, her grief. She knew what was happening and she couldn't bear it either.

Well, sod her. If Cassandra had to bear it, they'd all bloody well bear it.

"She needs you," he said. "She needs you now."

Lady Charles might well need her drug. She might well need

to hide. He understood that. But he knew now it was no solution. It felt like a solution, but it wasn't. And if he could do nothing else for the woman he loved, he would do this.

"Hold on for a few hours," he said. He let go of her arms, took her hand. She still wore her wedding ring. "Just a few hours. You can do that. You can do that for her because she needs it and we love her."

"I let her down."

"That doesn't matter. All that matters is that she needs you now. Her mother. We've both let her down. We will not let her down again."

He waited. He wanted to scream, *Your daughter is alone in there; she does not want me but she must not be alone.* But he must be patient. Cassandra would want him to be patient. He waited. And as he waited, Lady Charles took in a deep breath. She let it out. He saw her take control of herself. Her shoulders straightened, her chin rose. She pressed her lips together and nodded rapidly.

"Yes," she said. "Yes."

She brushed past him and went into the room. Cassandra was no longer alone.

"Mama?" he heard.

"I'm here, Cassandra, my dear. I'm here."

The door clicked shut.

Joshua leaned back against the wall and pressed the heels of his hands into his burning eyes and kept them there, even when he heard the shuffle and patter of footsteps. A hand squeezed his arm, briefly.

"She's going to be all right." The housekeeper.

He lowered his hands, looked at her caring, concerned face. A convoy of maids hovered behind her, bearing basins and linens and heavens knew what.

"This happens," Mrs. Greenway added, sure and calm.

Comforting him. He wasn't the one who needed it. "More often than you know. But she'll be fine." She turned to the maids, grabbing a bundle of linens that she tucked under her arm and taking the basin of steaming water in both hands. "Wait here," she said to the maids. "You too, Mr. DeWitt."

"Tell her…"

She paused. He leaned across to open the door for her. Caught a glimpse of his wife's skirts, his view of her face blocked by the body of her mother seated at her side. He looked away.

"Tell her I'm here. I'm not going anywhere."

Not you, she'd said. *Just go*, she'd said. *Not you*, she'd said.

"You'll tell her. Promise me?"

"I'll tell her. Let us look after her now."

CHAPTER 32

Joshua had never known Sunne Park to be so still. Miss Lucy, Miss Emily, and Mr. Isaac had just now left to visit a neighbor, the butler informed him, so he told him to send clothes after them with a message to stay away. He paced through the empty house and the servants faded away from him like ghosts. Finally, a pair of footmen herded him into the main study, where a fire roared and food and drink were laid out, as were a deck of cards and some books. He understood what they wanted him to do, so he obeyed, mildly surprised by his own docility.

Not you. Just go. Not you.

He could not eat. He thought about drinking but he needed a clear head in case she needed him. It was too hot by the fire. Too cold away from it. His legs didn't work properly but all the chairs felt wrong.

In his roaming, he spied familiar sheets of paper on the desk. The plans she'd shown him, that day she'd sent him away and he could not leave fast enough.

Well, they were good plans and he would consider them now.

And according to these plans, as he recalled, this room was to be his study. There it was, right there—"Mr. DeWitt's study."

Except that it wasn't. It had been altered. The ink was a slightly different color, slightly off the line. An extra "s" had been added.

"Mrs. DeWitt's study."

With one pen stroke, she had written him out of her life.

And here was a fresh page, with lists for Newell and herself, items to research, requests for shopping catalogues. A query for Miss Sampson, about educating orphans here.

She had been busy.

And he had been right. She had never needed him. She had sought to include him out of duty, because she always tried to do what was right. But after he abdicated, she finally claimed her position and her space and her own home. Her own life.

A life that did not require him.

He was proud of her. He wanted to weep. But she had put too much on their child and now she had lost that. She would grieve, as he would grieve. And one day, their grief would lessen and fade, as grief always did, and she would turn to him again. She would need him for one thing at least. If that was his only chance—if he had to start again as a stallion—he'd take it. He'd take any chance he could get.

He shuffled through the pages. To the bedrooms. She still claimed the mistress's room, connected to the master bedroom for him. No: Not for him. "Mr. DeWitt's chambers" had been crossed out, with two strong lines, the end of one tearing the paper. Now it said: "Empty."

Empty. An empty space. Like the empty rooms in his house in Birmingham. Her empty womb. The place that belonged to her husband. Empty. Like that feeling in his gut when she told him to go.

Empty space.

But ah! Ha ha! Here was the thing about an empty space: An empty space needed to be filled.

He scrabbled about for pen and ink and cursed his bad handwriting. He crossed out "Empty" and rewrote his name. And the study: He looked about. It was a big room. Why shouldn't they share it? "Mr. and Mrs. DeWitt's study." Or maybe not. Maybe she wouldn't like to have him underfoot all day; he'd ask her. "Nursery for baby." He changed that too: "babies."

A knock at the door, a second knock. He dropped the pen with a splatter of ink, and Mrs. King the midwife stepped into the room.

"How is she?" he asked.

"Your wife is tired and sad, but she will be all right."

"I left her. Three days ago she was well and I left her. She was upset and it...Was it...?"

"Naught but coincidence," she said briskly. "I told her the same."

Not you. Just go. Not you.

"She blamed me?"

"She blamed herself, poor lamb. But there's not one thing either of you could have done different to change this, that's the truth, and don't you listen to any fool doctor what tries to say otherwise. I've been doing this a long time, and my mother and my aunts and their mother before, and let me tell you, if a baby wants to come, it'll come, and it won't care if you're in the midst of heartbreak or war. But sometimes babies just don't want to be born and there's an end to it. But you have to stay away from her now."

"What?" It was a conspiracy. "Never."

"Out of her bed, I mean. For a month or so. Give the poor lamb time to recover."

"But I can still *sleep* with her?" Another thing he learned in Birmingham: He hated to sleep alone.

"Aye, sleep, if you want. But mind that's all you do."

"Can I see her?"

Not you. Just go. Not you.

"She's sleeping now. Let her rest."

ALONE AGAIN, he went to the window. The light was fading but it was still the same day. It was still the same garden. She would sleep, and she would wake, alone. Would she reach for him, as he reached for her?

There had been a moment, when she first saw him. She had been happy to see him. She *had*.

He had to give her something, so she knew, when she awoke, that she was not alone. She would never be alone again. Had he ever given her anything? Not in London, and when everything was arranged with Das, he had left Birmingham too quickly to even think of buying her a gift. That was what husbands did for their wives, wasn't it? Bought them gifts. He should get her something she liked. What did she like? What was wrong with him, that he loved her so much and didn't even know what she liked?

I like it when you leap through windows.

She did like him, she *did*. She liked flowers and music and pigs and cats and making love to him. She liked soft fabrics and strawberry tarts and those awful herbal wines her mother made. She liked meeting new people and winning at cards and balancing the ledgers and rubbing her cheek against his scruff. She liked it when he teased her and when he brushed her hair and when he kissed the underside of her breasts.

And he had a lifetime to learn everything else she liked and make sure she always had it.

The plans! They could be a gift to show her! He grabbed them up and was halfway to the door when he stopped. Wait. No. She was ill. She didn't want him blathering on about plans and money and businesses. Not now, not yet. That wasn't a gift.

Then out the window—Flowers!

He'd take her flowers. Roses and...the other ones. The Donkey's Elbows or whatever they were called.

He ran into the still-wet garden and grabbed at a rose, which bit him, and he sucked the blood off his finger and tried again, and his sleeve snagged on a thorn, and he tried to free himself, but then his other sleeve snagged too, and then he couldn't even get the wretched rose to snap off, and it occurred to him that flowers might be more complicated than he thought.

He ran back inside—sprinting, because he didn't have time for this, no time to argue with flowers when his wife might think she was alone—and he found a knife, a nice sharp pen knife, and he ran back out and this time the rose could not withstand him. Ha ha! Behold the mighty conqueror of roses! One pink rose, and then another rose, and this purple-blue flower and that yellow one, and this white one, and it needed some more pink ones, and then he had a whole bunch of flowers, and they didn't look nearly as pretty and symmetrical as the flowers in the house, those flowers made harmonious by her competent hands, but he decided that didn't matter, because at least he had a lot of flowers. Now he needed to tie them together.

He dashed back through the entranceway, under that carving of "*Every sunne is a new one,*" which went to show how much they didn't know, because it was the same sun every day, rising and setting, constant and sure and endless, and sometimes one simply needed to look at it anew. That was a nice thought, and he'd tell Cassandra that thought; he had so much to tell her. But first, no time to waste—string!

He charged inside, but before he found any string, he found a ribbon. How fortuitous! It was a pretty green color, not unlike the color of Cassandra's eyes when they were being green and not brown, and he decided that yes, this ribbon would be ideal for tying up the flowers. Unfortunately, the ribbon was attached to a bonnet, but Joshua decided that he needed the ribbon more than the bonnet did, so he pulled out his handy pen knife and sliced the ribbon from its bonnet and tied up his flowers, which still didn't look nearly as good as bunches that she made, but he had no more time to waste, so he jogged up the steps, only to see that the door to his wife's room was closed and her mother had just come out.

He opened his mouth to speak, but Lady Charles pressed her fingers to her lips.

"Hush," she whispered. "She's sleeping. She needs to rest now."

"I need to see her."

"She's sleeping."

"She's my wife."

Lady Charles's eyes flicked to the sorry bunch of flowers in his hand. "But don't wake her. Not yet."

Then she was gone.

Silent as a cat, he let himself into the room, darkened now, though it was still light outside. She slept peacefully, in her blessed nightcap, her mouth open, a faint blush on her cheeks. He entered as quietly as he could, and put the flowers on the table by her bed, and sat in the chair. He wanted to touch her, but didn't dare wake her.

"I'm your husband and you're my wife and I know what that means now," he whispered. "It means for better or for worse, and I'm going to devote my life to making your life better, whether you want me to or not."

Then he rose, went out, and crept down the stairs to wait out the evening and the night and all the long hours until he could see her again.

CHAPTER 33

Cassandra awoke. The pain was gone. The blood was gone. A lantern burned; they had not left her in the dark. She was alone, in a clean shift, a clean nightcap, with clean linens on the bed. Mr. Twit was curled at her side. Nothing had changed.

As if it had all been a dream. As if right back at the start, she'd dreamed Lucy singing and dancing alone in the ballroom. Joshua and the ball and Mrs. O'Dea and the lovemaking and the baby: She'd dreamed it all, and now she would get up and get on with her life. The same as always. The life she would accept because it was the one she had.

She smelled flowers, the promise of them, but they were wrong. If this were a dream, she would smell only violets, the violets she'd picked that long-ago morning, excited by the start of spring.

No violets. Instead, laid by her bed was the most peculiar bunch of flowers she'd ever seen, a wildly mismatched and exuberant hodgepodge of blooms. It looked like something Joshua would throw together for her, if he was ever to take leave of his senses and start picking flowers. The sight filled her like a smile: He had come back.

For the baby, not for her. It was the first thing he had said. He had let himself love that baby, and he would never survive the loss, and it would send him running again; perhaps he was already gone. What could she do? She had to let him go.

She picked up the flowers. They were tied with ribbon. Emily's ribbon. Yes, it was more likely Emily had picked them. Why on earth would Joshua ever pick her flowers?

Except that Joshua should have done it. He could have done it. Why had he not done it? The fiend!

Let him go?

Let him try!

She flung down the flowers and hurled herself out of bed, slightly dizzy, tired and sore, damp between her legs, but she was fine. Well, no, she wasn't fine, her heart ached with the void left by her baby, but she would be fine. One day. This happened, they all said that. Sometimes babies just aren't ready to be born.

Well, all she could do about that now was grieve and wait for her heart and body to heal, and find hope in the other women's words. But as for him? *Oh no, indeed, Mr. DeWitt. This will not do. Not this time.* She was always going along with what life threw at her. Did she think she had fortitude and patience? No: It was cowardice. No more. She was not going to accept whatever life threw at her, not this time, not without a fight.

Her dizziness having passed, she soothed Mr. Twit's growl of complaint, tugged off her nightcap, and carried the lantern into the dark, sleeping hallway.

His empty bedroom sent fear shivering through her, but she kept on, ignoring the weakness in her limbs, marching down the stairs, and slipping into the study.

And there he was, keeping vigil by the fire, staring at the coals, as she herself had done, all those nights on her own. He did not turn; he did not seem to have even heard her enter.

Her eyes drank him in, every beloved, cursed inch of him, this infuriating, intense, captivating man, who had turned her inside out and transformed her into someone new.

No, not someone new. Into who she had always been inside.

And he thought he would leave her?

Not a chance!

She set down the lantern with a little bump.

"You are not running away again," she announced.

He jolted and leaped to his feet, crossing the room toward her, arms outstretched, talking all the while. "You're awake. How are you? You should be resting. Why aren't you resting? Let me take you upstairs. I'm so sorry. Are you all right?"

"This will not do. I'm not having it."

A shadow crossed his face. His arms fell. He stopped walking, though his body kept swaying toward her. He was as taut as a violin string, his eyes soft and dark and flicking wildly over her face.

"Please," he said gently. "Let me—"

"No." His shoulders jerked, but she hardly noticed. "All my life, I was well behaved and polite and never made trouble. Not any more. I won't accept it. This is not how it will be and you will not run away."

"Cassandra—"

"Stop." She showed him her palms and glared. "I will *not* behave nicely and I will *not* be polite and you will *not* object because it is you who taught me to be rude. You are a coward and a fool, and you will not run away again, do you hear me? I know it hurts, it hurts so much, but you'll have to stand there and take it like a—like a—woman! Yes, that's what you'll do. I want a husband, and you're the only one I have and the only one I want, so you'll...*bloody well* be a husband to me."

"Cassandra—"

"And don't you tell me not to curse! I'll curse if I want to! I'm tired of being good. I'm going to make trouble for you, Joshua DeWitt, and you will be my husband if I have to knock you over the head and tie you up. You told me to fight for what is mine. Well, you're mine and this time I'm going to fight."

She stepped forward, but a wave of dizziness hit her, and her knees threatened to fail. In a flash, Joshua sprang, scooped her up, and carried her over to the settee. He laid her on it like she was the most precious thing in the world, then sank to the floor, holding onto her hands.

"Are you all right?" he whispered. "What do you need? Tell me what you need."

"I'm all right, I..."

The dizziness had vanished, and taken with it her wits, for why on earth was Joshua kneeling on the floor? Holding her hands in his, big and warm and strong, stroking her fingers, staring at her as though his world was about to end?

"You want me to stay?" he said. "Really?"

Clearly he had lost his wits too.

"Did you not hear a word I just said?"

His eyes did not release hers as he pressed her fingers to his lips. His fingers were so strong and sure, they could hold her whole body and soul, and his eyes could melt her bones, they were so hot and dark and liquid.

Liquid.

He had tears in his eyes.

"You didn't want me. You sent me away." He spoke in a whisper that tore at her already torn heart. "Earlier today. I broke us so badly that even in your greatest need, you pushed me away."

"I never…"

"You said, 'Not you.' I wanted to help you, but you said, 'Not you'."

He pressed his lips together and briefly squeezed his eyes shut. Her own tears welled. She slid onto the floor and freed one of her hands to press it to his cheek.

"I did not want you to have to see what was happening," she said softly. "I was losing our baby and I did not want you to see that. I feared you could not bear the pain."

"But you had to bear the pain, so I should too. You had to be strong and brave, but you did not have to be alone." He spoke firmly now, and took both her hands in his again. "Whatever the pain, whatever the burden, we bear them together." A faint smile curved his lips. "Must I explain to you, Mrs. DeWitt, how marriage works?"

"You love me," she told him. And herself. A simple fact, simply stated, for both of their simple minds.

"With everything I am."

She heard her own words and his, and a breathless, tear-filled laugh shook out of her, releasing her pain into the night.

"I ought to have mentioned that earlier," he said ruefully. "It took me a while to see it."

"It took a tragedy."

"Before then."

She shook her head, looked down at their joined hands. "You say that now, but you left me, and you only came back for…"

Her words trailed off at the sight of his hands. Specifically, his left hand. More specifically, the gold band that encircled the ring finger. She took his left hand in both hers and studied the ring carefully. It was bigger than hers, of course, but the same gold, with the same patterns etched along its rim.

It matched hers exactly.

"You found your wedding ring," she said.

"I never lost it. But it meant nothing to me before. Now it means everything: My fidelity and devotion to you."

"Where was it?"

"Birmingham."

"Then..." She ran her thumb over the ring and looked up at him. "You got it before. Before you came back. Before I lost the baby."

A strange new relief filled her. It was not the tragedy that made him love her. He did not come back only for their baby. He came back for her. She had lost their baby, the dream of that child, but she had not lost him too.

"It was in Birmingham that I realized that you matter to me more than anything. I *am* married to you. I don't mean the vows we said two years ago, or the rings or our names or the paperwork. I mean that I can never leave you, because my heart and soul and body are already married to you, bonded and forged in the furnace like steel. They have been for some time, but I could not see it."

He lifted her left hand to his, kissed the gold band on her finger.

"In different circumstances, now would be the time when I confess my undying love, get down on my knees, and ask you to marry me. But I'm already on my knees and we're already married."

A shaky laugh escaped her. "You always were very efficient."

"I'm sorry I left you. I'm so, so sorry for all the times I hurt you. I'm sorry I have been such a dreadful husband. I'm so sorry I wasn't here for you. But I vow to be better, and make your life better. And maybe, if I love you hard enough, with everything that I am, in time you will love me too."

The anguish in his eyes left her amazed. "Joshua, you fool, of course I love you."

"But you love everything. And you're stuck with me, so of course you...I mean, I wish you could...That I was..." He closed his eyes briefly, opened them again. "You are very good at loving, but I am very hard to love."

"Loving you is the easiest thing in the world, and there is nothing I love like I love you." She spread her hand over his chest, over his heart, felt it beating with all his wild exuberance. "My love for you is as much a part of me as the air that I breathe, which means it will never stop until I do. Which is why I told you that I shall never let you go."

His eyes searched hers, as if seeking the truth. She saw the moment he surrendered his fear, and allowed himself to be loved. It was followed by a smile, spreading slowly over his face like sunrise, stretching into a grin.

He pressed his forehead to hers. "You said something about tying me up, I believe."

"I might indeed tie you up," she warned.

"Mrs. DeWitt! I am shocked!"

She had to laugh, shaky and wondering, with relief as much as joy, and he was chuckling too. They were still laughing when their mouths met. It was not easy to kiss while laughing, and they had to start and stop several times before they figured it out. But figure it out they did.

Then he settled back on the thick rug and she curled into him, her body tired, her heart grieving, and her whole being bathed in joy. His heart beat against her ear, as strong and true as the arms that held her tight.

"I hurt you because I was scared," he whispered. "I was scared that you would leave me, that if I loved anything again I would lose it, and so from the start I tried to keep you away."

"You were scared of *me* leaving *you*? Oh, what fools we are." She pressed her face into his chest. "Joshua?"

"My love?"

"I don't want to be scared anymore."

"Here's my idea: I hold onto you and you hold onto me, and we never let go and we never turn away from each other, no matter what happens, however hard it gets." He briefly squeezed her tight. "Even when the bad things happen, and the bad things will happen."

"A bad thing happened today."

"Yes." He pressed a kiss to her temple. "But the good things will happen too. And we will have each other, to share our joys and look after each other when our hearts break."

"That's what hearts do," she said. "They break. Hearts love and hearts break and then they heal. Every hour, every day, we love and hurt and heal." She pressed her hand over his heart. "Our hearts are broken now."

"Perhaps we can do something for the little one we lost today." She looked up at him questioningly. "In your garden," he continued. "A little statue, perhaps."

Love rushed through her, and through the ache of her grief, it brought the promise of a new, different kind of peace.

"Yes," she said. "With some new flowers. A reminder of the love we gave."

"And that there is always, always, more love to give."

JOSHUA INSISTED she had to rest, and Cassandra found she had to agree. He lifted her into his arms and once more carried her upstairs and helped her into bed.

"Were these flowers from you?" she asked, leaning back against the pillows, watching him strip.

"Do you like them?"

She smiled at the haphazard posy, bursting with life and energy. "Very much. How is it that they are tied with Emily's ribbon?"

"Ah. That's *Emily's* ribbon."

Oh dear. "Was that ribbon, perchance, attached to a bonnet?"

He grinned. He stood naked, and she enjoyed the sight.

"I'll buy her a new one," he said. "And you. I will shower you with gifts."

"I don't need gifts, I only need..." A thought struck her. She had forgotten. "What about Birmingham? Your home is there."

"My home is with you."

He slipped into the bed beside her and pulled the covers up over them.

"But your work," she said.

"Das and I have it all sorted. He is buying into the company as a partner, and he'll manage it from now on. I'll stay involved enough to annoy him and keep him on his toes. But now I want to support ideas that are not yet ready, that might not bear fruit for decades, if ever, but are worth the risk for the benefits they might bring. Like electrical power and clean water. And I can do that living with you and getting under your feet."

"But to leave Birmingham? Birmingham was where you made yourself. It's who you are."

"It's who I was. You made me who I truly am. You showed me a world where it was safe for me to love and be loved. "

She flipped over to face him. "You showed me a world where it was safe for me to express myself and fight. Which, apparently, means that I yell now."

"I adore it when you yell. And when you start throwing

champagne and chairs? Oh." He shuddered with melodramatic delight. "All that passion and emotion…"

She trailed her finger over his chest. "I want you near but I can't…Mrs. King says I must heal. I can't…do my wifely duty."

"But my husbandly duty is to let you heal, both heart and body. I can wait." He stroked her hair gently. "I am a man of infinite patience."

"You are nothing of the sort."

"But I am an inventive problem-solver. While you are healing, I shall list all the things I want us to do to each other, and you will make a list too, and when you are ready, we will work through our lists. In fact, I already have some ideas."

"So do I."

She turned back over, her back to his chest, and when his arm came around her waist, she covered it with her own.

"My ideas will be better," he said.

"We shall see about that."

"Indeed, we shall. I mean to astonish you with my ingenuity, Mrs. DeWitt."

"Oh please do, Mr. DeWitt, I'm all agog."

She let her eyes drift closed, wrapped up in their love, knowing that even though life would keep breaking her heart, it would also be full of joy.

All of the time.

AUTHOR'S NOTE

The song "Oyster Nan," which Cassandra sang to Joshua, appears in the songbook "Wit and Mirth, Or, Pills to Purge Melancholy," edited by Thomas d'Urfey and published in 1719–1720.

It is not a nice song.

More stories in this series are coming soon. Read on for details, or visit miavincy.com.

COMING NEXT

For news on release dates, future books, and more, sign up at miavincy.com/news or visit miavincy.com.

A BEASTLY KIND OF EARL

Life's a beast. And then you get married.

Rafe Landcross, Earl of Luxborough, wants to take his bad temper and jaguar-mauled face back to the peace and quiet of his orchids and ganja. But first he must trick Miss Thea Knight into an invalid marriage—except that Thea, a social outcast planning revenge on those who ruined her life, just might have a trick or two of her own...

A DANGEROUS KIND OF LADY

They say to keep your enemies close. They don't say *how* close.

Proud heiress Arabella Larke must marry or lose her inheritance and everything she loves. But Arabella is determined to choose her own husband, and for that she needs to buy time. Her solution? A fake engagement with Guy Roth, Marquess of Hardbury, her lifelong enemy and the one man she is sure will never want to marry her...

A SCANDALOUS KIND OF DUKE

He can have anyone he wants...except her.

Leopold Halton, Duke of Dammerton, longs to escape his scandalous past, but a series of popular cartoons continues to drag it up. To stop the unknown cartoonist, he enlists the help of artist Juno Bell. Leo has loved Juno for years, but her parentage makes her no match for a duke...as does his discovery that *she* is the very cartoonist he seeks to destroy.

CPSIA information can be obtained
at www.ICGtesting.com
Printed in the USA
LVHW111458150819
627777LV00005B/720/P